BARBARA
NADEL

BLOOD BUSINESS

HEADLINE

First published in Great Britain in 2020 by
HEADLINE PUBLISHING GROUP

First published in paperback in 2020 by
HEADLINE PUBLISHING GROUP

1

Cataloguing in Publication Data is available from the British Library

ISBN 978 1 4722 5486 3

Typeset in Times New Roman by Palimpsest Book Production Limited,
Falkirk, Stirlingshire

Printed and bound in Great Britain by Clays Ltd, Elcograf S.p.A.

Headline's policy is to use papers that are natural, renewable and recyclable
products and made from wood grown in well-managed forests and other controlled
sources. The logging and manufacturing processes are expected to conform to the
environmental regulations of the country of origin.

HEADLINE PUBLISHING GROUP
An Hachette UK Company
Carmelite House
50 Victoria Embankment
London EC4Y 0DZ

www.headline.co.uk
www.hachette.co.uk

Cast List

Çetin İkmen – former İstanbul detective

Çiçek İkmen – his eldest daughter

Samsun Bajraktar – İkmen's Albanian cousin, a transsexual

Dr Arto Sarkissian – police pathologist, İkmen's oldest friend, an ethnic Armenian

Inspector Mehmet Süleyman – İstanbul detective

Sergeant Ömer Mungun – Süleyman's deputy

Inspector Kerim Gürsel – İstanbul detective

Sergeant Eylul Yavaş – Gürsel's deputy

Constable Ercan Tuna – police officer

Selahattın Özer – Police Commissioner

Constable Gülse Aksoyer – local police officer

Sinem Gürsel – Kerim's wife

İbrahim Dede – dervish

Tansu Barışık, aka Sugar Hanım – an ageing prostitute and police informant

Gonca Şekeroğlu – gypsy artist

Leah Delmonte – former prostitute

Wahıd Saatçı – drug dealer

Uğur Bulut – Kurdish businessman

Lokman Bulut – Uğur's younger brother

Sister Eudokia – the Bulut brothers' adopted sister, a Greek
  Orthodox nun
Ara Bulut – Uğur and Lokman's father
Serkan Tolon – friend of Lokman, rich boy
Cihan Teke – Bulut family lawyer
Deniz and Can Palandoken – heroin addicts
Türgüt Akgün – cemetery gate-keeper
Raşım Dorsay – cemetery guard
Münir Sever – cemetery guard
Dr Sibel Çoban – surgeon
Dr Alp Özdemir – general practitioner
Cemal Yüksel – Machine bey
Sevval Kalkan – the Actress
Olimpio – the Designer
Cumhur Polat – Gold bey
Ateş and Ece Kazantzoğlu – husband and wife
Devlet – their son
Yaşar Akgün – gangster
Abdülkadır Soyar – Yaşar's uncle
Ekrem and Ali Haydar Özınce – Yaşar's muscle
Hafız Barakat – Syrian refugee
Eyüp Celik – celebrity lawyer
Berat Aznavoryan – owner of carpet shop

Pronunciation Guide

There are 29 letters in the Turkish alphabet:

A, a – usually short as in 'hah!'

B, b – as pronounced in English

C, c – not like the 'c' in 'cat' but like the 'j' in 'jar', or 'Taj'

Ç, ç – 'ch' as in 'chunk'

D, d – as pronounced in English

E, e – always short as in 'venerable'

F, f – as pronounced in English

G, g – always hard as in 'slug'

Ğ, ğ – 'yumuşak ge' is used to lengthen the vowel that it follows. It is not usually voiced.
As in the name 'Farsakoğlu', pronounced 'Far-sak-orlu'

H, h – as pronounced in English, never silent

I, ı – without a dot, the sound of the 'a' in 'probable'

İ i – with a dot, as the 'i' in 'thin'

J, j – as the French pronounce the 'j' in 'bonjour'

K, k – as pronounced in English, never silent

L, l – as pronounced in English

M, m – as pronounced in English

N, n – as pronounced in English

O, o – always short as in 'hot'

Ö, ö – like the 'ur' sound in 'further'

P, p – as pronounced in English

R, r – as pronounced in English

S, s – as pronounced in English

Ş, ş – pronounced like the 'sh' in 'ship'

T, t – as pronounced in English

U, u – always medium length, as in 'push'

Ü, ü – as the French pronounce the 'u' in 'tu'

V, v – as pronounced in English but sometimes with a
slight 'w' sound

Y, y – as pronounced in English

Z, z – as pronounced in English

If he looked to his right, where only the very last outpost of the setting sun could be spotted glinting on the horizon, he could see a long, wavy line of tombstones. Melancholy grey posts topped with uniform carved turbans, these were the last resting places of nineteenth-century Ottoman men. The female version, he knew, featured a woman's head veil, which always looked to him as if it were weeping.

Uğur Bulut knew he didn't have to be here. The pathologist, a portly man standing beside him, had told him his attendance, or not, was up to him. But what else could he have done but be here? The grave the two burly diggers were uncovering belonged to his mother. And the exhumation had been requested by his brother. He saw the pathologist turn to Ali Dede. 'If you'd like to sit, I can arrange for a chair . . .'

'No, no, no.' The cleric tilted his head. 'But thank you.'

Fucking Lokman! If it hadn't been for his brother, none of them would be here now. Not the pathologist, the gravediggers, the cleric. It was bad enough being an Alevi in a majority Sunni Muslim country without advertising the fact by standing beside a Dede or Alevi priest in the designated Alevi portion of the great Karacaahmet cemetery. Uğur wanted to hide, to disappear amongst the thick foliage of the cemetery's many cypress trees. But he couldn't. If he was going to prove to that bastard Lokman, and his lawyer, that he was indeed his mother's elder son, and so entitled to her considerable estate, he had to go through with

1

this. But that didn't mean he didn't think the whole situation was insane.

When Lokman had started this nonsense, voicing to all and sundry that he didn't believe the two of them were brothers, Uğur had laughed – at first. He'd suggested they both take DNA tests, for comparison, each with the other, but Lokman refused. Instead he'd insisted, possibly at the behest of his lawyer, that their DNA be tested against that of their mother. Uğur had scoured his mother's old house for a hairbrush or a piece of her clothing, knowing that he'd cleared the place of all personal items after her death. That was what she had instructed him to do. There had been nothing, which was why he was here now, in this cemetery, watching his mother's body re-emerge into the light.

The pathologist, who usually worked for the police department, was an Armenian by the name of Sarkissian. He was an eminent man renowned for his expertise and honesty. He said, 'When the men reach what we are seeking, you may wish to look away, Uğur Bey.'

Uğur nodded. His mother had died five years ago. She'd been old, sick and tired, and when the end came, it had been merciful. Buried in just a seamless winding sheet, no coffin to temporarily protect her body from the earth, she was unlikely to be anything more than a skeleton. Hopefully her bones would yield the DNA sample he needed so badly. Because it wasn't just about his mother's estate; it was also about her honour. By stating that Uğur could be an adoptive rather than a natural child of their mother, Lokman was implying that Perihan Hanım had lied to her own children. His only 'proof' for this assertion was that their sister, Aysel, had been adopted, plus the obvious physical differences between the two men. Uğur was tall and light skinned, while Lokman was short and dark like their mother.

Of course, what his brother really wanted was Perihan Hanım's house in the upscale İstanbul suburb of Sarıyer, and the pastane shop in Beyoğlu she had established on her own, and which she had left to her elder son. Efforts to find the two men's father, who had left the family when Lokman was two, had come to nothing. Uğur, who vaguely remembered him, had thought for years that he'd probably drunk himself to death.

'Ah . . .'

Uğur looked at the doctor, who added, 'It appears the men have found what we are looking for.'

Suddenly Uğur felt sick. He'd convinced himself he was going to be fine with this exhumation, that he was a tough, upright Kurdish man who did not cry. But now he was falling apart . . .

Dr Arto Sarkissian had seen it all before. Exhumations were rare, but when they happened, and where relatives were involved, there were always tears, sometimes vomiting. This statuesque, besuited Kurdish businessman was no exception. Gently moving Uğur Bey to one side, the pathologist stood on the edge of the hole the two gravediggers had excavated and contemplated the small piece of tattered winding sheet that stuck up from the earth.

'All right, proceed,' he said to the two men down inside the grave. 'Gently.'

'Yes, sir.'

One of them looked like a bull on heat, while the other came across as vaguely deranged. He doubted whether 'gently' was a word they were accustomed to. But they loosened the earth around the corpse with more ease than had been expected and, grunting as they tried to get hold of what couldn't be much more than a skeleton, raised the clod-encrusted figure to the surface.

Normally, having contact with the dead was considered unclean and disgusting by Muslims. Arto Sarkissian, one of the few Christians left in the medical profession, though they had utterly dominated it until comparatively recently, could see that the two men were disgusted at what they were required to do, but he could also tell they were stoical. An empty coffin stood waiting for the body of Perihan Hanım on the other side of the hole. As they lifted the corpse from the ground, the smaller of the gravediggers grunted.

It was then that something happened none of them had expected.

It was just a foot. Falling through the folds of the simple cotton shroud, it was grey and gnarled and very obviously dead. But it was not the foot of a person who had died five years ago. It had nails, still polished and painted bright red. Even the gravediggers knew it wasn't right, which was why they dropped the body, and why Uğur Bulut began to scream.

Chapter 1

It was difficult to know who was the more eccentric looking, the boy or the man.

Çetin İkmen – former police inspector, widower and native İstanbullu – had been asleep in his chair in his large apartment in Sultanahmet when the doorbell rang. Moving his cat from his lap to the floor and hastily lighting a cigarette, he'd dragged himself to the front door. As he opened it, the cat, Marlboro, jumped onto his shoulder. İkmen groaned. Then he saw the boy.

Thin, dark, wearing a most inappropriate T-shirt featuring a topless woman, the kid was probably only about fifteen. He was also completely, stinkingly filthy.

'What do you want?' İkmen asked through a blowback of smoke. Eyes smarting, he coughed.

For a moment, the boy was mesmerised by the cat. A huge ginger tom, Marlboro only lived with İkmen part-time. His real life happened on the street, where he fought, stole or had sex with almost everything in his territory.

'You are Çetin Bey?' the boy said eventually.

İkmen took the cigarette out of his mouth. 'Who wants to know?' he asked.

'Machine Bey, he ask for me to get you.'

The kid had an accent, which was probably why he was talking what sounded like nonsense.

'Machine Bey?'

'He make things. Kumkapı.'

5

Kumkapı was a pleasant district on the Sea of Marmara, a fishing port and former home to large numbers of Armenians.

The boy took a crumpled piece of paper out of his trouser pocket and shoved it into İkmen's hand. It was a letter. Written in a very fine hand, it said:

Dear Çetin Bey,

I apologise for introducing myself in this somewhat bizarre fashion. I don't go out and so I have had to resort to sending this missive to you with a boy who does odd jobs for us sometimes. He is Syrian and, like so many of them, almost destitute. He has minimal Turkish, but he does speak some English, a language I know you can use.

I need to speak to you about a matter concerning a friend. As a former police officer and a man of good conscience, you are the only person I can trust with this problem. I can and will remunerate your efforts.

From the bottom of my heart I would urge you to follow the boy, Hafız. He will take you to a carpet shop in Kumkapı, where a man called Berat Bey will bring you to me. All will become clear.

Your faithful servant,
Machine Bey

So the boy hadn't been confused about the man's name.

İkmen leaned against the doorpost, Marlboro's bloodied furry face pressed against his. He had no idea who this Machine Bey might be. The boy in front of him could maybe enlighten him, if indeed his English was up to it. But should he even bother to consider this? He knew that many dissident types lived difficult and hidden existences, trying to keep under the radar of official scrutiny. Machine Bey could be one of those. But then again, he could just as easily be someone of quite a different nature.

İkmen had always been and would always be a vocal critic of what he felt was wrong about the political temperature of his country, both before and after the ascent of the current ruling party back in 2002. His daughter Çiçek had been implicated, but then exonerated, for her supposed part in the attempted coup of 2016. And mud, as İkmen knew all too well, stuck.

He spoke to the boy in English. 'This Machine Bey,' he said, 'have you actually met him?'

'Oh yes, sir,' the kid said. 'He make beautiful things.'

'Where?'

'I cannot say.'

'Somewhere in Kumkapı?'

'Yes.'

İkmen got the distinct feeling that was the end of the conversation as far as the boy was concerned. Which meant that whether to go with the kid or not was up to him. After a few seconds' thought, he took his phone out of his pocket and made a call.

According to the paperwork regarding the death of Perihan Bulut, she had succumbed to bone cancer at the age of eighty-five back in 2013. The woman they had found in the grave couldn't possibly be Perihan Hanım.

Arto Sarkissian looked up from the body and into the eyes of a tall man clad like himself in white coveralls, way across the other side of the laboratory.

'I remember Çetin İkmen telling me years ago that one gets accustomed to the smell of death,' the man said. 'But in this case . . .'

The doctor shook his head. 'A particularly odiferous example of putrefaction, yes,' he said. 'But that is to be expected a week, two at the most, after death.'

'That recent?'

'Oh yes,' he said. 'Although the skin has begun to detach,

the marbling on it is only green, although dark in places, as opposed to black. This is why I called you, Inspector. This is not Perihan Bulut by any stretch of the imagination. And then there's this . . .'

He pulled down the plastic sheet that had been covering the body. Whoever this was had been old. Thin, and with swellings around her joints consistent with arthritis, her entire body was covered with waves of wrinkles and patches of callused skin. But that was natural, or could be. What wasn't natural was the large hole in her chest.

'Her heart has been, in my view, surgically removed.'

The tall man, Inspector of Police Mehmet Süleyman, blinked. 'Doctor . . .'

'Which is the other reason I called you, Inspector. Tragically, you and I have both seen the results of post-operative sepsis that can set in when one has willingly donated a kidney. But a heart?'

'Maybe she was already dead?'

'Maybe. I will have to endeavour to find out. But if she wasn't, what fresh hell is this, eh?'

Organ harvesting from desperate people for paltry sums of money had been going on for years. The poorer the victims, the less regard their wealthy customers showed when it came to their welfare, and many had died after being treated in unscrupulous back-street clinics or even private houses. But the possible harvesting of a heart from a living person, a woman of some age to boot, was a new low.

At the age of fifty, Mehmet Süleyman had seen many examples of the darker side of human nature, but this was, as the doctor had said, a fresh hell he hadn't even imagined.

'How is Mr Bulut?' he asked.

'Distraught,' the doctor replied.

'I have ordered a fingertip search of the area around the grave up to a half-kilometre radius.'

8

Arto shrugged. They both knew that whoever had taken Perihan Hanım's corpse had probably disposed of it a long way away. After all, the grave didn't look as if it had been recently disturbed, so care had obviously been taken to cover up the substitution. It would have made more sense, to the doctor's way of thinking, to bury this fresher body on top of the original corpse, but without knowing exactly what motive was at play here, it was impossible to say why this hadn't happened.

'Can you compose a description of this woman I can issue to forces across the country?' Süleyman asked.

'Of course.'

'I'll see what we have in terms of missing women outstanding. Grandmothers are not usually numerous.'

'The old die,' Dr Sarkissian said.

'Don't we all,' the policeman replied.

'Fish.' The boy wrinkled up his nose.

The little İkmen had managed to get out of him about his origins had resulted in his finding out that Hafız came originally from Damascus. Not a place known for its fish. Unlike Kumkapı, where every other building was a fish restaurant, and those that were not were wet fish shops.

'Yes, it is rather pungent,' İkmen said as he sent a text to his daughter Çiçek and then lit up a cigarette. They were supposed to be going to some nameless carpet shop, but all he could see was fish. The boy asked for a cigarette, and İkmen gave him one as they walked down towards the centre of the district, Kumkapı Meydan, in silence.

A lot of people forgot how important the district of Kumkapı still was in the lives of İstanbul's ethnic Armenian minority. Although much depleted, it was still home to a small Armenian community, and remained the seat of the Orthodox Armenian patriarchate. İkmen's oldest friend, Arto Sarkissian, had got married in the church of Surp Asdvadzadzin more years ago than he cared to recall. Back then, there'd been a lot of fish too; there had always been fish in Kumkapı, just not quite this much, being mainly consumed by foreign tourists.

As they passed a brightly lit open-fronted restaurant, İkmen heard Russian being spoken, saw violinists warming up for a night of hard playing and watched sweating men cooking large quantities of seafood over open coal fires. For one reason or another, mainly because he couldn't be bothered, he hadn't eaten that day. Now he felt a stab of hunger. He ignored it. He didn't want to pay a lot of money for a nice piece of fish only to eat just half of it. As he began to draw away from sixty towards sixty-five, he was finding that his already small appetite was dwindling with each passing year.

'Here.'

For a moment he didn't really see the one very brightly coloured and startlingly modern carpet completely filling the window in front of him. This was because it, and its adjacent door, was squeezed between two fish restaurants. The sign above the window was just about visible; it said Galeri Bagratid.

'We're here?'

Before the boy could answer, a small, dark man of about fifty came out of the shop and offered İkmen his hand.

'I am Berat Aznavoryan,' he said. 'No relation to the famous French singer, as far as I know.'

İkmen took his hand. 'I am Çetin İkmen.'

'Yes, I know.' Aznavoryan smiled. 'Come in.'

İkmen walked up the few steps into the shop, but the boy, Hafız, didn't follow him. In fact, when İkmen looked round, he had disappeared.

Tiny pinpoints of light between the trees attested to the fact that many funerals had been celebrated in the great Karacaahmet

10

cemetery earlier that day. Some families would leave lamps burning after the funeral of a loved one, to provide illumination to the soul of the departed. Sergeant Ömer Mungun found the sight of them both comforting and at the same time unsettling.

Although he had lived in İstanbul and worked as Inspector Mehmet Süleyman's deputy for the last ten years, Ömer originally came from the ancient city of Mardin in the far south-east of the country. Nestled high on a vast rock looking out over the Mesopotamian plain, Mardin had always been a place of many faiths – Islam, Christianity, Judaism and also far older pagan beliefs. Ömer and his family subscribed to one of the latter, worshipping an ancient snake goddess called the Sharmeran. This meant that his beliefs about death didn't concur with those of his mainly Muslim colleagues – including the men and women conducting the fingertip search he was supervising.

He stood a few metres away and watched as rows of officers in uniform slowly fanned out through the grass, torches in their hands, some disappearing into the darkness beneath the trees. A forensic team was excavating the grave that should have contained the body of Perihan Bulut. It was possible that some fragments of her bones were still in there somewhere. But they weren't evident, not yet.

There was a rumour, which his boss would neither confirm nor deny, that the unknown woman who had been found in the grave was a victim of organ harvesting. One of the constables who had first responded to Dr Sarkissian's call for assistance claimed to have seen a large hole in the body. Word was it had been open and unstitched. But that didn't make sense. People who sold their organs were always stitched up after surgery, even if they later succumbed to internal bleeding or infection.

Back in Ömer's home town, a place now surrounded by refugee camps built to accommodate hundreds of thousands of displaced people from Syria, stories about organ harvesting were rife.

11

Kidneys were the most common currency, although eyes were also popular. The way it worked involved a potential donor being tissue-matched to a recipient. This was done by a broker, who would also sometimes care for the donor until his or her wounds began to heal. Once a match had been established, both patients would be operated on either locally – sometimes in a private house rented for just this purpose – or in the rich recipient's country of origin. The entire trade was predicated on the inequality that existed between the two parties. And of course it happened in İstanbul too. It happened in most places where the poor were numerous and the rich were few but empowered.

Ömer began to shiver. His father needed a heart bypass, but that wasn't going to happen any time soon, because the family didn't have enough money. They would if his father sold his house, but he wouldn't do that. The old man wanted to leave something to his two children. As he'd told Ömer last time he'd gone home, 'If you and your sister don't inherit this house, then everything I have done to put you through school and university has been for nothing.'

There was a logic to it. Ömer's father had no education and little money, but he'd been able to buy a house because back in the 1980s Mardin property had been cheap. That the Mungun place was now worth five hundred thousand euros was for him a vindication of all the hard work and suffering he had endured as a mere farm worker. Ömer couldn't argue with that even if he'd wanted to. The old man was so proud of his house and his children, his own existence was almost irrelevant to him.

Not so different, Ömer felt, from those who sold their kidneys to put their children through school.

Although it only had one window looking onto the street, Galeri Bagratid actually opened out into a vast premises, which, İkmen reckoned, probably ran behind the fish restaurants on either side.

The Armenian owner seemed to specialise in modern, startlingly coloured carpets.

'While our dealers are still all right to go into Afghanistan, I can get my hands on these amazing modern designs,' Aznavoryan said. 'I see them as expressions of both the rage and the creativity in that country.'

'They're certainly striking.'

The dealer smiled. 'You like carpets?'

'I have very few,' İkmen said. 'But those I do have, I treasure.'

'When a carpet speaks to a person, it does so for life,' Aznavoryan said. 'Follow me. It's down here.'

A small stone staircase with no banisters led down underneath the shop. On one side of the small landing, a door was open onto a room with a group of women sewing inside; on the other were more stairs. Darker and more scarred than the first staircase, this second flight led down past a room full of young men staring fiercely at computers. İkmen looked up and was slightly disconcerted at how far they had descended. Many shops and restaurants in the Old City concealed other businesses both above and below their shiny exteriors. Some of them even had ancient cisterns in their basements.

The lighting above the stairs became more sparse, and soon İkmen was aware of the fact that he couldn't easily see his own feet.

Aznavoryan, aware of his predicament said, 'Don't worry, Çetin Bey, almost there now.'

İkmen was about to ask where exactly when something creaked in front of him and his host opened a door into a brightly lit room that took his breath away.

All Cemal Yüksel had ever wanted to do was build a cool glass and metal bridge over the gorge that ran through his village in Cappadocia. He'd done well at university, going on to teach at

13

the faculty of engineering, where, somehow, he'd been denounced by either a colleague or a student. Why, he didn't know, because right up until the time he found himself in Silivri prison, he hadn't really taken much interest in politics. Being accused of participation in the failed coup of 2016 had, however, concentrated his mind, and when he was suddenly released, with no explanation, several months later, he decided to take more notice of current affairs. But with no prospect of employment – he might be innocent, but still no one wanted to know – it was difficult for him to do anything much but sleep rough and eat out of dustbins.

'But then I met Gold Bey,' he told his gawping guest.

Barely aware of the steaming tea glass in front of him, Çetin İkmen said, 'What is this place?'

It had been a Byzantine chapel. Age-blackened stone walls rose up on either side to meet in a curved barrel roof, covered with what looked like the ghosts of saintly frescos. More clearly visible were the paintings at the far end of the structure – studies in cobalt and terracotta of the Virgin and Child, the Archangel Michael, the hand and breath of God. And then there were the machines.

'Through Gold Bey, I met Berat Bey, who allows me to live and work here,' Cemal said. 'I am far too old to be on the street these days.'

İkmen saw Aznavoryan smile.

'Yes, but this . . .'

Not all of the machines moved. Some merely glinted in the light from the candles that lined the walls. Those that did move made variable noises – some whirred, some clicked, some operated in complete silence. Big or small, all of them were highly polished, constructed of different-coloured metals, and where they did move, their motion was smooth, almost hypnotic. But what they were for was not apparent.

'I never actually practised as a civil engineer,' Cemal said as he watched İkmen's astonishment with some amusement. 'I went straight into academia. Then I went to prison, and penury followed. Although Berat Bey allows me to live here rent-free, I still need to make money.'

'From these?'

'I always made things, even as a child,' he continued. 'One has to be interested in construction to even contemplate becoming an engineer. My parents were poor. I come from a village in Cappadocia, where my father raised goats. But my father's brother lived here in İstanbul, where he worked as a kapıcı. One year he sent me a present, a Meccano construction set. You know of them?'

'Yes,' İkmen said. 'I think it is a British toy.'

'That's right. I made all sorts of things. Bridges, houses, a train – I even made things of my own creation. Like these.'

The machines, whether moving or static, appeared to look at İkmen, as though they were sentient in some way.

'What do they do?' İkmen asked.

'Nothing,' Cemal replied.

'Oh come, Machine Bey, they feed the soul,' Berat Aznavoryan put in.

'Maybe, but they are without function.'

Aznavoryan turned to İkmen. 'I think you will agree, Çetin Bey, that these hand-made items are works of art.'

'Absolutely!'

Cemal shrugged. 'Maybe,' he said. 'But as you know, Berat Bey, they deliberately have no function. That,' he looked İkmen in the eye, 'is their point.'

Chapter 2

They were all going to eat together. That had been the plan. But then her father had contacted her to say he was going out to see someone in Kumkapı, and her boyfriend had sent a text to say that he'd be late. This left Çiçek herself and the other resident of the Sultanahmet apartment, her dad's elderly transsexual cousin, Samsun Bajraktar.

Radiant in red velvet, Samsun sat opposite Çiçek on the family's balcony, drinking Campari and soda.

'You should have a drink and relax, Çiçek,' she said as she lit a cigarette and then coughed expansively. 'You know how they are.'

Çiçek didn't reply. In her early forties, she couldn't recall a time when meals hadn't been disrupted by her father's job. When her mother had been alive, she'd given him hell about missing or being late for meals. When Çetin İkmen retired, Çiçek remembered her mother breathing a sigh of relief. But then Fatma İkmen had died. Involved in a road accident on the night of the attempted coup, she had succumbed to her injuries and died in her husband's arms. And now Çiçek's father was working again, albeit unofficially.

'I'll leave it a bit longer . . .' she said.

Samsun poured her a drink anyway. She'd seen it all so many times before. Women waiting for men and men just doing their own thing anyway. But in spite of this, she was glad that Çetin was getting out and about again. When Fatma died, the entire İkmen family had wondered whether her husband would survive.

16

But he had – just – even though he didn't come truly back to himself until he started working.

In an attempt to wipe the miserable expression off Çiçek's face, Samsun said, 'I've decided to call our kitchen guest Yiğit.'

Ever since just before Fatma İkmen's death, some members of the family – principally those who took after Çetin's mother Ayşe, a well-known witch – had reported the presence of a djinn in the family kitchen. Creatures of smokeless fire who lived between the human world and that of the angels, djinn were generally mischievous creatures who shared some characteristics with Western poltergeists. Samsun, Çetin, Çiçek and her brother Bülent could all see its hairy, snarling face and unpleasantly slack body much of the time.

'Why?' Çiçek asked. 'Personally, I wouldn't call it brave. Creeping up on us in the dark.'

'Which is why it is Yiğit,' Samsun said.

Belatedly, Çiçek worked it out.

'Ah,' she said, 'after the—'

Samsun held up a warning finger. Even in the privacy of their own homes, people avoided making jokes about politicians or others in power. She handed Çiçek a very strong Campari and soda.

'Samsun . . .'

'Oh, if you can't cook by the time the men get here, I will,' she said. 'It's only pasta, after all. Your father will barely eat any of it anyway, and if I know him, Prince Mehmet will be too busy looking into your eyes.'

Çiçek pulled a sour face. 'You think?'

'I know,' Samsun said. 'I've been studying Mehmet Süleyman ever since he started working with your father all those years ago. He's been married twice and had numerous lovers, including that mad gypsy woman over in Balat. But I've never seen him as stuck on someone as he is on you.'

'And yet he stands me up . . .'

17

'Oh don't be silly,' Samsun said. 'He's working. You know all about that. So far you've kept him keen by playing unconcerned. Don't come across desperate now or he'll think he's got you and take you for granted. You're a clever, beautiful girl and he's lucky to have you. Make sure he never forgets that.'

Çiçek had been going out with her father's former colleague for almost a year. She was, although she'd never admit it, deeply in love. She sensed he felt the same way about her. But she also knew that this scion of an old Ottoman family connected to that of the sultans was often presented with temptation. Even at over fifty, he was still handsome and charming, while that whiff of danger in his manner made him irresistible to many women.

But she also knew how passionate he was when they were alone together, and the thought of it made her smile. Samsun noticed, and smiled too.

'So the machines are works of art?' İkmen said.

'No.'

'Then . . .'

'People can dub them works of art if they wish, if they need to put a label on them,' Machine Bey said. 'But their true purpose resides in their lack of functionality. My time in Silivri was a crash course in political engagement, Çetin Bey. Happily cut off in my own department, I hadn't noticed how the modern world had distorted and darkened. Now we build vast transport systems designed to impress, we knock down people's homes to make way for glittering towers we know will collapse in even the smallest earthquake. We worry about how we look on social media. All over the world, we do nothing. That's what my machines express – a superficially beautiful nothing.'

Berat Aznavoryan's phone beeped.

'I must go back up to the shop,' he said. 'I will leave you gentlemen alone.'

18

When he had gone, Machine Bey said, 'Berat is a good friend. On those occasions when I sell one of my machines, he helps me.'

'Who buys your machines?'

'Ah, now there's a thing,' Machine Bey said. He led İkmen to a group of battered leather sofas and they both sat down. 'I am going to trust you with my life, Çetin Bey.'

Thankfully for İkmen, Machine Bey offered him a cigarette and lit one up for himself. He'd been literally on the cusp of begging to be allowed to smoke.

Once he had exhaled the first lungful, he said, 'You've told me of your detention and, of course, given the current climate, I know that you must have had to convince yourself I could be trusted before you invited me here.'

'And my present predicament is serious,' Cemal said. 'Çetin Bey, what I am going to tell you involves others like myself. For a variety of reasons, we have fallen foul of . . . of the norms of society.'

He was a dissident, albeit one who had come to dissent lately, but he was trying really hard not to say so. This made him an instant underdog, and İkmen always took their side.

'You clearly know my reputation, Machine Bey,' he said. 'So speak freely. How can I help? If I can, I will.'

'Thank you.' Cemal smiled. 'A friend of ours, a lady, has gone missing. I am afraid for her.'

'A lady who does what?' İkmen asked.

'These days she is a graffiti artist,' his host said. He handed İkmen a Polaroid photograph of something that made the former policeman snatch a sharp intake of breath.

'That is,' he said, 'pointed to say the very least.'

It was pitch black now. There was no point searching any more. Mehmet Süleyman assigned officers to guard the crime scene overnight, and then began the long walk with Ömer Mungun back to the nearest exit from the cemetery. Even the heavy light pollution from the city failed to illuminate the darkness that existed underneath and between the trees.

As the two men walked, they talked. Ömer was keen to discover whether his boss had found out anything more about the unexpected occupant of the grave.

'Nothing on the body to identify it,' Süleyman said. 'An elderly woman, and . . .' He took a deep breath. 'This is not for anyone's ears but your own.'

'Of course, sir.'

'Her heart had been removed.'

This was not quite what Ömer had been expecting. He wondered whether he should tell Süleyman that rumours about organ harvesting were already circulating, but decided against it.

'By that, I mean surgically removed,' Süleyman continued. 'In Dr Sarkissian's opinion.'

Ömer felt his face go cold. So the rumours were true.

'Her heart was removed for transplant?' he said. 'That must have killed her.'

'Quite.'

He had to stop for a moment. Süleyman stopped too.

'Sir, this is another level,' Ömer said. 'I mean, kidneys, eyes, we've had those for years. Those you can survive. But this . . . What happened? Was she kidnapped? Or was she persuaded to get involved in something without knowing the facts?'

'We don't know,' Süleyman said.

'And when you say elderly . . .'

'I couldn't really tell. Dr Sarkissian estimated she was over seventy-five.' He frowned as the implications within that hit him. 'Which is old . . .'

Ömer shook his head. 'Who would want a heart from a seventy-five-year-old?'

Süleyman said, 'I have no idea.'

20

'Unless the recipient was older?'

The two men began walking again, this time in silence.

Somewhere in the vastness of this dark cemetery, criminal activities could be taking place around other graves involving people's beloved friends and relatives. For many years, people who thought about such things, like Süleyman's ex-boss Commissioner Hürrem Teker, had been warning about the opportunities the city's huge and unmanageable burial grounds presented to criminals. Massive spaces in the middle of the city, deserted at night.

When the two men finally got back to their cars, it was almost ten o'clock.

As he climbed into his Fiat, Ömer said, 'I'm just about ready for my bed. See you in the morning, sir.'

Süleyman nodded. He wanted to go home but knew that he couldn't. Çiçek and who knew how many other members of the İkmen tribe were waiting for him in Sultanahmet. He had to go, he had to eat Çiçek's food, listen to Çetin's moans, entertain whoever else was in the apartment and kiss his beloved once they were alone. He wanted to do all that really. He would have just preferred to do it on another night.

'When did she go missing?' İkmen asked.

'Three weeks ago,' his host replied.

It was difficult not to keep staring at the machines. Though incomprehensible, they were all, in their own ways, striking, if not beautiful, even the ones that didn't move. Was this intentional?

İkmen pulled his thoughts back to the issue at hand.

'So tell me about her,' he said.

Machine Bey sighed. 'Like me, she has served time for some unnamed offence,' he said. 'We call her Actress Hanım, because of what she did in her life before.'

21

'We?'

'There are four of us, all in the same position; we all live under the care of others who either love us or have sympathy with us. Collectively we call ourselves the Moral Maze.' He smiled. 'A title thought up by one of our number, Gold Bey, a jeweller, who finds grim humour in the fact that we are all innocent – hence moral – and that some of us live underground in the maze that lies underneath this city.'

The life of the city beneath the ground was well documented. Punctuated not only by Byzantine chapels and ancient cisterns, İstanbul's vast underbelly also hid tunnels, storage areas, even a palace. If a person wanted to hide, there were plenty of opportunities.

'How do you communicate?' İkmen asked.

'Mainly online. We have all met together only a few times. It's not easy. Although none of us was ultimately tried and convicted of anything, our cards are marked, as it were. Moving around freely could put us in danger of arrest for some minor infraction that might see us back in prison.'

İkmen offered his host a cigarette, and they both lit up again. 'So this lady, this actress, tell me about her. How do you know she's missing?'

'She lives with another woman,' Cemal said. 'Though not as a couple, you understand. Do you watch soap operas, Çetin Bey?'

Ah, the glossy and dramatic Turkish TV series! Very successful both at home and abroad.

'No,' İkmen said. The lives of fictional rich folk were not his thing.

'Then maybe you won't know our Actress,' Machine Bey said. 'Her name is Sevval Kalkan. She played a character called Zeynep in a series called Family Is Everything. It was about a wealthy crime family who lived in a yalı on the Princes' Islands. A bit like a Turkish version of The Godfather.'

22

'I know the trope.'

Machine Bey smiled. 'It was very successful,' he said. 'But then, after the coup, Sevval was arrested. She was released around the same time as me, but by that time the character of Zeynep was being played by someone else, and Sevval was effectively blacklisted. Luckily she knew of another woman who had been through the same experience. You may have heard of her – the fashion designer, Olimpio?'

İkmen shook his head.

'Well, she has some money and has managed to retain her small flat in Beyoğlu, where the two of them lived until Sevval disappeared.'

'She wasn't arrested for graffiti?'

'No, that very fine example of her work is now in the possession of someone who appreciates such things.'

Spray-painted onto a wall, the image had shown a leading politician in a compromising situation with a woman. It was the sort of thing that could easily get a person arrested.

'How?' İkmen asked.

Machine Bey smiled. 'I don't know,' he said. 'I am merely repeating what Actress Hanım told us. Whether the authorities are aware of Sevval the graffiti artist, I don't know either.'

'I imagine they are.'

'And yet do you not think, Çetin Bey, that if she had been re-arrested, we would have heard about it? There has been nothing in the media as far as I am aware. Berat Bey knows the situation and he would have told me. No, she left the apartment she shares with Olimpio on the evening of the twenty-ninth of June. It's now the nineteenth of July, which makes the last time she was seen three weeks ago.'

'Do you know where she was going that evening?'

'No,' he said. 'All I know from Olimpio is that she said she was going out.'

'Didn't Olimpio ask her where?'

Machine Bey shrugged. 'It seems not. I don't know what the nature of their relationship is. I know they live together out of necessity, but whether they are friends or not is something I am not aware of. All I do know is that we are all worried, and that includes Olimpio.'

'We? You give me some names, some pseudonyms. Who exactly are we?' There was a pause, then İkmen said, 'I will have to know who these people are and where they live if I am to help you, Machine Bey. I will need to speak to them, find out what they know.'

'They know nothing; that is why I've called upon you.'

'And yet they probably know more than they think,' İkmen said. 'Now, let us start with you, Machine Bey . . .'

'Who did you say he was going to see?' Süleyman asked as he spooned pasta and sauce into his bowl.

'I didn't,' Çiçek said. 'The only message I got was that it was someone over in Kumkapı.'

'Who?'

She threw her arms in the air. 'I don't know! He didn't say! You know what he's like.'

Samsun watched. It was clear to her that Mehmet Bey had some problem, probably work related, that he wanted to get off his chest with the help of her cousin. Çiçek, on the other hand, wanted to talk about everything but her father. There was, Samsun knew, some jealousy on Çiçek's part over her father's relationship with her lover. She was in danger of alienating Prince Mehmet if he ever worked that out.

Samsun said, 'It's not the first time Çetin Bey has just gone out, and let's face it, even if he was here, he wouldn't be eating much.'

Neither of the other two said anything, although Prince Mehmet smiled. He had nice manners. He was also, Samsun could see, pale and tired looking. It was obvious to anyone, apart from Çiçek, that all he really needed was his own bed – alone. But the younger woman was, albeit unconsciously, touching him all the time. It wasn't healthy.

Apropos of nothing, Samsun broke the silence again. 'Have you seen the price of tomatoes today? Up a full lira from this time last week. People can't go on like this.'

Turkey's relationship with its principal ally, America, was under strain due to a number of factors, not least being the USA's seeming reluctance to extradite the alleged leader of the failed coup of 2016 to Ankara. Ever cautious, the already nervous international money markets had sent the lira tumbling against the dollar, which meant that Turks were having to pay ever more for their staples. It affected everyone.

Eventually Çiçek said, 'Why do you think this sauce is so thin? Just olive oil and herbs . . .'

'It's very tasty,' Süleyman said.

'You think so?'

He squeezed her hand. 'I do.'

It was a hot evening, but Samsun felt a chill run up her spine. Çiçek had started this relationship so well, but now she was turning into a doormat and a nag. When she'd finished her pasta, she excused herself and went to her room. It was best to leave the two of them alone, given their respective moods. If he had any sense, Prince Mehmet would make his excuses, go home and get some sleep. But as she closed the living-room door behind her, she heard the unmistakable sound of kissing.

If Machine Bey, otherwise known as Cemal Yüksel, hadn't decided to put his trust fully in Çetin İkmen, then the latter would have just forgotten about the whole thing. People either working for or sympathetic with those who had apparently denounced the Moral Maze members were everywhere, and

İkmen knew that he himself was not the kind of person of whom they would approve either. But Yüksel had, finally, been liberal with his information.

As İkmen walked slowly through the great hippodrome built by the Roman emperor Septimus Severus in the second century AD, he thought about how the city of İstanbul had always been awash with plots and subterfuge. Nothing really changed. The Roman emperors had given their people beer and circuses to keep them happy, not to mention the blood of the victims of their games, and now, in the modern world, it was roads, bridges and traitors.

As well as telling İkmen everything he knew about Sevval Kalkan, the Actress, Yüksel had filled him in on the other two members of the Moral Maze. Under the Olimpio label, Tuba Genç had designed clothes for the rich and famous both in Turkey and abroad. For some years her collections had been exhibited on the catwalks of Paris. Now penniless, apparently rattling around in her old apartment in Beyoğlu, she sold her skills to anyone who wanted them, and at knockdown prices. But of course, any prospective client also had to be discreet, or fearless, or both. Gold Bey, the jeweller Cumhur Polat, lived in a basement in Tarlabaşı making 'punk' jewellery out of old mobile phones and computer components for young people who liked to look a bit edgy.

The really sad thing about all this was the way these people's families had rejected them. Men and women in the same position but with family support could manage. But by either accident or design, these poor souls had found themselves alone. If indeed they were poor souls. Many years in the police force had taught Çetin İkmen that prisons were full of 'innocent' people. Nobody ever owned up to being rightfully arrested and convicted. But then he had not worked in the arena of political crime, an extremely grey area at the best of times. He'd always counted himself fortunate to have dealings only with killers.

Way too late for dinner, he sat down on a wooden bench and lit a cigarette. The authorities would, he knew, be very interested to know what Yüksel, Polat and Genç were up to and who was enabling them. He could, if he wanted, earn himself some kudos by exposing what were no doubt tax-evading activities. After all, they could be as guilty as sin, couldn't they? And yet he knew that his habit, for want of a better word, of always backing the little man wasn't going to have that. Not without evidence, which would or would not make itself apparent in the fullness of time. He had agreed to help them find Sevval Kalkan, and Cemal Yüksel was going to arrange meetings for him with the others. Yüksel had offered to pay, but İkmen had turned the money down. He didn't know what Machine Bey charged for his beautiful useless creations, but he imagined that they were relatively cheap. When he got home, provided everyone was out of the way, he'd try to find something equivalent on the Internet.

He rose to his feet and began to walk again. When he was almost home, he saw Süleyman come out of his building and get into his car. The younger man didn't see him, and İkmen wondered how he'd fared on his own with Çiçek and Samsun for company. His daughter had suddenly become noticeably possessive of her lover, and he wondered why that was. Did she know something that he didn't? Süleyman had a bad track record with women, and İkmen hoped that his friend wasn't cheating on his daughter. Poor Çiçek, with one broken marriage and a curtailed career behind her, didn't need any more misery in her life.

Uğur Bulut watched his brother's eyes fix on that nebulous blob in the middle of the Bosphorus once known as Galatasaray Islet. Lokman had always maintained that Uğur had only bought this house in Arnavautköy so that he could see the islet, now in darkness, from his top-floor terrace.

'Who owns it now?' Lokman pointed out into the night, his

27

finger seeming almost to touch the darker patch of black in the waterway's widening girth beyond the first Bosphorus Bridge.

'The club,' Uğur said, by which he meant Galatasaray football club, his passion for over thirty years.

'So why'd they demolish the restaurants?' Lokman continued.

'I don't know the ins and outs of it,' Uğur replied. Officially the club's general assembly had ordered the demolition of the islet's once famous and popular restaurants because the structures were unstable. But there had also been rumours at the time that İstanbul municipality had wanted the stunning location for the site of a new mosque. The truth of the matter was still unclear, while the half-demolished islet lay, a ghost of its former self, in darkened limbo.

Uğur sat down opposite his brother. A warm breeze was blowing off the Bosphorus, which was a relief after a long, hot and terrible day. Lokman hadn't accompanied him to their mother's graveside for the exhumation the previous evening, which was probably why he looked so fresh. Uğur watched his brother as he gazed out over the vast waterway behind the house. He'd always been a lazy bastard. Even as a child, when their mother had been working hundred-hour weeks to get her business in Beyoğlu up and running, he had not even been able to do his part, which had rarely consisted of more than getting himself to school on time. Then, when the Gaziantep pastane, their mother's patisserie, had really taken off, he had been too busy with his university friends to lend a hand.

It had been Uğur who had made the deals with the pistachio nut producers of Gaziantep to supply only their very top-class product for transformation into sweet, sticky baklava. The Bulut family originated in Gaziantep, and so to trade with local business people hadn't been onerous. But Uğur had made the most of his contacts, and now had his own interests in tourism to the area, as well as running his mother's old business. Lokman, by contrast, had done little beyond take money from his mother and his brother and borrow from others. Now he wanted more. In fact he wanted what Uğur had, and was prepared to besmirch his own mother's name in order to get it.

After a long silence, he said what was on his mind.

'Are you sure what was found in Mother's grave wasn't her?'

Of course now he suspected Uğur of staging an elaborate hoax. Another conspiracy theory to add to the many such fictions he claimed to believe. Lokman routinely read the more sensationalist newspapers and was, to Uğur's way of thinking, addicted to conspiracy websites online.

'The body we found was not that of a woman who had been buried for five years,' Uğur said.

'How do you know? You're not a doctor.'

'A doctor was in attendance.' He leaned forward to catch his brother's eye. 'You could have been there.'

Lokman said nothing, which only served to infuriate Uğur.

'If you had been, you'd know and I wouldn't now have to try and justify myself to you.'

'You'll do anything to keep everything for yourself,' his brother hissed.

'I give you money! I clear up after you! You do nothing.'

'You're not my mother's son. Look at you! Blond and big and—'

'Like our father!'

Lokman stood up. 'I don't remember him. I grew up fatherless, you—'

'Mother and I raised you,' Uğur said. 'We gave you everything. You wanted to go to university; I never got to go.'

'No, you got our mother's business. And her house as well as your own. I have to live in a slum!'

It was like a slap in the face. Uğur had bought Lokman an apartment in Tarlabaşı because he'd wanted to live somewhere 'edgy'. That it was, in parts, a slum was what he'd liked about it. As he had always been, he was the author of his own displeasure. He was also the instigator of this exhumation. Uğur would have preferred that they both have comparison DNA tests, but Lokman had maintained that his brother would cheat in some way. How he would do that was a mystery.

There was a bit of Uğur that took some pleasure in things having worked out the way his brother had not anticipated. But it was only a small frisson. That his mother was not in her own grave was deeply troubling. Where was she, and why had some unknown woman's corpse replaced her?

Chapter 3

Sometimes whether or not a person noticed something was dependent upon what they were looking for. In all his years of visiting the tiny bookshop owned by an ancient called İbrahim Dede, Çetin İkmen had never before noticed how many ornaments sat amongst the old man's books. There were crystal models of the imperial mosques, some rather sinister-looking knitted dolls from Anatolia, miniature coffee pots and, almost hidden from view by a photograph album from the nineteenth century, something that looked very much like one of Machine Bey's creations.

Situated in the Sahaflar Çarşısı, or Book Bazaar, İbrahim Dede's little shop was packed to the rafters with volumes on just about everything, some of which had been acquired by his father almost a hundred years ago. Like many of the booksellers in the Sahaflar Çarşısı, İbrahim Dede was a dervish, a deeply spiritual man whose mind was forever open to new, or old, esoteric frontiers.

As usual, İkmen bowed to the old man before he spoke.

'İbrahim Dede, it's been far too long since we last saw each other.'

İbrahim Dede put his hand out, and İkmen kissed it.

'A week may pass, or a year,' the old man said, 'but you are always welcome here, Çetin Bey. Now come and join me for a glass of tea and I will see how I may be able to serve you.'

The two men sat on a pair of battered stools at the back of the shop while a boy, who magically appeared from nowhere, brought them glasses of tea. He was, the old man explained, one of his many grandsons.

İkmen hadn't gone to İbrahim Dede's shop expecting to find anything connected to his latest commission. In fact, in the absence of any further communication from Machine Bey, he had come to the Sahaflar in order to amuse himself and, possibly, to talk to the old man about the djinn that lived in his kitchen. The often malignant creatures frequently appeared, or so it was said, in houses where someone was about to die. İkmen's djinn had turned up a few months before his wife's death. But now that he had seen the strange gold-coloured spider-like thing on İbrahim Dede's shelf his mind was entirely upon that.

He'd spent much of the previous night looking at whatever he could find online about the people who called themselves the Moral Maze. Much had been taken down since their respective falls from grace. Sevval Kalkan probably had more mentions than the others. She had started life as a model and progressed to Family Is Everything via TV commercials and a couple of kids' shows. Tall and very slim, she was an attractive woman who looked a lot younger than forty-five. In the soap opera, she had played the favourite daughter of the mafia boss character Volkan Akan and was a magnet for the attentions of all the local rival mafia bosses. It was pure hokum, but millions loved the programme.

İkmen reached up and took the metal spider thing off its shelf. 'Interesting,' he said. The look of the object was so typical of Machine Bey's stuff, it couldn't have come from anywhere else.

'Ah. If I may . . .' The old man took it from İkmen and put it down on the floor. Slowly, one leg at a time, it travelled forwards, propelled by its own weight.

'What is it?' İkmen asked.

'I am told it is a machine of sorts,' İbrahim Dede said. 'Produced by an artist no one seems to know anything about. It's beautifully balanced, hence the appearance of motion.'

'Where did you get it?'

'From my oldest son.'

'I like it.'

'I can ask him where he got it if you like,' the old man said. 'But my understanding is that this artist's works are unique, and so I doubt you'd be able to buy something the same.'

'I'd like to see more,' İkmen said. 'If you can let me know . . .'

'Of course. If my son remembers, I will tell you.' He paused for a moment, and then he said, 'So what can I help you with today, Çetin Bey?'

'Djinn,' İkmen said.

'Oh dear. Are you bothered by one?'

'It would seem so,' İkmen said. 'It came before my wife died and . . . Well, it now seems to be a permanent fixture.'

Machine Bey had told him that his work was being sold, but İkmen wondered who, apart from İbrahim Dede's son, was buying. The old dervish had always been the type of person who supported those in trouble, and his son was probably of a similar mind. He suspected that those in law enforcement would probably be interested too. After all, Machine Bey and his friends, though now at liberty, remained under suspicion.

Mehmet Süleyman's phone rang. As he picked it up, he noticed that the caller was Arto Sarkissian.

'Doctor?'

He heard the Armenian clear his throat. 'I thought I'd update you on my investigations into the unknown body from the exhumation at the Karacaahmet cemetery,' he said.

It had been on Süleyman's mind all night. He'd gone back to his apartment after seeing Çiçek but hadn't been able to sleep. The thought of somebody moving bodies around in the city's cemeteries had haunted him.

'I've found what appears to be the site of a cannula insertion in the left hand,' the doctor continued. 'Botched somewhat, causing considerable bruising. This would seem to suggest that the woman had some sort of medical procedure . . .'

'Or IV vitamins?' It was still quite common practice in certain Turkish hospitals to prescribe intravenous vitamins or rehydration fluids to patients feeling generally unwell.

'Possibly. But given the fact that a surgical procedure has been performed on her, my feeling is that she was anaesthetised prior to the removal of her heart. I say this because the organ has been tidily and expertly extracted; there are no signs of any defensive wounds; and now this cannula site.'

'But no one, surely, would give up their own heart? That is certain death.'

'Unless she didn't know that was going to happen,' the doctor said. 'Maybe she was told she was going in for gall bladder surgery. She has several gallstones, which I would think could be extremely painful.'

'Yes, but in a hospital . . .'

'Not necessarily. Inspector, you know as well as I that there is a considerable trade in harvested organs in this country, and as far as I am aware, they don't always pass through hospitals.'

In the past, harvested organs had mainly moved onto the market via corrupt staff in private medical facilities. But now, particularly on the borders with Syria and Iraq, areas thick with desperate refugees, a lot of trade originated from private dwellings using the services of disgraced or corrupted doctors. It was a development that had resulted in many more donors succumbing to infection.

'As well as a battery of blood tests, I've also ordered a hair follicle test, firstly for DNA purposes and then to try and determine what drugs she might have been given,' the doctor continued. 'Most of them will have cleared her system, but if I can isolate one or more constituents of the drugs used in general anaesthesia, we might be on firmer ground regarding our organ-harvesting thesis.'

'Of course.'

'As for personal effects, she was buried in her clothes, şalvar trousers and a shirt, before being wrapped in a shroud. Only one possible identifying artefact: a gold locket that was in the pocket of her trousers.'

'Send me a visual?'

'Of course, but it's old by the look of it, and contains a photograph of a man.'

'Oh?'

'Ah, don't get too excited,' the doctor said. 'It's sepia, which means it's probably early twentieth century. And it's faded.'

'All right, but send it to me anyway.'

'Will do.'

When the call was over, Süleyman put his phone on his desk and leaned back in his office chair. The woman must have been tricked with a promise of elective surgery. Maybe whoever had offered it to her had claimed to do so cheaply. Maybe they had even taken money from her before her death. His train of thought just got worse. And where were her family? Nobody answering the description of this woman had been reported missing in the İstanbul metropolitan area in the last four weeks. Who was she, and why had someone deemed it necessary to hide her corpse in an existing grave? And where was the body of Perihan Bulut? There couldn't have been very much left of her after five years, surely. Why remove her bones?

He picked up his copy of Hürriyet and scan-read the report of the incident. Now that it was in the public domain, the department had set up a phone line for information, and so soon every crazy in the city would be calling up to give vent to their pet theories. One or two genuine leads might emerge, but in

35

Süleyman's experience that was unlikely. Especially now, when the world appeared to be polarising around ideas that were not only idiotic but dangerous.

There she was, the old whore! Known locally as Sugar Hanım, Tansu Barışık was the owner of a large, battered house down by the Syrian Orthodox church. All sorts lived there above the small, damp basement flat she inhabited – pornographers, pimps, drag artists, students, strippers, kids who called themselves artists. Bless them.

Cumhur Polat scoured the rough ground at his feet for components he could use to make his jewellery. The local drug dealers often threw away their mobile phones, smashing them up first so that no one could use them. It was amazing what a skilled hand could do with a couple of SIM cards and a broken screen, though it was a far cry from fashioning stylish creations in gold, silver and precious stones, which was what Cumhur used to do.

It was his brother, Bilal, who had effectively ended Cumhur's career, though not on purpose. Bilal had been a follower of the sheikh who it was thought had orchestrated the coup against the government in 2016. Even though, like most people, he had been completely against the coup and had stopped following the sheikh by that point, his association with him had not been forgotten. In turn, Cumhur's relationship to Bilal had damned him, helped by the jealousy shown to him by a much younger goldsmith with whom he worked. This man, Sadi Bey, had openly envied Cumhur's talent whilst at the same time never showing any signs of wanting to put in the hard work needed to improve. And so he'd taken a shortcut and denounced the older man.

A stay in Silivri prison had followed, after which Cumhur had lost not only his job but his apartment and his wife too. She worked for the local municipality, and so any contact with a felon, even one who was never actually convicted, was beyond the pale. And their marriage was effectively over anyway.

Luckily Cumhur's friend Berat Aznavoryan had taken pity on him and provided him with rooms in one of the houses his family still owned in Tarlabaşı, plus a small amount of cash to start his own business. Cumhur had done well. Catching the vibe among young people for edgy junk jewellery, he made beautiful things out of stuff other people didn't want, and so his overheads were minimal. He soon got to know his neighbours in Tarlabaşı, people like Sugar Hanım, who didn't judge, and then he met people like himself.

It was concerning that the Actress hadn't been in contact for three weeks. He picked up a broken iPhone cover off the ground and looked at it. Rose gold; not real, of course, but he could incorporate it into something. He put it in his pocket. He thought, if the Actress has been taken away by someone, does that mean the rest of us are in danger?

His phone beeped to let him know he had an email. It came from the Designer, Olimpio, and said: Machine Bey has found someone to look for the Actress. This man wants to speak to us all. I've said yes and am seeing him today. Will let you know what I think.

Machine Bey had mentioned the name Çetin İkmen to him a few days ago. An ex-policeman, İkmen was also the father-in-law of a one-time colleague, Berekiah Cohen. He thought they were probably in safe hands.

Cumhur Polat, Gold Bey, returned to his basement room and spread out his latest finds on his workbench. He was almost out of stock and would have to work hard to replenish it. It would seem that for good or ill, a significant number of Turkish youths liked both what he made and the fact that buying stuff from him could be seen as an act of subversion.

* * *

Although he was not a native of İstanbul, there were people in the city who, when it came to authority figures, would only talk to Sergeant Ömer Mungun. These were men and women who originally came from the far south-east of the country, most especially those who, like Mungun, spoke Aramaic. A case in point was one-eyed Wahıd Saatçı.

'Strangely, I'm not going to ask you how business is going,' the officer said to Wahıd. They were sitting outside one of the smallest cafés in the city, the policeman and the drug dealer. Situated beside the storage facility that had once been the Mayor Synagogue in the Golden Horn district of Hasköy, it was a place without a name that served only one product: the thick, milky menengiç coffee, made with pistachios, so loved by people like Wahıd from the city of Urfa.

Wahıd sighed. 'So why are you here?' he said. A long-time police informant, Wahıd offered a very particular product. A devotee himself, he bought his pure opium only from two small farmers in Antep province, and his clients were almost exclusively rich and sometimes famous.

'We may have a situation with organ harvesting,' Ömer said.

Wahıd had only been in İstanbul for five years; prior to that, back in his home city of Urfa, he had almost certainly come across this trade. It all happened down on the border with Syria: gun running, drug peddling, people trafficking, organ harvesting. Refugees were just so vulnerable . . .

Wahıd stared levelly at him with his one grey eye and said nothing.

'You and I both know this is rare, but not unknown, in İstanbul,' Ömer continued. 'We both know it is more common in Urfa, and these days in the Tur Abdin.'

The Tur Abdin or Slaves of God region was where Ömer's home city of Mardin was situated. Almost on the Syrian border, it was a place thick with monasteries, hermits and other slaves of whatever god one could care to name.

'I am aware that different trades on the border may intersect,' Ömer said. 'Those of us at the edge of the world have always assisted one another.'

'They've usually fought.'

'Sometimes, yes. But they are aware of each other.'

'I don't know of such a trade here in the city, Ömer Bey.'

'Not even one possibly organised by Syrian brothers?'

Wahıd Saatçı came from a family of Syrian Christians resident in Urfa for generations. He'd come to İstanbul to make his fortune, and had succeeded. Deep inside the Syriani community of the city, he would know whether his brothers from the east were involved in such an operation. A man of expensive tastes, there wasn't much he wouldn't do for money. And Ömer knew from past experience that when Wahıd said he didn't know about something, he usually did.

'You'll be well remunerated.'

Wahıd cocked his head to one side, 'Maybe.'

'Maybe what? Maybe I'll pay you well, or . . .'

'Maybe I'll see what I can discover,' he said. 'But there will be overheads. As you know, Ömer Bey, no one talks in this city without at least a small consideration.'

Ömer put his hand in his jacket pocket and took out a roll of banknotes. He passed them across the table to Wahıd.

'That should get you started.'

Wahıd nodded, pocketed the money and stood up.

'I assume I'm paying for your menengiç . . .'

Wahıd laughed

'I'm a poor man with only one eye, Ömer Bey. It would be churlish of you not to take pity . . .'

* * *

39

By rights, because Perihan Bulut had been buried in one of the newest parts of the Karacaahmet cemetery, within walking distance of the main entrance, her grave should have been well protected. As well as custodians who worked at the cemetery bureau, there were also guards who, according to some visitors, were rather strict about the taking, or not, of photographs.

Now Süleyman was confronted by a group of these men while he waited for Ömer Mungun to arrive. An early-morning appointment with an informant, who could be useful to the investigation had made the sergeant late.

'Is this colleague of yours—'

'He's on his way,' Süleyman said to the small man at his side.

The gatekeeper and his guards would need to be interviewed separately, and while Süleyman was accompanied by a small cohort of uniforms, he needed another pair of eyes and ears in the interview process.

After almost ten minutes of uncomfortable silence, Ömer arrived.

'Sir . . .' he panted.

'We can use the gatekeeper's office,' Süleyman said.

'Oh yes, indeed,' the small man at his side said. 'Anything we can do to assist you in the pursuit of your investigation, efendi.'

The servility of many public officials when dealing with the police made Süleyman cringe, but he swallowed his distaste and followed the elderly man to his office.

'This place is terribly overcrowded, as you can see, efendi,' the man said as he sat down behind his desk. 'Can I get you some tea?'

'No thank you,' Süleyman said. He and Ömer Mungun sat down opposite.

'We can't cope, to be honest,' the gatekeeper, Türgüt Bey, said. 'I mean, the older graves are just sinking into the ground. We need more land, but there isn't any. In some places you can't even walk without treading on some poor soul's grave.'

Ömer said, 'It's not easy—'

'But that is not our problem,' Süleyman interrupted. 'It is, as I understand it, your job and the job of your guards to keep the cemetery safe from grave robbers, necrophiliacs and the like.'

'It is! But it's hard—'

'Then do another job,' Süleyman said.

Both Ömer and Türgüt Bey audibly gasped at the bluntness of his words. But then Süleyman could be blunt if occasion demanded it; even cruel at times.

'I do remember Perihan Bulut's funeral,' the gatekeeper said. 'She was a famous lady. Her pastane is one of the most celebrated in the city. Tourists go there. It was reported in the papers and everything. Flowers were placed on her grave regularly by her sons. I must admit I was shocked when we got the order for exhumation through. I think it was something to do with a DNA test—'

'That's not important,' Süleyman said. 'What is important is that the body that was found in Perihan Hanım's grave had been dead for what is estimated to be around two weeks. Our forensic team are analysing the soil to see if disturbance within its structure can give us any more clues. But it would seem that the unknown woman was buried within a few days of death. She was encased in a shroud as custom dictates, and not simply flung into the grave. But she shouldn't have been there at all.'

'Of course she shouldn't! I don't know what else I can say. Nothing sinister has been reported to me. You can check my logs. Of course we do get kids breaking in from time to time, but that's usually teenagers looking for somewhere to be together.'

'Is that a big problem?'

'No! As I say, it happens sometimes. It's quiet here, especially at night, and you know what teenagers are like. The boys, the guards, usually chase them out. We've a couple of men who take that sort of activity quite seriously – religious men, you know.

41

But I've always believed that unless desecration is taking place, there's no need to do anything more than frighten them off.'

'What about repeat offenders?' Ömer asked.

'What, kids who keep coming in to meet each other? Not that I know of,' the gatekeeper said. 'But ask the boys. As I say, it's not something I take too seriously. Youngsters do these things. It's their hormones!'

'Unless it's a cover for something more sinister,' Süleyman said.

Türgüt Bey sighed, and brought out a large book, which he placed on his desk. 'This is my incident ledger,' he said. 'Everything out of the ordinary or untoward is recorded in here. That includes incidents that are reported to me by our guards. As far as I'm concerned, nothing sinister has happened this year.'

Süleyman took the book from him. Where the gatekeeper's fingers had been, he could feel wetness from his sweat. Although hot outside, the office had powerful air conditioning, which was set very cool. Türgüt Bey had to be nervous. But then he probably would be whether or not he had any connection to the incident. Officials like gatekeepers could easily lose their jobs if their integrity was even so much as questioned. He passed the book to Ömer.

'Have a look,' he said.

Ömer perused the book while being watched by the gatekeeper and his own imperious superior. Fortunately, even skimming the tome convinced him there was nothing to see.

'Nothing here, sir.'

Süleyman turned back to the gatekeeper. 'What about digital records?'

'On the computer?'

'Yes.'

'Only in part,' he said. 'We do things the old-fashioned way here. Generally. For the past fifteen years burials have been recorded digitally, which is why I can tell you that Perihan Bulut was buried on the twentieth of December 2013. We do have written records from the past, but they are not comprehensive. This place has been in existence since the thirteenth century; don't ask me what that is in the Hijri calendar . . .'

Türgüt Bey was clearly not a religious man; he had probably not chosen to work in close contact with ministers of religion. Süleyman wondered what he had done before he came to the Karacaahmet.

'And of course,' he continued, 'we also get the pilgrims coming to pray at the tomb of Karaca Ahmet up on Bağlarbaşı Selimiye Caddesi. Begging for miracles or giving thanks.'

The thirteenth-century mystic after whom the cemetery was named was a saint in the Alevi Muslim canon. Famed for his humane treatment of the mentally ill, Karaca Ahmet was close to the hearts of many Alevis, including, Süleyman imagined, the Bulut family.

'They're not generally a problem,' the old man continued, 'but sometimes they bring animals they wish to sacrifice. I'm not against it; I just find it strange.'

'Presumably the dead animals are taken away and the meat distributed?'

'Yes. It's no bother, but . . .'

Initially Süleyman hadn't taken the gatekeeper for a secular person, but as he got to know more about him, it became apparent that that was what he was.

Türgüt Bey leaned across his desk. 'If we had trouble here, I would tell you. The fact is that this place is quiet, and to be honest, that's why I work here. I want an easy life, Inspector.'

'What did you do before you worked here, Türgüt Bey?' Süleyman asked. 'I have a feeling it was something quite different from this.'

The gatekeeper sighed. 'Oh yes,' he said. He paused for a moment and then looked up, smiling. 'I was a lawyer.'

Süleyman raised his eyebrows. 'A person more used to being called efendi than one using that term to others.'

'The world has changed a lot in recent years,' Türgüt Bey said. 'Looking after the dead is far easier than trying to help the living.' He changed the subject. 'I understand the body you found in Perihan Hanım's grave was that of a woman. There was a suggestion in the paper that she might have donated an organ . . .'

'Yes,' Süleyman said. 'An elderly lady. But I can tell you no more than that at this time.'

'I see.'

Had the gatekeeper wanted to know how she had died? It would have been a natural question to ask. But he didn't pursue it. Maybe that was the lawyer in him coming through. Such people, in Süleyman's experience, knew very well when to pursue a line of questioning and when to be quiet.

What kind of lawyer had he been? And what had he done, or not done, that had pushed him into such a lowly field of employment?

While the inspector was thinking about these things, Türgüt Bey rose to his feet and said, 'Do you want to question the boys now?'

Chapter 4

She was very tall. When she stood in front of her window with the light coming in behind her, she looked like one of Giacometti's long, thin sculptures.

Çetin İkmen gazed around the room, which was crammed with books, fabrics and a few upholstered chairs that had clearly seen better days.

'Sit down,' she said.

He'd got close to her once, when she had let him in, and he'd noticed how bad her colour was, how sunken her cheeks.

'Thank you.'

Machine Bey had told him that the Designer, Olimpio, lived in an apartment in Beyoğlu, but he hadn't expected it to be so high up and light.

She continued to stand, silently, as if making some sort of dramatic statement with her body in front of the window. Was she doing it as a reflex, without thought, or was she trying to make an impression? İkmen had come across many artistic types during his career with the police and had never been able to make his mind up about whether those in the arts were posing or just simply attention-seeking.

'So, Miss . . .'

'Call me Olimpio,' she said. 'It reminds me of what I once was.' At last she allowed herself to sink into the nearest chair, then she smiled. It looked like a skeleton grinning. İkmen wondered what the hell could have done that to her. He took his notebook out.

'Olimpio,' he said. 'You know who I am and why I'm here . . .'

'For Sevval,' she said.

Now that he knew that her teeth were brown and broken, he couldn't look anywhere else. 'Yes.'

'She left to go out on the twenty-ninth of June, a Friday,' she said. 'It was early evening, not a good time for people like us to be out and about, not with so many police around. But Sevval does as she pleases.'

Without asking whether he minded, she lit a cigarette. İkmen, though pretty desperate to light up himself, practised self-control and got on with the interview. He had a feeling that this woman was only just holding her emotions together, and that any sort of interruption could very easily throw her off course. Even if the only real emotion he could actually detect was anger.

'What time was this approximately?'

'It must have been seven, seven thirty,' she said. 'The street was just beginning to get crowded.'

Olimpio's apartment was situated on Sahane Sokak, a Beyoğlu street thick with bars and restaurants. And although it was on the top floor of a six-storey building, İkmen imagined it could get noisy.

'Did she tell you where she was going?'

'No,' she said. 'And I didn't ask.'

'May I ask why not? From my point of view, when one is in some sort of collective, particularly when one may be in danger—'

'We found ourselves together,' Olimpio said. 'Not by choice, but circumstance. I knew her from her time on Family Is Everything. I designed costumes for the first season. I went out to Büyükada, saw some of the episodes being filmed. Sevval struck me as a bit of a diva at the time, but that's nothing new in her industry or mine. When she was arrested, I felt for her, though, and when I was arrested I understood what she was going through.'

'Do you know what her alleged connection to the—'

46

'No,' she said. 'We got out of Silivri within days of each other and met up by chance when I was leaving my apartment to go shopping. She was homeless. Her family had completely disowned her. What kind of person would I be if I hadn't taken her in?' But she didn't look happy about it.

'Did you know Machine Bey or Gold Bey before . . .'

'Before I found myself a non-person?'

She was bitter, which was understandable. But if her appearance was anything to go by, she had allowed that bitterness to entirely take her over. İkmen had looked at some online photographs of her from London Fashion Week three years ago, and while this woman was clearly the same person, she was now ravaged by something.

'I knew Cumhur, Gold Bey,' she said. 'I worked with him on several of my collections. He produced some incredible pieces of jewellery for me in 2015. But . . .' She shrugged. 'Just to be clear, and in case you listen to gossip, I was not arrested for being the mistress of this holy man everyone hates. I've never had any connection to him or his organisation. I don't even believe in God.'

'So on what grounds were you brought to Silivri?'

'Like so many, like Sevval, I was denounced by a competitor who, let us say, has better connections than I.'

It was a familiar story, and, although those who had been wrongly denounced were usually released from jail, their careers and sometimes their social lives were over.

'I know I will never work in fashion in this country again,' Olimpio said, 'and without my passport, I can't even go elsewhere.'

Passports were always confiscated when people entered the prison system. But those whose supposed crimes were political sometimes didn't get them back. So far so familiar.

'To go back to Sevval, Machine Bey told me that she had recently started making graffiti art. Can you tell me anything about this?'

'I think it was shit.'

'What?'

'Didn't Cemal show you any pictures of her "art"? Politicians being sucked off. Oh, how new is that idea?' She waved her hands and shrugged. 'Childish rubbish. And dangerous too. If the police had caught her, they could have got to all of us. Selfish bitch!'

'And yet Machine Bey told me that artwork was sold . . .'

'To some super-cool so-called dissident,' she said. 'Some child of conservative parents who wants to look edgy. Whoever it was must have paid handsomely to have the local cops turn a blind eye when bricks disappeared from somewhere round here.'

'Do you know who this person was?'

'Not a clue,' she said. 'Sevval and I did not do a lot of talking after her first week here.' She ground her cigarette out in an ashtray and immediately lit another.

'Do you mind if I smoke?' İkmen asked.

'Go for it,' she said. 'There's an ashtray behind you.'

He lit up.

'My mother always said I was too soft to live,' Olimpio said. 'I always thought she was talking nonsense until I lived with Sevval. She was – is – selfish, rude, thoughtless . . . I could go on. I know I should have thrown her out, but I couldn't. Unlike the rest of us, she's a famous face and so she couldn't even lie to get what she needed to live. I'll be honest, I'm glad she's gone. Cemal and Cumhur liked her – she's one of those women who gets on better with men. They're genuinely afraid for her. I'm more afraid of what she can do to harm us.'

'You think she might do that?'

'Who knows? She made, so she said, ten thousand lira from the sale of her "work of art", so she's not without money now.' She leaned forward in her chair. 'You can probably tell that I didn't like her.'

'Well, yes . . .'

48

'And I'm not embarrassed about that. But I can also tell you that I wouldn't hurt her. Why would I? As Machine Bey told you, we all make our living by selling our skills to those who don't care what we might have done and who are not perhaps as afraid as they should be. My father left me this flat. It's all I've got and so if I can earn enough to keep the lights on and feed myself, that's my only concern. The world outside my door can disappear for all I care.'

'And Sevval?'

She made a barking sound in her throat; a bitter laugh. 'OK, she's a lot younger than me, but the little bitch was addicted to herself. That's why when she went out on that Friday night and didn't come back, I didn't immediately think anything of it. She'd fuck anyone. She told me she even fucked a cop one night.' She shook her head. 'I'll be honest with you, if and when she returns, I don't know whether I'll be able to take her back.'

'Do Gold Bey and Machine Bey know about this?'

'No,' she said. 'I've said nothing to them. They're men; she charms them, and I have to say, Gold Bey really does get on well with her. They met some years ago when she was in a play in Harbiye. I don't think they've ever been lovers, but I don't know. Not now, I doubt. Poor Cumhur lives in some dive in Tarlabaşı, looking like shit and making plastic gewgaws out of junk for morons who think that living as we do is cool.'

'Your customers,' İkmen said.

'Yes.' She turned her large bloodshot eyes on him. 'Fucking ghouls who feed off our poor broken souls.'

For a moment İkmen felt stunned by the violence of her words, then he said, 'May I have a look at Sevval Hanım's room?'

'If you like,' she said. 'There's nothing in there but a few clothes.'

On the face of it, she wasn't wrong. Sevval had lived in a box room with a single bed and a wardrobe half full of garments. There were no photographs, no handbags; a couple of pairs of earrings on a bedside table, but that was it. Did this mean that she had taken everything that might be personal to her when she left? He looked underneath the bed. There weren't even any slippers, but there was something, and it was encased in a foil pouch on the floor.

According to his employment record, twenty-three-year-old cemetery guard Raşım Dorsay was local, from Üsküdar, and lived with his father and siblings. Before becoming a guard, he'd worked on a building site in Şişli. His educational record was poor and he had probably never left İstanbul. They'd already interviewed four cemetery guards, and Süleyman was beginning to feel as if their faces were all merging into one young, amorphous image. Raşım Dorsay, however, was rather different. When Ömer Mungun asked him why he was a cemetery guard, instead of saying as the others had, 'It's a job,' he replied, 'It's important to keep our martyrs safe.'

There were a considerable number of people who believed that all their deceased forebears were martyrs. In fact, any dead Muslim could be described as such, irrespective of how they died. Many people who used this term were pious.

'You're religious?' Süleyman asked Dorsay.

'Not really.'

He looked up. The guard was a slim, attractive young man with a very open face.

'I pray when I'm able, I fast during Ramazan if I am well enough,' Dorsay continued. 'I love God and His Prophet but I am aware that by a lot of people's standards I am not overly pious.'

And yet, Süleyman felt, he was probably all the better for his lack of outward religiosity. His colleagues were rather more keen on people knowing just how devout they were. Up to this point there had been rather too much swearing on the lives of mothers or the souls of local saints for Süleyman's taste.

'You've worked here at the Karacaahmet for the last three years,' Ömer said.

'Yes, sir.'

Which meant that, unlike his colleagues, he wouldn't have been around to see the burial of Perihan Bulut.

'You worked in the building trade prior to coming here.'

'Yes. I prefer this.'

'Have you witnessed any incidents during your time here?'

'Of course,' Dorsay said. 'Kids getting in and attempting to have sex or take drugs happens a lot, especially in the summer.'

'So now?'

'Yes. The school holidays are very long. A lot of parents work and can't look after them. They come here because they're bored and they want to be bad to relieve that boredom. I used to do it myself when I was a kid.'

'What?'

'I'd climb over the wall and smoke,' he said. 'Then I started reading the gravestones and found them really interesting. I began to wonder who these people were, what they'd done. If you're poor, there's not much to do when you're young.'

'So you've sympathy with the kids who come in here to mess around?' Süleyman said.

The other guards, while never turning kids over to the police, admitted to finding them a nuisance and giving out the odd slap here and there.

'I talk to them,' Dorsay said. 'But only if I'm on my own. Usually I'm paired with Münir Sever, but he's not always well enough to come to work.'

'Why not?'

'He's older than the rest of us. He gets stomach trouble.'

Süleyman found Sever's name on his list. He was fifty-three and had yet to be interviewed.

He said, 'So you talk to these kids, even if they're desecrating gravestones?'

'No! Of course not! But I've only come across something like that once.'

'Like what?' Ömer asked.

For a moment Dorsay looked unsure of himself, then he said, 'A pervert.'

'Defiling a corpse?'

He put his head down. 'About to. I stopped him.'

'When was this?'

'Last December.'

'What happened?'

'I pulled him off her and . . . and we talked.'

'You talked? And then what? Did this get written up in the incident book?'

The guard shook his head.

'Why not?'

He looked up. 'He was a poor thing,' he said. 'Desperate. Misguided, of course. The body had been buried just that morning; he said he'd been watching the funeral, but I never saw him. He was shivering and so I gave him some biscuits I'd brought with me. He was so sorry.'

'You let him go?'

'We talked for a long time. Together we placed the lady back in her grave and filled it in. It took time.'

Süleyman shook his head and repeated, 'You let him go?'

'He said he'd reform,' Dorsay said. 'I saw sincerity in his eyes. Don't you think that sometimes you just have to trust people, Inspector? Give them a chance?'

'If people commit offences, they need to be punished,' Süleyman said.

'Yes, well you're a policeman . . .'

'I do my duty.'

'And I do mine,' Dorsay said. 'Maybe not as strictly as . . . He's never been back, Inspector. Not to my knowledge.'

Süleyman felt himself getting angry at the boy's naïvety. 'This site covers seven hundred and fifty square metres,' he said. 'How do you know he's never been back? Do you have eyes in every corner, underneath every mausoleum?'

'No . . .' Dorsay looked shocked.

'Then you don't know!' Süleyman said. 'You say you love God, and yet you put yourself in His place by deciding you know best about the fate of a man who has committed an offence!'

'I—'

'What did he look like? Do you know his name? Do you know how old he was? What?'

Enemies. Inspector Süleyman had asked him whether his family had any enemies, and Uğur Bulut had told him there were none that he knew about. But that hadn't been strictly true, and now he regretted saying it. Everyone had enemies, particularly those in business, like Uğur. But then again, could he honestly see any of his competitors digging up his mother's body? He couldn't. There was of course that other business, but that seemed to be over with now. But it did bring to mind his brother. The disappearance of their mother's body was rather convenient for Lokman, given that he had to know, surely, that they were indeed brothers. And yet that didn't make sense, because it had been Lokman who had insisted upon the exhumation. Could he really have set the whole thing up in order simply to create doubt?

Lokman Bulut was lazy, avaricious and easily led. He'd spent almost all his teenage years getting into trouble with either his family, the police or both. But that was because he was also stupid, or so Uğur had always thought. When their mother had been dying, she had been very clear about who was to inherit the business, and under what circumstances. The family lawyer,

Cihan Bey, had been called and she had schooled him in exactly what her wishes were. Lokman had been provided for. Every month his considerable allowance came out of company profits to fund his pathetic lifestyle. Uğur had been horrified at the amount right from the start, but he'd never said a word.

Perihan had been well aware who and what Lokman was. 'Your brother is weak and an idiot,' she had said to Uğur. 'I'm making provision for him so that you don't have to worry about the stupid boy.'

It hadn't been as simple as that, however. Though far from being an addict, Lokman liked to shove coke up his nose when he went out for an evening with his unsavoury friends. Maybe it had been one of those, and not his lawyer, who had persuaded him to exhume their mother? All rich and bored, Lokman's friends were almost exclusively young men who lived off their parents or wives or both. Uğur didn't know them, as such, and now felt that maybe he should have made more of an effort to do so. But Lokman's life was so chaotic and in so many ways false – living in a slum to appear cool – that he'd always steered clear.

Uğur sat down behind his desk. His office, which was above the pastane, was on the top floor of the four-storey building his canny mother had bought so many years ago. With kitchens at the back of the property and the distribution operation on the middle two floors, the Gaziantep pastane was not just an İstanbul institution, but a worldwide brand. Their baklava was shipped all over the world, and could be found in high-end grocery stores from Moscow to London. In addition, Perihan's old house in Sarıyer had been rented out for years, bringing in yet more revenue to the company. Surely Lokman had enough money! His allowance was a percentage, so if the business did well, so did he. Why had he rocked what was a very stable boat? Did his increasingly frequent requests for an advance on his allowance have anything to do with it? And what was he using that money for? Uğur shivered at the thought of it. If he was borrowing from outside the family again . . .

His phone rang. He looked at the screen and saw that it was his brother. That happened a lot. He'd think about someone, and the next minute they would either appear, call or send an email. Had Uğur been of a superstitious nature, he would have read all sorts into that phenomenon. But he wasn't and didn't.

'Lokman. I'm glad you've called,' he said.

'Really?' his brother said. 'You know what—'

'You want an advance on your allowance, I know,' Uğur said. 'What's it for?'

There was a pause at the other end.

'Well?'

'I need—'

'What for?' Uğur yelled. 'You have a generous allowance, you own your own property, even if you call it a slum. So it's only bills . . .'

'They've gone up.'

'When?'

'Been going up for months, like everything,' Lokman said. 'I need another five hundred a month.'

'So what were the advances I made to you last month and the month before about?'

'Oh. Well, expenses. Everything has gone up.'

'You'll have to budget then,' Uğur said. 'Like everyone else.'

Yeah, I will. I . . .' Lokman's voice trailed off.

'You're not in debt again, are you? Borrowing—'

'No!'

Uğur wanted to yell again, but then it occurred to him that if his brother had come under the influence of his friends or dodgy associates, grilling him wasn't going to get him very far.

He sighed deeply. 'So you want me to put another five hundred into your account.'

'I'll starve if you don't.'

Uğur didn't answer. Could he hear Lokman sweating, or was that just in his mind?

Eventually he said, 'All right. I'll transfer it now. But you have to budget in future.' He put the phone down before his brother could answer.

As he was transferring the money into Lokman's account, he thought about the various ways in which he might keep tabs on him. One of his neighbours, some tattered type from Adana, was a venal character. Uğur was sure that for a relatively small material incentive, he could buy the loosening of his mouth. And then of course there was their sister . . .

It was all too easy to look a complete mess in the heat of high summer in İstanbul. Not only was it hot; it was also humid. Çiçek İkmen didn't need to look at herself in any mirror to know that her hair was flat to her head and dripping with sweat. Not that her father would probably even notice.

'Dad!'

He'd walked straight past the café where she worked and was currently strolling down Sıraselviler Caddesi, cigarette in hand, lost in his own thoughts. She had to call out again.

'Dad!'

He turned. 'Çiçek!'

She ran towards him and the two embraced.

'Where are you going?' she asked.

'Nowhere in particular,' he said. 'I'm just sort of . . . window shopping, I suppose you'd say.'

İkmen didn't really do shopping, window or otherwise. Çiçek, who had just finished for the day, frowned.

'Yes, I know that's unusual, but there is a point to it,' he said. 'There are a lot of independent shops round here, aren't there?'

'That's what Cihangir is about,' his daughter said.

This wasn't strictly true. Until the 1970s, Cihangir, a sub-district of Beyoğlu, had been a semi-derelict quarter characterised by tall European-style houses built in the nineteenth century. Then, as artists and writers looking for cheap lodgings moved in, the district began to cater for their needs, with increasing numbers of coffee shops, restaurants and also a large number of antique and arts and crafts shops. In the twenty-first century, the place had become super-cool for all sorts of reasons, not least of which was the long list of celebrity writers and actors who lived in the area. Shops were only a part of what for many of İstanbul's young people was a very attractive local vibe.

Çiçek took her father's arm. 'Are you looking for anything in particular?' she said.

She knew he was working on something, but she had no idea what. With luck, she was going to see Mehmet Süleyman later that evening, and so her mind was rather taken up with that. Nobody's fool, Çiçek knew that she had been acting in a very needy fashion with him for some time. She also knew that it wouldn't do. But it was hard to sit on her anxiety. It was easy for Samsun to say that if the relationship was giving her so much grief, why didn't she finish it? It just wasn't as simple as that.

She watched her father turn something over in his mind. Then he said, 'Quirky jewellery.'

'What, you're looking for some?'

'I'm looking for a specific type of thing,' he said. 'Not just weirdly fashioned silver. More . . . well, made out of junk, I suppose you'd say.'

'Like?'

'Weird stuff. Bits of old phones, broken watch components.'

'A girl came into the café a few days ago wearing old SIM cards as earrings,' she said.

'That's the sort of thing.'

'Well, that's urban street style for you,' she said. 'Been big here for a long time, but especially since . . .' she looked around to make sure their conversation wasn't being overheard, and lowered her voice, 'Gezi.'

The Gezi Park protests back in 2013 had escalated from an environmental demonstration about the destruction of a city-centre park to a full-scale protest against the government. Thousands had come out onto the streets until what became for a while countrywide demonstrations were finally put down by the state. Few people alluded to Gezi any more, especially since the attempted coup of 2016, but in some areas, like Cihangir, a certain free spirit continued to prevail, made visible by urban style markers like tattoos, brightly coloured hair and weird jewellery.

'Mmm. So would you say,' her father said, 'that those who wear things like that are always of a more liberal mindset?'

'Oh come on, Dad,' she said. 'Since when did you see a covered woman with a broken old-school watch on a chain round her neck?'

They reached the large tea garden on the corner between Sıraselviler Caddesi and Akarsu Caddesi.

Her father said, 'Tea?'

'Why not.'

They sat down at a table underneath a tree and were brought two large glasses of tea almost immediately. As İkmen dropped two sugar cubes into his drink he said, 'Do you know who produces this "street style"?'

'Loads of people,' she said. 'You can buy street-style anything now. Clothes, art . . .'

'What kind of art?'

She shrugged. 'Anything really. As long as it's kind of recycled. Junk, I guess. But some of it sells for a lot of money.'

'What kind of thing?'

He was clearly on some sort of mission. She said, 'There's this thing called steampunk . . .'

'Isn't that something to do with Britain?'

'I think it's quite big there, yes,' she said. 'But there's a Turkish version called Ottoman steampunk.'

'Really?' He lit a cigarette and offered Çiçek one, which she took. 'What's that all about then? Sultans in spaceships designed by H. G. Wells?'

She smiled. Her father knew exactly what any number of modern trends involved; he just liked playing the part of a grumpy old man. Çiçek went along with it.

'Sort of,' she said. 'There's a book out by a journalist, Özgür Mumcu, called The Peace Machine, which is science fiction meets Ottoman history. People who are into that sort of thing like old technical and sometimes surgical instruments. You can pick up clocks and things made of brass round here, and there are a couple of nautical instrument places in the Kapılı Çarşı.'

'Mmm.'

Suddenly she couldn't bear not knowing what he was doing. 'Is this about the thing you went out to Kumkapı for yesterday?' she said.

He thought for a moment and then said, 'Yes. But I don't want you to ask me anything else about it.'

'Why not?'

Again she could almost see the cells in his brain whirring away, making something up. In the end he said, 'Confidentiality.'

'I see.'

Perfectly valid in the world of private investigation, but not, Çiçek knew, true. She knew her father, and now she was certain that whatever he was involved in was something not without some considerable risk.

Appearing to change the subject, he put his hand in his pocket and took out a small foil packet. 'Know what this is?' he said.

The packet was open at one end.

'Tip it out,' İkmen instructed.

A small pen-like object fell onto the table. Çiçek frowned. 'Looks like something diabetics use to test their blood,' she said. 'Where—'

'Yes, I thought so too,' he said. He smiled, and put the item and its foil packet back in his pocket.

Chapter 5

Cemal Yüksel set everything going. Things that moved with multiple legs, unnameable shapes that opened and closed, metallic arms that waved to gently humming balls made of strips of thin steel – everything in motion, everything making noise.

He looked around his rough stone-walled workshop under the ground. Unless Berat Bey came to take tea with him or follow up on a commission, he lived in total isolation, not even knowing whether it was night or day. Without his friend in the carpet shop up above, he would die. Or rather, he wouldn't die, but he might put himself in harm's way if he went outside. And Machine Bey longed to do just that. Subsisting, even if he was doing what he'd always loved, was not the same as living, and now that he could no longer communicate with Sevval online, he felt his life shrink still further.

It wasn't that he was in love with the Actress – he was old enough to be her father – but he knew he desired her. Not that he'd ever act upon it. The ex-policeman had picked up that there had been some sort of issue between Sevval and Olimpio, which was true. Olimpio was older than Sevval, less attractive; she was jealous. Flung together by circumstance, the women disliked each other, and Cemal had no doubt that Olimpio would be quite glad if Sevval disappeared for good. But only on one level. Her unexplained absence felt ominous, and as he sat down at his computer to send a message to Gold Bey, he wondered what observations Çetin İkmen would make about him. Cumhur would have to be careful what he said. They all needed this man in order to find Sevval, but engaging him had been a risky strategy, notwithstanding his honest credentials.

He typed: I'd be guarded about what you tell him. If he told certain people how we are surviving out here, he could earn himself kudos, not to mention money. Remember, we have a duty to protect those who enable our existence.

'I've never come across a heart being traded before. I have known donors to die whilst having their kidneys removed. But the removal of a heart is a certain death sentence.'

The speaker, once Çetin İkmen's sergeant, now Inspector Kerim Gürsel, had his feet up on his desk, just like his predecessor had done for the preceding thirty years. It amused Mehmet Süleyman. Kerim Bey and İkmen couldn't have been more different, but the younger man had, by his own admission, been heavily influenced by his boss.

'If the woman had it done in the full knowledge of the procedure's consequences, then this could represent a new low in the levels of desperation some are experiencing in this city,' Süleyman said. 'If you sold your own heart, it could only be to provide cash for your loved ones.'

'Did she have anything else wrong with her?' Kerim asked.

'Nothing terminal, according to Dr Sarkissian. Just gallstones.'

Kerim frowned. 'And that's another thing,' he said. 'Who in their right mind would buy an old heart?'

Süleyman said, 'That's probably the most mysterious aspect. I don't know. Unless it was someone who didn't know anything about the donor.'

Kerim shook his head. 'It's like something out of a science fiction novel. The organs of the poor harvested for the benefit of the rich. And the recipient will be rich . . .'

'You think so? I wonder.'

'Why?'

'If the recipient knew how old the donor was, possibly he or she got it cheap,' he said. 'Or maybe the recipient didn't know the age of the donor but was just desperate. Maybe an entire family had to raise money for this operation. And yet . . .' he looked up at the ceiling as he thought his argument through, 'heart transplant surgery is extremely complicated. There are a lot of problems associated with rejection, and after-care is essential.'

'Which brings us back to a wealthy recipient,' Kerim said. 'For a start, your surgeon had to be highly skilled; that costs money. Then, as you say, there's the after-care. The purchase of the organ is in many ways the least of your problems. I know there are doctors who have been dismissed, taken early retirement or been involved in damaging litigation who theoretically could perform such a procedure. But if such a person got caught, that would be the end. That would be prison.'

'I know. My father once had a doctor who was drunk,' Süleyman said. 'He functioned. He didn't harm my father, I don't think, but he didn't do him much good either. No, if we follow the line of thinking that this heart was procured for a wealthy recipient, then the surgeon would have to be competent. And if the surgeon was competent, then he or she must have known the donor was old.'

'Which would mean that the doctor was in on the deception.'

'If it was a deception.'

'What do you mean?'

Süleyman stood up and put on his jacket. 'Maybe, if the recipient's heart was so degraded he or she was close to death, any heart would do as a stopgap. I mean, I don't know whether that is even possible, but it'll have to wait now until tomorrow. I said I would take Çiçek out to dinner tonight, and I mustn't be late.'

'Where are you going?'

'She's booked some place in Karaköy,' he said. 'Mediterranean cuisine – whatever that means. But I suspect the restaurant is just an entrée to the main event, which is hitting the nargile joints in Tophane. I know she doesn't look like him, but she's very similar in character to her father at times.'

'Rather smoke than eat?'

Süleyman shook his head. 'What can I say?' He picked up his car keys. 'What are you doing, Kerim Bey?'

Kerim smiled. 'I can get you a list of surgeons who have disgraced themselves, if you like.'

'Would you? That would be really useful.'

'No problem. How's your missing person search going?'

'No one fits the profile in the city, but I've got a couple of leads outside. Mainly elderly people suffering from dementia, which is a consideration. A person who is dementing may be persuaded to do a lot of things they would ordinarily refuse to do.'

Kerim shook his head. 'That's another level of cynicism.'

'Isn't it. Oh yes, and a visual of a locket found on the body by Dr Sarkissian is being circulated.' He walked towards the door.

Kerim said, 'By the way, apparently a woman came in today asking for Çetin Bey.'

Süleyman shook his head. 'They still come. What happened?'

'She was told he'd retired and she just walked out,' Kerim said. 'I wish I'd been there. Silly constable who spoke to her just let her go.'

Süleyman left. Kerim stared at the screen saver on his laptop. He knew he should go home, but he didn't want to. His mother-in-law had come to stay to help look after his wife, Sinem, who suffered from arthritis. She was a nice enough woman, but if she was around, Sinem's carer – and Kerim's lover – the transsexual Pembe Hanım, had to keep away. Kerim ached for her.

* * *

64

'We live in vicious times,' Çetin İkmen said. 'Where those not even convicted of an offence may have their lives ruined by rumour. And if you have been imprisoned, even if nothing has been proven against you, when you are released anyone who tries to help you may come under suspicion too. It's going to be difficult, I feel, to pursue this Actress woman under such circumstances.'

Fatma İkmen, who was on this occasion almost transparent, just smiled. Like most ghosts, she only appeared in certain places, in this case on the balcony of the İkmen apartment in Sultanahmet. In life, she'd always liked it there.

İkmen sat down. 'A lot of bad blood is flowing from the Designer, Olimpio, towards Sevval, the Actress,' he continued. 'I'd like to know whether it flowed the other way too. What I picked up was jealousy. The kind some middle-aged women can have for their younger counterparts. I know that may come across as sexist, but I have to say what I see. Not that I can imagine Olimpio killing anyone, if indeed Sevval is dead. I found the detritus of what looked like a blood testing kit in her room. Olimpio claimed to know nothing about it. Çiçek said it's something used by diabetics—'

'Shit!'

The expletive came from the kitchen. İkmen ran inside to find Samsun standing over several broken plates and food scattered across the floor.

'What happened?' he asked.

'Yiğit!' Samsun pointed into thin air.

'Yiğit?'

'Your fucking djinn!' Samsun said.

'It's not mine!'

'I was making us a meze, and the next thing I know, the fucker is sticking its face over my shoulder! Look, Çetin, I know this sheikh from Bukhara. Everyone says he's marvellous . . .'

65

'I'm not having some insane Uzbek coming in here warbling on and—'

'You don't want your wife exorcised too, I get it,' Samsun said. 'But for the love of God, Çetin, this thing has to go! You know if you ever wanted to sell this apartment . . .'

'I don't!'

'I know, but . . .' She sat down and sighed, only at the last moment noticing that there was olive oil on the chair. 'Oh, and now that's just wonderful. This skirt is new . . .'

İkmen, who didn't worry about things like stains, sat down opposite. 'Samsun, I will deal with it,' he said. 'But—'

'In your own time, yes, I know,' she said. 'But I'm older than you are, Çetin, and I just can't cope with it. All I want to do is live out my days in relative peace here with you and Çiçek and have a few drinks and laughs along the way. I don't want to live with a djinn. Dad had one for years, which he used to keep us all away because he was a mad antisocial old fool.'

Her father, Çetin's Uncle Ahmet, had been, like İkmen's mother, a peasant from a particularly inaccessible part of Albania. The supernatural had always been at the centre of their lives.

İkmen put his hand on Samsun's heavily ringed fingers and squeezed. 'I will deal with it, I promise,' he said. 'When I've finished this job . . .'

'Oh!' Suddenly animated, Samsun put a hand up to her head. 'Oh yes!'

Alarmed by her rapid change of tack, İkmen said, 'What is it?'

'Oh yes, a woman!' she said. 'She wants to talk to you.'

'What woman? What about?'

'I don't know. Claimed to be one of Madam Lilli's girls from Ayvansaray. You remember that brothel, up by the Kariye museum . . .'

'What?'

'Madam Lilli, old Jewish woman,' Samsun said. 'Employed a lot of girls, including dear old Lale Hanım. Remember her?'

'No.'

'You should. Very famous amongst the trans girls at the time. We worked together in Tarlabaşı for a bit. She died years ago, but—'

'Can you get to the point? The woman who wants to talk to me . . .'

'Oh yes,' she said. 'I spent the day with Neşe Hanım. You know, my friend who came from İzmir in the seventies. She's in the Or Ahayim now. Having chemotherapy and then going home to an empty apartment wasn't working for her. They're so kind there. A Jewish hospital, and dear old Neşe an atheist. Bald as a virgin's buttock, poor thing. Anyway, she has this other visitor when I get there. So I offer to go and come back when she's alone, but Neşe says no, and so these nice nurses take us into the garden and I go and get tea from the canteen. Neşe isn't supposed to smoke these days, but of course I brought her some cigarettes and we all lit up—'

'Samsun.'

'Get to the point, yes,' she said. 'Well, Neşe's other visitor was a woman called Leah. About seventy. We're talking about all sorts of things, and it turns out she was a working girl at Lilli's old place. She was with her when she died. Neşe's asleep in her chair by this time. I take the cigarette out of her hand, and get more tea, then me and this Leah, we talk about our families. She has a daughter in IT. I say I live with you and Çiçek, and then the next thing I know she's all wide eyed and shocked.'

'Leah, not Neşe?' He had to make sure; Samsun's stories tended to splurge.

'Yes, Leah,' she said. 'You investigated the death of one of her neighbours back in the twentieth century.'

'When? It was a long century.'

'I don't know. But she still lives in the same apartment she lived in then, which is in Balat. She told me she'd been to police headquarters looking for you, but when they told her you'd retired, she left. I took her address and said you might be retired but you're still about. Very impressed by you she was.' She riffled in her bag and took out a piece of paper. 'She doesn't have a phone, poor bitch, but this is where she lives.'

She handed it over. İkmen read it and felt a jolt go through his body.

'That was back in the nineties,' he said. 'And I was working with Süleyman.'

'Are you sure?'

'Oh yes,' he said. 'The dead man was called Leonid Meyer, and he'd had battery acid forced down his throat.'

Right in the middle of the cemetery, where the gravestones were most tightly packed and the trees that shielded them from the sky were at their densest, night-time was almost entirely black. Even though he wasn't alone, cemetery guard Raşım Dorsay didn't much like being on night duty at the Karacaahmet.

'Do you believe in ghosts?' the young man asked his older colleague, Münir Sever.

'No.' Sever was a blunt sort. Now in his fifties, he'd been a professional soldier and had a reputation for straight talking.

'I do, although I've never seen one,' Raşım said. 'My mum believed in ghosts.'

'A lot of people's mothers do.'

Raşım shone his torch at a group of gravestones, one of which was the one that had been disturbed. It still had police tape attached to it.

'What do you make of this grave robbery business, Münir Bey?' he said.

'As I told the police, it's always happened. Never come across it here, though, I told them that straight. When I was a boy back in our village, there were several instances of it. Perverts.'

'Always?'

'Far as I know. My father was a village guard, and he used to say it was retards from the mental hospital. They'd get out and go straight for the graveyard.'

This kind of talk was typical of Münir. Although he could read and write and claimed to be able to speak English, he wasn't an educated man and was riddled with all sorts of prejudices against disabled people, the mentally ill, homosexuals, women, non-Sunni Muslims. It was all rubbish, and the vision of patients absconding from a psychiatric hospital and running straight to a graveyard, ready for sex, almost made Raşım laugh.

'My father caught a few,' Münir continued. 'Nutters.'

Raşım didn't go into his own experiences with cemetery invasions. He'd been unable to tell Inspector Süleyman much about that necrophile he'd caught and then let go. He'd found him while wandering off from the prearranged schedule they all had to follow, and so he'd not recorded it in case Türgüt Bey told him off. Then he'd pushed it from his mind. Or rather, he'd tried to. When Süleyman had asked him for a description, he'd held back. The man had told him he'd never do it again, so why make trouble for the poor soul?

'This'll be nutters too,' Münir said, pointing at the taped-up grave.

'Who else would take one body out of a grave and put another one in? You'd have to be a nut. Or a criminal. Some of them put in Silivri for political crimes, they'd do it. Twisted bastards. Traitors. I was on the Martyrs Bridge in 2016, holding back the enemies of the state . . .'

And he was off. Legend-building his own life. Maybe he had been on the bridge that fateful night of the failed coup. Who knew? If he had been, he'd probably spent all his time asking people whether they were Alevi, or homosexual . . . But Raşım was no longer listening. He began to walk away. Training his torch on the ground so that he didn't fall over, he headed for one of the few paths that remained.

Which was when he spotted something on the ground that made him frown.

The Karaköy restaurant that Çiçek had chosen was called Kayık, after the traditional wooden fishing boats native to the Bosphorus and eastern Aegean. It was a tall, narrow building in the middle of a terrace of similar nineteenth-century ex-mercantile properties. And although it was very stylish inside, it was also too hot, so Çiçek and Süleyman took a table outside on the pavement.

Now bathed, rested and changed after work, Çiçek was looking very glamorous in a 1950s-style summer dress in bright pinks and yellows. As she crossed her slim legs, her full skirt rustled in the light wind coming off the nearby Bosphorus.

'You look amazing,' Süleyman said as he poured water on top of the viscous rakı that nestled at the bottom of their glasses. They both watched as the magic happened and the liquid turned the colour of milk.

'Thank you,' she said. 'I was absolutely wrecked by the end of my shift today. I looked as if I'd been rained on, I'd got so hot.'

'You're still hot now – in a different way.' He picked up his glass and proposed a toast. 'Şerefe.'

She clinked her glass against his. 'To us,' she said.

He went back to looking at his menu. After a few moments, he said, 'I think I'll have lamb cutlets.'

Çiçek chose chicken. Their orders placed, they drank their rakı in silence for a few moments until she said, 'I met Dad on the way home this afternoon.'

'Oh?'

'He's working on something, as I told you,' she said. 'I've no

70

idea what, but it would seem to have something to do with urban street jewellery.'

He frowned.

'You know the sort of thing,' she said. 'Bracelets made out of twisted nails, earrings created out of old bits of mobile phones. A lot of the kids with tattoos and piercings wear that stuff.'

'Yes, I've seen them.'

'He was wondering where you might get such items. I know it's all about this thing he's working on, but for a moment I had a vision of him with a bike chain around his neck. Sort of a late middle-age crisis.'

They both laughed. The thought of Çetin İkmen wearing anything but a cheap suit and tie was ludicrous.

She said, 'How was work?'

As a police officer's daughter, she knew it was best not to let on that you knew anything about an ongoing investigation. She knew he was engaged in the so-called 'grave robbery' case centred on the Karacaahmet cemetery in Üsküdar. But she left it up to him to tell her as much, or as little, as he felt he could.

He paused for quite a long time before saying, 'Confusing.'

'Can I ask?'

'No,' he said bluntly. Then, realising he had overreacted, he took her hand. 'Sorry.'

'No, I'm sorry,' she said. 'I know how it is from living with Dad.'

'Who is also being evasive,' he said. 'What to say and to whom is a problem. But in general we do share with our colleagues and cut our families out.'

'Dad always used to tell us it was for our own good.'

'He was right. The last thing any of us wants is to put those we love in harm's way.'

It wasn't until after he'd said it that he realised he'd used the word 'love'. And knowing how Çiçek felt about him, he instantly

71

regretted it. Or did he? Was he imagining things, or did her face just briefly light up when he said that word? And was he mistaken in thinking that the sight of it brought him pleasure?

While he was turning all this over in his mind, his phone rang. He looked at Çiçek. 'Sorry.'

'It's OK.'

It was Ömer Mungun.

'Sir,' he said, 'something's been found at the Karacaahmet.'

'What?'

'Remains. Possibly human . . .'

The Leonid Meyer case had been the first geniunely puzzling murder investigation Çetin İkmen and his then new sergeant, Mehmet Süleyman had ever worked on. Up to that point, Süleyman had only experienced domestic homicides, where the killer either confessed immediately or was seen committing the crime. As İkmen's deputy, he'd had to learn fast. He'd also, İkmen remembered, needed a lot of guidance. He'd been so innocent back then! Still living at home with his parents, he wasn't even married for the first time when the Meyer affair happened. Had that twisted case, perpetrated by people in the grip of a delusion so strong it led to torture and death, changed his friend Süleyman for ever?

Çetin İkmen watched the lights come on in the streets below and marvelled, not for the first time, how the past continually broke through into the present. Leah Delmonte, the woman Samsun had met at the Jewish hospital, had been a neighbour of the old man. If he remembered correctly, she'd actually found his body. He hadn't seen her for twenty years. She'd been a middle-aged prostitute back then, one of what had then been a larger Jewish community. The world had changed a lot in the intervening time. Apart from anything else, the reason for Meyer's death had been entirely discredited.

Killed by members of a Turco-Russian family called the Gulcus, Meyer had been a refugee from the old Soviet Union. He'd also taken part in the slaughter of the former Russian royal family, the Romanovs, back in 1918, which was why the Gulcus had killed him. And while there was no evidence to suggest that Meyer was not who the family believed him to be, advances in DNA technology had proved beyond reasonable doubt that the Gulcus Russian matriarch couldn't possibly have been the Tsar's third daughter, Maria, as she had claimed. The real Maria's bones now lay in a shrine to the family that the Russian government had constructed on the site of the slaughter. Now, for some reason, the woman who had found Leonid's tortured body had reappeared. And she wanted to talk to İkmen.

Samsun said that Leah didn't have a telephone, and so he'd have to either write or go and see her. He remembered that apartment block well. Shabby, its stairwells smelling of piss, it had been one of the last bastions of poor Jewish life in the city. The rich had moved to Nişantaşı and Şişli a long time before. He wondered what Leah Delmonte could want with him now.

But first thing in the morning he had an appointment to see Gold Bey, the jeweller over in Tarlabaşı. It would be interesting to find out what his take on Sevval Kalkan, the Actress, was going to be. İkmen had never looked for someone in such an ambiguous position before. Machine Bey had told him that if the police got involved, as they normally would, lives lived in the shadows might be put at risk. How, for instance, did he even begin to ask those outside the Moral Maze about her? In the normal course of events he would have retraced her last recorded steps, which had been on Sahane Sokak, where she had lived with the Designer. But how to do that? Her face was too well known, as was her fall from grace, to make asking about her anything but risky. According to Olimpio, she'd gone out frequently and taken many lovers. But who had these men been, and where had she met them? 'A cop' had been mentioned as one of her beaus, but had that really happened? And who had bought her contentious work of graffiti for ten thousand lira?

He hoped that Gold Bey might be able to shed new light on the Actress's habits. According to Olimpio, he liked Sevval, but that didn't necessarily mean he was blind to her shortcomings.

After that, İkmen would drive over to Leah Delmonte's old place in Ayvansaray.

Chapter 6

'It's a femur.'

It was first thing in the morning after a night of no sleep. Mehmet Süleyman looked at Arto Sarkissian and said, 'Thigh bone?'

'Yes. Human,' the doctor continued. 'With signs of scorching at the head where it would have articulated with the pelvis at the hip joint. Is this all that has been found?'

'So far.'

Süleyman had gone straight from the restaurant in Karaköy to the Karacaahmet cemetery, leaving poor Çiçek to eat her grilled chicken on her own. One of the cemetery guards had found this bone less than a metre from Perihan Bulut's grave.

It certainly hadn't been there when the area was being searched by forensic investigators. How had it got there?

'Is the scorching recent?'

'I think so, yes,' the doctor said. 'I'm assuming you would want me to fast-track DNA testing, inasmuch as that's possible.'

'Yes.'

The doctor laid the bone down on his bench and considered it.

'I'm loath to declare anything about this yet,' he said. 'However, femur length is a very good indication of overall body height. The thigh bone makes up approximately one quarter of the body's overall height. I have measured this and it is thirty-eight centimetres long. That means that its owner was approximately one hundred and fifty-two centimetres tall.'

'Short.'

'Possibly a woman. The only other thing I can say for certain is that the bone shows little evidence of weathering.'

'What's that?'

'Weathering occurs when a bone is left out in the open for any length of time.'

'Including in the grave?'

'No,' he said. 'The term refers to exposure to surface conditions, including the weather. I can see little if any evidence of it.'

'So this could be a bone from a grave?'

'That, given its context, is the most probable explanation. This can happen in very overcrowded graveyards like the Karacaahmet. As pressure underground increases, sometimes things are pushed to the surface. Doesn't explain the scorching, however. Did the guard who found it report any fires in the vicinity?'

'No, but fires have been lit in the Karacaahmet before. Usually by homeless people in the winter.'

'Hardly the weather for it at the moment,' the doctor said. 'Inspector, my rather brief interaction with Mr Uğur Bulut involved a discussion regarding possible sources of existing DNA for his mother. He says there are none, hence the exhumation. So in order that I may compare any DNA found on this bone to DNA from the Bulut family . . .'

'Of course. Test Uğur and his brother. Don't take no for an answer.' Süleyman began to move away. 'I'd best get back over there and see if anything else has come to light.'

'As ever, as soon as I know anything . . .'

'It's appreciated.'

Süleyman left, leaving the doctor alone with the single femur. The only evidence, so far, that someone as yet unknown had ever lived.

İkmen was still known by some in Tarlabaşı. Even though all the drug dealers and bonzai casualties were still in their beds, early mornings didn't put off Rifat Sasmaz, the owner of İkmen's favourite place to drink when depressed. He hadn't walked past the bar, let alone entered it, for almost two years. But even from the outside it still reeked of rakı, piss, cigarettes and cannabis. He was going to just carry on towards his destination when Rifat came running out and grabbed his arm.

'Çetin Bey! It's so good to see you!'

'Ah . . .'

Rifat hugged him. 'I heard you'd retired,' he said. 'I couldn't believe it, but when you didn't come by, I thought, oh then, that must be true. How could they do such a thing? How could they push you out—'

'Retirement was my choice, Rifat Bey,' İkmen said.

'Really?'

'Yes.'

'Do you want a drink? No charge.'

Rather stupidly, he thought later, İkmen said, 'It's nine a.m.'

Rifat threw his grubby arms wide. 'All the more reason to put a gloss on what will be a long day!'

It was almost a good idea. If İkmen hadn't been going to a basement flat in Emin Camı Sokak, he might have allowed himself an early-morning rakı. But he refused.

As he got closer to his destination, he noticed that the washing lines strung across the streets were increasing in number. There were more homes in this part of the district, another marker being the hordes of kids in the unmade streets, playing football, dancing or taunting the old junk man who made his way slowly along the middle of the road dragging his cart. Frazzled-looking cats with ears that appeared to be made of lace scampered into corners behind abandoned bags of rubbish and in one case the skeleton of an old sewing machine. İkmen wondered vaguely whether these feral fleabags could take on his own dear Marlboro. He decided that in spite of Marlboro being king of the Sultanahmet streets, these wall-eyed monsters would tear him apart.

Eventually he stopped in front of a tall, thin house that he could see had once been pink. A number was scrawled on the wall, which corresponded with the one on his notepad. As usual in this part of the city, the front door was up a small flight of steps, and was open. He went inside. Unsurprisingly, the place smelt of damp.

Cumhur Polat lived in the basement, and so he walked towards a flight of stairs that led downwards. As he got closer, he groped for a light switch on the wall. Probably one of those timed ones that switched off automatically just before you reached your destination. But there wasn't even that. A deep, dark well of blackness loomed before him, and as he descended, İkmen struggled to keep a hold on the rickety banister to his right. If he fell into this abyss, who knew where he'd end up, and he'd probably break every bone in his body. As he lowered one foot onto the step below, he felt something squishy touch the bottom of his shoe. A discarded piece of food, or a dead rat? It didn't bear thinking about. His body went into shock and began to tremble.

He was almost, unwittingly, at the bottom of the stairs when suddenly he heard a click, and light flooded over him. A door not a metre away opened, and he saw a tall, thin figure silhouetted against the light.

'I was driving to my hospital.'

'Along Dr Eyüp Aksoy Caddesi?'

'Yes. I live in Kuzguncuk.'

Dr Sibel Çoban had been driving to work as a surgeon at the Koşuyolu Medipol hospital, to the north of the Karacaahmet cemetery, when she'd seen smoke coming from inside the graveyard.

'I was due on shift at nine, so this must have been about eight thirty,' she said. 'I took very little notice because, as I say, it was only a small fire. I've seen such things many times before in the Karacaahmet. When they are burning leaves, and sometimes when I think homeless people camp there, but that's usually in the winter. I thought nothing of it until I heard the news this morning.'

'And it was here?'

They were a considerable distance from where the femur had been discovered, by the wall that enclosed the cemetery on the south side.

'Around about,' she said. 'It's such a big place, I think that even with the guards, people get in.' She shook her head. 'My father is buried somewhere here. He died twenty years ago, and this place has become ever more crowded as the years have gone by. Not even my mother comes here any more. She's nearly ninety, and I'm afraid if she comes she might fall and break something.'

Looking around at the uneven rows of gravestones, at places where tree roots appeared to be straining to burst through the ground, Süleyman said, 'I imagine a lot of people who have relatives buried here feel that way.'

'What will you do now?'

'We'll perform a fingertip search of the area and see what we find,' he said. 'I can't see any obvious signs of a fire.'

'As I said, it wasn't big.'

He smiled. 'Let me escort you back to the entrance,' he said. 'Thank you very much for reporting what you saw.'

They began to move away from the wall.

'This is the second incident here, isn't it?' she said as she stepped over a fallen gravestone.

'Yes,' he said. 'The investigation is ongoing.'

In spite of the hot weather, she pulled her jacket tightly around her body as if she was cold.

'When not even the dead are safe, we need to take a long, hard look at our city,' she said. 'I don't know the story behind what's going on here, but I'd put money on our Syrian visitors being behind it. Ow!'

She'd turned her ankle. Süleyman grabbed her arm and steadied her.

'Oh dear!' she said, flustered. 'I'm so sorry.'

'No problem.' He smiled.

She was an attractive woman, probably in her early fifties. In reality, she'd told him very little that he didn't already know. But he appreciated the twinkle in her eye when she looked at him, even if her observation about Syrian refugees seemed to indicate a worrying degree of prejudice.

If there was such a thing as a typical jeweller, then Cumhur Polat was it. One of İkmen's sons-in-law, Berekiah Cohen, was a jeweller, and he too was a tall, thin man with glasses that made him look like an owl. It had to be all that peering at small pieces of metal through powerful magnifying glasses. Maybe it pulled at the eyes.

'Come in, Çetin Bey,' the jeweller said as he stepped aside to allow İkmen into his apartment.

'Thank you.'

While it was thankfully light for a basement flat, Gold Bey's apartment was so damp, even in the height of summer, that İkmen could clearly see a watery sheen on the rough, peeling walls. And the smell down there was almost overpowering. What such conditions could be doing to the jeweller's health didn't bear thinking about.

'I am sorry this place is so messy,' Polat said. 'When Berat Bey gave me the keys, I found I had to move everything that I could into here from a four-bedroom apartment.'

İkmen knew that Gold Bey had been married and that his wife had divorced him as soon as he was released from Silivri. It was a familiar story.

'Where did you live before?' he asked.

'Nişantaşı.'

Of course he had. Polat had never been just any Grand Bazaar jeweller; he'd been an artist whose work had sold all over the world. People like him could afford to live in Nişantaşı.

'I'll take you to my workroom and then I can explain what I do,' Polat said.

He led İkmen through a door and into a larger room that smelled very slightly of burning.

'I've been soldering,' he explained.

There were, İkmen counted, three soldering irons on benches that were covered with piles and piles of what could only be described as rubbish. Broken glass and china, scatterings of nails and rusty screws, broken mobile phone screens, pieces of chain that might or might not have been made of silver or gold. Then there were the stacks of empty cigarette packets, lost boncuk evil-eye charms, broken vape machines, curling stickers and seemingly endless labels from jars of jam, spices and olives, and a small pile of fabric. Luckily, in the midst of all of this were a couple of hard chairs.

'Do sit down,' Polat said. 'The samovar is on. Would you like tea?'

'Thank you.'

İkmen sat while his host went into a tiny kitchen and poured them both glasses of tea. When he returned, he said, 'May I ask what made you take on the job of trying to find our Actress?'

İkmen hadn't really thought about it. He was intrigued; who wouldn't be? Working for a group of people who lived such secretive and yet also creative lives was fascinating. But it was dangerous, too. At best the Moral Maze was a group of wrongly accused dissidents; at worst they were enemies of the state. Was it the danger? The feeling of being up against odds so great success was almost impossible? No. Not really. It was the usual thing, the thing that had always motivated İkmen and probably always would.

'People are precious,' he said. 'Irreplaceable. And when they are murdered or go missing, those who love them deserve answers. It is very easy to state that those who are at odds with much of the rest of society are not worthy of such recognition.'

'There was no way we could have gone to the police.'

'I know. Not saying that all officers are the same, but anyone who might try to help would put him- or herself at risk. But that doesn't apply to me.'

'And yet there is some risk, even for you.'

İkmen nodded. Then he said, 'Tell me about Sevval Kalkan.'

Polat took a sip of his tea. 'We've only actually met twice,' he said. 'She's youngish, as you know, and charming. I like her, and were I twenty years younger, I might have fallen in love with her.'

'I get the impression Olimpio thinks you have.'

He laughed. 'Oh, Olimpio! You know she's the oldest of all of us?'

It hadn't been easy for İkmen to access much about any of the Moral Maze members online, but he did know that Cemal Yüksel, Machine Bey, was in his early sixties, Cumhur Polat was fifty-nine, while Sevval Kalkan was forty-five. Only the Designer's age had eluded him. Remembering her now, he realised that while she obviously wasn't young, he couldn't actually tell precisely how old she was.

'No.'

'She's seventy,' Polat said. 'But don't tell her you know. Seventy and madly jealous of a kid of forty-five.'

'I picked that up. Do you know how Sevval responded to it?'

'She laughed at her,' he said. 'We got on, Sevval and me. Sometimes she would email me and tell me all about it. Olimpio would do things like hide her make-up, threaten to lock her out when she left the apartment.'

'Did she go out much?'

82

'I expect Olimpio said that she did. But not to my knowledge. During one of our meetings Olimpio flew into a rage about all the men Sevval met and had sex with. Sevval denied it, and I think she was probably telling the truth.'

'Because you like her?'

He smiled. 'I'm almost old enough to be her father. I like her, but that's all,' he said. 'I just know that she is as afraid of going out and being recognised as the rest of us.'

'Where did you hold these meetings where you all got together?'

'Different places.'

He clearly didn't want to say, and so İkmen went back to the subject of the Actress.

'And yet an attractive woman like Sevval—'

Gold Bey's face suddenly hardened. 'You shouldn't take Olimpio's word for much,' he said. 'She always exaggerates.'

'Yet Sevval turned rather riskily to graffiti.'

'Mmm. I didn't like that,' he said. 'But she has a skill, and she needed money.'

'What for?'

'Well, to live with Olimpio. You don't think she let her live there for nothing, do you? The person who bought the rude graffito was some rich boy. Sevval told me he was one of my neighbours.'

'One of your neighbours?'

'Poor areas like this are attractive to some,' he said. 'God knows why. Rich kids who want to get down and dirty with the poor for "experience". I don't understand it myself. I worked hard to get out of the slums.'

'Where are you from?'

'Çarşamba.'

İkmen knew Çarşamba, now a very conservative district, well. When he was young, probably about the same time as Gold Bey, it had been a place where the poor scratched a living in the shadow of the great Süleymaniye mosque.

'Do you know this man who bought Sevval Kalkan's artwork?'

'No,' Polat said. 'And I didn't ask. I don't think she meant my direct neighbours, though. No one would play at living in this street. I mean, look at it.'

'Isn't the whole area blighted?'

'No,' he said. 'Round by the Suriyani church the property's not so bad. Here we're riddled with damp and rats, many of which come from the ever-encroaching building sites. Even when I lived in Nişantaşı, I disapproved of this gentrification that seems to rear up wherever you look now. It may improve a district in a cosmetic sense, for a while. But what happens when the new properties don't sell – and a lot of them don't. And it does people who have to live here no good at all. The Roma and the immigrants pushed from pillar to post . . .' He shook his head. 'I'm sorry, I'm ranting.'

İkmen smiled. 'You have much to be unhappy about, and for the record, I agree with you about the gentrification. I hate it. May I ask if it's all right to smoke?'

Polat picked up a saucer and gave it to him.

İkmen lit up.

'Would you say,' he said, 'that most of these people who are living here for the "experience" limit themselves to the area around the church?'

'Maybe not exclusively, but I know there are a few who call themselves artists up there.'

İkmen leaned back in what was not a comfortable chair. 'So tell me about yourself,' he said. 'And about your work.'

Looking down on all that colour pleased Wahıd Saatçı. Not that he'd chosen to live overlooking the eighty-five-metre-long Rainbow Stairs linking the districts of Cihangir and Fındıklı just for the sake of some pretty steps. Salı Pazarı Yokuşu had a large population of 'hip' people. Those who lived liberal lifestyles, espoused liberal values and had money. Not the super-rich, though, and that was a good thing, even if some of his most enthusiastic customers came from their ranks. Opium, pure and smoked in a pipe, was a luxury item. But it was something that young hip types would beg, borrow or steal to obtain. They always had and they always would.

Wahıd's apartment was high up, light and roomy. He even had a balcony, enclosed in glass, where he would sit for hours on end watching the world walk by on the rainbow-painted stairs below. Sometimes he'd see people he knew; sometimes the stairs would be swarming with sightseers, keen to get close to a symbol of the failed uprising against the government in 2013. Sometimes the Gezi fans and the people he knew were one and the same. And then there was Deniz Palandoken.

Puffing up the stairs like a ninety-year-old, Deniz was heading his way on a mission set for her by her husband, Can. Neither of them had yet reached forty, but Deniz and Can had been addicts all their adult lives. Both from rich families, their discovery of the joys of first heroin and then pure opium had led the couple down some dangerous alleyways. They'd both sold themselves on the streets for years, but while Can tried, although usually failed, to save himself for the opium smoke he adored, Deniz would buy anything that might be called heroin to inject into her body, smoke or stick up her nose. It was said the couple had once had a baby, which they'd sold. But that was just gossip. People like the Palandokens lived in a world thick with criminality, rumour and outright delusion.

Wahıd's doorbell rang and he went inside to answer his intercom. It was indeed Deniz. And when she'd finally made it up six flights of stairs she walked into his apartment and sat down on the floor. His pipe between his fingers, Wahıd let her catch her breath before he instigated conversation.

* * *

85

'Each piece is different.' Gold Bey put a pair of earrings into İkmen's hand. Consisting of long curls of what looked like black onyx but felt far lighter, they were attached to wires that would go through the ear lobes and held in place by small sparkly spheres. 'The curls I make by heating plastic from, in this case, an old sex toy. The transparent crystals come from broken glass from the street.'

Next he showed İkmen a brooch made from a tin can lid, some cat fur and liquid latex; a mobile phone necklace; and a bracelet made of chicken wire and dog's teeth. It was amazing stuff, and weirdly beautiful.

'You are very skilled,' İkmen said.

'I was at the top of my profession.' Polat took a deep breath to calm himself. 'Each one of my pieces has a story connected to it. The story is part of the piece.'

'What do you mean?'

'Whenever I sell an item, I give my buyer a story to go with it.'

'You sell directly to the public?'

He laughed. 'Oh no. I sell through people.'

'What people?'

'Ah, people whose identities I don't reveal. Our customers, for want of a better word, are our lifeline, Çetin Bey. To reveal their names could not only get them into trouble but would be suicide for us. You will see many, many pieces that might be mine in shops all over the city, but you will only know they are mine if they come with a story.'

'Which will be told to the buyer by the person you sold that piece to?'

'No,' he said. 'That story will be read to the buyer by a shop-keeper who will have bought the piece from someone they will never see again.'

'I've seen one of Machine Bey's creations in the premises of a friend,' İkmen said.

'Businesses will be able to buy our artworks from time to time. But once sold . . .' Polat shrugged. 'Only the Designer interacts with her clients.'

İkmen frowned. 'What do you mean?'

'Some of her old clients came back to her when she got out of Silivri,' he said. 'They go to her apartment for fittings.'

'She didn't tell me that,' İkmen said.

'She wouldn't. We protect our markets, Çetin Bey.'

İkmen smiled. He could understand that. 'Cumhur Bey, do you know whether Sevval Kalkan was diabetic?'

'No,' Polat said. 'Why?'

'I found the remains of a blood testing kit in her room in Beyoğlu. Olimpio said she didn't know anything about it either.'

'I can't help you,' Gold Bey said. 'She never mentioned it. Mind you, when you enter Silivri prison, you are given a medical that can throw up things of which you were not aware about your health.'

'Like?'

'Machine Bey found out he has high cholesterol, or so he told me. I don't know whether he takes medication for it. Diabetes can be serious, though, can't it? No, she never mentioned it. When we met, she appeared to eat normally . . .'

'I don't give credit, Deniz.'

He'd told her many times, but with junkies it just didn't go in. Fortunately Wahıd Saatçı didn't have to deal with people like her much these days. His typical clients were far higher up the food chain.

'It's Can's birthday,' she said. Her hair was matted with filth and her feet were bare. Rumour had it the couple had finally become homeless.

'I can't help you,' he said. 'I'm not a charity.'

She begged. She threw herself at his feet and, with her posh voice whistling through her broken teeth, she, a woman who had once lived in luxury, begged him, a no one from Urfa, to help her. It was almost hypnotic. But Wahıd Saatçı, in spite of himself, was not the sort of man who could be comfortable in the presence of misery. He'd seen too much of it. He'd experienced more than anyone would, with luck, ever know.

'Get up,' he said.

But she wouldn't. Crying now, she was making his feet wet and he was experiencing something approaching a crisis of confidence. He wanted to help her and yet he was a drug dealer and they didn't do that, not unless they wanted someone to take over their territory.

He heard her say, 'For the love of God, it makes Can feel himself again! It's the only thing that does!'

And Wahıd remembered Can Palandoken when he still had money, sitting on a vast couch in that yalı in Yeniköy his father had given him, smoking from a pipe tipped with silver. The poor bastard had lost himself a long time ago. The things the pair of them had done to feed their habits since. And then a conversation he'd had with Ömer Mungun, the Mardinli policeman, came back to him. He turned it over in his mind and then he said, 'Sit down on a chair and I will get you some water, Deniz Hanım.'

Her crying stopped and she looked up at him.

He put a hand down to lift her to her feet. 'Maybe if you can help me, I can help you.'

The poor wretch began to take her clothes off, but he stopped her.

'No, not that,' he said. 'I want to ask you some questions, and provided you don't lie to me, perhaps I can help you. But if you do lie to me, I will know and I will punish you. Do you understand?'

Chapter 7

There were scorch marks, some admittedly old, all along the wall bordering Dr Eyüp Aksoy Caddesi. Investigating them for traces of human remains was going to take some time.

'This part of the cemetery will have to remain closed,' Mehmet Süleyman told the gatekeeper, Türgüt Akgün.

'No, no, no!' Türgüt waved a small red hand at the policeman. 'This is the most active part of the site. People visit all the time. The dead need to be buried!'

Süleyman stuck the order for temporary closure under the man's nose. 'Not my problem,' he said. 'This warrant is not negotiable. A legal exhumation was performed in this cemetery that led us to what may be a very serious criminal offence.'

'A body found in the wrong grave.'

Süleyman moved closer to the man so that he towered over him. 'You have told me you were a lawyer in a previous life . . .'

'Property, not—'

'Even so, you will know that everything stops when a crime is committed. Everything.'

'The wrong body . . .'

'You know there's more to it than that!' Süleyman snapped. 'Don't think I've not heard your guards gossiping.'

The gatekeeper became silent.

'We have a serious problem here,' Süleyman said. 'It extends beyond one body in the wrong grave, as you put it, into a general issue around security. Fires are often seen in here, particularly in the winter; people get in and out at will, all undocumented. No wonder crimes are committed.'

'Efendi, you can't blame me . . .'

'I'm not,' Süleyman said. 'I'm blaming what appears to be a general lack of professionalism.'

'The boys, the guards, they are not educated people. I have to devise rotas for them. They have no initiative.'

'I don't care,' Süleyman said. 'Educated or not, people should have pride in their work. Protecting our dead is an important duty. I imagine every one of those men would go berserk if I suggested they were unpatriotic. But they're behaving as if they are by not taking what they do seriously. And who knows, maybe some of them are even implicated. I don't know. Not yet, but I will.'

'Efendi—'

'Oh don't call me that, Türgüt Bey. Just don't!'

Süleyman went outside the cemetery office building and lit a cigarette. He didn't know whether Türgüt Akgün knew he was from an old Ottoman family or not, and he didn't care. A lot of people were becoming increasingly servile to public officials and it made him angry. İkmen had always hated it. In the old days servility had been the only game in town; there had been an entire elaborate protocol around it in Ottoman times. But Süleyman had hoped that was dying out. Now, in his middle years, he was seeing a resurgence.

He saw Ömer approach through the falling dusk and called him over.

'Sir.'

'We need to get this place locked down tight,' he said. 'I don't want any more fires, any more breaches of security. If we have to do everything ourselves, then so be it. Seems to me this place needs a security rethink. Commissioner Teker was worried about the cemeteries years ago, but no one listened.'

Ömer's phone rang. He looked at the screen and frowned.

'Who is it?' Süleyman asked.

'Informant.'

'Then take it.'

Ömer put the phone to his ear.

'A lot of my trips away from home are to hospitals these days,' Leah Delmonte said as she placed a china cup and saucer in Çetin İkmen's hands. 'Sugar's on the table.'

'Oh, thank you.'

He couldn't remember whether he'd ever been into the apartment Leah had once shared with her old madam all those years ago. It didn't matter, but somehow he hadn't imagined that it would be so chintzy.

'I didn't know you had a trans cousin until I went to visit poor old Neşe,' Leah said as she sat down in a battered armchair with a grunt.

İkmen smiled. 'I was very glad when Samsun told me you wanted to speak after all these years,' he said.

'I've grown old.'

He shook his head. 'Not old, no,' he said. 'Never that.'

She laughed. 'You were ever the charmer.'

He offered her a cigarette, which she took, and then lit one for himself. 'So how can I help you, Leah Hanım?'

She crossed one heavily stockinged swollen ankle over the other.

'Well, it's trivial,' she said. 'But at my time of life most things are. My knees are arthritic and so I can't clean the cupboard under the sink out properly, the pharmacy no longer sells the hair dye I like, I could go on for ever. But I don't, I stop myself. Unless it's something I really care about.'

'Which is?'

'When the landlord was finally persuaded to clean up old

Leonid Meyer's apartment, he rented it out to a family from Trabzon called Kazantzoğlu . . .' She looked over her shoulder as if expecting someone to be there, then added, 'Pontic Greeks.'

'Ah . . .'

Basically Anatolian Greeks, the Pontics had lived mainly on the Black Sea coast for hundreds of years until almost all of them were obliged to leave the new republic of Turkey in 1923. The Kazantzoğlu were clearly one of those families who had chosen to remain.

'Timur Kazantzoğlu had a wife, Ceyda, a son, Ateş, and his wife Ece, who, over the years, produced a huge tribe of children. Every year a new baby. The old man, Timur, he died in 2010 and still his son and his daughter-in-law were producing. Ece was forty-six by this time, happily pregnant. I'll come back to that.' She drank some tea. 'Ceyda Hanım and I were friends almost from the first. I was still working when we met; she could have spat at me on the street, but she never did. Between you and me, I think she had a past, if you know what I mean. But anyway, we were friends. When poor old Lilli died, she was there for me, and I was there for her when her husband passed away.'

'It's good you made such a loyal friend,' İkmen said.

'Ah, you say that, but . . .' She raised a finger in the air. 'That was the case until last month.'

'June?'

'The fourteenth of June. I remember it clearly. I went to see Ceyda, and Ateş, her son, told me she'd gone out. She didn't go out to many places I didn't go too, but she did go out, and so . . .' She shrugged. 'I went back the next day – still not there. Then the next, and so on and so on until I couldn't do it any more! To explain, while most of Ateş and Ece's children have now left home, there are still two of them in that apartment, and then there's Devlet . . .'

'Who is Devlet?'

'Eight years old and like an infant, the poor thing,' Leah said. 'Devlet was the last child Ece had. My mother used to call such creatures children of the menopause; said they were never right.' She shook her head. 'So now I don't ask any more where Ceyda is. Last time Ateş said something about her going to Trabzon.'

'Which she may have done,' İkmen said.

'I know. She'd been before, to see her sister. But she always told me she was going,' Leah said. 'We were close. We went to the shops together, the auctions, I taught her how to use Starbucks; one day we went to Gülhane Park. Çetin Bey, I'm afraid that something has happened to her.'

'On what basis, Hanım?'

She shrugged again. 'A feeling? A notion? I don't know,' she said. 'But what I can tell you is that ever since Timur Bey died and that poor brainless boy was born, things have not been the same in that apartment.'

'Did Ceyda Hanım say anything to you about it?'

'No, she was always loyal to her family, even with me . . .'

'But?'

'But I notice things myself,' she said. 'The anger, apart from anything. Struggling to deal with that boy, who just lies on his bed making noises, that is hard. Ground them all down. Ece and Ateş, they try to get some treatment and some help with him, but what can you do when you've no money? Ateş Bey drives a taxi and does some sort of nightwatchman work. Poor Ece is left with the child and of course Ceyda, who in spite of her age does her bit.'

'And the rest of the children?'

'The two still at home are at college.'

İkmen put his cigarette out and then lit another. Chain-smoking took him back to his youth. It was bad, but it was also enjoyable.

'So what do you want from me?' he asked.

'I don't think Ceyda Hanım is in Trabzon,' Leah said. 'She would've told me. I think the family are being evasive.'

'What makes you think that?'

She sighed. 'They avoid me. All of them. I used to see them all the time and we talked, you know. Now, without Ceyda Hanım, it's as if they've a bad smell under their noses. I'll be honest with you, Çetin Bey, I know I can say this with you: I wonder whether they sent her away.'

'Sent her away where?'

'I don't know!' She helped herself to another of his cigarettes and lit up. 'The whole family has been struggling for years. Sometimes they pay the rent, sometimes they don't and then the landlady has a screaming fit. Sometimes the food they eat . . . Ugh! You wouldn't give it to the cat! I've made food for all of them in the past, during the winter when it's cold. But their problems are too big for me. There was another son, Ateş's brother Berat. Maybe she's gone to be with him? But she would have said.' She leaned forward, 'I wonder if she's gone somewhere against her will. There, I've said it!'

İkmen frowned. 'So how do I get to meet these people?'

'Something I used to like to do with Ceyda Hanım was go to the auctions in Balat Mahallesi. Ece, the daughter-in-law, still goes.'

İkmen had heard that auctions of mainly cheap things had started in an old coffee house in Balat. They were, it was said, extremely popular.

'You can see her there; there's one on tomorrow,' Leah said. 'You'll know her because she'll have that poor damaged child with her. She always does.'

It was dark by the time Ömer Mungun reached Taksim Square. He waited, as arranged, in front of the Republic Monument, an Italian-designed memorial to those who had taken part in the

94

war of independence when Turkey became a republic. It stood where it always had, but the huge mosque in front of it was new, and contentious. Here in the heart of secular, republican İstanbul, it still looked strange to many eyes, even if it did, to other eyes, represent the new religious reality.

'Ömer Bey.'

Wahıd Saatçı had this way of looking almost regal when he felt like it. Maybe he was of the opinion that if he looked excessively smart, the dozens of uniformed cops who patrolled the great concrete square would leave him alone. Ömer thought that if that was the case, he was probably right. Some of the thicker uniforms gave those they thought might be vagrants a bad time.

Ömer bowed. 'Wahıd Bey. Do you want to talk here, or . . .'

'Let us walk.' Wahıd began to move.

Following, Ömer said, 'Where are we going?'

'Let's head towards İstiklal Caddesi.'

Making for a street that was not only packed with people but bursting with light and heat from bars, restaurants and shops seemed a bit crazy given the evening was already so hot. But Ömer could see where Wahıd was coming from. There was nowhere else in the city that was as anonymous as İstiklal.

Passing in front of the new mosque and heading down past the baroque French consulate, Wahıd lit a cigarette and then said, 'I saw an old acquaintance of mine today. A rather sad case. Wealthy, fallen on hard times.'

It would have been easy for Ömer to say something about how maybe Wahıd's trade in opium had something to do with this, but he didn't.

'It was nice to see her,' the drug dealer continued. 'And fortunately I was able to help her with a small problem concerning her husband.'

'I'm glad.'

'Yes.'

The flashing fairy lights from a nearby cigarette and sweets kiosk reflected disconcertingly in Wahıd's one grey eye.

'In return,' he continued, 'she gave me some information you may find useful.'

'Hence your call.'

'Indeed. My friend had reason to contact an agent of a group of people who organise organ transplant services,' he said.

Ömer asked, 'Do you have names?'

Wahıd sighed. 'There was a play I saw once when I first came here. It was called The Lower Depths. It was Russian, set in a doss house, a last port of call for the poor before death on the streets. This is the target group for these people.'

'Junkies whose organs are shot.'

'Why not?' Wahıd said. 'Who is to know the difference?'

'The surgeon who performs the transplant?' Ömer shook his head. 'This is nonsense.'

'Not if the surgeon doesn't care,' Wahıd said. 'Ömer Bey, do you not understand? This is transplant surgery for those with little money, not none. This is the poor exploiting the destitute. In life, everybody punches down.'

'Punches down?'

They turned into Zambak Sokak, a relatively quiet street lined with publishing offices and high-walled Greek church buildings that led from İstiklal Caddesi to the vast and noisy Tarlabaşı Bulvarı. The noise on İstiklal had been too much for both of them.

Wahıd stopped. 'In life we always exploit those lower down the food chain,' he said. 'The poor will cling to anything that may save them. Even if these recipients of damaged organs die, they will still thank the doctors who tried, as they see it, to save them. And not all of them will die, because not all of the people in the lower depths are addicts.'

That was true. Some might just be undernourished or old.

'How did this contact of yours know about this?' Ömer asked.

'She sold them something once.'

'What?'

Wahıd didn't answer. Music, ABBA by the sound of it, blasted out from somewhere and then subsided.

Realising that Wahıd was not going to reply to his question, Ömer said, 'So we knew prior to this conversation that people in this city were involved in organ harvesting. What information have you got for me that might help me arrest these people?'

'My contact was taken to two places in order to transact her deal,' Wahıd said. 'One, she said, was somewhere in Kasımpaşa, an old wooden house apparently. You know that in spite of that wonderful new stadium our president has built there, Kasımpaşa is still the cheapest district on the İstanbul Monopoly board?' He laughed. 'But that's no use to you. In that rabbit warren of Black Sea coast families I can't help you, that's for sure.' People from the Black Sea coast were famously insular. 'But you may have more luck with an apartment in Gümüşsuyu.'

That was an upmarket part of town centred on a street called İnönü Caddesi. Made up of large low-rise apartment blocks plus some old buildings like the German consulate, Gümüşsuyu had some good restaurants and a lot of academic residents. It was where a now deceased colleague, Ayşe Farsakoğlu, had once lived.

'Meaning?' Ömer said. Süleyman often used this word as a question, but when he did it, it sounded far more arrogant.

'My contact went to an apartment in Gümüşsuyu to pick up her money. She said she could see the Bosphorus.'

'So where did she have her surgery?' Ömer asked. 'In Kasımpaşa?'

'She didn't have any surgery,' Wahıd said.

Ömer frowned.

'She gave them something,' he said.

* * *

97

Was that her? Olimpio stared down into the street below and willed the woman standing in a small puddle of darkness beside the doorway to the bakkal opposite to look up. Was it Sevval? She moved like her, but she was dressed very unlike the Actress. In fact the woman in the street below was dressed more for winter than summer. She wore what looked like an anorak, with a hood.

Olimpio moved away from the window. If it was Sevval, she'd come up soon enough. And then the men would be delighted. Not for the first time, Olimpio thought about how awful it was to be old. She'd never married or had children, but during her younger years she'd taken lots of lovers. Men had still pursued her well into her fifties. But not any more. And as if her fading looks were not bad enough, her time in Silivri had made her persona non grata to most people. Her remaining customers were all faded old women like her, people who pathetically trusted her to make them look beautiful again. She played along, pandering to their vanity, telling them lies, because she knew her life depended on it. Her ladies would never talk about her to anyone, much less the authorities. As long as they had beautifully made clothes to wear, that was their secret. Sometimes she wondered when they would work out her clothes were not doing them any favours.

No ring came from the doorbell. She lit a cigarette. Was Sevval maybe waiting out in the street because she couldn't decide whether to return to the Moral Maze or not? Had she left some panting lover somewhere to resume her old life? Perhaps it wasn't the Actress out there at all. She hoped it wasn't. She hoped that last argument they'd had just before Sevval left had been the last of her. She wondered whether the guilt she'd felt since would ever go away.

'All three of these worked in the south-east,' Kerim Gürsel said as he placed three photographs – two men and one woman – in front of Mehmet Süleyman. 'The one on the left in Mardin, the woman and the other man in Gaziantep,' he continued.

Süleyman frowned. 'All surgeons?'

'All surgeons and all found guilty of removing organs from patients for financial gain.'

'What about the circumstances surrounding their arrests?'

'Two of them worked out of their own hospitals and were informed on by colleagues. Always a risk. You have to pay a lot of people off, which is why it took longer to track down the male doctor from Gaziantep. He bought a house in the Tepebaşı district of the city, a mansion apparently, which he used as his clinic and his operating theatre.'

Kerim Gürsel had called Mehmet Süleyman into his office when he saw that he too was working late. Apparently waiting to meet Ömer Mungun, who was currently with an informant, Süleyman had been impressed by how much information Kerim had managed to accrue about the activities of unscrupulous surgeons.

'It's claimed that most of the donors involved were Syrian refugees,' Kerim said.

'I don't know whether what has happened here was run out of a house or a hospital,' Süleyman said. 'But I accept it's very possible that those harvesting organs here in the city may well have contact with gangs or even individuals on the borders with Iraq and Syria.'

'Where refugees are plentiful.'

'Indeed. Did you find any surgeons implicated in organ trafficking here in the city?'

'No,' Kerim said. 'Doesn't mean there aren't any.'

'No.' Süleyman sighed. 'You know as I left the Karacaahmet cemetery this evening I realised how close it is to two hospitals. One of the local doctors reported seeing fires in the cemetery. And given that we found a human femur, it would seem possible that the cemetery is being used as a dumping ground for at least one unfortunate donor.'

A knock on Kerim's office door disturbed their discussion.

'Come.'

Ömer Mungun put his very white face around the door.

Süleyman stood up. 'Ömer Bey,' he said. 'You look sick. Sit down.'

Ömer sat, but he didn't speak, not for what seemed like forever.

Not all ghosts were mute. İkmen had once been to an apartment in Bomonti where the occupant, a thief, claimed that his dead mother shouted at him through the keyhole. İkmen hadn't heard her, but he'd had no doubt the thief had heard something. Fatma İkmen was, however, entirely silent. But that didn't mean her husband didn't know what she would say when he spoke to her.

'I know, I'm a fool to myself,' he said as he sat opposite her on their balcony. 'But what can I do? Leah Delmonte is a poor old thing, alone and lonely. She had one friend and now she's gone. And yes, I know I won't make any money . . .'

He lit a cigarette.

'Anyway,' he said, 'a missing old woman could be a bit of light relief from the deadly seriousness of this Sevval Kalkan affair. I'm unsure about Machine Bey, but I'm certain that Gold Bey and the Designer aren't telling me everything. Even when people live hidden lives, they are still subject to passions, jealousies and competition. Was Sevval thrown out by Olimpio? I wonder.' He lit a cigarette. 'Did Olimpio kill Sevval? I do know that when one is out of favour with the majority of society, life becomes even more cheap than it already is. We both remember the coup of 1980. All those people arrested, blacklisted, the torture and the executions. Nothing new is happening today.'

He puffed on his cigarette, watching as Çiçek came into the living room.

'On the balcony!' he yelled to her.

He heard her say, 'OK.'

Then he turned back to Fatma. 'She looks glum. It seems

100

Mehmet is chin deep in his latest case and Çiçek is being left to amuse herself. She'll have to either get used to it or end the relationship. I know you never really liked the job. But in our case, there was no choice. Although saying that, I could have retired earlier. I know that now. I wish I had, but . . .' He was quiet for a moment. Then he said, 'Of course, what is new these days is surveillance. In reality it's been around for years, but . . . Blurry film of people shopping, fighting, kissing. Always made me shudder, the intimacy of it. And in my day it wasn't always that helpful. But I can't discount it. There's a bakkal almost outside Olimpio's door. Maybe they've got some footage. Maybe they've wiped it already . . . I don't know. But I should find out.'

'Dad?'

Çiçek had come out onto the balcony and was looking at him. 'Talking to Mum?'

'Yes. Can't you see her?'

'No.'

She could often see her mother, just like she could usually see the djinn that infested the kitchen. But not today. She sat down on one of the chairs she knew her mother didn't use.

'I'm assuming you're bothering her with your work,' she said.

İkmen scowled. 'True, but any observation delivered with such bitterness is going to get a reaction. What's the matter?'

She shrugged. 'Hoped I was going out tonight, but apparently not.'

'With Mehmet Bey, I take it,' her father said. 'So go out with someone else. You've got friends, siblings . . .'

'It's not the same.' She lit a cigarette.

Of course it wasn't and İkmen knew it, but he hated seeing his daughter hanging around the apartment like a moody teenager.

'You know—'

'I know you're going to say I should put up or shut up,' Çiçek said. 'But it's not as easy as that. I worry about him. And although he's told me very little, I know he's working on this case over at the Karacaahmet cemetery. He was at a press conference with the commissioner . . .'

'Which you made sure you watched.'

'Dad, the TV is always on at work, rolling news, you know?'

He did. He tried to ignore it when he could, but he had almost as much need for access to instant news bulletins as the rest of his countrymen. He had not, however, known what Süleyman had precisely been involved in until Çiçek had just told him.

'Grave robbery is not the most dangerous crime . . .' he began.

'How do you know?' she said. 'It's ghoulish! Who in their right mind would take a body out of a grave? It was replaced with another body. What's that about?'

İkmen could think of a few things, but he baulked at mentioning any of them.

'She'll be back at eleven,' Ömer said.

'To this informant's apartment?'

'Yes. He promised her more gear, so she'll come. We could pick her up on Salı Pazarı Yokuşu. According to my informant, she's typical user material.'

'Meaning?' Süleyman asked.

'Thin, slow moving, prematurely aged, stinking.'

'They're not all like that,' Kerim Gürsel said.

'This one is.'

Süleyman nodded. 'Does your informant have any idea who the people she dealt with might be?'

'No,' Ömer said. 'If he'd pressed her for information, he might have frightened her off. He's a drug dealer; why should he give a damn?'

'Because this is another level?' Süleyman said, and then shook his head. 'No. What am I saying? You're quite right, Ömer Bey, why should he care? Why did he tell you, by the way?'

'Apart from the fact that I give him money?' Ömer shrugged. 'He's not a bad man.'

He wanted to say more about Wahıd Saatçı, but he didn't. Whenever he talked about the problems of living in the far east of the country, he knew his colleagues switched off. Both Süleyman and Kerim Gürsel had been there, but that wasn't the same as living there, which was hard. Places like Gaziantep and Mardin were periodically on a war footing, obliged to accommodate tens of thousands of refugees; residents often had to leave to make something of themselves. Those who stayed faced uncertain futures amid the shifting loyalties that pervaded those old, once colonial lands.

'Does he think she'll talk?' Süleyman asked.

'He doesn't know, sir.'

'Not that we can, despite your informant's accusations, pick her up now or maybe ever,' Süleyman said. 'But we can watch her.'

Ömer said, 'She sold her own child . . .'

'Yes,' Süleyman said. 'It is alleged. But let us see where she goes and who she is in contact with before we jump to any conclusions. According to your source, she had the child in a wooden house in Kasımpaşa. Let's see whether she goes there again and who, if anyone, she talks to. Flesh trafficking, be it organs or live children, is a multimillion-dollar industry. We may be on the edge of just one of its tentacles here. We must proceed with caution.'

Chapter 8

At some point, it was said, all the tunnels underneath the city converged. Nobody knew where. Perhaps somewhere along the mythical underground route from the Aya Sofya to the Church of St Mary of the Mongols in Balat. Cemal Yüksel, Machine Bey, had often wondered whether his one-time chapel underneath the carpet shop somehow linked up with other Byzantine monuments in the city. If it did, then maybe by following as yet undiscovered exits from the chapel he would eventually come to rooms that had once been part of the great palace of the Byzantines. Interesting, but he had to admit that the real motive for his minutely investigating the walls from time to time was to find out whether they led up to the surface.

He longed to get out. If Sevval had left Olimpio's apartment of her own volition, he could understand that. Being stuck in one place was terrible. Being stuck with someone to whom you were beholden was even worse.

Unlike Cumhur Polat, Gold Bey, Cemal had never had any designs on Sevval. She was too young and they'd all been brought together by circumstances no one could feel good about. Had Gold Bey maybe met up with the Actress and then, when he didn't get what he wanted . . . No, that couldn't be it. And yet Cemal felt bad that he hadn't told İkmen these things. How could he? The last thing anyone wanted was for suspicion to fall on the Moral Maze itself. Her disappearance had to be connected to someone else – or to no one. Maybe she had simply gone. Maybe they'd never see her again. Maybe this was what happened when people could no longer live in the world. They were just snuffed out of existence.

They came out of nowhere. She'd been halfway down the Rainbow Stairs when the one not in uniform said, 'Kimlik?'

Deniz knew she had her identity card on her somewhere. She put her old tapestry bag down on the stairs and began searching through her pockets.

'Yes, Officer.'

He was probably her age, maybe older, but he looked like a boy. She knew he regarded her with contempt; the police always did, always moving her and Can on, always abusing them, looking for stuff. Can had been done three years before but they'd let him go because he'd given them a name they wanted. She'd never been picked up on her own until now.

She eventually found her kimlik in the pocket of her trousers. She handed it over and watched as he examined it. The uniform at his side shifted uneasily from foot to foot. The examination seemed to go on for ever. Eventually he said, 'I want to search your bag.'

She could ask 'What for?' but they both knew the answer to that question. If it walks like a junkie and talks like a junkie . . .

She said, 'Go ahead.'

He tipped the contents of the bag out at her feet.

'Hey!'

He fixed her with his gaze as he began to sort through old packets of cigarettes, lighters, a sanitary towel, loose change. It would do him no good.

People in the vicinity began to look, and move away.

She let him rifle. If he knew where her gear was, it was doubtful he'd volunteer to retrieve it. Although of course he could always find someone who would. She put her arms up so that he could pat her down, but he didn't.

She shrugged. 'You wanna—'

'You can go,' he said as he kicked her bag back towards her.

'Oh?'

It wasn't the first time she'd been stopped and searched, although most of the cops usually did a cursory pat-down. But of course there had been times when she'd been too smelly and they'd just walked away. Maybe this was one of those times. She couldn't smell herself, but then what did she know?

'And get home,' the policeman said. 'You're as high as a kite.'

Deniz picked up her bag and staggered down the Rainbow Steps.

Now that was a name İkmen knew.

It was too hot to sleep and so he'd gone online to see if he could find anything more about Sevval Kalkan. Although her name had been pretty successfully expunged from most Turkish websites, it did appear in several English references. On the back of her Turkish work, she'd appeared in two English-language films produced in the UK back in 2013. In both, it seemed, she'd been some sort of 'ethnic'. Outside Turkey she'd not had a big career, but it could possibly have built, given time.

Trying to find her graffiti art, however, was another matter. There was nothing. This wasn't surprising, but it was a search that led nevertheless to a lot of very varied examples of street art. One of these, a vast peacock made from discarded tin lids and rags, was particularly striking. Created on the side of a building, now demolished, in the old Sulukule district of the city, it was the work of Gonca Şekeroğlu, a famous Roma collage artist and one-time lover of Mehmet Süleyman. İkmen hadn't realised that she had diversified into street art. But then it had been over a year since he'd last seen her, and late though it was, he decided to remedy that right away.

* * *

106

It was said by Perihan Bulut that she had adopted Aysel because she saw the child's mother drop her in the street. The story had always been that the girl's mother had been a junkie who had just wandered off and left her in the gutter on İstiklal Caddesi. Neither Uğur nor Lokman knew whether that was actually true. All they did know was that their sister Aysel was a force of nature.

'If I had realised that you were making trouble for our brother Uğur I would have come sooner.'

Lokman cringed as she pointed a long, pale finger in his face. Although three years her senior, Lokman had always been in thrall to his tall, blond, terrifying sister. And now that she was a nun, it was even worse, in spite of the fact that neither Lokman nor Uğur was a Christian.

Aysel, or Sister Eudokia, had got in on a bus from Thessaloniki two hours ago. Uğur, who had called her the previous evening, had met her at Esenler bus station, and now the three of them were in Lokman's apartment in Tarlabaşı.

Lokman said, 'It's nothing to do with you. Why are you here?' But he wouldn't catch her eye.

Uğur pulled up a very trendy plastic seat for his sister and she sat down.

'Because you're acting like a moron,' she replied. 'If I'd known you were having our mother dug up, I would have come sooner.'

'She's not your mother!' As soon as he'd said it, Lokman cringed.

She slapped him across the face. 'Horrid little boy!' she snapped. 'Mother would die all over again if she could hear you. She put Uğur in charge of the family affairs because she knew you were useless, and I was already in the convent. I need nothing. But you, you selfish little brat, you want everything. Look at this apartment! You must be able to afford something better than this.'

'He should be able to,' Uğur said. 'If he didn't spend all his allowance, and borrow money too.'

'You call this bullshit all over the walls art?'

Lokman ignored her. 'If it hadn't been for me, we'd never have known that someone else was in Mother's grave.'

'Oh, so you did a good thing, did you?' She slapped him again. Lokman made no attempt to defend himself. 'I left the world to get away from situations like this, the stink and the worship of money. Render unto your brother Uğur that which is—'

'He's not my brother, I don't believe it.'

'Yes you do,' she said. 'You lying little toad. Uğur has told me everything and I can see exactly what you are doing and why. You're so profligate you can't even sustain a lifestyle in Tarlabaşı, and so you attempt to take our mother's entire empire from our brother. You make up lies so you don't have to do something simple like take a DNA test. Oh no, Uğur would fix that in some way. What nonsense!'

'We've had DNA tests now, me and Uğur,' Lokman said. 'That fat doctor made us do it.'

'Good. Clarity at last. You are both our mother's blood children and you both have access to her fortune.' Uğur put a hand on her shoulder. 'If you can't manage, get a job. But in the meantime, I have been given leave to come home until our mother's body is found. Me! Not even a blood relative! But I care. She saved me and I care.'

'Saved you to become one of . . . of them!' Lokman said, then shrank back from her again.

Eudokia narrowed her eyes. 'One of what?' she said. 'Go on, say it.'

But he didn't. Perihan had always been open with Aysel about her parentage. When the girl had a chance to take a genetic test, Perihan encouraged her. Aysel, it seemed, was almost entirely

Greek. That was not why she'd become a nun. Perihan had sent her to a school that had been run by nuns, where she had acquired her desire for the secluded life. Doing such a thing via the Orthodox Church had made sense.

'Yes, I am ethnically Greek,' she said. 'But—'

'But you are also our sister,' Uğur said.

'And I love you both,' she said. 'Even though you, Lokman, are a lazy little shit. So I'm going to be staying with Uğur until our mother's body reappears. I will pray for that. I will also act as Mother would have done with you, Lokman. I will be here tomorrow morning at six to get this place in some sort of order and take you shopping.'

'Shopping?'

'For food,' she said. 'When I came in, I checked your fridge. Man cannot live by vodka alone.'

Çetin İkmen had parked his car outside the ancient church of St Mary of the Mongols and made his way over to a tall house surrounded by walls that looked as if they had been designed to protect a fortress. Behind those walls, he knew, there was a considerable garden, although one would never suspect it to look at the place. If anything, the walls that surrounded Gonca Şekeroğlu's home were higher than he remembered. But the music was the same, and the smell – cooked meat, rakı and cigarettes. He walked around the back of the property where he knew there was a gate and let himself in.

For a moment it was as if no time had passed since his last visit. There were still multicoloured lights strung in the branches of the trees, smoke from a fire pit in the mouth of the old cistern belched its meaty aromas into the air, violin music played and Gonca sat cross-legged on the ground, weaving strands of what looked like golden hair. As he approached, she said, 'Hello, İkmen. What can I do for you?'

With some difficulty, he sat on the ground beside her. 'What are you doing?' he asked.

Under her still nimble fingers, the golden strands were becoming a small piece of fabric.

'This is byssus,' she said. Then she looked up at him and smiled. 'Or is it?'

İkmen searched his memory for a word he'd probably last heard when he was a child. 'Sea silk?'

'The golden fabric as worn by the pharaohs of Egypt and the emperors of Rome,' she said. 'The most expensive substance on earth.'

'I thought the magical silk-producing clam was extinct?'

She shrugged. 'Maybe it is.'

'Then what . . .'

She put her work down. 'Who knows? But when one of the masters of our new universe wants a small trinket made from byssus for his wife, then who am I to deny him?'

Sea silk had been used in the costumes of the Mediterranean elite for over a thousand years. As far as most people knew, the clams from which it was harvested had all but disappeared. Not so many years ago, İkmen would have said that if anyone knew where to source such a treasure it would be the famous collage artist Gonca Şekeroğlu. But not any more. In a world so enthusiastically stripped of its resources, that was unlikely. And yet clearly customers remained, and he could imagine what those people were like. He saw them on his television every day.

'An offer you couldn't refuse?' he said.

'Gypsies refuse no offers.'

Her face was sad now, and suddenly he knew that the place he had walked into was not the same as it had been years ago when he'd first met the free spirit that was Gonca. Even she, it seemed, was trapped in the same box of deception as everyone else. He offered her a cigarette, which she took. He noticed that parts of her floor-length hair were now white. But she was still beautiful. She always would be.

İkmen cleared his throat, then said, 'Street art.'

'Graffiti? What about it?'

'I've seen one of yours online. A peacock.'

'I dabble.'

'I'm told there are collectors,' he said.

She frowned. 'What? People who physically take artworks away from buildings? Only that English artist, Banksy. Why?'

He took out the photograph Machine Bey had given him of Sevval Kalkan's offensive graffito. 'Look at this.' He passed it over.

'Mmm,' she said, 'you don't see one of these every day.'

'What, the sentiment or . . .'

'A Polaroid.' She squinted at it. 'Strong stuff, but I've seen worse. Where was this?'

'I don't know,' he said. 'Wondered if you'd seen it.'

'No.'

She continued looking at it.

'Sold to someone, apparently,' he said.

She shrugged. 'Anyone can get an artist to come into their home and paint an artwork. Especially these days, when so many creative people are under suspicion. Hence my own works of prostitution.' She looked down at the sea silk square on the ground.

'Sure,' he said. 'But Gonca, this artwork was on an outside wall. It was removed brick by brick.'

She looked up at him and then solemnly passed the photograph back. 'You mean this? This wasn't created outside, İkmen.'

He looked at the photograph again while she pointed at something down in the far right corner.

'There,' she said, 'that is a wooden floor.'

Was it? İkmen looked closely, and for a moment, he couldn't

see it. But when he did, he couldn't un-see it. How had he not noticed that? How had Machine Bey? Sevval had created her masterpiece inside someone's home. But whose?

'Where do you come from?'

The boy just looked at him, bewildered. All he would say was, 'Hafız. Hafız.' Probably his name.

Cemetery guard Raşım Dorsay was on his own this shift. His usual partner, Münir Sever, was off sick. He'd seen the kid as he'd made his way, on his usual route towards the shrine of Karaca Ahmet. When the boy had seen him, he'd tried to run, but Raşım had caught him. Now, close up, he could smell the kid and it wasn't pleasant. Not starved by the look of him, he certainly hadn't had a wash in a long time.

'Do you come to the shrine?' Raşım asked in a loud voice, as if trying to verbally batter the boy into understanding.

'Karaca Ahmet shrine. Do you come?'

The boy pointed to himself and repeated, 'Hafız.'

He was probably a Syrian; a lot of the people sleeping rough were. But if he didn't respond to the name Karaca Ahmet, then he probably wasn't an Alevi visiting the shrine. So he was either in the cemetery to sleep in what he might feel was comparative safety, or to meet someone, or else he was lost. He hadn't been desecrating graves, which was a mercy, but Raşım knew he should record the kid's presence. The police were everywhere and so even Türgüt Bey couldn't object. In fact he should take him into the office.

'You need to come with me,' he said as he grabbed one of the boy's hands.

Hafız, if that was his name, struggled.

'Ah! Ah!' Raşım increased his grip. 'Come on! You have to come with me now!'

The kid began to cry, but Raşım held on, and eventually they

112

arrived at the gatekeeper's office, where Türgüt Bey was sitting at his desk.

'What's this?' he said as he rose to his feet.

'Caught this one lurking behind a gravestone,' Raşım said.

Türgüt looked at the boy, whose head was now down and whose tears flowed freely.

'What was he doing?'

'Lurking, as I say, Türgüt Bey. He can't speak Turkish; I think he might be Syrian.'

The older man thought for a moment and then said, 'So what do you want me to do about it?'

Raşım didn't say anything.

'Chuck him out on the street,' the gatekeeper said.

'Yes, but—'

'If he wasn't up to mischief, then let him go. Smack him around the head a few times if it makes you feel better.'

He sat down again and returned to his paperwork.

Last time Raşım had looked, the incident book had been entirely empty. But he knew that didn't reflect his reality or that of several of the other guards. And of course there had been that incident with the necrophile he'd told Inspector Süleyman about. Or rather, the incident he'd only told him half the truth about.

He tried again. 'Should I—'

'No, you should not record this, because it's nothing,' Türgüt Bey said. 'Isn't it bad enough that we've got the police all over the cemetery talking about our lack of security? Do you want to lose your job?'

'No, sir.'

'Then take the boy away and get about your business.'

Raşım did as he was bid, pushing the boy out of the main gates and into the street. Türgüt Bey treated all the guards as if they were idiots. Even before the police came on the scene, he'd raged on about how recording negative incidents could cause them to lose their jobs. But then surely such things were just part of life, and the guards were doing what they were paid to do when they apprehended intruders.

Was that in his head, or was it coming from the phone in the hall downstairs? He'd been dreaming that he was a police officer, of all things. His parents would be appalled. Only boys from the slums who could fight well but couldn't read properly joined the police . . .

Mehmet Süleyman opened his eyes, and for a moment he couldn't work out where he was. He should have been in his bedroom back home in Arnavautköy, but somehow he was in a tiny room somewhere else with a mobile phone beside his ear trilling exactly the same ringtone he remembered from his youth. Shakily, he picked it up.

'Süleyman.'

'It sounds as if I have woken you,' a voice said. 'I apologise, Inspector, but I thought you should know that I have just received some of the DNA data I requested on the Karacaahmet cemetery femur.'

Süleyman sat up. He often dreamed about being back home with his parents and his brother these days. Not that he'd had anything like an idyllic childhood, but it had been better than now. DNA? Already?

'Doctor,' he said. 'No, no problem. I was asleep, but . . .'

'The team who perform the tests for me have worked absolute magic. Now, to the good news first,' Dr Arto Sarkissian said. 'The DNA from the bone definitely matches the DNA supplied by Perihan Bulut's sons. That may be of some comfort to her relatives.'

'I imagine so.'

'However, there is a problem with the sons' DNA samples.'

'What do you mean?' Süleyman said.

'I mean that only one of the samples is a first-rank relative,' the doctor said.

'The other comes from someone who is not a direct descendant of this woman.' Süleyman heard the doctor clear his throat. 'It would seem that there was something in Lokman Bulut's assertion that he and his brother are not what they appear.'

Chapter 9

İkmen placed the Polaroid on the table. 'Where did you get this?'

'She gave it to me,' Machine Bey said. 'Sevval.'

'Why?'

Machine Bey set a glass of tea in front of his guest and sat. Around him, the world of mechanical art was already whirring and humming.

'Why?' He shrugged. 'She wanted us to see what she was doing. The rest of us, Gold Bey, the Designer and me, we have been able to take up our old skills to some extent since our release from prison. But Sevval had to find something new to do. Acting is a very public pursuit. I didn't know she had any artistic talent, and although what she has produced here isn't to my taste, I can see that it is something that is skilful.'

İkmen nodded. 'Can you recall where she said this was located?'

'No,' he said. 'As I think I told you before, she said nothing beyond that it was somewhere in Beyoğlu. But because it was bought, it's gone now.'

'And you didn't think that was odd?'

Machine Bey thought for a moment. 'I've heard of such things happening.'

'The English artist Banksy.'

'Yes,' he said. 'In England.'

'So don't you think that if something like this had happened here, you would have heard about it?'

'I don't go out . . .'

'But you are online,' İkmen said. 'Surely the removal of a piece of wall in Beyoğlu would be reported somewhere.'

'I thought that maybe the subject matter . . .'

'Maybe that would have been glossed over, but someone would have seen it and put it up online somewhere,' İkmen said. 'But no one did.'

Machine Bey looked up. 'You think Sevval lied?'

'Not necessarily,' İkmen said. 'If you look at the corner of the photograph, you will be able to see a wooden floor.'

Machine Bey took his glasses off and squinted. 'Oh. That little bit there?'

'Yes.'

He looked harder. 'And so . . .'

'That Polaroid was taken indoors,' İkmen said. 'It's on someone's wall somewhere. Did Sevval ever talk to you about her friends?'

Still apparently in shock, Machine Bey said, 'Who would want such a thing? I mean, I can understand removing a stack of bricks and placing it on display in a dedicated art gallery. But to have something like this in your own apartment . . .'

'Machine Bey?'

He looked up. 'Oh, yes . . . or rather no, I don't know Sevval's friends. I think they melted away after her arrest. With the exception of Olimpio, we have all found ourselves with new allies.'

'Olimpio was of the opinion that Sevval had multiple lovers,' İkmen said.

Machine Bey shook his head. 'I don't know. Not to my knowledge. But Olimpio lived with her and so would have known more about her habits. But . . .'

'She's an older, jealous woman.'

He shrugged. Then he said, 'I know Gold Bey would have had an affair with Sevval in a heartbeat.'

'He says not,' İkmen said.

'Then I think he may be lying to himself. Not that he'd ever force himself on her or anyone else, but I could see his desire in his eyes.' He shook his head. 'I didn't want to have to even think about what part any member of the Moral Maze might have played in Sevval's disappearance.'

'If you know of anyone she met . . .'

'No.' He shook his head. 'The only person I know of who is connected to Sevval is her mother.'

'Who rejected her.'

'Well, not quite,' Machine Bey said.

The two men had brought a nun with them. Once Ömer Mungun had ushered them into Süleyman's office, he knocked on Kerim Gürsel's door and said, 'They're here.'

After a few moments, Süleyman and Dr Sarkissian came out into the corridor, both looking grave. Ömer said, 'There's a woman with them. A nun.'

'A nun? Are you sure?'

'She looks like a nun to me,' Ömer said.

Süleyman looked at Dr Sarkissian and raised his eyebrows.

The story this woman had told Sergeant Mungun's informant was that she had given birth to a child in a wooden house in Kasımpaşa. And here she was, in Kasımpaşa, standing outside a wooden house one road back from the Golden Horn. And yet this wooden house was a public building, a community centre for migrants from the Black Sea city of Trabzon. Now in plain clothes, Constable Ercan Tuna had got a good look at Deniz Palandoken the previous evening with Sergeant Mungun. Then, as now, she'd looked like a typical homeless addict.

A female colleague had followed her from the Rainbow Steps to a derelict house in Cankurturan, where she'd met a man, seemingly her husband, with whom she'd shared an opium pipe.

Then the pair had slept until dawn, when the woman had roamed the streets, diving into dustbins for food. Now she was in Kasımpaşa, at a community centre where supporters of Black Sea football club Trabzonspor hung out to smoke, drink tea and watch matches on a TV set placed near the top of a high-ceilinged room. Such places were common across the city. The exclusive preserve of men, they acted as refuges from family life, unofficial employment agencies, and places where migrants could follow their native team and reminisce about the old days. Sometimes they could serve as loci for meet-ups of the crime families that had come into the city with the legitimate migrant population. One thing they rarely featured was women. And yet Deniz Palandoken had gone inside without a hair being turned.

Constable Tuna could see the men inside looking at him, and so he walked on by. At the end of the street there was a small bakkal in the basement of a tall stone house. He went inside, where he found a small man wearing a white kufi skullcap, who bowed gracefully as he entered. It was well known that many of the people from the Black Sea district were very observant when it came to religion; the family of the president himself hailed from that part of the country. Kasımpaşa was his home borough, a fact that made a lot of the local people feel very proud. Tuna, a native of the much more free-and-easy district of Yeşilköy, out by Atatürk airport, was very much out of his comfort zone in a place like this.

He looked at the old man and smiled. 'Good morning, uncle,' he said.

The man bowed again.

'I'd like to buy twenty Camel cigarettes, please.'

He already had cigarettes, but buying things from a local shop often allowed one to get into conversation with the shopkeeper, which could prove useful. On this occasion, however, he had miscalculated – badly.

The old man's face dropped and he said, 'We do not stock such things in this shop.'

'Oh.' And now he could see that. No cigarettes behind the counter.

'Have you not heeded the message our president gives about the perils of smoking?' the man continued.

'Er . . .' This was the president's heartland and the president was a virulent anti-smoker. 'I have . . .'

'But you do not act,' the man said. 'Go home and mend your ways.' He turned his back.

Tuna returned to the street, where a group of women were standing outside the community centre. All covered, they talked to each other behind nervous hands, and when one of them looked at him, Tuna turned away.

'Perihan Hanım named me Aysel,' the nun said in answer to Süleyman's question about her identity. 'My real mother left me on İstiklal Caddesi shortly after she gave birth to me. Mother Perihan brought me up as her own.'

'So you are not a blood relative?' Süleyman said.

'No. Mother Perihan never hid that. She treated me like her own children, giving me the best she could manage, including sending me to school at the Lycée Notre Dame de Sion.'

Situated in fashionable Harbiye, the Catholic girls' school was one of the best and most expensive in the city.

'Mother Perihan was Alevi, like my brothers, but actually she was very much for freedom of religion. When I came home from school saying I had a vocation to be a nun, she just smiled and said I could if I wanted to. At the age of nineteen, I took a DNA test to try to discover my origins, and when I found that I was in fact Greek, my vocation seemed to be set in stone.'

'So why are you here now?'

'I've been given leave,' she said. 'Our mother's body has been desecrated. I won't return to my convent until this is resolved, until I can confidently leave my brothers to resume their lives. Our mother was the closest thing to a saint on this rotten earth. This needs to be put right.'

Tall and thin, she sat back in her chair with a determination Süleyman rarely saw on the faces of people called into his office.

Dr Sarkissian cleared his throat and looked at the three siblings. 'Well,' he said, 'the good news, if one can call it that, is that the thigh bone we found in Karacaahmet cemetery is indeed related to you.'

Uğur Bulut leaned forward in his chair. 'Have you found any more . . . pieces?'

'No,' the doctor said. 'Not as yet. Inspector Süleyman's team are still looking. But what we can say with certainty thus far is that your mother's body was removed from her grave and scattered. There had also been an attempt to burn the bones.'

'God!'

'I'm sorry,' Süleyman said. 'This must be hard to hear.'

He watched both men's eyes fill with tears and saw their sister take their hands. After a few moments' silence, Sister Eudokia said, 'So? What's the bad news?'

Dr Sarkissian cleared his throat again. Süleyman knew what was coming and found himself looking away.

'Genetic testing on the bone matched against DNA taken from the two of you reveals that you are both related to Perihan Bulut. However, only one of you is a first-rank relative.'

Lokman Bulut turned on his brother. 'I told you!'

Uğur Bulut, no less shocked, but more controlled, looked at the doctor and said, 'Can you please tell us what that means?'

'Of course. A first-rank relative generally means you are a child or a parent of the person. This is true in one of the sets of results in this case. In the other set, however, there is a complication. While related to Perihan Bulut, this subject is only a second-rank relation. In all probability the child of one of Perihan Hanım's siblings.'

'So which . . .'

'Uğur Bey I am sorry to have to tell you that you are not Perihan Bulut's son.'

'I told you!' Lokman Bulut reiterated. 'I told you!'

Sister Eudokia smacked him hard on the face and then put her arms around Uğur, who was now in tears.

'You will need time to absorb this, I know,' the doctor continued. 'On top of what has happened out at the Karacaahmet, it is a very hard time for you. I wish it were otherwise.'

The nun looked up. 'So what now?'

'So we continue to look for more of your mother's bones,' Süleyman said. 'Above and beyond that, we are going to bring whoever did this to your mother to justice.'

'You sound very confident, Inspector,' she said.

He didn't reply.

Dr Sarkissian said, 'I would recommend that you all go home now and spend some time talking to each other.'

Lokman Bulut stood up. 'I'm going to call my lawyer,' he said, and left the office.

The others watched him go. Uğur Bulut said nothing, but Sister Eudokia was another matter.

'At present,' she explained, 'Uğur runs our mother's business. Perihan Hanım knew which of her sons was the most capable. Lokman gets a generous allowance and doesn't have to work. But it's not enough for him. He's a greedy little shit. I fear what will happen now.'

Dr Sarkissian sat down beside her. 'I wish I could undo what has been discovered here,' he said. 'But I can't.'

'I know.'

'He's always said I wasn't Mother's son, and I've always laughed at him,' Uğur Bulut said. 'How did he know?'

'He didn't,' his sister said. 'The little bastard got lucky. But we will fight him if we have to, Uğur. He will wreck Mother's business.' She got to her feet. 'Come on, we need to contact Cihan Bey.'

Süleyman rushed to open the door for the traumatised pair. As she left, Sister Eudokia said, 'We will speak to our family attorney. If any court finds in favour of our brother, then it means that justice in this country is truly dead.'

When they had gone, Süleyman and Dr Sarkissian sat down, exhausted.

Eventually the doctor said, 'God, that was awful. The younger brother is clearly, as his sister said, a little shit. You know, Inspector, I wonder about the ethics of DNA testing.'

'It helps us apprehend wrongdoers we would otherwise miss,' Süleyman said. He stood up and locked his office door, then opened the window and lit a cigarette.

'Yes, but look at this situation,' the doctor said. 'If that boy takes control of his mother's company, it could be a disaster.'

'If the sister is correct.'

'I think she may be. Did you see the glee on Lokman Bulut's face when he realised he was his mother's only natural son?' He shook his head. 'And unfortunately a court may find in his favour. I imagine Perihan Bulut left a will, but who knows how much weight that will carry given the situation? God, I hate this job sometimes.'

Süleyman, half in and half out of his window, said, 'Can we talk about DNA on the other body?'

'Now that's out of the way? Yes,' Dr Sarkissian said. 'Ethnically diverse, as one would expect from a subject, I imagine, originating from Anatolia. Bit of Turk, Greek, Armenian. A very common profile. No matches to anyone currently on any of our databases, although I can tell you that she was dying anyway.'

Süleyman frowned.

'She had leukaemia,' the doctor said. 'And, given that I can find no evidence of chemotherapy or any other treatment regime in her system, I would say untreated.'

'Was it possible she didn't know?' Süleyman asked.

'She would have been sick, but yes. If she didn't consult a doctor, she may well have been in the dark.'

'How would that have affected her status as an organ donor?'

'Depends how ethical the doctor performing the procedure was. In this instance, I think we can assume he or she was devoid of ethics. This woman was not well. That said, if she knew that, and especially if she knew she was dying, it could explain why she donated her heart. Perhaps her family were given money; maybe she did it freely out of a desire to help someone else live after her inevitable death. But then again, maybe she didn't know; maybe she was just a victim.'

Süleyman finished his cigarette. 'You know, Doctor,' he said, 'a long time ago, Commissioner Teker was worried about our vast city cemeteries and the opportunities such enormous, poorly protected spaces offered to criminals. I know she thought it was only a question of time before something happened that was going to be too big to ignore. I think this may well be it.'

If she was bad enough to have been admitted to Bakırköy psychiatric hospital, then Mihrimah Kalkan, Sevval's mother, was as good as dead. Not that it meant that trying to speak to her would necessarily be a waste of time. People underestimated what patients with dementia were aware of. The problem İkmen had was getting in to see her. But in the meantime, he was in Balat, outside a house not far from Gonca Şekeroğlu's place, on a road that was so steep it made his legs tremble. Although Balat had at one time been home to a large proportion of İstanbul's Jewish population, İkmen knew that this particular row of tall, brightly coloured houses had once been owned by Armenians. The one he was currently standing outside had been a coffee house for almost as long as he could remember. But now it was a very popular auction room, and people were already beginning to assemble for the sale, which started at one.

So far, there'd been no sign of a woman pushing a child that was no longer an infant in a buggy. What was in evidence was an immensely diverse group of people, including headscarfed housewives, cheap-suited old men, young hipsters with beards, and a large cohort of elegantly dressed secular ladies. This last group talked excitedly about what they might find at the auction.

'I'm looking for a set of hamam tası for the new bathroom,' one said. 'Not that we have an actual hamam, but I think it's just nice having some bowls, maybe filled with soap or potpourri.'

Another, a woman wearing the biggest sunglasses İkmen had ever seen, said, 'While I resume my never-ending search for ikat fabrics.'

The other women laughed. Ikat fabrics from central Asia were incredibly colourful and highly sought after. İkmen couldn't really see such items turning up in a place run by a man who looked like something out of a seventies American cop show.

Ali İpek, the auctioneer, wasn't exactly famous, but İkmen had seen pictures of him in the press. Aged about sixty, he wore a trilby hat and a sheepskin coat, even in the heat. A roll-up cigarette hung out of the corner of his mouth as he called his customers in to the sale.

'Come on, mesdames et messieurs,' he yelled, lapsing into poor French. 'The auction of dreams awaits, and who knows what will come your way today!'

The women went inside, one by one. Some carrying babies and leading toddlers by the hand, others alone, biting their lips as they stood in the harsh afternoon sunlight. Constable Tuna watched as they went up some stairs behind the open doorway.

Through the window beside the doorway he saw that the men were watching a football match on the large television.

'What are you doing?'

Tuna turned and found himself looking into the face of a huge man. Not only tall, this character was morbidly obese, and he reeked of stale sweat.

'Wondering what's going on here,' Tuna said.

'Not your business what ladies do. Who are you?'

His cover story wasn't as finely honed as it would have been had he been actually undercover. He hadn't really anticipated this sort of problem. He should have done. People from the Black Sea coast towns and cities tended to stick together.

'I'm a location scout,' he said.

The man narrowed his eyes. 'What's that?'

'Locations for film and TV companies,' Tuna said.

'Which ones?'

'I work for an agency. Who are you anyway? Are you police?'

The man grimaced. 'No. Why do you ask me that?'

'Because you're questioning me.'

The man fell silent for a moment, then he said, 'We don't want people coming round here filming us.'

Tuna didn't want to provoke him, but he said, 'And are you some sort of community leader I should know about?'

'Me? No. But I'm telling you we like to be left alone here. Filming is not Islamic and we are very observant here.'

Tuna nodded. 'I can see that,' he said. 'And I will pass it on.'

'You'd better.'

Tuna walked away. As a lone man, well dressed and keeping himself to himself, he hadn't expected such hostility. Maybe his mistake had been to ask for cigarettes at the bakkal. But then he saw one of the women who had gone into the community centre come out. It wasn't Deniz Palandoken, but she was carrying something that Deniz would have coveted. The woman showed her friend, another covered woman, a large gold coin, known as a Tam, these are manufactured for the purpose of saving. What on earth could a junkie like Deniz have to do with what was clearly a women's savings scheme?

Chapter 10

'Ten lira, fifteen . . . I'm looking for twenty. Come on, you won't find quality like this just anywhere. All hand stitched . . .'

The auction house was gloomy, airless and full of stuff that was probably mostly junk. There were some truly terrible faded reproduction paintings on the walls – a grey rendition of Van Gogh's Sunflowers caught İkmen's eye. And yet the audience was huge. People, as well as sideboards that had seen happier times, and bags of old curtains, were stuffed into every possible nook and cranny. But as yet there was still no woman with a disabled child. Maybe, in spite of what Leah Delmonte had told him, Ece Kazantzoğlu was no longer so keen on the auctions.

As the auctioneer held up the leather satchel he was attempting to sell, one wag shouted out, 'You'd need to pay us for that, Ali Bey!'

The auctioneer laughed, as did most of the punters.

'Oh, Cengiz Bey!' he said. 'Ever the joker. Come on, ladies and gentlemen! Look at the quality of this leather. Honestly, this bag could survive anything. Give me twenty and bring a smile to my poor old face.'

If nothing else, this kind of auction was a laugh, İkmen thought. Completely unlike the sale he'd once been to, in his capacity as a serving police officer, at a very plush auction house in Şişli. That had been a strictly no-joke situation, unlike this. Even the audience was entertaining. An old man sitting to his left nudged

him and said, 'I'm waiting for the lots they call "miscellaneous".
Usually bags full of all sorts, often old pornography.'

'Right.' İkmen smiled. Did he look like the sort of man who
might be in need of some old pornography?

The satchel eventually sold for nineteen lira, and before the next
lot was announced – the old man predicted it would definitely be
'miscellaneous' – a boy came round with small paper cups of tea.
It was all very civilised, and although you couldn't smoke, which
was a nuisance, İkmen felt quite comfortable in these surroundings.

He was just thinking that he might come again at some point,
purely for his own enjoyment, when the front door opened and
a covered woman appeared.

The auctioneer called out to her. 'Ah, Ece Hanım! We
wondered where you were.' He turned to the tea boy. 'Ersu, go
and give Ece Hanım some help with Devlet Bey.'

İkmen wanted to turn around and look, like everyone else,
but when he heard what was presumably the poor damaged boy,
he stopped himself. It was a godawful noise and he wondered
how the auction could carry on against a background of such
wild screaming and grunting.

But the auction attendees made way for the woman and her
child, and the man who had been sitting beside İkmen, and two
ladies who had been next to him, moved out of the way to allow
Ece Hanım and her son to sit at the front. Like the modest woman
she clearly was, Ece Hanım didn't acknowledge İkmen in any
way, but just sat, eyes front, one hand holding onto the buggy
containing her son.

Another covered woman, behind İkmen, whispered to her
friend, 'Now we'll hear nothing.'

Exhumations were rare, and so cemetery guard Berkin Koca
knew he was on shaky ground when he said, 'Well, they probably
come from exhumations.'

A large sheet had been laid on the floor of the gatekeeper's office. It was covered in pieces of bone gathered by police officers from almost every corner of the Karacaahmet cemetery over the past two days. Two guards, the gatekeeper, and an imam who just happened to be in the building at the time looked down at the small ossuary Ömer Mungun was showing them.

Ömer looked at the gatekeeper. 'How many exhumations do you have?'

'I don't know, not many . . .' Türgüt Bey glared at Berkin Koca and said, 'They don't come from exhumations. Don't be ridiculous.'

Berkin felt his face flush. Bits and pieces of bone were common amongst the gravestones. Somebody had once told him that it was because there were too many bodies all piled up together. As if to underline his thoughts, Türgüt Bey said, 'Old bone fragments get pushed up to the surface from time to time, Sergeant.'

Mungun pointed to half a ribcage. 'And that?' he said. 'How do you explain that?'

Türgüt Bey said nothing. What could he say? Ever since an unknown body had been found in that Alevi grave, the police had been everywhere, looking for other instances of the same thing. Türgüt Bey had told the guards they had to cooperate, be respectful and just do their jobs. He'd warned them, though, too. The police, he'd said, wanted ultimately to replace many of them with their own officers, using this incident to portray the cemetery as unsafe.

'We will need to test the larger examples,' Mungun said as he looked down at the bones on the sheet. 'If we can reunite them with their resting places, that will be all to the good.'

'And, er, Sergeant, if you do identify these bones, does that mean you will wish to reopen those graves?' Türgüt Bey asked.

'A decision will be taken if that happens,' Mungun said. 'For the moment, we will remove these bones and continue looking. I am aware that some of the smaller fragments may have simply come to the surface over time, but the more substantial pieces have, we believe, been removed. There is also evidence of attempts to burn some of the larger remnants.' He took a deep breath and continued. 'Inspector Süleyman has ordered a continued police presence here for the time being. We've had independent reports of night-time fires here, which I would like you to look out for. Also, anyone who shouldn't be in the graveyard, someone who isn't a visitor, who maybe appears to be sleeping here, is to be reported to us.'

Berkin saw the face of his colleague, Raşim Dorsay, resolve into a frown.

A bag of 'miscellaneous' was the next lot. Keeping one eye firmly on Ece Kazantzoğlu, İkmen also took in the fact that several of the secular ladies wanted this bag. Maybe they were interested in old-fashioned pornography?

'Lot four,' the auctioneer announced. 'Bag containing miscellaneous fabrics. Some very fine, I'm told. Who'll start me off at five lira?'

The lady with the massive sunglasses flung her arm in the air.

'Madam.

'Six? Who will give me six?'

One of the woman's friends put her hand up, and the little group all giggled like schoolgirls.

'Let's go for ten! Who'll give me ten!' No one took the bait and so the auctioneer lowered the price. 'Eight?'

There was a pause, and then Ece Kazantzoğlu raised her hand.

'Ece Hanım! Thank you!'

'I'll give you ten,' a female voice said.

'Ten! Here!'

There was a buzz of voices, one of which İkmen heard say, 'I think it's real. Go on.'

'Twelve!'

'Twelve from the lady with the green headscarf! Some

131

beautiful fabrics here for you today, ladies,' the auctioneer said. 'Came from a yalı out in Yeniköy, I'm told.'

Did İkmen hear someone whisper the word 'ikat'? Could that scruffy-looking old bag really contain valuable central Asian fabrics? If it genuinely had come from a yalı in Yeniköy, it was possible.

Ece Kazantzoğlu raised her hand again. 'Fifteen.'

'Fifteen lira here,' the auctioneer said.

The boy, Devlet, obviously excited by the action that was taking place around him, hooted loudly. İkmen noticed that, in spite of the warm weather, the child was dressed in a thick jumper and woollen trousers. A lot of village people believed they had to protect their children from the cold even in the summer. But the boy, who was plump, was sweating. The hooting was as much about this as the action around him.

'Twenty lira!'

Devlet screamed. A man murmured, 'Take him outside, woman.'

'Twenty-five,' Ece Kazantzoğlu said.

'Twenty-five from Ece Hanım here! Thank you! Any advance . . .'

'Thirty!'

The woman in the green headscarf had given up. Now it was between Ece Hanım and the small group of secular ladies İkmen had seen outside.

'Thirty-one,' Ece said.

'Thirty-one!' the auctioneer echoed. 'Nothing for a lot like this, I can tell you. Bag of treasure, this!'

Devlet screamed, wriggling in his large buggy, as if he wanted to get out.

'Forty!' The bid came from one of the friends of the woman with the massive sunglasses.

Watching Ece Kazantzoğlu, İkmen saw that she was conflicted.

She clearly wanted the bag, but forty lira was a lot of money for an ordinary working-class woman. Devlet began to howl and then cry, and İkmen took his bottle of water out of his pocket. The child was clearly baking. He was just about to offer him a drink when Ece Hanım said, 'One hundred lira!'

İkmen was shocked. A woman at the end of his line of chairs exclaimed, 'Oh, I say!'

The auctioneer, completely unfazed, said, 'One hundred lira. One hundred lira for this bag of fine fabrics from a yalı in Yeniköy. Beautiful stuff.'

İkmen saw Ece Kazantzoğlu looking at him. 'I thought your boy maybe needed a drink,' he said.

She took the bottle from him. 'Thank you.'

'No problem.'

'One hundred Turkish lira! Any advance on one hundred Turkish lira?'

Now that the boy was drinking, he was silent. İkmen heard one of the secular ladies say, 'I'm not paying one more kurus. Not for that.'

The auctioneer raised his hand. 'One hundred Turkish lira for lot four,' he said. 'Going once, twice, three times.' He brought his hand down. 'Sold to Ece Hanım.'

The audience clapped, including Devlet, who dropped İkmen's water bottle on the floor.

'Can you, like, make a watch out of old watch parts? You know, old-school, not digital?'

In the early days of his sojourn in Tarlabaşı, Cumhur Polat had answered the door to no one. Back then, Berat Bey had brought him everything he needed, and although he did sometimes go out now, the front door had remained taboo. But he'd got careless and left it open, and these two had just let themselves in.

Probably in their thirties, the pair were typical of the trendy hipster types one saw in Tarlabaşı these days. Both slim and dark, one sported a man bun and tattoos while the other wore a T-shirt featuring a picture of the Mexican artist Frida Kahlo in a hijab.

'I'm not a watchmaker,' Gold Bey said. 'I think you've come to the wrong place.'

'But you are the guy who makes jewellery out of junk, right?'

'Steampunk stuff,' the other one said.

They'd pushed their way in and so there was no point denying what he did. They could see his jewellery everywhere.

'We'll pay you,' the one dressed in the Frida Kahlo T-shirt said.

'I don't think I can do what you want,' Gold Bey said. 'I'm not a watchmaker. I can only make something decorative.'

The young man shrugged. 'Decorative's cool,' he said. 'How much do you want?'

Some of these rich youngsters were just given money by their parents. They were allowed to do whatever they wanted, provided they didn't rock the boat. These days some of them were the children of the new pious middle class, and so whatever drinking, drug-taking or womanising that went on had to be done out of sight. Almost anything else they could do with impunity.

'I don't know yet,' Gold Bey said. 'You'd have to tell me what materials you would like me to use and I'd have to calculate how much time I'll spend making the item.'

'Whatever.'

'Yes?'

'Do what you like, man,' the T-shirted one said. 'I just want a cool watch like nobody else has got.'

'He's all about street style,' his tattooed friend said.

'So when can you do it?'

Cumhur had to think. Most of the time he made things to his own schedule. Commissions were rare and only came through third parties. 'Two weeks?' he said.

The tattooed man looked a little sniffy, but his actual customer just shrugged. 'OK,' he said. 'So what, do we come here in two weeks?'

They knew where he was and so there was no point in going elsewhere. Cumhur even accepted that he might make the watch and then the two of them could just rob him. But if he turned them down, there was a risk they knew who he was and would get his small business stopped.

'Yes,' he said.

Frida Kahlo nodded. 'OK,' he said. 'We'll talk money then?'

'Yes,' Cumhur said again.

The tattooed one grabbed hold of his friend's arm and laughed. 'Hey, man, maybe you'll be able to pay this dude in cake by then!'

Çetin İkmen wasn't a cruel man, but he let the woman struggle with her various bundles before he walked over and offered to help. She was probably religious, and he wanted to make sure she was desperate enough to say yes.

'Can I be of assistance, Hanım?' he asked.

The auction had finished half an hour ago, and Ece Kazantzoğlu had paid for and collected the fabrics she had bought for a hundred lira plus a set of plastic bowls she'd got for five.

She looked at him, her face flushed. Devlet was hooting again, probably still too hot, and Ece's purchases were down on the ground by her feet.

'Oh . . . you . . .' She clearly recognised him as the man who had given water to her son.

İkmen bowed. 'Will you let me help you?' he said.

'Oh, er, no . . . Um. I'm near home . . . in Ayvansaray . . .'

She wasn't near home and would need to either walk down to the Golden Horn and get a bus, or hail a taxi if one came along in Balat. İkmen picked up the stuffed plastic bag, leaving her with the bowls.

'Let me help you down the hill, and if we see a cab in the meantime, you can flag it down,' he said.

For a moment she just stared at him. He felt she was going to say something about her husband disapproving of her speaking to other men, but she didn't. Probably because everything she had bought had defeated her. She balanced the bowls on the back of her son's buggy and just smiled weakly.

'As slowly as you like,' he said as he passed his own car, visions of having to walk up the hill again to retrieve it tormenting his mind.

Slightly behind him, she walked in silence until Devlet began making noises again. Then, maybe out of embarrassment, she said, 'Thank you so much for helping me, er . . .'

'Halil,' he said, using his brother's name.

'Halil Bey,' she said. 'I am Ece, and this is my son Devlet, although I imagine you know that from the auction.'

'Yes.'

His phone rang, but he ignored it. Answering it, given the situation, was too complicated.

'Is that your phone?' she said.

'Yes, but it's not important.'

They continued on in near silence as Devlet chuckled to himself. İkmen knew that he had to let her speak if possible. If the impetus came from her, it would not seem as if he was either trying to pick her up or cross-examining her.

Eventually she said, 'I like the auctions. They allow me to get out with Devlet.'

'It's a bit of fun,' İkmen said.

'But you do get some great things sometimes,' she said.

He looked round at her. 'Like your bag of fabrics?'

She lowered her eyes. 'An extravagance,' she said. 'What must you think? So much money!'

'Word in the auction room was that some of those fabrics are

136

'ikat,' he said. 'But you couldn't have known that because you came late.'

'No . . .' She looked away for a moment, then she said, 'To be honest with you, Halil Bey, I didn't know what was in the bag beyond the fact it was full of material. But those ladies . . .' She shook her head.

He smiled. 'The fashionable Nişantaşı set?'

'People like that look down on us,' Ece said, and she wasn't wrong. 'I've been going to the auctions for a couple of years now, and they always act as if they are better than us.'

It was a familiar line coming from a person from the provinces. There was truth in it, but it was also a retreat into victimhood that was not always justified since the party of the religious right had taken control of the country.

'You have a lot of material here,' İkmen said as he looked down at the bags in his hands. 'You must be planning to make many things.'

'Oh yes,' she said. 'Eventually. Hopefully we will move soon, so we'll need new curtains and cushions.'

He grunted. The hill was a bit shallower now and he didn't feel quite so bilious when he looked across the rooftops of Balat to the Golden Horn beyond. His interest piqued, he waited for her to speak again. For a covered woman, she was a bit of a closet gossip.

'My mother-in-law, God rest her soul, passed away recently and left my husband some money,' she said.

İkmen felt his heart skip a beat. According to Leah, the Kazantzoğlu family had told her that Ceyda had simply gone away. Now apparently she was dead.

'So we will move. Find a place with fewer stairs to push and pull my son up and down.'

'That will be a blessing,' he said.

'Yes. My mother-in-law was a lovely woman; she'd be so happy.' She had tears in her eyes.

Had Ceyda's family had problems with Leah? Was this a case of wishing to exclude her from any claim upon her old friend's estate? Not that she'd have a claim. Also, it occurred to him that if Ceyda had had money, why hadn't she spent it on her impoverished family when she was alive?

'Ceyda Hanım, my mother-in-law, used to like the auctions,' Ece continued. 'It was she who brought us the first time. It's one of the reasons I keep coming.'

They reached a crossroads, and there, suddenly, was a yellow taxi.

İkmen said, 'Do you want me to get that for you?'

'Yes please.'

The cab driver was a miserable soul who took one look at the woman and her disabled son and said, 'I'll take them, but you'll have to get the kid in the car. And if he messes himself, she'll have to pay for the damage.'

Disgusted at his attitude, İkmen threw twenty lira in his face. 'Here's your clean-up money in advance, you miserable bastard.'

He helped Ece and Devlet into the taxi. 'It has been nice to talk to you,' he said. 'God bless you.'

Ece smiled.

Mehmet Süleyman remembered how one of his aunts had always saved to buy gold. His mother and her sister, his Aunt Barçın, had been born in a village in western Anatolia. Unlike his mother, Aunt Barçın had never left, and visits to her and his maternal grandparents had always seemed like time travel.

The old wooden house the family lived in had no electricity or running water, and the toilet had been a stinking hole hidden by a shack in the back yard. Aunt Barçın, as his grandparents' only unmarried daughter, was little more than a servant to her parents and her older brother, his Uncle Kemal. But with what little money she had, she was prudent. Once a year she would travel to the nearby town of Ayvalık to buy gold coins, which she put away for her nephews. When she died, Mehmet and his brother Murad each inherited several thousand liras' worth of these coins.

'It's what ladies in the countryside do,' he said now to Constable Tuna.

'So why not go to a goldsmith?'

Had his mother not come from a peasant background, Mehmet Süleyman wouldn't have understood either.

'Because if the gold merchant comes to the neighbourhood then it's safe for the women to go and visit him unaccompanied,' he said. 'The community centre is run by locals who will look out for any signs of impropriety. Now, you say Deniz Palandoken went in before any of the other women?'

'Yes, sir.'

'Did you see her come out?'

'Much later, when everyone else had gone,' Tuna said. 'That part of Kasımpaşa is quite hostile to outsiders, so I wasn't comfortable staying too much longer. I was questioned by a man who was clearly the local busybody.'

'What did you say?'

'That I was scouting for film and TV locations. He wasn't impressed.'

Süleyman smiled. There was a lot to admire about the tough, insular Black Sea communities, even if their exclusivity could be infuriating. However, Deniz Palandoken wasn't one of them. She was a posh girl and a user, and yet according to Tuna, she seemed to have moved amongst the locals unnoticed.

'When Deniz came out of the community centre, was she carrying anything?' Süleyman asked.

'No, sir.'

'Did you see a man or a woman who might have been the gold merchant?'

'No. But then if it was a man, maybe he went downstairs to drink tea and watch football with the men.'

This was possible. What had Deniz Palandoken, an apparently penniless junkie, been doing at a gold-buying event in Kasımpaşa? What was she doing in Kasımpaşa full stop? It was where she'd had the baby she'd sold, probably for drugs. Unless she was pregnant again . . .

'Machine Bey.'

There was a sigh of what sounded like relief from the other end of the line.

'Oh, Çetin Bey,' he said, 'Thank God you've got back to me.'

After putting Ece Kazantzoğlu and her son in a cab, İkmen had walked back to his car, where he'd looked at his phone. The call he had missed had been from Machine Bey. He'd phoned him back, not, it appeared, before time.

'What's wrong?'

'I had a call from Gold Bey,' he said. 'He fears that someone knows his identity and may use his situation to persecute him.'

'Does he have any evidence for this?'

Machine Bey told him about the two young men who had pushed their way into Gold Bey's apartment and asked him to make one of them a watch.

'Hipsters, Gold said,' Machine Bey continued. 'There are a lot of them in Tarlabaşı these days. But of course Gold, like the rest of us, is on edge because the Actress is still missing. Is this connected in any way to that?'

'I don't know.'

'Nor I,' he said. 'Gold can describe the men.'

'Get him to write descriptions down,' İkmen replied. 'With regard to the Actress, I have several lines of enquiry I can follow . . .'

'That's very good to hear.'

'Mmm.' Strictly, it was true, but it was also going to be problematic. Getting hold of CCTV footage even from an everyday bakkal could prove difficult, and as for seeing Sevval Kalkan's mother in Bakırköy . . . 'I'm working on it,' İkmen said. 'Ask Gold Bey to email me those descriptions as soon as he can.'

'I will.'

İkmen cut the connection. Accessing information as a private citizen was difficult. As a police officer, in a sense he'd had it easy. Now, unless he was very clever, he was at the mercy of bribe culture, which was expensive. Though it didn't have to be . . .

Chapter 11

Can was sick. Deniz was sure it was an infection, because a cut he'd got on his leg weeks ago wouldn't heal – and it stank. They'd both tried to ignore it, mainly so that they could buy gear. But that morning she'd been unable to breathe without smelling the rancid pus that had gathered around his knee.

The derelict house they'd been living in was alive with vermin, which hadn't helped. But now that Deniz had antibiotics, everything would be okay. She pushed the box of tablets into one of Can's hands. Time was people had been able to be buy antibiotics over the counter, but not any more. Now you needed a legitimate prescription or a doctor dodgy enough to write you one with no questions asked, but for a price. Deniz had spent all day working to get the money to give the doctor, and the prescription had now been made up in a pharmacy on Divan Yolu.

'Penicillin,' Deniz whispered in her husband's ear. 'Take two now and two more in the morning.'

Can looked down at the box and then up at her. He hadn't had any teeth for at least five years, but like his wife, he still sounded posh.

'That's all very fine,' he said, 'but where's my gear?'

'No money for that,' Deniz said. 'If you don't take the antibiotics, you'll die.'

He looked at the box again, and then threw it across the room. 'Fuck that,' he said.

Deniz ran into the darkened corner and retrieved the tablets. She shoved the box in his face. 'If you don't take these, there'll be no more opium, because you'll be dead!' she said.

Can turned his face away.

Furious, she slapped the side of his head. 'I never wanted to go back to that place, I vowed I never would. But I did it for you,' she said. 'It ripped me apart going back there! That hellhole where I had Didem!' She began to cry.

Her husband shook his head. 'Where'd you get the money?' he asked. He didn't care about how she felt; just how much money she'd wasted on antibiotics.

Weeping, she said, 'Why do you care?'

He shrugged.

Eventually, after composing herself, she said, 'I stole it, and yes, it was a lot because antibiotics cost more than heroin if you have to get them under the counter. If I didn't have the contacts I have, you would be fucked.'

He said he'd take them, but she'd have to get 'something' for him too.

She threw a half-filled bottle of water at him and stood up. 'I'll go and score.'

He laughed. 'Hurrah!'

She bent down, took two tablets out of the box and put them in his mouth. 'Swallow.'

For a moment he did nothing, but then he reached for the bottle of water and appeared to wash the drugs down his throat.

'I'll need to get money first,' Deniz said as she clambered over some broken masonry and stepped outside. 'Don't wait up.'

These things happened. Some called it coincidence, while others, like Çetin İkmen, called it magic. And to make matters even spookier, he'd been looking at the djinn when his phone rang.

'Hello, Çetin.'

143

Of course, it was Süleyman. He'd been thinking he might call him just at that moment.

'Mehmet,' he said. 'I was just thinking about you.'

'Invoking me,' he heard his friend say.

They both laughed. The djinn disappeared. It didn't like levity.

'And while I could do the very old-fashioned thing of asking after your health, I won't insult your intelligence. I need your help,' Süleyman continued.

'Of course,' İkmen said. 'Provided you agree to at least listen to my woes.'

'Always.'

'And because you and I both know that tonight is Çiçek's Spanish class, I feel there is probably no time like the present.'

Çiçek, who already spoke several foreign languages, had wanted to keep her linguistic skills sharp by learning a new one. She paid for private tuition once a week with a Spanish lady in Beşiktaş.

'I'll meet you at the Mozaik in an hour, if that's convenient,' Süleyman said.

İkmen smiled. The Mozaik was his favourite bar, not five steps down his street. 'I will bring cash and a cat,' he said.

'Order a plate of anchovies for Marlboro Bey on my behalf,' Süleyman said.

'Consider it done.'

Uğur Bulut and his adopted sister, the nun Sister Eudokia, were exhausted. What the police pathologist had told them had come as a huge shock. If Uğur wasn't his mother's son, then who was he? The family lawyer, Cihan Bey, had been in meetings all day, and so the earliest they could see him was going to be the following morning. They had spent much of the day either not speaking or indulging in speculation.

Now it was the evening, and Uğur was drunk, while Sister Eudokia had taken up smoking again. It was dark outside, but neither of them got up to put on any lights in Uğur's large upstairs lounge. Illumination from passing vessels on the Bosphorus was enough for them to see what they were doing.

After a long period of silence, Uğur said, 'Do you remember Auntie Filiz?'

'Not well,' Eudokia said. 'I remember her dying. I must have been about eight. We all went to the village for her burial. I liked the sheep.'

The Bulut family came originally from a village just outside the south-eastern city of Gaziantep. Both Perihan and her husband Ara had grown up in the village and lived there until Ara moved them to İstanbul to find work.

'Auntie Filiz was Mother's eldest sister,' Uğur said. 'Never married, never had kids, died young.'

'What from?' the nun asked.

He shrugged. 'No idea. I was a teenager. I can honestly say I remember nothing about her funeral except that I was bored.'

'Funerals are boring, you're right.'

'Am I her son?' he said.

'I don't know.' Eudokia had answered this question several times before.

'Auntie Aylin is the only one of the sisters still alive, but she's so religious, how do I even start a conversation with her?'

Perihan Hanım had had two sisters and a brother, Yıldırım. Only her younger sibling Aylin and her brother were still alive. The parents were long dead, and many of the extended family had moved far away.

'We will ask Cihan Bey's advice when we see him tomorrow,' Eudokia said. 'But don't forget that Mother made a will. In the full knowledge that you were not her son, she left you the business and her house in Sarıyer. Those were her wishes; it's going to be hard for Lokman to overturn that.'

'I don't know.'

'Dr Sarkissian is going to email us his report, which we will take to Cihan Bey. Before we make any judgements on anything, we need the full facts.'

Her brother began to cry. 'If Lokman takes over the business, he will wreck it!' he said. 'Look at the way he lives. The people he mixes with. He will impoverish himself and me, and our staff, who love and trust us, will be put out of work.'

Eudokia reached over and took his hand. 'Let's not get ahead of ourselves,' she said.

He gripped her fingers. 'I don't know what I'd do without you, Aysel.'

She smiled. He still used her old name from time to time, and it was strangely comforting. They'd all had the most wonderful childhood. Perihan Hanım, effectively a single parent, had always worked, but she'd also been a loving and attentive mother. None of them could have wanted more. Except of course Lokman, who had always hassled and moaned even as a small child. He wasn't like his mother or his brother in any way. Eudokia wondered whether he'd got these traits from his father, a violent alcoholic. Ara Bey had left the family by the time she came along; Perihan had thrown him out when the business began to turn a profit. Everyone assumed that because he'd not come back to beg for money, he'd probably died. But no one actually knew.

İkmen enjoyed reminiscing about old cases. The Leonid Meyer affair had been a particularly mysterious one.

'I had entirely forgotten Leah Delmonte,' Süleyman said. 'What's she like now?'

İkmen painted a picture of a woman not greatly changed from the one they'd both known all those years ago.

'You'd think that a life of prostitution . . .' Süleyman began.

'But she was never on the streets.' İkmen took a long swig from his glass of rakı and lit a cigarette. 'Madam Lilli kept a clean house. These things matter. It was nice to see Leah again. But I am troubled by these neighbours of hers. To cut her out after she has been so close to their mother strikes me as odd.'

'Maybe they'd always disliked her. She was a prostitute, and if the family are pious . . .'

İkmen shrugged. 'But to tell her that Ceyda Kazantzoğlu has simply gone away when Ece told me she is dead . . .'

'Maybe they did that to spare her feelings.'

İkmen gave him a sceptical look. 'Really?' he said.

Süleyman smiled. 'Well, no, what would be the point?'

'Exactly,' İkmen said. 'Which is why if you could find out whether a Ceyda Kazantzoğlu of Ayvansaray is alive or dead, I would be grateful.'

Süleyman toasted him. 'Consider it done.'

They sat in silence for a few moments. It was a warm, sticky evening, which was why it was so nice to be drinking outside, underneath the multicoloured fairy lights of the Mozaik bar, even if the smell of fish from Marlboro's plate was almost over-whelming. The massive tom sat between them, eating and purring.

Eventually İkmen said, 'So what is on your mind, Mehmet Bey? In my capacity as an amateur these days, I'll do what I can, but—'

'You'll never be an amateur, Çetin.'

İkmen ignored the compliment. 'What can I do?' he said.

Süleyman lit a cigarette. 'I wonder if you remember a couple of names,' he said. 'Junkies. I know you always had a lot of sympathy.'

'No one plans to become a junkie,' İkmen said. 'No one opts to face a possible prison sentence when one robs the local bakkal for money to get a fix. Yes, I always tried to help rather than punish if I could.'

'Can and Deniz Palandoken,' Süleyman said.

İkmen smiled. 'Oh yes. I remember reading about their amazing wedding in Cumhuriyet. Beautiful rich kids from very well-connected military families. They had the ceremony on a boat in the middle of the Bosphorus. Probably only five years later, I caught Can trying to steal a leather jacket from a shop in the Kapılı Çarşı. He did it under my nose. I made him take it back and then gave him a talking-to. He was as high as a kite. What's your interest?'

'You probably know that I'm investigating this business out at Karacaahmet cemetery,' Süleyman said. 'We think the removal of one dead body followed by the substitution of another is connected to organ trafficking. Ömer Bey has what he believes to be reliable information that the Palandokens have, how shall I say, donated in the past.'

'Ooh.' İkmen shook his head.

'As we all know, this type of trade is prevalent in the east, but not here,' Süleyman continued. 'The Palandokens are one of the few leads we have. But we have to be careful not to spook the people they did business with.'

'Of course.'

'So we're tracking them. Can Palandoken is ill and is currently holed up in a derelict building in Çemberlitaş. Deniz goes out to get money and score, if she can, from Ömer's informant. Earlier today she was at a community centre in Kasımpaşa, apparently at an event where women buy gold.'

'Black Sea coast people,' İkmen said. 'Like, incidentally, the Kazantzoğlu family. A lot of old Pontic Greek families up that way. But carry on.'

'I can't think that Deniz was going to buy gold, but the people in the community centre appeared to be comfortable around her, which is odd given their antipathy towards outsiders.'

'She must be known to someone with influence.'

'Possibly, but she's such a mess.' Süleyman leaned in towards İkmen. 'It is alleged that she came into contact with organ smugglers when she sold her own newborn child. It is further alleged that she gave birth in Kasımpaşa and then handed the child over somewhere in Gümüşsuyu.'

İkmen shook his head. 'God help us. I've heard some things . . .'

'Five minutes before I phoned you, I had a call from the officer who has been watching Deniz this afternoon and evening. It seems she had a prescription for antibiotics made up at the pharmacy on Divan Yolu. The pharmacist claims he doesn't know the signatory, a Dr Alp Özdemir, but he knows of him. He works in general medicine in Kartal.'

This was a district on the Asian side of the city characterised by numerous luxury tower blocks.

'The prescription carries today's date and is possibly the reason why Deniz stole a wallet from a café this morning. But where did she meet Dr Özdemir? She didn't go over to Kartal at any point today. After she stole the wallet, she went to the public toilets at Karaköy, then she took a bus to Kasımpaşa, where she was inside the community centre for approximately an hour. When she left there, she got a bus back to Karaköy, walked over the Galata Bridge and then up the hill into Sultanahmet, where she first went into the Pudding Shop for a coffee then had the prescription made up at the pharmacy. The way I see it, she had opportunities to meet with Dr Özdemir during the course of today, although the Pudding Shop and the toilets at Karaköy have to be long shots . . .'

'Leaving the community centre in Kasımpaşa?' İkmen said.

'Yes, but how? She went to a gold-selling event.'

'Maybe the doctor was there too.'

'With all the women, it's unlikely.'

'Unless . . .' İkmen raised a finger, 'he is known to those at the centre, and to Deniz.'

'Which in the case of the latter could mean that he has a connection to this organ trade. It's a leap, because we don't know if the people Deniz gave her baby to two years ago are organ harvesters, agents for childless parents or fucking paedophiles. The only thing Ömer's contact has said is that there was a doctor present at her confinement – or so she says.'

İkmen rested his chin on his hand. 'What have we become, eh?' he said.

'Çetin, there's no point getting misty eyed about the old days,' Süleyman said.

'I'm not, but it's so fucking—'

'Yes, I know how awful it is! You don't have to tell me.' He sighed. 'Look, I find myself in a position here of being on the one hand sceptical that any of this has anything to do with the incident at the cemetery, and on the other afraid that if I move to interview this doctor, he will alert those with whom he works, who may be involved in organised crime.'

'He's not a surgeon,' İkmen said.

'Doesn't mean he isn't involved.'

They both drank, and then lit up cigarettes.

'So why speak to me?' İkmen asked. 'What can I do?'

'I want to know what you would do if this was your problem,' Süleyman said.

'Come away from there, boy!'

'I can see smoke!' Raşım Dorsay said. 'Look, there!' He pointed towards the main gate.

His fellow guard, the much older Münir Sever, said, 'We're on this route tonight; we don't go down there.'

'Yes, but—'

'Leave it! You know what Türgüt Bey said about reporting things. Do you want the police to make us redundant?'

'No . . .'

'Then leave it!' Münir bent double as pain hit him. 'Now look what you've done!'

Raşım didn't know what to do. Münir was always having trouble with pain. He said it was something to do with 'stones', whatever they were. He'd had them for years.

'Can I—'

'No!' Münir put a hand up to stop him helping. 'Just shut up and let's get on with the job. And don't question me again. Remember, I was on that bridge on the night of the coup, protecting this nation. I know more than you. Every time you argue, the pain comes.'

And yet Raşım could still clearly see smoke. What was happening down there? He didn't even know who was supposed to be guarding that part of the cemetery tonight.

'You need a woman,' İkmen said.

'I know that!'

Marlboro had finished his anchovies and was tapping Süleyman's arm demanding more. It was irritating him. It made İkmen laugh. He called one of the waiters over and said, 'Another plate of fish for Marlboro Bey, please. Put it on my bill.'

As if he'd understood what had been said, Marlboro sat down and waited for his next course.

İkmen continued. 'A local woman. Do you know how often these gold sales happen?'

'No,' Süleyman said. 'As for a local woman . . . We don't get many female officers from districts like Kasımpaşa. I won't say none, but I don't know of any.'

'So you have to think creatively,' İkmen said. 'For various reasons I won't bore you with, I've had reason to spend some time in Tarlabaşı recently. Not Kasımpaşa, I know, but the two districts abut one another and there is a certain amount of movement between them. And you and I both know a woman from Tarlabaşı who, I suspect, could not be stopped from going where she wanted even by a muscle-bound wrestler from Trabzon.'

Süleyman lit a cigarette. 'You don't mean Sugar Hanım?'

'Why not?'

Tansu 'Sugar' Barışık was an elderly prostitute who had lived in Tarlabaşı all her life.

'Why not?' Süleyman said. 'She hasn't left her apartment for ten years, to my knowledge. She's enormous! She's got legs like tree trunks . . .'

'And there's not much she won't do for hard cash,' İkmen said. 'If Sugar Hanım turns up wanting to buy gold, I can't imagine anyone will stop her. And everyone knows her and knows she's got money, so it isn't going to be odd that she's there.'

'What, out of the blue? We don't even know when these things happen!'

'So go and ask her if she knows,' İkmen said. 'She may well. She's got her spies everywhere in Tarlabaşı and probably beyond, knowing her. I've a few things I'd like her opinion on myself. Why don't we go together in the morning?'

'Çetin, Sugar Hanım will never leave that vile apartment,' Süleyman said. 'And if she did, how's she going to get anywhere? She can barely walk!'

'Taxi?'

'With her smelling like a dead cat?'

The waiter returned and placed a bowl of fish in front of Marlboro, who started eating and purring again. İkmen stroked his back.

'You know she knows everything and everyone, Mehmet.'

'Even about the Black Sea contingent? Not really her type, are they.'

'No, but I'd put money on the idea she's serviced more than a few of them in her time,' İkmen said. 'They're not all religious, you know.'

'I know. But . . .'

'Give it a go,' İkmen said. 'I would. What have you got to lose?'

He was still shaky. Machine Bey had passed on his descriptions to Çetin İkmen of the two young men who'd come to his workshop, but Cumhur Polat was still afraid. What could İkmen do about it? If the men didn't like what he produced for them, would they accuse him of trying to cheat them? Would he be arrested? Flung back into prison? He'd rather die.

Some trans girls who lived across the road were having a loud party, but it didn't matter; he couldn't sleep anyway. He knew them; they all worked as prostitutes, because although things had eased for transsexuals a few years ago, everything had clamped down hard after the attempted coup and no one would give any of them a conventional job. What choice did they have but to go on the streets and offer themselves to the very men who publicly derided them?

It was stuffy inside the apartment, and Cumhur decided to go outside and get some air. Maybe the girls would invite him in. He knew Arzu Hanım, the matriarch of the trio, and he could do with a drink.

Apart from the party, the street was silent. It was three o'clock in the morning. A rat snuffled in a dustbin, pushing out empty yoghurt cartons in its search for more meaty comestibles. Cumhur let it be. Living in Tarlabaşı, one had to get used to rats; they were everywhere. Even in the new-build homes in the gentrified part of the district you could see them, snuffling around the BMWs and Mercedes owned by the pious middle class. The air was rank after a day of stifling heat, but it was better than being indoors, sniffing up fumes from his soldering iron.

He was looking around to see whether he could spot anything he might be able to use in his work when he saw her walking slowly along the street. She hadn't spotted him and so he could have just let her go, but how could he?

He put out a hand and touched her arm. 'Sevval?'

She looked into his eyes, but then her legs gave way beneath her. Just before she hit the ground she said, 'I'm dying . . .'

153

Chapter 12

In common with many people outside the medical profession, Inspector Süleyman was under the impression that doctors all somehow knew each other.

'I've never heard of him,' Dr Sarkissian answered in response to Süleyman's question about Dr Alp Özdemir from Kartal. 'I know a few family practitioners, but not him. I may know the practice.'

'He works alone,' Süleyman said.

'Then no.'

It was early, and the doctor had only just washed and dressed. A hot night, struggling to sleep whilst sweating, was making him think that perhaps the time had come to install air conditioning. Although how that could be done in such a huge, historic property was beyond his understanding and was exactly why he'd never considered it until now.

'Doctor, would you know whether family doctors like Özdemir would have any sort of training in surgery?' Süleyman asked.

'Some,' he said. 'We all see a fair few operations performed when we are in training. As for any sort of skill in that discipline, they would know enough to perform, say, an emergency tracheotomy if a patient's upper respiratory airway is blocked. Some will be more skilled than others, of course. But it's not a normal part of their work.' He paused for a moment, gathering his thoughts. 'I assume this doctor has some connection to the Karacaahmet case?'

'Possibly.'

'I see.'

'But I must tread carefully,' Süleyman continued. 'Organ traf-ficking is big business, and we all know that, while doctors may perform the actual task, it's almost always organised crime behind it. Not that I've had any intel about which of our charming local families it may involve.'

'A reflection upon how crime these days is international, do you think?'

'Possibly.'

The number of victims of gang-related violence who were not Turkish had increased over the years. Arto Sarkissian had been one of the first to really notice this. The modern purveyors of death didn't discriminate, however tribal they claimed to be.

'If I hear anything about this Dr Özdemir, I will let you know,' Arto said.

'Thank you, Doctor.'

Cumhur Polat had been awake for so long, he knew that he must now look quite weird. But that was hardly pertinent here.

Once he'd got over the shock of meeting her in the street, he'd taken Sevval Kalkan into his apartment, where they had just stared at each other for what seemed like ages. Clearly exhausted, and also possibly in pain, she'd asked if she might lie down for a while. He'd given her his own bed and then sat in his workroom, looking at her through the bedroom door.

When she finally got up, at 9.30, she hobbled rather than walked out of the bedroom and Cumhur offered her tea.

'Yes please,' she said.

He went into his small kitchen and made them both tea. When he returned, she was sitting in the living room, staring at the wall. Her face was so white, it was almost green. He put her glass of tea down on the table in the middle of the room and

155

sat opposite her. Eventually he said what had been floating around in his mind for hours. 'Where have you been?'

She closed her eyes, then opened them, then she drank some tea. The warmth gave her face a very small trace of colour.

She said, 'I can't tell you.'

After all the anxiety they'd been through about her, Cumhur felt angry. 'Can't or won't?' he asked. 'We've all been worried to death about you.'

'I'm sorry.'

She looked away. He heard her say, 'I should go.'

It was as if she were playing with him. Some cruel game he didn't understand. 'I don't think so,' Cumhur said. 'What were you doing walking around outside my home if you didn't want to see me, or at least use my bed? I mean, you were coming here, weren't you?'

She turned back to face him, but she didn't look at him. She looked down. 'Yes.'

'Well then . . .'

'I was exhausted,' she said. 'I didn't know where else to go.'

Cumhur leaned forward. 'Where had you come from?' he asked.

Sevval shook her head.

'You don't know or you won't say?'

She looked up. 'I can't say.'

Cumhur felt utterly bewildered. 'What's going on here?' he said.

Sevval took a bottle of pills out of her handbag and took two.

'What are they?'

She said, 'I couldn't just go without seeing you. I can't be here for long.'

'Why not?'

It took her a very long time to answer. Was she formulating something to say, maybe some lie to tell him? Or was she genuinely wrestling with her thoughts? He couldn't decide.

'I'm going to die,' she said eventually, in a thin, small voice. 'I told you last night. And I'm afraid.'

Cumhur Polat, caught entirely off guard, was winded by her words.

'You look like shit, İkmen.'

It had been a very long time since Çetin İkmen had seen Tansu Barışık. But neither she nor her cat-scented accommodation had changed much in the intervening time. If anything, she might have got a little fatter, but it was difficult to tell as she'd been huge for years.

İkmen gently persuaded a cat to climb off a reasonably sanitary chair and then sat down himself. 'Luckily I've never claimed to be a glamour boy,' he said.

Sugar looked at Süleyman, smiled and said, 'No, that's his job.'

Süleyman bowed and sat down beside İkmen.

'So what do you want?' the old woman said. 'I doubt either of you is here for the purposes of pleasure. And anyway, I shut that particular shop up years ago.'

İkmen looked at Süleyman. 'You go first, Mehmet Bey.'

Süleyman smiled. 'Sugar Hanım,' he said, 'do you know anything about gold sales at a community centre in Kasımpaşa?'

She lit a cigarette. 'I've never been to one,' she said.

'But you know of them?'

'Everyone does. It's where all the covered women go to buy gold Atatürk coins with the little bits of money their husbands let them have.'

'They're a good investment.'

'Yes, well if you promise not to tell, I'll show you mine,' Sugar said. 'It's amazing how many of those five-hundred-kurus coins can be fitted underneath a mattress.'

'Your secret is safe with us,' Süleyman said.

'I used to buy them from the Kapılı Çarşı when I was mobile,' she said. 'Now I don't bother. Waiting a month for some Kasımpaşa hard man's gold merchant brother from Rize to turn up isn't for me.'

'It happens once a month?'

'So I've heard,' she said.

'And local hard man?' İkmen asked. 'Who?'

'Well, I use the term loosely,' she said.

'I thought Paşa Beyaz was dead,' Süleyman said, naming a very old and decidedly lacklustre gangster who came from Kasımpaşa.

She waved a dismissive hand. 'Oh yes,' she said. 'That particular empire fell apart years ago. Stupid old fool: there's never been real money in protection round there. Nobody's got much to protect. Anyway, some of your lot have always had their hands on whatever business goes on there. No, this is a man called Yaşar Akgün. Long streak of piss; he looks about sixteen, but he's actually forty-something.'

İkmen looked at Süleyman. 'Know him?'

'No,' he said.

'He's a funny one,' Sugar said. 'Can't work him out, if I'm honest.'

'Why?'

'Well,' she said, 'to begin with, it was Akgün who set up the gold sales, with this brother who still lives in the back of beyond. Yaşar himself works as a taxi driver. Used to live in some hovel in Kasımpaşa until he moved into Paşa Beyaz's old place just after the old bastard died. Bought it apparently. He's got no record as far as I know, no business interests, and yet it's said that if you want to really frighten someone down there, you tell them you're going to get Yaşar Akgün onto them. Mesut Hanım, one of my drag queens upstairs, comes from that area and still has family there. She told me people round there call him "efendi".'

Which meant he had respect.

'Maybe he's running something alongside or incorporated into the gold sales?' İkmen said.

'Well, he's got money, he's got respect and he's just a taxi driver,' Sugar said. 'I'd ask your colleagues who work Kasımpaşa. I mean, even poor old Paşa Beyaz had them in his pockets, and he was a useless old bastard.'

It wasn't even midday and it was already as hot as hell. But Sevval Kalkan was cold. Cumhur Polat put a blanket around her shoulders while he sweated in his airless living room.

'Tell me what's wrong,' he said.

'I can't.'

But he could see that she was leaning over to one side, her left hand pressing down on the top of her hip.

'Sevval, you must,' he said. 'You say you're dying but won't tell me why or what of.'

'It's too late,' she said.

'What is?'

She thought for a moment. 'If I show you something, you must promise me you won't do anything about it.'

'About what?' Hot and worried, Cumhur was losing his mind. 'Look, I can't promise not to do anything. All I can promise is that I will only tell Cemal. I can't deal with this on my own.'

She rocked backwards and forwards, obviously in pain, her face white and slathered in cold, shiny sweat. In both her body and her mind she was in agony.

'All right. But you must promise me, only Machine Bey. Not even Olimpio, especially not her.'

'I promise.'

Grunting in pain, Sevval pulled her shirt out of her trouser waistband and then undid the zip fly.

'Oh God! Sevval!'

'It's OK, it's OK,' she gasped.

As she pulled her shirt and her trousers apart, he could see a large bloodstained gauze dressing on her hip.

'What's that?'

She had to pant to work up the courage to remove the gauze. The suppurating wound beneath it stank.

Mehmet Süleyman left Çetin İkmen at Sugar Barışık's apartment.

'He's always in a hurry,' the old woman observed.

'He is working a very complicated and sensitive case,' İkmen said.

'Grave robbing.' She shook her head. 'Can't see a profit in it myself, but these are desperate times. If food gets any dearer, I'll have to break into my savings under the mattress. Anyway, what do you want, İkmen? I have got all day, as you know, but I could do with a nap now.'

'I want to try and find two young men,' İkmen said. He read her the descriptions Gold Bey had written.

When he'd finished, she said, 'Fucking hipsters. As if it's not bad enough that they're knocking down our homes to build concrete monstrosities for the middle-class pious brigade, now our own buildings are infested with those people's overprivileged children playing at edgy poverty.'

'And yet they are a fact,' İkmen said.

'Bastards!'

The subject had hit a raw nerve, as he'd suspected it would. Then she said, 'No, I don't know these people. Why would I?'

He flattered her. 'Because you see everything?'

She gave him a baleful look. 'You can't stroke my ego to make me remember something I don't know, İkmen,' she said. 'I may well have seen these boys; I've certainly seen boys like them as they walk past my window with their arses hanging out of their trousers, and their tattooed arms. But I can't tell one from another. I know it's a really old-woman thing to say, but they all look the fucking same to me.'

İkmen left her with a couple of packets of cigarettes and an apology for making her so angry. More than any group of incomers, the hipsters of Tarlabaşı had caused the most controversy. No one could understand why such privileged people would want to live in a place where crime was rife and rats roamed the streets.

He walked up the stone steps from Sugar's apartment and into the street. It was a hot morning and the usual Tarlabaşı suspects were about in force. A couple of bonzai addicts were passed out outside the Syriani church; a kid with a filthy face was playing with dust in the gutter; women – covered as well as almost naked and caked in make-up – went about their morning shop; and some lad wearing a Che Guevara T-shirt was talking to a middle-aged man İkmen knew to be a dealer. He'd begun to walk back towards Tarlabaşı Bulvarı, his head pounding with vestigial cat odour from Sugar's place when he saw something that caught his attention.

Cumhur knew he didn't need to call Machine Bey to ask what had to be done, but he did it anyway because he had promised her that he would. When he walked from his workroom, where he'd made the call, back into his living room, she was either asleep or unconscious. It didn't really matter.

What was clear was that she'd either injured herself, had some sort of surgical procedure that had become infected, or been stabbed. He called for an ambulance as he stood in front of her. Not even her eyelids flickered.

Guilt, his mother always used to say, was God's way of telling you you were wrong. It was Raşım Dorsay's day off, and he was utterly consumed by it. Fortunately, in a way, his mother was dead and so he didn't have to contend with those eyes of hers that had always suspected him of something. She had rarely been wrong.

If he hadn't shown mercy and understanding to that poor deluded necrophile all that time ago, would any of what had gone on at the Karacaahmet recently have happened? Had his less than punitive attitude towards that wretched soul caused others to come to the cemetery feeling that the place was a soft touch? Not that there was any evidence the corpse of that unknown woman in Perihan Bulut's grave had been interfered with in any way. But there were rumours that bits of her had been stolen.

But then what could he do? Even back then, Türgüt Bey had been adamant that nothing went into the incident book. Now with the police on his back he was losing the plot. Ranting on about redundancies, saying the police would replace them all. It was unlikely to happen, and even if it did, Raşım couldn't see how it would affect Türgüt that much. He'd been a lawyer before he'd taken the job at the Karacaahmet, so he had to have money. Raşım couldn't see why the gatekeeper was even in the job unless when he gave up his law practice he felt he needed something to do.

But none of these musings made him feel any better. What he really needed to do was act to reduce his guilt, and the only way he could do that was to give a description of that necrophile to Inspector Süleyman. In reality, the man's face was carved into his memory, probably for all time, given the weirdness of what had gone on that night. But he'd stopped short of describing it to the policeman, firstly because he'd never seen that particular man again, and secondly because he knew it would anger Türgüt Bey. It was one thing for something to happen in the cemetery, but quite another to be able to back it up with hard facts. Like the fires that came and went: when they were gone they were gone, leaving any witnesses struggling to remember where they had taken place in such a vast site.

Chapter 13

Was it possible that this was one of the young men who had frightened Gold Bey? He was dark, with a man bun, and his arms were covered in tattoos. But then a lot of the youngsters in the area had either one or the other.

İkmen followed him. He noticed that he walked a little unsteadily, as if drunk or on drugs. No one talked to him, but then if local people felt the same as Sugar Hanım about the stylish incomers, that wasn't surprising. He turned right out of Karakurum Sokak and onto Cuckuk Sokak, where he entered an old house that looked a lot less down-at-heel than its neighbours. No washing hung from its balconies, and there were two bicycles chained up outside.

As İkmen watched the young man go inside, his phone rang. He looked at the screen and saw that it was Machine Bey. He had been just about to ring him. Another case of fortuitous everyday magic.

'Oh, Çetin Bey,' he heard the man say breathlessly. 'I've just heard from Gold Bey.'

'I was just about—'

'He has found her!' he said. 'The Actress!'

'Oh my God! Where?'

'Tarlabaşı.'

İkmen looked around reflexively.

'She's very sick,' Machine Bey continued. 'Poor Gold had to call an ambulance. She was bleeding and unconscious.'

'Bleeding from where?'

'I don't know,' he said. 'Gold has gone with her. He had no choice.'

'Gone where?'

'To the Memorial Hospital in Şişli. Gold was treated for cancer there years ago. He still has medical insurance.'

'Does the Actress?'

'I don't know,' he said. 'We can't ask her. I'm worried for him, for them both.'

'I don't think the staff at the hospital will have a problem with either of them.'

'But she is well known! Çetin Bey, if you could go to the hospital, I would be so grateful.'

'There's nothing I can do . . .'

'I know, but if you could be there, with him . . .'

İkmen leaned against the wall of the house at his back and sighed. Various kids ran around his legs. He told them to bugger off, then he said to Machine Bey, 'All right, I'll go. I was going to let you know I think I may have a lead on those two young men who visited Gold. But now—'

'Please! Please go! We can talk later.'

'Your mother named you as her son and left everything to you on the proviso that you maintained an allowance for your brother,' Cihan Bey said. 'You, Sister Eudokia, did not wish to be a beneficiary of your mother's will.'

'I didn't,' Eudokia said. 'When I entered the convent, I left the world behind. Mother understood that.'

'And yet here you are.'

Cihan Teke had been a lawyer all his adult life. Now in his nineties, his mind was still as sharp as ever, which was why the very astute Perihan Bulut had chosen him as her family advocate. Of an age, they had been friends.

164

'I'm here for my brothers,' Eudokia said. 'When Mother's body was not found in her grave, I asked Mother Superior if I could come home, and she agreed. When a piece of Perihan Hanım's body was found, I thought more would follow, but that may or may not happen. However, this test upon the thigh bone that has been established to belong to her has now thrown up this . . . awfulness.'

The old man nodded.

'Dr Sarkissian, the police pathologist, has told Uğur that he is a second-rank relative of our mother,' she continued. 'He isn't her son, but he is closely related. Now Lokman has gone off, apparently back to his lawyer, in order to mount a challenge to Mother's will.' She shook her head. 'If he succeeds, he will wreck the business and spend all of Mother's hard-earned money on God knows what. Mother knew he was a total waster who hung around with other wasters, which was why she bequeathed everything to Uğur. But then you know this.'

'I have an uncle and an aunt on my mother's side of the family,' Uğur said. 'My mother's other sister is deceased. I can't help wondering whether one of those is my real parent. I wonder if I am even related to my father, although how I would ever find that out is beyond me. I don't know whether he's alive or dead.'

Cihan Bey looked at the document on his desk. 'As one of only two direct beneficiaries of a will I can attest was made when your mother was of sound mind, I can't think there's too much your brother can do. If your mother wanted you and you alone to run her business and take control of her property—'

'Two direct beneficiaries?' Eudokia butted in. 'Don't you mean one, Cihan Bey?'

The old man looked down at the document and sighed. 'There was one other person to whom your mother left a small amount of money,' he said. 'A hundred thousand lira on her death.'

'Who?'

'I am not allowed to divulge that information,' he said. 'Your mother strictly forbade it.'

'A hundred thousand lira is a lot of money,' Eudokia said.

'I know.' He sighed again. 'All I can do is contact this person and ask their permission for the information to be divulged to you.'

Uğur put his head in his hands. 'This nightmare is getting ever darker.'

Eudokia put one of her hands on his back. She looked at Cihan Bey and said, 'Lokman runs through all the money Uğur gives him every month. He spends it on rubbish. Uğur even bought him a flat in Tarlabaşı because he wanted to live there so people would think he was trendy. Tarlabaşı! Who in their right mind would choose such a place?'

Cihan Bey said, 'I will do what I can.'

Uğur, who was still trapped in his own misery and wasn't really listening to anyone else, said, 'My brother mixes with scum. And I don't mean the poor and displaced. If he mixed with them, I'd be happy. But no, he likes to hang out with other privileged hipsters, people who come from rich families.' He looked up. 'Connected people.'

The room fell silent. Cihan Bey had always been a religious man. He was a member of the ruling party and lived his life according to Islamic values – which was why the elevation of certain groups and individuals didn't sit well with him.

'I will proceed according to the letter of the law and your mother's wishes,' the old man said. 'As you know, Uğur Bey, I had the utmost respect for your mother, and I will do everything in my power to ensure that her legacy is protected.'

Although it could give outsiders the impression that it was just a vast monoculture of observant people from the Black Sea district, Kasımpaşa was actually, in small pockets, quite diverse. Even the local constabulary were not exactly what Süleyman had expected. Constable Gülse Aksoyer, for instance.

He had already spoken to the lowly female constable's superiors in Kasımpaşa. The name Sugar Barışık had given him, Yaşar Akgün, had been familiar to everyone, but no one could or would say that he was anything to do with organised crime. He was a taxi driver who had a clean record and had come into some money after the death of his parents back in Rize. And yes, he did organise the monthly gold sales, with his brother, for the safety and comfort of local ladies.

Süleyman hadn't expected much else, although the glowing testimonies had made his skin crawl. He knew this game of old. Where local cops were in someone's pocket . . .

He was just about to get into his car when he felt a hand on his shoulder.

He'd hardly been aware of her at Tarlabaşı police station. She'd stood at the back of the squad room and not said a word. Probably forty-something, Constable Gülse Aksoyer was tall and thin, and had a crooked nose, which made her quite distinctive.

'Inspector Süleyman . . .'

'Hello,' he said. 'Did you follow me from the station?'

'Yes and no,' she said. 'I'm off duty now. I'm going home, but . . .'

'But?'

'I've a friend who lives on this street. Can I take you to her place to talk?'

İkmen found Cumhur Polat in the antiseptic waiting area outside the emergency department.

Polat looked at him. 'Why are you here?' In spite of the air conditioning, he was sweating.

'Cemal asked me to come,' İkmen said. 'Do you know anything yet?'

Polat shook his head. 'Some doctor took her from me. They asked me whether I was her next of kin, and so I had to say no. I told them about her mother.'

'Who is in Bakırköy.'

Cumhur nodded. 'Sevval told me the old woman's pretty far gone. Hasn't been able to recognise her for several years.' He looked into İkmen's eyes. 'They asked me whether Sevval had medical insurance, and I said I didn't know, which I don't. I think one of the nurses may have recognised her.'

His mind was clearly racing as he changed subject and stared with his round red eyes.

'I couldn't take her to a public hospital,' he began. 'I . . .'

İkmen held one of his hands, firmly. 'I know,' he said.

The public hospitals were always noisy and overcrowded, and the chances of people recognising Sevval were high.

'Do you have any idea what might be wrong with her?' he asked.

Polat shook his head. 'She had a large piece of blood-soaked gauze on her left hip. There was some sort of wound underneath. I don't know whether she'd been attacked or had an accident.'

A man in a white coat came out of a door and walked up to them. 'Mr Polat?'

'Yes?'

The man, who was young and, by the sound of his accent, foreign, sat down beside him.

'I am Dr Abdullah,' he said. 'I am treating your friend Miss Kalkan.' He looked at İkmen. 'Who are you?'

'Çetin İkmen,' he said. 'I am a friend of Mr Polat.'

'I see.' The doctor cleared his throat. 'We have tried to get in touch with Miss Kalkan's mother, but that has proved . . . problematic.'

168

'I knew it would.'

'Yes. Are you sure there's no one else I can contact?'

'Not that I know of,' Cumhur said. 'Doctor, what is wrong with Sevval?'

The doctor stared at the floor. He was obviously trying to work out whether he should divulge any details about his patient.

İkmen said, 'Doctor, if it helps, I am a former police officer. If you call police headquarters, you can check my credentials.'

Dr Abdullah nodded.

'Or I can call on one of my colleagues.'

The doctor sighed. Then he said, 'I can tell you I have already contacted the police.'

'Oh . . .'

'I can't tell you why, but what I can say is that your friend Miss Kalkan has sepsis. She is unconscious and we're doing what we can.'

Cumhur's face was grey.

'Without permission from the patient to discuss her case with you, I can tell you no more,' the doctor said. 'The next twenty-four hours will be critical.'

'Can I stay here?' Cumhur asked.

'Of course.' The doctor stood up to leave. 'I'm sorry.'

İkmen stopped him before he went back through the door into the emergency department. 'You suspect foul play?' he asked.

Dr Abdullah paused for a moment. 'I don't know whether you know him, but an Inspector Gürsel is on his way here. If you are who you say you are, I'm sure he will decide what he may or may not tell you.'

'My colleagues are new in the job.'

Constable Aksoyer had taken him to the home of a friend, an elderly covered woman. The two women spoke together in the Kurdish dialect, Zaza. Shortly afterwards, the old woman left.

Gülse Aksoyer availed herself of her friend's samovar and made them both tea. They sat down at a very scarred kitchen table.

'I am now the longest-serving officer in the station,' she continued.

Mehmet Süleyman had noticed that she was probably the oldest officer he had seen in Kasımpaşa; she was also the only female.

'I know Kasımpaşa well,' she said.

'Unlike your colleagues?' he asked.

She tipped her head to one side and smiled. 'The officers I served with for many years have all gone.'

She didn't actually use the word 'purged'; she was probably too nervous about saying it to a stranger. But when Süleyman too smiled, she must have known he understood. What she said next proved that he was right.

'Yaşar Akgün is a gangster,' she said. 'Everyone knows it, including my colleagues.'

'I see.' He drank some tea. 'Do you know whether they take—'

'No,' she interrupted. 'And I don't want to know. If they take bribes from Akgün, that is between them and God. If you were to ask me whether I think bribery is involved, however, I'd have to say yes, though I've never seen it in action. What I know, what is fact, is that local people fear and respect Akgün.'

'A taxi driver.'

'Who lives in a big house once owned by Tarlabaşı's previous godfather. You can find what nobody will admit are petitioners outside that house most of the time,' she said. 'They'll tell you they're friends paying a social call. He has a lot of friends who are petty criminals, some of whom I've arrested myself and who have got off with not much more than a slap on the wrist.'

He nodded. 'Do you know anything about his gold sales?'

'His brother comes from Rize once a month,' she said. 'Local women go.'

'Have you been?'

'No,' she said. 'They won't let me.'

'Who won't?'

'The men at the community centre and my superiors. I've been unsure about that for a while,' she said. 'On the face of it, women go in, buy gold and come out again. But because Akgün is involved, I am suspicious. He clearly helps people in various ways. He owns a large house. He has staff, for which you can substitute the word "heavies". He can't possibly make much from his brother's gold sales. Security is always tight around those events. All sorts roam about outside making sure no one gets in who shouldn't.'

Süleyman remembered what his own officer had told him about the atmosphere in the area on gold sale day. He also recalled that Deniz Palandoken had been allowed in to the sale. Did this mean that drugs were involved?

'You think the gold sale is a cover for criminality?'

'Yes. I just don't know what. Drugs could be the short and easy answer, but I don't think there'd be so much community support for that. I may be wrong; we live in difficult times . . .'

'Do you ever go into the community centre?' Süleyman asked.

'If necessary,' she said. 'It's ninety per cent men in there and so I'm not welcome. But I have been inside.'

'What's it like?'

'Well, there's a coffee house downstairs, where men do what they do in such places. Upstairs, there's a large room at the top of the stairs, plus I think three small meeting rooms. Activities take place up there, but I'm not sure what. I have noticed that sometimes, even when a gold sale isn't on, the place is locked down.'

'By which you mean . . .'

'Muscle outside,' she said. 'The men I call his heavies. Some people being turned away.'

Of course this Yaşar Akgün had to have other business interests

171

apart from taxi driving and the gold auctions. But were those interests necessarily connected to the community centre?

'What about protection?' Süleyman asked.

'Kasımpaşa isn't like Tarlabaşı,' Aksoyer said. 'Even if they're not moral and religious, most people at least pretend they are. Whorehouses are easily taken care of. Small bakkals less so, and since the renovation of our sports stadium, the district has become even more focused on being perceived as "good".'

Kasımpaşa football stadium had been renovated back in 2005, when it was renamed after the current president of the republic, the district's favourite son.

'I don't think protection in Kasımpaşa would have a very good return,' she continued. 'But then maybe Yaşar has interests outside the area. Not that that makes a lot of sense, given the apparent hold he has over people in Kasımpaşa.' Then, finally letting down her guard, she said, 'This bastard has bought much of my station, and I want him gone!'

Süleyman's phone began to ring as he jotted down his number and handed it to Aksoyer. 'Call me any time,' he said. Then he took the call.

People like Cihan Teke didn't venture out of central İstanbul unless it was to go to a summer house on the Princes' Islands or the shores of the Bosphorus. A town like Gebze, sixty-five kilometres outside İstanbul, wasn't the sort of place a man in an Italian suit would usually be found. Nor was working-class and workaday Gebze the sort of place where chauffeur-driven limousines routinely turned up.

The person he had called from his office had arranged to meet him at a budget hotel called the Marmara. Talaat, Cihan Bey's chauffeur, pulled up outside the rather down-at-heel 1960s building, but the lawyer didn't actually get out of the car until his host had emerged from the hotel to greet him.

'Whenever I see you, you always look far more spry than you should, Ara Bey,' Cihan said as he allowed himself to be led into a brown lounge that was clearly still firmly trapped in the 1970s.

'It was Nazlan, God bless her soul, who saved me. She told me it was the drink or her. I chose her, and when she died, I still chose her.'

They sat down on chairs that had too much in common with beanbags for Cihan's taste, but he tolerated it, and the coffee that eventually materialised was, he had to say, really very good for somewhere out in the provinces.

Once they were alone, his host said, 'So tell me about the children.'

'It's the children, or rather one of them, that I'm here to see you about.'

'Which one?'

'Uğur.'

He smiled. 'Is he OK?'

'Yes. Or rather no, but that is what we must discuss. You may have heard that there has been some trouble at the Karacaahmet cemetery recently. A body was absent from its grave.'

'Replaced, wasn't it?'

'Yes. Although the police have now discovered a part of the body that went missing, namely a thigh bone,' the lawyer said. 'Distressing though this is, I have to tell you that the missing body was that of your late wife, Perihan Hanım.'

Ara Bulut raised his large shaggy eyebrows. 'That's awful!' he said. 'Who would do such a thing?'

'The police are investigating,' Cihan Teke said. 'I'm very sorry. However, the reason I am here is because in order to find out who the bone belonged to, DNA tests were performed on the item itself and on your sons. Are you familiar with DNA testing, Ara Bey?'

'I know it can show certain things,' he said. 'Diseases and so on.'

'It can also indicate ethnic origins and parentage.'

Surely Ara Bey had already known that? DNA testing was common now, and was talked about on the TV just like the one he had banging out a stream of nonsense in his hotel reception.

'The results have shown that while Lokman is Perihan's son, Uğur was not given birth to by your then wife.'

There was a long silence. Ara Bulut was a large, pale-skinned man who coloured easily. He was colouring now.

'Whoever his mother was was closely related to Perihan Hanım,' Cihan Teke continued. 'I should tell you, Ara Bey, that your son Lokman, now furnished with this information, is contesting his mother's will.'

'He can't do that!'

'Yes, he can.'

Ara looked around the brown room as if confused. 'Is he still a complete waster?' he asked. 'Is he still like me?'

'Like you were, Ara Bey, yes,' Cihan said. 'Although apparently he has friends in high places in spite of his lifestyle. This is what worries me.'

'Perihan chose Uğur because she knew he'd look after the business.'

'Indeed.'

'Lokman gets a good allowance.'

'Which he burns through every month – and more.'

Ara Bulut put his head in his hands. 'I thought that if I left, the boys would stand a chance . . .'

'You'd also fallen in love with Nazlan Hanım,' the lawyer put in.

'Yes, well . . .'

'Which is why you own this charming hotel. Now, I think I

174

can say with some confidence that you would not agree with your son Lokman taking over your late wife's business?'

'Of course!'

Cihan bowed. 'Very well. In that case, I fear you will have to make a public statement to that effect. I know that neither yourself nor your late wife wanted either of the boys to know of your whereabouts, but these are strange and confusing times where pieces of bone may tell stories we do not want told.'

Ara pulled his chin into his pale grey beard and began to mutter, to make excuses.

Cihan put a hand up to silence him. 'And of course I will need to know who Uğur Bey's real mother was,' he said. 'I believe, if I remember correctly, that Perihan Hanım had two sisters . . .'

Kerim Gürsel had been in with Dr Abdullah for half an hour when İkmen's phone beeped to let him know he had a text message. It was from Süleyman. Ömer Mungun had investigated whether Leah Delmonte's friend Ceyda Kazantzoğlu was still alive, and had discovered that officially she was. So why had her daughter-in-law told İkmen she had died? And if she wasn't dead, then where was she?

He'd told Cumhur Polat to go home, and while the jeweller had been reluctant to leave, he had also become aware of the fact that while the doctor might tell the police certain things about Sevval Kalkan, he was not going to tell him.

Kerim reappeared about fifteen minutes later and invited İkmen to accompany him back to headquarters in his car. On the way, he told his old boss what the doctor had told him.

'She has donated bone marrow,' he said as they moved slowly through the traffic, much of it ultimately headed, as they were, for the Atatürk Bridge.

'Bone marrow?'

'They harvest it through the hip bones,' Kerim said. 'Don't

know why and didn't ask. What I did ask was whether the doctor knew where Miss Kalkan had done this. He didn't. She's only regained consciousness once, briefly, since she was brought in, and even then she couldn't talk. She's got sepsis, which means that either she discharged herself from the hospital that performed this procedure, or the harvesting was done illegally, possibly outside a clinical setting. What does her friend know about it?'

'Nothing,' İkmen said. 'She just turned up at his place and told him she was dying.'

'She may well be.'

'And yet theoretically she can be saved.'

'Oh yes, it's possible; just not, apparently, particularly probable.'

Sevval, according to Cumhur Polat, hadn't wanted to go to hospital. She'd talked about her death as something that was inevitable. But why? Had she been so frightened of revealing herself in public that she was prepared to die to preserve her anonymity? And where had she been in the meantime? She'd now been missing for almost four weeks. Did it take that long to donate bone marrow, and how had that even happened?

'So do you think this was an illegal donation?'

'The doctor does,' Kerim said. 'But of course I will have to contact a lot of hospitals just to make sure. Mr Polat told Dr Abdullah that he'd asked Miss Kalkan about her injury but she flatly refused to tell him how she'd got it. That, to me, smacks of illegality. How do you know about all this, Çetin Bey?'

İkmen had always trusted Kerim Gürsel. It was one of the reasons he'd been so pleased when the sergeant had been promoted to his old job. But as a gay man in a deeply politicised system, Kerim was vulnerable.

İkmen said, 'If I tell you what I know, I have to be able to trust that you won't move against the people I am working for.'

Kerim looked across at him with a shocked expression on his

face. 'Çetin Bey,' he said, 'I have trusted you with my innermost secrets . . .'

'But officially, Polat and Kalkan . . .'

'Are enemies of the state, yes, I know,' he said. 'You think I wouldn't recognise that woman? And the man I've also seen on TV, when he was arrested. My only interest in these people is the notion that the woman may have been pressured into donating bone marrow in the kind of surroundings that can lead to sepsis. I will need to consult with Mehmet Bey. You know he's working on a possible organ-harvesting case?'

'Yes,' İkmen said. 'Kerim, I didn't mean to offend you . . .'

Kerim Gürsel smiled. 'You haven't,' he said. 'You couldn't. And I know we live in dangerous times; I of all people understand. I swear to you I will not put these people in harm's way. Now just light a cigarette and tell me about it.'

Chapter 14

Crime lords, in Mehmet Süleyman's experience, frequently had interesting and often colourful backstories. But there were always exceptions to any rule, and Yaşar Akgün was that thing. Piecing the little he had found out about him from Constable Aksoyer together with an examination of his Facebook profile wasn't all that helpful. If Akgün was indeed a successful gangster, he kept that side of his life well hidden online. Just a middle-aged taxi driver with one broken marriage behind him and a daughter back in Rize.

But when it came to the gold business run by his brother İzzet, that was another matter. His shop, called Altınbaş, was a nondescript-looking emporium on a street in Rize. Apparently established in 1996, it specialised in gold jewellery, mainly for women, and also gold coins for investment. Significantly, however, and very much not on the shop's website, was the fact that İzzet Akgün had a police record. Assault on a man when drunk in 1994; another assault charge in 2000, this time apparently sober; three speeding fines, one under the influence of alcohol in 2014; plus a dispute over access rights to his shop that had begun in 1996 and continued until 2001, when the matter was finally resolved in Akgün's favour. The family were natives of Rize, where İzzet lived in an apartment close to the central plaza.

Famed for its tea production, Rize was the kind of small provincial city that gave Mehmet Süleyman the shudders. Industrious and hard working, it was nevertheless low on places where one might socialise in a mixed group of men and women, its values being decidedly pious and rural. It was small wonder that Yaşar Akgün had left the place. But why was his brother still there; and perhaps even more weirdly, why had İzzet used a firm of attorneys from Ankara to fight his case against his neighbour, and not a local company?

A knock on his door caused Süleyman to look up from his computer screen. 'Come.'

Kerim Gürsel entered, followed by Çetin İkmen.

Süleyman smiled. 'Çetin Bey,' he said. 'What a nice surprise.'

'It was Filiz, Perihan's older sister,' Ara Bulut said. 'Old Raşıt Bey, my father-in-law, died just before we got married, and so we were living with my mother-in-law, Barçın Hanım, and also Filiz, who was too old to marry by that time.'

'How old was she?' Cihan asked.

'Thirty,' Ara said. 'You know how old that is for an unmarried woman in the middle of nowhere.' He sighed. 'Perihan wasn't getting pregnant. My drinking got worse, and then she wouldn't sleep with me. In retrospect, I don't blame her. I was a pig to that woman. She was ten times cleverer than I've ever been, just like Nazlan, just like most women, I've come to think. Filiz wasn't a beautiful woman, but there was a seductiveness about her . . .'

'Why didn't she marry when she was young?' the lawyer asked.

'Her father became ill when Filiz was sixteen. As the oldest child, she had to help her mother. By the time the old man died, she was twenty-eight. I could say that I was drunk when it happened, and of course I probably was. But can I use my drunkenness as an excuse? No. She was there, she wanted me and I wanted her.'

'You made her pregnant.'

'Barçın Hanım was blind by that time and so keeping it a

179

secret from her was easy,' he said. 'The brother was away doing his military service. Only Aylin, the younger sister, knew. Things get covered up in small villages; they always have. In order to preserve the family's good name, Perihan brought Uğur up as her own. And she loved him, God bless her. But we moved to the city to get away from Filiz. Perihan couldn't bear to look at her. Lokman is the only child we had together.'

'He says he always knew that Uğur was not who he appeared to be,' Cihan said. 'I don't know whether that was wishful thinking on his part.'

'Nor I. But Perihan wouldn't have wanted Lokman to take over the business, that I do know. The boy's like me, unfortunately.'

Cihan Bey leaned forward. 'If you want to help Uğur, you must be prepared to underwrite Perihan's will.'

Ara closed his eyes.

'I know you don't want to re-enter your sons' lives . . .'

'I promised Perihan I wouldn't.'

'I know. But unfortunately, if we want to be sure of defeating Lokman's attempt to take over the business, you have to support Uğur. And the boy deserves to know who his mother was, don't you think?'

'He'll hate me even more than he already does,' Ara Bulut said.

No one had told İkmen that Kerim Gürsel's sergeant, Elif Arslan, had left. As the three men discussed possible connections between Süleyman's Karacaahmet case and what might have happened to Sevval Kalkan, İkmen suggested it might be an idea to involve Sergeant Arslan in order to gain some female insight. Süleyman looked at Kerim Gürsel, who said, 'Elif was transferred.'

'Oh,' İkmen said. 'Did she . . .'

'She's been replaced by another woman,' Kerim continued. 'A young graduate, fast tracked.'

'I see. Good.'

Another look passed between Süleyman and Gürsel, and this time İkmen said, 'What's going on?'

'She's . . . well . . .'

'She's called Sergeant Eylul Yavaş,' Kerim said. 'She's twenty-six and very keen.'

'So where is she?' İkmen asked.

Again that look passed between his colleagues.

'What is it?'

'She's contacting hospitals for me,' Kerim said. 'It's a big job . . .'

'And she's covered,' Süleyman said.

Suddenly İkmen knew why his colleagues had been so reticent about this new officer. 'As in . . .'

'Hijab,' Süleyman said. 'They can now, and quite frankly, why not, seeing as there are so many of them in our ranks.'

İkmen felt a chill run up his spine. But not because the woman was covered, not necessarily.

'By "them", you mean . . .'

'Çetin, you retired because people like them – and we know who we mean by that—'

'We also know,' İkmen said, 'that back in the days of the Gezi protests, a lot of women who covered their heads came out to oppose the status quo. A lot of religious people came. Democracy is something that is open to all!'

'Yes, but—'

'This young woman is clearly observant, but if we assume that she is also, to use your words, one of "them", this is doing her a disservice,' İkmen said. Although he knew why his colleagues had spoken as they had, he felt angry with them. Reading between the lines, Elif Arslan had been replaced with a more acceptable version of a female officer, but that didn't necessarily mean that this Sergeant Yavaş was the enemy within. 'Innocent until proven guilty,' he continued. 'I know that doesn't really work out these days, but if we don't uphold our own values, then who will?'

There was a tense silence, and then Kerim said, 'You're right, as ever.'

'And if she loses us our jobs?' Süleyman said. He had a point, and İkmen knew it.

Eventually he said, 'It's a risk.'

'A risk that with my own living expenses, plus those of my mother and alimony to my ex-wife and my son—'

İkmen raised a hand to silence him. 'I understand,' he said. 'I do.'

After first checking that his office door was locked, Süleyman sat down behind his desk again and said, 'I read this book not long ago. It was called Let the Right One In. It's about vampires, which is irrelevant, but the title of the book is pertinent. What if we think we're letting the right one in only to find that we've been duped? God, Çetin, you know what the risks are!'

He was right. If this woman had been sent in not only to learn about policing but to spy on Kerim and his colleagues too, then she could be dangerous. But to exclude her simply because she covered stuck in İkmen's craw. So for the moment, he changed the subject.

'A thought,' he said. 'Sevval Kalkan has either donated her bone marrow or had it taken against her will to benefit someone. We don't know who. What we do know is that she was not often out and about prior to her disappearance four weeks ago.'

All the officers were up to speed on İkmen's case now.

'So how did this operation come to pass?' İkmen continued. 'Did she maybe meet someone on the street who asked her to give them her bone marrow?'

The other two men laughed.

İkmen shrugged. 'Ridiculous! But seriously, how did it happen? Sevval, it seems, decorated some hipster's flat with political graffiti and got paid handsomely for it. But was that generous payment actually for her bone marrow donation?'

'It could have been,' Kerim said. 'But then that begs a question about tissue matching. How do you know that your marrow will be suitable?'

'You get tested,' Süleyman said. 'I don't know how that's done.'

'Dr Sarkissian will know,' İkmen said.

'Probably.'

'And what about your Karacaahmet case?' he asked. 'We don't want to draw any false conclusions here, but it is sort of connected.'

'Organ trafficking, yes,' Süleyman said. 'Or rather, that is what we suspect. I have a lead on that Dr Özdemir over in Kartal I have yet to pursue.'

'The one who wrote the prescription for the Palandokens?'

'Yes. And it would seem that old Sugar Hanım was right about there being a new godfather down in Kasımpaşa: Yaşar Akgün, who may or may not be involved.' He frowned. 'There's something else too.'

'Which is?'

'Akgün is a common name, but it is also the surname of the gatekeeper up at the cemetery. He doesn't live in Kasımpaşa and was a property lawyer before he gave it all up for a quieter life amongst the dead. But . . . Yaşar, the godfather, has a brother who lives in Rize – he's the one who performs the gold sales I told you about. He had a dispute with his neighbours some years ago and hired a law firm in Ankara to fight his case. Why enlist help from so far away?'

'Do you know where the gatekeeper used to practise?' Kerim asked.

'Here in İstanbul,' Süleyman said.

'Always?'

'No. But not in Ankara.'

'Then maybe the firm in Ankara was known to him in some way.'

'Or maybe there is no connection,' Süleyman said.

'Do you think the old Jew will make me a fine watch?' Lokman said as he breathed cannabis smoke slowly out of his lungs.

His friend, a man called Serkan Tolon, who was considerably older than he looked, took the joint from Lokman and said, 'He's not a Jew.'

'He's a jeweller!'

Serkan laughed. 'Not all jewellers are Jews, just like not all makers of baklava are from Gaziantep.'

'Yes they are!'

'No they're not!'

'The good ones are!'

Serkan sucked on the joint, holding the smoke in his lungs for several seconds before saying, 'Whatever.'

It was difficult to imagine that these two young men, sitting on huge embroidered cushions on the floor of Serkan's living room, had attended one of Turkey's best schools. Galatasaray Lisesi, on İstiklal Caddesi, had once, long ago, provided education for the Ottoman elite, and still to some extent fulfilled that function for the republic. Boys who attended the school tended to go on to university and then gravitate towards professions like medicine or the law. But neither Lokman nor Serkan had been studious, and now both lived on an allowance provided by a parent. But there the similarities stopped.

Although she became wealthy, Lokman's late mother had been working class and had laboured hard for her millions. Serkan, on the other hand, came from a family that had the benefit of inherited wealth. Under the Ottomans, the Tolon family had prospered as loyal retainers working in the various palaces of three late-nineteenth-century sultans. In more recent times, many family members, including Serkan's father, had been active in the conservative movement that posited a return to the days of empire. That his youngest son lived in an apartment in a wild part of the city peopled by immigrants, drag queens and prostitutes didn't bother Tolon senior in the slightest provided Serkan didn't get himself arrested or become involved in any sort of scandal.

'Have you been to see your lawyer yet?'

'No,' Lokman said. 'Uğur's been to see old Cihan Bey, our family man. But my lawyer's cheap, and a bit of a bruiser, which is good.'

'My uncle will help you out,' Serkan said. 'He knows everyone.'

Lokman took the joint back from his friend and said, 'I don't have any money.'

'No, but you will have. Your mother was clearly out of her mind when she left everything to your brother. He's not her son. Why would she do that?'

Lokman shrugged, joint in his mouth, looking at Serkan's insane walls decorated with radical posters and artworks poking fun at the president and the government.

He said, 'You know, I always thought Uğur and I couldn't possibly be full brothers. Don't know why. Wishful thinking, I suppose. I just wanted to make trouble for him really.'

'It took balls to arrange to get your mother exhumed.'

He shrugged. 'She never liked me. I've always been too much like my father. But what the fuck? As you've always said, sometimes to get what you want, there have to be casualties.'

Türgüt Bey hadn't noticed him when Raşım Dorsay entered the cemetery out of uniform. He didn't really know why he'd come. He was meant to be off, and yet he couldn't relax at home because his mind wouldn't let him.

As Türgüt Bey had said for a long time, if the cemetery guards didn't prove they were managing the site correctly, the police would take over. But the perimeter was breached all the time, and it had got worse. The truth was, there was something very rotten in the system. But what? Getting another job wouldn't be easy, but to carry on in this atmosphere of uncertainty was driving him crazy.

The place was quiet. The only people he could see were police. Was it a sign? And even if it wasn't, should he just do what his mind was screaming out for him to do anyway?

'I'm not an expert,' Arto Sarkissian said, 'but I do know that if someone is put forward for this treatment, both the recipient and the donor have to have what is known as an HLA blood test.'

'What's that?' İkmen asked. Although he was no longer employed by the national police force, he had come to Arto Sarkissian's laboratory to find out what he could about bone marrow transplants, both for himself and on behalf of Kerim Gürsel.

'HLA stands for human leukocyte antigen, something that is found in most cells of the body. The test determines which antigen genes a person has inherited and detects any antibodies to HLA antigens that might cause a bone marrow transplant to fail. Usually done, as I say, by blood test, but can also be performed using a cheek swab now.'

'Would a person's doctor know whether this test has been performed?'

'Yes,' Arto said. 'It should be in that person's medical notes.'

'But could someone who isn't a doctor perform the test?'

Arto frowned. 'Depends what you mean,' he said. 'A nurse or a phlebotomist could perform a blood test. Theoretically anyone could take a cheek swab. But the actual analysis would have to be done professionally.'

Somehow Sevval Kalkan had been selected as a bone marrow donor for someone. They still had no idea who the woman's doctor was, but something else occurred to İkmen.

'Could someone other than a person's doctor have access to their medical notes?' he asked.

'Excepting hospitals? You know that if a patient is treated in hospital these days, their notes can be accessed by their consultant there?'

'Kerim Bey is trying to find out whether this person was treated in hospital,' İkmen said. 'But let's assume he or she just has a family doctor: could someone not medically trained get hold of their notes?'

'Of course,' Arto said. 'You and I both know that when money or sexual favours are put on offer, anything is fair game. Çetin, can you tell me a bit about the background to this? I don't mean the person's name, but a general outline of what has happened.'

İkmen told him what he could. When he'd finished, the doctor said, 'Even as an enemy of the state, this person will still have a doctor. I'm getting the sense of someone middle class.'

'Yes.'

'Then Kerim Bey would do well to put out a request to family doctors as well as hospitals. Have you spoken to Mehmet Bey?'

'Yes,' İkmen said. 'I know about his involvement in the Karacaahmet case.'

'So you know that organ trafficking is strongly suspected.'

'Yes. Although we're not assuming any connection.'

The doctor frowned. 'Another thing, and controversially: if your man or woman has been arrested for his or her opposition to the state, then a DNA sample will have been taken from them.'

'Of course.'

'Which in the wrong hands . . . I will say no more,' he said. 'But you know what I mean.'

İkmen felt cold. If what Arto was implying was correct, that a police officer could be involved, then who had that theoretical officer taken a swab on behalf of? And why?

* * *

He knew it was probably a character flaw, but Mehmet Süleyman secretly enjoyed catching people off their guard. It wasn't as satisfying if the person was innocent, but if they were guilty or, like Türgüt Akgün, a work in progress, it always gave him a bit of a frisson.

'Oh, Inspector Süleyman!' the gatekeeper said. 'I didn't know you were coming. Your men didn't say. I, er . . . can I get you tea?'

Turks always resorted to the offer of tea if they didn't know what to do next. Hospitality in the face of apprehension.

'No thank you,' Süleyman said. 'I'm here to liaise with my officers.'

'I've not been told they've found anything untoward . . .'

'You wouldn't be.' Süleyman smiled, then said, 'I've actually had a call from one of my officers, which is why I'm here.'

'Oh. About . . .?'

'I don't know,' he said. He began to walk in the direction of the exit, and then stopped. 'Oh, Türgüt Bey, I forgot to ask you last time: were you born here in the city?'

'Oh, er, yes,' the gatekeeper said.

'Where?'

'Er, Hasköy,' he said. 'Why?'

'Do your family still live in Hasköy?'

'No. No, we're all over the city now.'

'Mmm,' Süleyman said. 'Any of your relatives in Kasimpaşa?'

'Kasimpaşa? No.' He laughed, slightly nervously Süleyman thought. 'No, we've all done rather better than that, Inspector.'

Süleyman smiled back. 'Thank you.'

As he headed across the cemetery, he mulled over what the gatekeeper had told him. Kasimpaşa still had a reputation for being somewhere people ended up rather than a destination. Maybe the gatekeeper, if he still had relatives there, was ashamed? And maybe not. When he found Raşım Dorsay, he said, 'So, Raşım, what do you have to tell me?'

Chapter 15

It was only early evening, but Çiçek İkmen knew that her lover, Mehmet Süleyman, had entirely forgotten they had a date. This was because, although it wasn't yet time for them to meet, he hadn't contacted her that day at all. To make matters worse, her father was out on the loose too.

She'd already flung her keys down on the dining table and sat on the sofa before she realised that she wasn't alone in the family apartment. Had Samsun got home early from her dental appointment? Çiçek stood up in time to see Samsun coming out of the kitchen with a very tall, dark man wearing a djellaba. When she saw Çiçek, Samsun said, 'Oh. You're early.'

'And you're not at the dentist,' Çiçek replied. 'Who's he?'

'A friend.' Samsun's cheeks coloured. She had always been a terrible liar.

'No, who is he really?' Çiçek asked.

Samsun sighed. 'A friend of Layla's,' she said.

'And Layla is . . .?'

'She's a falçı, I've known her for years. She works at the Café Laf in Bakırköy. It's one of the best in the city.'

There were a lot of cafés in the city that employed falçıs, or fortune-tellers. Café Laf wasn't really on Çiçek's radar.

'You were supposed to go to the dentist,' she said.

The man in the djellaba said something and Samsun waved a hand at him. 'He can only speak Arabic,' she said. 'I think he's from Oman.'

'Yes, but why is he here?'

'I was trying to tell you!' Samsun said. 'I went to the Laf so that Layla could read my cards. Apart from your grandmother, she's the only one I've ever trusted. I wanted to see if she could tell me anything about this dental work I'm due to have.'

'And did she?'

'No, because then I met this lovely man, Abdulfattah something. He was with Layla when I got there; she was very excited.'

'Excited to see a man whose language I presume she doesn't speak? Who is he, Samsun?'

'Oh, he's a very spiritual person . . .'

Abdulfattah said something else. Çiçek held up a hand to silence him. She knew exactly who this man was, Samsun had been going on about it for months.

'He's an exorcist, isn't he?' she said. 'For the djinn.'

Samsun said nothing.

'That must be a yes then,' Çiçek said. She sat down again. 'You do know that Dad will go mad if he comes home and finds an exorcist here?'

'Yes, but—'

'I don't like the damn djinn any more than you do,' Çiçek said. 'But this is Dad's apartment, and if he wants it to stay, then it stays. I'm sorry, but you'll have to ask this man to leave.' A thought occurred to her. 'Unless he's already . . .'

'No, I don't think so,' Samsun said. 'He hasn't read from the Koran or blown on things or anything like that.' But she looked anxious.

'You'd better hope he hasn't, or Dad will kill you,' Çiçek said. 'And quite honestly, I've got enough troubles of my own without worrying about you!'

After some very fraught shouting and gesticulating, Samsun ushered the now very confused man out and took him down to

Divan Yolu to get a taxi back to Bakırköy. When she returned to the living room she said, 'I'm sorry, Çiçek, but I'd had enough. Just lately it always seems to be there. Can't go into the kitchen without it rearing up.'

Çiçek sighed. 'I'm sorry I got angry. To be honest, I can largely ignore the wretched thing these days, but I have to say it does cast a sort of depressive mood over the place, and I don't need that right now.'

Samsun sat down. 'Mehmet Bey?'

'We're supposed to be going out this evening and then I was going to stay over at his place, but I've heard nothing from him all day. He usually rings or texts to see whether I can still make it. I always can; it's he who sometimes has problems.'

Samsun put a hand on Çiçek's knee. 'You know how it was growing up around your father,' she said. 'It'll always be the job first, you know that. Now more than ever.'

'Why now?'

'The world is screwed,' Samsun said. 'Look around and tell me if you see anywhere that isn't in chaos.'

Çiçek was silent.

'Precisely,' Samsun said. 'There isn't anywhere. And when the world is politically as fucked up as it is now, crime gets worse. I can't believe some of the shit that goes down in this city these days. And now the dead are getting dug up for reasons I daren't even think about . . .'

'How do you know—'

She waved a hand. 'I hear stuff,' she said. 'Mehmet Bey is trying to find out who did this; trying to make the dead, and the living, safer in their beds. I know it's hard, Çiçek, but I can see that he loves you by the way he looks at you. Don't give him a hard time when he gets here. I know it goes against every feminist bone in your body, but just don't.'

191

Çiçek turned her head away. Could she do that? And indeed, should she?

'I lied to you about not being able to remember what that necrophile I interrupted looked like,' Raşım Dorsay said. 'I'd never come across anything like it before, and so his face is forever etched onto my memory.'

'Why are you telling me now?' Süleyman asked.

Raşım had wrestled with his conscience for hours to come to this point. 'I want it to stop,' he said.

'Want what to stop?'

'Your investigation. We all do,' he said.

'I'm sure you do. But it only finishes when I find out whose body has replaced Perihan Bulut's body in her grave, and why. That is just the way things are. Do you have a problem with police officers being on site?'

'No . . . Well, yes. Türgüt Bey is worried,' Raşım said.

'Worried about what?'

'To be fair, he was worried before you turned up.' Instinctively he looked around to make sure no one was listening. 'Türgüt Bey says that if we don't keep this place safe, then the police will take over and we will lose our jobs.'

Süleyman laughed. 'You think I have enough officers to police a site like this on a permanent basis?' he said. 'I wish I did. I wish I had enough officers to do my own job effectively.'

'Yes, but Türgüt Bey—'

'Türgüt Bey is misguided,' Süleyman said. 'Unless you have committed an offence, your job is safe. Now tell me about this man.'

Raşım breathed in deeply and then said, 'He was about thirty. Tall, like you, but thin, really thin.'

'Unnaturally so?'

'Maybe. He was in a bad way. Told me he was homeless, which

192

I suppose would explain that. He had quite a handsome face, regular features, not too big or too small. Brown eyes. Main thing about him, though, was the strawberry birthmark on the left-hand side of his face. Maybe that explained what he was trying to do. Maybe it explained why he was homeless. You know how ignorant people can be about children who are less than perfect.'

Süleyman did. While many rural parents saw children with learning difficulties as gifts from God, physical infirmities were not always looked upon so kindly.

'Was this man from the city?'

'I don't think so originally,' Raşim said. 'He had a bit of an accent. From the east, maybe? I don't know. Like I don't know his name or anything else about him really. Just a handsome face ruined by that birthmark, which was sort of uneven and rough looking. Am I in trouble now?'

Süleyman sighed. 'You can redeem yourself by coming to police headquarters and making a statement,' he said. 'I'll need everything you can recall about this man.'

Raşim visibly relaxed. 'Thank you, efendi.'

'Oh don't call me that!' Süleyman said irritably. 'Türgüt Bey crawls around using that term as if he's some kind of serf! Man was a lawyer, for God's sake!'

'Sorry. Sorry.'

He shrugged. 'Not your fault,' he said. 'But about Türgüt Bey, do you know why he was so worried about the security of your jobs?'

'Not really.'

'Does he talk about it a lot?'

'No, but we're rarely allowed to log things we find wrong in the incident book.'

'He prevents you from doing that?'

'Sort of. He just sort of waves a lot of problems away. Like if we find someone wandering about . . .'

'Like your birthmark man.'

'Yes. If we apprehend someone who shouldn't be in the cemetery, he just tells us to let them go. Münir Bey, the man I work with, he's the same. He says if we have too many incidents, we'll lose our jobs.'

Kerim Gürsel got the call from the hospital about Sevval Kalkan as he and İkmen were walking out of police head-quarters. They both stood in the street as they came to terms with the news.

'She died at 6.02,' Kerim said. 'Dr Abdullah said there will have to be a post-mortem, when we will learn more, although I will have to speak to Dr Sarkissian first.'

'Because of the possibility of homicide?' İkmen said.

'Yes, although is it clinical malpractice? To discharge someone after surgery with no after-care, what is that?'

İkmen said, 'Depends what we're talking about, doesn't it. In some hospitals and in some districts this is normal. We know that.'

'It's not right.'

'Of course it's not! But is it criminal? I'm sorry, I have no answer to that question, Kerim, but you must consider it.'

'I am.'

'Has Sergeant Yavaş managed to find the hospital where Sevval was treated?'

'Not yet, or she would have told me.'

'Maybe. But I'd go back and talk to her,' İkmen said.

'I was going to give you a lift home . . .'

'Don't worry about that! Go back. Talk to her. Anyway, I had better go and tell Cumhur Polat and his associates the bad news. I'll get the tram home and pick up my car.'

The two men embraced.

* * *

His phone rang. He looked at the screen. It was Çiçek. His heart sank. He was supposed to have picked her up to go to dinner. He answered the call.

'I am so sorry,' he said. 'I'm still working.'

'I gathered that,' she said. He heard her sigh. 'It's OK.'

'No it isn't,' Süleyman said. 'It really isn't.'

She didn't answer. He could tell she was angry. He could feel her anger pouring down the phone.

'I had to sort out . . .' He shook his head. 'Look, I have no idea when I'm going to be able to leave, so why don't we go out tomorrow—'

That was when it exploded. 'I want to see you tonight,' she said. 'I know that traditionally relationships are all supposed to be about men and their needs, but—'

'Çiçek . . .'

She lowered her voice. 'We haven't slept together for weeks!' she said. 'I can't go on like this.'

Was he shocked? Yes and no. If she'd come from any other family he would have been, but she was an İkmen and they were straight talkers.

'I need you, Mehmet!'

'And I need you too. But—'

'No buts! I've got a key to your apartment, I'm going to go over and wait for you there.'

There was a pause. He saw that he was almost at the gate-keeper's office. God, what it was to be wanted by a beautiful and seductive woman. He wanted Çiçek as much as she wanted him.

'All right,' he said. 'I'll get away when I can. I don't know when that will be.'

'Good,' she said, and cut the connection immediately.

Süleyman didn't know how to feel. Was he angry at her for crashing in on his other life as a defender of the people? Or was he flattered by her passion for his body? He didn't know.

He stepped into the gatekeeper's office and found Türgüt Bey at his desk.

'Ah, efendi . . .'

'Inspector Süleyman,' he said. 'I'm leaving now.'

'Oh, did you find what you were looking for?'

'Yes.'

Raşım Dorsay had already left the cemetery, bypassing the gatekeeper's office, and was sitting in Süleyman's car.

Süleyman drove him to police headquarters in silence. They both, it seemed, had much on which to ponder.

They were all together at Gold Bey's apartment – Gold, Machine, the Designer – all out of hiding because what they had each been suffering alone over Sevval had been too much.

İkmen told them as kindly but as straightforwardly as he could that the Actress was dead.

Cemal Yüksel, Machine Bey said, 'But how? How could she die from just an infection?'

'It was untreated and it was at an incision into a bone,' İkmen said. 'That can be very dangerous.'

'But why didn't she say?' Gold Bey asked. 'When she did finally come to me, all she would say was that she was dying. She wouldn't say why. I felt at the time it was almost as if she wanted to die. We would not have judged her. To just disappear like that . . .'

'Maybe that was part of the deal she struck with whoever did this,' İkmen said. 'The more we know about this, myself and the police, the more we believe that this was no legal transaction. Do any of you know whether she was registered with a doctor?'

'No.' Olimpio looked up. 'I thought she was going out to meet men. She told me she was. We rowed about it. She revelled in the attention.'

'But she probably wasn't,' İkmen said. 'She was probably

preparing for this donation. There are a lot of blood tests she would have had to go through in order to see whether she could donate.'

That wasn't strictly true. She probably did have to make arrangements with whoever had asked her to do this. But İkmen suspected that she might have had one-night stands as well.

'I found a blood-testing kit in her room, the type used by diabetics. Do you know anything about that?'

'She wasn't diabetic as far as I know,' Olimpio said. 'Could she have used it to test her blood for something else?'

İkmen didn't know. Kerim Gürsel had found Sevval's arrest notes, and while she had been subjected to a blood test, it had not included an HLA analysis.

As if reading İkmen's mind, Cumhur Polat said, 'I had a blood test when I was arrested, at police headquarters.'

'We all did,' Olimpio said. 'And then again at Silivri.'

'Inspector Gürsel, can I talk to you, please?'

Kerim looked up and smiled. 'Yes, Sergeant,' he said.

Small and slim, she appeared a lot younger than twenty-six. Kerim reckoned that without make-up, she probably looked like a kid. But she was a hard worker who had come to him, he had to admit, under the cloud represented by her headscarf. And yet, as Çetin İkmen had said, if he allowed that to define her, then surely he was falling into the trap that he accused religious people of planting. To judge a book by its cover.

'Sir, I've contacted all the major city hospitals about Sevval Kalkan but without success,' she said. 'And I'm not surprised.'

'Oh?'

'We know that these procedures take place in private houses and apartments too,' she said. 'And the more I think about it, the more I'm convinced Miss Kalkan didn't go to hospital.'

'Why?'

197

'She'd be recognised,' she said. 'My family still watch her show all the time. Those characters are like friends to many people. I know I was shocked when she was arrested. My mother cried, couldn't believe she'd be disloyal.'

Disloyal to whom? Kerim wondered. Sevval had been released from prison without charge – eventually. By which time her career was over . . .

'Sir, Inspector Süleyman is investigating a possible case of organ trafficking out at the Karacaahmet cemetery . . .'

'I am well aware of that,' he said. Süleyman was in the building taking a statement from a witness. Kerim had already arranged a meeting with him in the morning.

'I'd like to learn more about serious crime,' she said. 'Sergeant Mungun . . .'

Ömer Mungun was going to be at the meeting in the morning, but Kerim hadn't invited Eylul Yavaş. Did she know this? She must have overheard or made an assumption or something. She was no fool.

Kerim nodded. 'Well,' he said, 'I am having a meeting with Inspector Süleyman and Sergeant Mungun about this in the morning, but it will be early and it won't be here.'

Should he include her? Technically he should, but trusting her when she'd been chosen for him by Commissioner Selahattın Özer was difficult. Özer had come out of retirement to take over from the previous commissioner, Hürrem Teker. Now discredited, Teker had voluntarily retired. Özer didn't share any traits with his liberal predecessor, which meant that officers like Süleyman and Gürsel distrusted much of what he did and everyone he appointed. But was that realistic? Kerim thought about İkmen again, and then said, 'Well, if you wish to learn more about what may or may not be a case involving organised crime, perhaps you should come along too, Sergeant.'

She smiled. 'That would be excellent, sir.'

'Very well. Six a.m. at the Vatan Kafe in Molla Gurani Mahallesi.'

It was just far away enough from headquarters that they would probably be able to talk in peace. He'd give Eylul Yavaş a chance.

She felt him get into bed beside her, his body still warm and damp from the shower he had just taken. Not that Çiçek had heard the shower running. Until he slipped in beside her, she'd been asleep. Blearily she turned to him. 'What's the time?' she said.

'Never mind.' He put his arms around her and she laid her head on his chest. He'd come home knowing she wanted to have sex, but given the fact that she was asleep when he entered his bedroom, he thought that maybe she had changed her mind. He was wrong.

Now suddenly wide awake, Çiçek rolled over and straddled him. It didn't take much, or long, for her to get him in the mood. And although he had come home exhausted, he seemed to find the required energy to satisfy her several times. He was not, he felt as she lay exhausted in his arms, doing badly for a man of fifty. Çiçek never tired of telling him how much he turned her on. But then women had always flattered him. It was just that this one really loved him too, and that was worrying.

The world was becoming more unstable by the week. A terrorist outrage here, the beginnings of a slide into authoritarianism there. Since the attempted coup in 2016, Süleyman didn't know whom he could trust. Prior to that, he had always felt confident in himself, whoever he was obliged to confront. But the landscape had changed and now the whole country was alive with whispers about who did and did not have the ear of this minister or that minister close to the seat of power. There were rumours and sometimes outright statements of support for politicians from known mobsters, as well as the threat that came from factional trolls online.

Lately he had become grateful for the fact that his son, Yusuf, was being brought up by his mother in Ireland. Not that Ireland was perfect, but at least there, as far as he could tell, the state kept out of people's private lives. He really feared for his colleague Kerim Gürsel, who was homosexual. If that new sergeant of his was a plant, he could find himself in a lot of trouble. But was she? Just because she wore a headscarf? Was İkmen right about not being terrified into becoming like 'them'? And what of Çiçek? The new sergeant aside, he knew of several colleagues who would be disgusted if they discovered that he slept with her. But he wasn't going to give her up. He knew that, if he wanted, he could get sex almost anywhere. He'd played the scene and even resorted to nameless fucks in back alleys in the past, but Çiçek was somebody he'd cared about long before they had become lovers.

He kissed her lips, and she stirred and opened her eyes. 'Do you want more?' she asked huskily.

'Do you?' he said.

She smiled. 'What do you think?'

200

Chapter 16

Silivri prison. There had been a moment when it had looked as if Çiçek would end up there. İkmen still felt sick every time he thought about that place, but now he had to think about it. Olimpio, the Designer, had invoked its name the previous evening and it had felt to İkmen as if he had been slapped. But she'd made a good point. If Sevval had undergone further blood tests when she went to prison, why had that been done? Cumhur Polat had been told that the prison blood test was to make sure that his health had not deteriorated since his arrest. It was possible, but not especially plausible. Since when had the health of political detainees been important? İkmen took his phone out of his jacket pocket and was just about to call Arto Sarkissian when he saw someone on the other side of Divan Yolu that he recognised.

What was Ece Kazantzoğlu doing wandering about on her own at such an early hour? And she was crying. He wondered whether he should go over to her in his guise as Halil Bey and ask her what was wrong, but decided against it. She was a pious covered woman; an approach by a strange man could frighten her. But he was intrigued.

He'd woken early that morning, his mind bothered by thoughts about poor dead Sevval Kalkan. But Leah Delmonte and the Kazantzoğlu family hadn't been far from his mind. Ceyda Kazantzoğlu, Leah's old friend, remained an enigma, neither officially dead nor, apparently, evidentially alive. He still had to get down to thinking about where he could go with this matter now.

Ece Kazantzoğlu scuttled off in the direction of the Blue Mosque, and he wondered what her purpose might be. Was she going to pray? Or was she perhaps visiting someone in the area? It was very early to be out visiting, although not, he felt, too early to phone a friend. He called Arto Sarkissian's mobile number.

When the doctor picked up he said, 'Arto, it's Çetin.'

A sort of spluttering noise came down the phone at him, and then the Armenian said, 'It's only six o'clock! What on earth do you want?'

'Is it usual for blood samples to be taken from people entering prison on remand?' İkmen asked. 'When they've already had blood samples taken on arrest?'

He heard the doctor sigh. He was accustomed to calls at strange times of the day or night, but he was clearly shattered. Eventually he said, 'Sometimes.'

'Under what circumstances?'

'I don't know! You're the detective. Maybe to check their state of health if it's been a long time between arrest and admission to prison . . .'

'I'm thinking specifically about Silivri,' İkmen said.

'Ah, well, political inmates, what can I say? Depends what those incarcerating them order. With that group of detainees, anything's possible these days.'

'Where would analysis of blood samples take place?' İkmen asked.

'I don't know. Forensic lab?'

'Can you find out for me?'

The doctor sighed. İkmen imagined him reluctantly rolling out of his enormous ornate bed and peering through his myopia for his slippers.

'Doesn't someone who goes to your church work at the Forensic Institute?'

Arto sighed again. 'Yes.'

'Well . . .'

'I'll ring him. I'll ring him.'

'Will you—'

'Today, yes, Çetin,' the exasperated doctor said. 'I promise on my mother's grave.' He cut the connection.

İkmen had met this man Arto was going to speak to, but he couldn't remember his name. All he could recall was seeing the two men coming out of church one Sunday, and Arto telling him this person worked at the Forensic Institute.

'So, Rize,' Süleyman said. 'Anyone know anyone in the job in Rize? Anyone have any connections to that city at all? And I mean the city, not to be confused with the district.'

He was so tired. He knew his eyes were red and his face was grey, but then he'd got only three hours' sleep.

Kerim Gürsel, who didn't, for whatever reason, look any better himself, said, 'No. Never been there, never even spoken to anyone in the police over there.'

Süleyman leant back in his chair and lit a cigarette. 'I wish I could go in there blind, but . . .'

Kerim cleared his throat and looked sideways at Eylul Yavaş. Süleyman caught the warning. His phone beeped, indicating that he had a text message. He looked at the screen and saw that it was from Commissioner Özer. He sighed, put the phone back in his pocket and took a sip of coffee.

The Vatan Kafe wasn't a regular police haunt, which was why Süleyman had arranged to meet there. But it was close enough to police headquarters to make it only a short drive in to work, and it was open twenty-four hours a day.

'Surely the issue is here in the city, sir,' Ömer Mungun said. 'This is where the problem is. I did some research about organised crime in Tarlabaşı, and it seems this Yaşar Akgün just came out of nowhere three years ago. He was born in Rize, but I've nothing

203

on when he first came to İstanbul, or why. It's like he arrived as a fully formed godfather. Except of course he looks and behaves quite differently. Quiet, physically unimpressive, divorced with one child, drives a taxi. And yet although this is not underwritten by anything except rumour and anecdote, he can rough up or even kill your enemies and avenge your family honour.'

Kerim's phone beeped and he looked down at it.

'From Özer?' Süleyman asked.

'Got to be in his office at eight,' Kerim said.

'Me too,' Süleyman said. 'Wonder what we've done wrong?'

Kerim smiled.

'The brother, İzzet, as far as I know just comes to the city to sell gold to women,' Ömer continued.

'To women from what is mostly a Black Sea community.'

They all turned to look at Eylul Yavaş. Ömer Mungun had scowled when she'd arrived. He didn't trust her and couldn't understand why Süleyman and Gürsel were giving her a chance.

'That's significant?' Süleyman asked.

'Yes, sir. Because they are, as I understand it, a close and closed community,' Eylul said. 'Kasımpaşa men have this repu- tation for being street fighters. I don't have figures for domestic violence in that area, but anecdotally, it is common. And paid employment amongst women there is low, so maybe that service provided by the Akgün family to the community is the seat of this new godfather's power.'

'I know what you mean, Sergeant,' Kerim said. 'But I don't think enough money is at stake here. And where are the men in all this? Kasımpaşa men, as you rightly say, are intensely mascu- line, and yet they seem to have chosen a skinny nonentity as their local godfather. I mean, old Paşa Beyaz, who had the district before this Akgün character, was quite useless in recent years because he was dementing. But back in the day, he could provoke fear.'

'Çetin Bey claims he was once called out to a fight in Kasımpaşa involving Paşa Beyaz using a cobra as a weapon,' Süleyman said. 'Yes, the old man became a joke, but he didn't start out that way, and so to be replaced by an apparent nonentity is strange. But are we looking at this issue in the right way? The connection between Kasımpaşa and the heartless body in the Karacaahmet cemetery only rests on the unlikely appearance of a known junkie at the community centre and the subsequent presentation of a perfectly legitimate prescription for antibiotics by her at a pharmacy in Sultanahmet. We don't know whether the doctor who signed that prescription met her at the community centre, and if he did, so what? What we know for certain is that the Karacaahmet is insecure. We know that people get in and even sleep and light fires there all the time. And I have recently discovered that the gatekeeper, who is aware of this, frightens the guards into not reporting incidents.'

'How?'

'Using dismissal as a threat. Türgüt Akgün is convinced, it is said, that if too many incidents occur, we will take over the protection of the site and they will all lose their jobs. Now he's an ex-lawyer, so he should know this is just not possible.'

'He's not related to Yaşar Akgün, is he, sir?' Eylul asked.

'Not as far as we can see,' Süleyman said. 'He says he has no relatives in Kasımpaşa. Not entirely sure I believe him. But he does come from a Black Sea family. Born in Hasköy, he worked in property law in İstanbul until 2012, when he spent a year with a firm in Gaziantep. When he came back here, he got the job at the cemetery.'

'Strange career progression,' Kerim said.

'Says he wanted to retire but then felt like working, but not within the rigorous discipline of the law. Makes sense,' Süleyman said. 'But he rules by fear and so I want to find out more about him. Why does he do that, and is there any connection, however tenuous, with Yaşar Akgün? These rural clans can be vast, and it is possible there is something. Türgüt is divorced and lives alone

in Kuzuncuk – posh Üsküdar. Don't know whether that is significant or not. In the meantime, I want to contact someone who
might be a credible source of intel in Rize about this family,
specifically Türgüt Akgün and Yaşar's brother İzzet, the goldsmith.'

So much couldn't be said since the attempted coup. Everyone
feared being accused of some sort of connection to it, either real
or imagined. Rize, as the heartland of popular support for the
ruling party, was particularly problematic. In official circles
especially, one never really knew whom one was talking to and
what their connections might be.

Ömer Mungun said, 'I'll go back to my informant who told
us about Deniz Palandoken. It's unlikely she will give up the
names of those to whom she sold her newborn child. If she even
knows them.'

'Unless we bring her in and lean on her . . .'

'Even then,' Ömer said. 'If she can sell her own child, then
she can sell her kidneys, whatever. Junkies are always looking
for the next source of funding for their habit. If she's got money
from these people before, she'll have them on the back burner
as a possible source for the future.'

He was right, but creeping so gingerly around these people
and their possible motives and connections was getting them
nowhere. Then, out of the blue, Eylul Yavaş said, 'We need to
talk to women. Women who go to the gold sales, women who
work in or around the cemetery, this woman who is a user, female
doctors. The one thing that sticks out to me in all of this is the
absence of women. And yet women are the victims in both your
investigation, Inspector Süleyman, and yours, Inspector Gürsel.'

And Süleyman, for one, knew that she was right.

It was well known to most of his clients that Cihan Bey, the
Bulut family's lawyer, always arrived at his office in Beyoğlu
really early in the morning. By his own admission an insomniac,

he liked to get to work early so that he could do any research he needed and stare out of his window at what could be seen from his fifth-floor window of the Golden Horn. But when he got out of the ancient lift that morning, he was surprised to see that someone had beaten him in.

'Uğur Bey?'

He'd been sitting on the floor, but now he stood up.

'I'm sorry to startle you, Cihan Bey,' he said. 'But I need to tell you something.'

He was very pale and looked a little shaky. The old man put a hand on his shoulder. 'Ah, well,' he said. 'I needed to speak to you and your siblings too.'

'I left Eudokia at home, and Lokman—'

'Don't worry, I will arrange everything,' Cihan Bey said as he unlocked his office door and walked inside. 'First let me make you some tea, and then you can tell me all about it.'

But Uğur Bulut couldn't wait. It had taken him all night to decide to come here, and now he was bursting to tell.

'No,' he said. 'No tea. Please listen, Cihan Bey. Please!'

Elderly watery blue eyes observed him with some gravity. Cihan indicated a chair and said, 'Please sit down, Bulut Bey.'

Bulut complied, and the old man sat down opposite. 'Tell me.'

He took a deep breath. 'I didn't tell the police everything when they found that body in Mother's grave,' he said.

'Oh?'

'I know I should have, but . . .' He was sweating now, and rubbed his face with his hand. 'I'm being leaned on to sell the business.'

'By?'

He shook his head. 'I'm not ready to name names, but they're serious people, and what's more, I know my brother knows them.'

'How?'

'Lokman mixes mainly with other spoilt rich kids like himself, but also with criminals. He finds them exciting, edgy; more significantly, they can lend him money when he needs it.'

'You know he's borrowed money from these people?'

'Yes.'

'How?'

'Because he told me. Begged me to pay them back, which I did. Then one of their thugs came around to the pastane and threatened me. His boss, he said, wants to buy the business.'

'Did you tell Lokman?'

'Later, yes. I thought at the time that I'd deal with it somehow, on my own. But then we had all the carry-on with Mother, the exhumation . . . Inspector Süleyman asked me whether anyone had a grudge against the family and I said no, but of course that wasn't strictly true.' He shrugged. 'I don't know what to do. If I tell the police, will they bear down on my brother?'

'If they do, why do you care?'

Bulut sighed. 'I don't know really,' he said. 'I guess because Mother trusted me to look after him when she died. She knew what he was like, which was probably why she left the business to me even though I wasn't her son. And God forgive me, I do care about him.'

Cihan Bey leaned back in his chair and steepled his fingers. Given what he had to tell the family later when they were all together, he didn't want this matter clouding the issue still further. He said, 'You must tell the truth to the police, and Lokman will have to take his chances.'

'He's a little shit . . .'

'But he's your little shit. I do understand,' he said. 'But I have to point out that I doubt your brother would deal so sensitively with you.'

'I know he wouldn't.'

'So tell the police.'

Uğur sat in silence. Eventually he said, 'So what do you want to see us all about later, Cihan Bey?'

'Oh, that can wait if necessary.' The lawyer smiled. 'Just let me know when you are finished with this Inspector Süleyman.'

'I can't claim to be anything other than what I am,' Eylul continued. 'Which is a middle-class, educated woman. I live with my parents in Nişantaşı and I've never had to do so much as wash my own clothes. But I am a woman and I do value my faith above everything else, unlike my family . . .'

Süleyman didn't know anything about Eylul Yavaş; in fact Gürsel, her boss, wasn't much more enlightened. They had all assumed she came from one of those newly well-off pious families who were being deliberately elevated in society. But according to her, that wasn't the case.

'Whoever the woman you found in the Karacaahmet was, she was old and so she was vulnerable. Sevval Kalkan was vulnerable because she was denounced and imprisoned for something it was later concluded she didn't do. Both these women could easily have been preyed upon by organ traffickers.'

The three men looked at each other.

Eylul said, 'I know you are all in many ways rightly suspicious of me because of the way I look, because I was fast-tracked into this job and because you probably think you know the way I cast my vote. In addition, I can't even begin to know what it feels like to be a woman in poverty in this city. But even though none of my forebears came from the Black Sea coast, I think, with respect, I have more of a chance of getting into a useful conversation with the women of Kasımpaşa than any of you do.'

She had a point. Most of the women in Kasımpaşa would never so much as look at a strange man. But they might speak to another woman. Might.

'How would you approach them?' Kerim asked.

'As a police officer,' she said.

Ömer shook his head. 'Eylul Hanım, with respect yet again—'

'I may have an educated accent, but I do speak their language,' she said. 'And that is because I am a pious woman. I know how hard it is for them trying to keep a halal home while at the same time having to put up with male . . . unreasonableness. It's as much or more because of tradition and lack of education rather than actual belief. If vulnerable women are being targeted by organ traffickers in Kasımpaşa, they are going to be members of the pious poor. Elsewhere in the city, in Tarlabaşı, say, they will be sex workers. But it is to the poor and pious women that we are being directed. I can tell you now, they will never speak to you, because you're men. Even if their husbands let them, which they wouldn't, the women wouldn't speak freely.'

'I've said before, Eylul Hanım,' Süleyman said, 'that the connections we have are tenuous.'

'I need to get back to my informant and see if I can squeeze any more intel out of him about the Palandokens,' Ömer said.

'And I must somehow tell Sevval Kalkan's dementing mother that her daughter has died,' Kerim said. 'Then I thought I'd try looking at her death from the point of view of who she might have donated her bone marrow to. In the normal course of events, people needing a graft are put on waiting lists until a suitable donor becomes available. Maybe someone had recently dropped off such a list . . .'

Süleyman, who had been looking at Eylul and frowning, said, 'I will take a chance and call Rize. The worst that can happen is that they lie to me about this Akgün family. Whatever happens, we need to be aware of rising mob activity in the city, and this, though unusual and quiet, is just such an example. Oh, and I'm for Sergeant Yavaş's idea, because she is quite right. Both our victims so far are female, and women, unlike men, do tell each other things.' He smiled at her. 'Even I know that.'

* * *

210

He'd arrived at Gold Bey's apartment at a time when he hoped the jeweller would be up and about, but İkmen was nothing if not a realist. Chances were that Cumhur Polat had fallen into his bed exhausted after learning of Sevval Kalkan's death. The front door to his building was open, and İkmen, stepping carefully over a pyramid of cats and kittens on the steps outside, went in and began to descend the gloomy staircase down to Gold's basement apartment. Halfway down, he stopped. He could see that Gold's door was open, and there were raised voices coming from the apartment.

Being careful to make as little noise as possible, he walked down the remaining stairs and then put his head around the open door. Gold and whoever he was talking to were in the workroom, the door to which was also open.

He heard Gold say, 'A friend of mine has just died. Show some respect. I'll finish your piece when I can. Anyway, why are you here? I didn't say I'd have what you wanted ready today.'

Another voice, which was cultured, young and male, said, 'That's immaterial. My friend here wants the watch you agreed to make for him. He's the customer and so he's always right.'

Someone laughed, and İkmen heard the sound of footsteps. He retreated to the darkness underneath the stairs.

A second young male voice said, 'Do you have any idea who my friend here is, Cumhur Bey?'

There was a pause, then Gold said, 'No, but I'm sure you're about to tell me.'

'My friend's father is Professor Aşık Tolon,' the second voice said.

Again there was a pause. 'Who?'

İkmen knew who Aşık Tolon was: a historian, an academic whose particular obsession was the reinstatement of the Ottoman Empire. For years he'd been regarded as a bit of joke. However, in recent times his views had taken on a fresh relevance as many conservative Turks began to wonder whether the republic had

211

been some sort of aberration and what the nation needed was a return to empire. Tolon and his ideas were very popular with those in power, and his books as well as his heavily publicised lectures had made him a media sensation. And even more wealthy than he had already been. He'd been a bit quiet recently on the TV and radio, but still, İkmen couldn't believe Gold had never heard of him.

'Where have you been living? Mars?' the first voice said. Then he laughed. 'Nice try to cut me down to size, but everyone knows who my father is and who he is very good friends with.'

No one said a word. Then İkmen heard Gold sigh. 'So what do you want?' he said.

'My watch,' the second voice replied.

'It's not ready.'

'So get it ready.'

The first voice said, 'We know who you are, and you have absolutely no chance of complaining about this to anyone who will listen. Well, anyone with power to help you.'

'We haven't agreed a price . . .'

'A price?' the second voice said. 'That will be what I think it is worth. So get on with it.'

The two visitors left. When he was certain they had exited the building, İkmen came out of hiding and found Cumhur Polat sitting in his living room with his chin in his hands.

'I heard what those men said to you.'

Cumhur shrugged. 'What can I do? The one with the hair bun is that moron Aşık Tolon's son. He knows he can make something up about me if I don't do what he and his friend want, and people will believe him.'

'Who is his friend?' İkmen asked.

'I don't know.'

'But these are the same men who came to see you before?'

'Yes.'

212

'Well, I think I might know where one of them lives,' İkmen said.

'So what?'

İkmen sat down.

'They come here, out of their minds on drugs, and no one cares,' Cumhur said. 'You heard who that boy's father is! Aşık Tolon can do no wrong.'

'Everyone can do wrong,' İkmen said. 'That's what has always puzzled me about why people want to be in with power. Eventually power becomes bored with you, and Professor Tolon may well have already fallen foul of that.'

'How do you know?'

'When did you last see him on TV, or hear his voice cracking tearfully on the radio as he describes how kind, gentle and clever the Ottoman Empire was?'

'I don't watch TV very much . . .'

'Trust me, his star has fallen,' İkmen said. 'And anyway, what happened here was extortion.'

'But not by the Tolon boy.'

'No, by his friend. Do you know his name or anything about him?'

Cumhur thought for a moment. 'I think he's got something to do with cake. Don't know what. Last time they came, they talked about some inheritance he is due to get involving cake. Maybe it was just a joke.'

Commissioner Selahattın Özer had retired once, but he'd come back to the national police force in İstanbul in order to oversee some restructuring of the department when his predecessor had been dismissed. Tall and slim, with a disturbing line in steely gazes from his cold light grey eyes, he wore a small, neat almond-shaped moustache with way more aplomb than he wore his cheap, wrinkled suit.

'I have been told that someone who is no longer a serving officer was in this building yesterday,' he said to Süleyman and Gürsel. 'Talking to both of you about police matters.'

'If you mean Inspector İkmen—'

'Ex . . .'

'Ex-Inspector İkmen, then yes,' Süleyman continued. 'He is acquainted with a friend of Inspector Gürsel's bone marrow donor victim, Sevval Kalkan.'

'A woman who came under suspicion for activities likely to endanger the integrity of this country.'

'Charges were dropped,' Gürsel said.

'Indeed.' Özer looked down at the paperwork on his desk. 'But as I understand it, an infection developed whilst voluntarily selling or donating bone marrow is hardly a matter for the police.'

Kerim Gürsel cleared his throat. Both he and Süleyman had wondered if Özer might look at the issue in this way. 'With respect, sir, the identity of the victim is immaterial.'

'I didn't say that it wasn't.'

And yet it was Özer who had brought up Sevval Kalkan's past.

'The issue,' Kerim continued, 'and this is backed up by the doctors I have spoken to, is one of negligence. A surgical procedure has been performed on this woman, we think outside of a hospital environment, and inadequate after-care has been provided, which has resulted in her death.'

'In addition,' Süleyman said, 'in light of my own investigation, it would seem that a trade in bodily organs and products is going on in the city.'

'We know that happens.'

'But it's not often we come by evidence of it, sir,' Süleyman said.

Özer just looked at him.

Slightly unnerved, Süleyman nevertheless continued. 'This could lead us to uncovering a network with a link to organised crime. In the south-east, where we know this happens more frequently than it does here, such trade is controlled by local godfathers.'

'That's not our concern,' Özer said. 'Besides, down there, people are desperate. Many of the victims are refugees who come across the border with nothing.'

Süleyman wanted to say that poverty was also the driver for organ trafficking in İstanbul, but he didn't. Özer was, he knew of old, one of those people who believed that 'the poor' were somehow complicit in their poverty.

'If this woman sold her own bone marrow and then developed an infection, it is unfortunate but not necessarily criminal.'

'Sir, with respect—'

'If these people want to make money, they should get jobs.'

'I agree.' Kerim's face was red now, and Süleyman feared what he might say next. 'But the fact remains that whatever the motive of the victim, doctors who have either been dismissed for misconduct or who are greedy and self-serving are operating on people in an unsafe environment. The doctor who tried to save Miss Kalkan's life begged me to put a stop to this. It makes more work for dedicated, honest doctors and it takes people's lives.'

Süleyman wondered whether, in support of his colleague, he should make the point about organised crime links again, but he decided against it. Özer wasn't really interested in organised crime. Rooting it out was labour-intensive and didn't have the immediate effect on clear-up figures that he liked. Or so it was said. Other things were also said about Özer and organised crime, but only by those officers who opposed the prevailing ruling elite, of which the commissioner was a member. Süleyman viewed Özer's apparent piety as genuine even if he was certain that at least some of those around him were far from what they seemed. Eventually he said, 'Sir, Inspector Gürsel and I have been collaborating on our investigations, and the intelligence that has resulted from this, as well as ex-Inspector İkmen's

215

intervention, is beginning to turn up leads not just to these crimes but potentially to others.'

'In what way? Give me an example.'

'We think that a new crime syndicate has formed in Kasımpaşa.' The commissioner looked up and frowned.

'Nascent as yet, but we're hearing rumours of what may be a significant threat to local people.'

'Rumours from local people?'

'No. But from reliable sources we have used before.'

For a while, Özer said nothing, thinking through what had been said. Then he leaned back in his chair and fixed his cold eyes on his two officers.

'I don't want İkmen in here or involved in any way,' he said. 'But I take your point about one lead resulting in another.'

What else could he have said? Süleyman wondered. Not very much without appearing to cut off an investigation for no good reason. And the fact remained that although many people believed Özer was in the pockets of the powerful, nobody actually knew that for sure.

'But I want an update every day, from both of you,' Özer said. 'And I want the operation at the Karacaahmet scaled down. There is no need for us to have so many officers out there.'

Once they were dismissed, the two men stood in the corridor, sweating. Whatever Özer might be, his very presence had a visceral effect on almost all of those who worked for him. Leaving his office, many felt as if they had somehow escaped from something dangerous or supernatural, or both.

People with drink problems were, in a weird way, close to Çetin İkmen's heart. Looking back on his forties, he now realised that he'd been a functioning alcoholic for most of that time. He still liked a drink, but not nearly as much as the man he found lying on the roof of the house in Cuckuk Sokak to which he'd followed the man-bun-wearing individual the previous day. The front door had been open, and so İkmen had walked inside and up the stairs until he could go no further. He'd seen no one until, on the roof, underneath a long line of washing, he had discovered the man.

Fearing he might choke on his own vomit, İkmen sat him up and then pulled him into a nearby plastic chair.

'You don't have to worry about me. I'm fine,' the man said as İkmen sat down beside him. He offered him his hand. 'Vedat.'

İkmen, smiling through the deluge of rakı fumes from Vedat's toothless mouth, took his hand and said, 'Çetin.'

There was a long pause, during which Vedat belched continually and İkmen appreciated what a marvellous view this rooftop afforded of the Golden Horn, which was shimmering with heat from the morning sun.

Eventually İkmen said, 'Do you live in this house, Vedat Bey?'

'This house? Yes,' he said. 'Twenty years.'

'That's a long time. You must like it here.'

'No.'

İkmen turned to look at him. It was impossible to tell how old he was, but his hair, such as it was, was grey. His face was heavily lined and very pale. Obviously he'd passed through the red-faced alcoholic state and into the more terminal yellow-grey phase.

'No? Why not?'

'New landlord,' he said. 'Stupid bastard party man. Can't drink, can't smoke, can't meet women. We all do, but . . .'

Tarlabaşı wasn't the sort of place that generally attracted pious ruling party voters – unless it was to buy up vacant land. But this was an occupied house that was probably full of people just like Vedat Bey. And yet the landlord, whatever his faults, had made the front of the building look almost beautiful.

'Who is your landlord?' İkmen asked.

'Well, the boy's officially the landlord, but it's his father, that shit off the television, who owns the place.'

'What boy?'

'Serkan "Bey",' he said sarcastically. 'Lives on the second floor. Ties his hair in a bun like a girl and yet there's his father having a go at trans girls and drag queens. This is Tarlabaşı, for fuck's sake! This is who we are!'

'What's this Serkan Bey like?' İkmen asked.

Vedat removed a small bottle of rakı from his coat pocket and took a swig before he replied.

'Young. Hipster,' he said. 'Weird clothes, weird facial hair. You know. Long as we pay our rent, I don't think he gives a shit what we do. He certainly doesn't give a shit what he does.'

'What do you mean?'

'He has women in his apartment all the time. Some friend of his comes round and they smoke so much cannabis you can smell it down in the street. They don't work, people like him. If I were his father, I'd kick his arse. But then with that type the rules don't apply, do they? They tell us what to do, but they do as they like.'

'What about his father?' İkmen asked.

'He's on the TV, I told you! He's that nutcase who talks about the Ottoman Empire. Completely ignores the republic, Atatürk . . . Anyone who's anyone loves him. I think he's an arsehole.'

So this Serkan was Professor Aşık Tolon's son, and Tolon owned the house. But he had to check . . .

'Do you know Serkan Bey's surname?' he asked.

'Oh yes,' Vedat said. 'Tolon.'

Ah. İkmen's phone began to ring.

218

Chapter 17

'I've never spoken to Yaşar Akgün,' Uğur Bulut told Süleyman. 'But I've seen him. When my brother told me he'd borrowed money from some hard man in Kasımpaşa, I went there to pay him off.'

'What happened?'

'I went to this community centre where Lokman had told me Akgün has an office. However, when I asked to see him, I was only allowed to do exactly that.'

'Look at him?'

'Yes,' he said. 'He sat at the back of the room behind two men who actually did the talking. Creatures encased in muscle. Akgün himself looks like some sort of geek. Skinny and hunched over. At first I thought he was maybe disabled or something, but then he fixed me with his eyes and I felt as if I was being looked at by the Devil. I'm not a fanciful man, but there was a genuine feeling of evil in that room.'

'What happened?'

'I told them I was Lokman's brother and that I'd come to pay off his debt. None of them said a word for what felt like hours, then one of the henchmen turned and whispered something to Akgün, who whispered something back, and the henchman said, "It's not good enough." I was floored. I said, "What do you mean?" and they told me how Lokman had been messing them around for months over this debt and that they were going to have to charge me for their trouble.'

Süleyman was not exactly excited, but he had been hopeful of a breakthrough when Uğur Bulut had asked to speak to him. Now here, apparently, was a connection between his family and the mysterious Yaşar Akgün.

'What did you say?'

'I said that was ridiculous. I put the suitcase full of the money Lokman owed them, half a million lira, on the table in front of me and told them to take it or leave it. I now know that was terribly naïve, but this bunch looked like a low-rent cast of a Godfather film. I underestimated them.'

'When was this?' Süleyman asked.

Uğur thought for a moment. 'Approximately three months ago.'

'Did they take the money?'

'Of course,' he said. 'They took the money, told me I'd be hearing from them and then dismissed me. I thought, in my stupidity, I'd got away with it.'

'What happened next?'

'They began to appear at my pastane. Sometimes one or two of the henchmen, sometimes Akgün and the whole lot of them, sometimes all the heavies without Akgün. For weeks they came in, ordered tea and plate after plate of baklava, took over a table for hours on end and then left without paying. At first my staff tried to make them, but things got ugly, and from then on I just let them do whatever they wanted. Then suddenly they stopped coming, and again I thought I'd got one over on them.'

'You hadn't?'

'They started to come again, asking to see me in my office, and that was when the threats began. Sell my business to Akgün at a price that would make strong men cry or they'd torch the place, kill me, shoot my customers . . . I knew that was what thugs like them did, and so to be honest much of that stuff didn't really bother me. We've had protection scams come our way many times and we've always managed to deal with them. I shouldn't tell you this, but we're Kurds; we know people.'

Süleyman said nothing. Some Kurdish gangs were known to protect their own as a matter of honour.

'What did make my blood run cold,' Uğur continued, 'was when all talk of physical threats ended and they began saying they would denounce me to the authorities as an enemy of the state. I think that was where their narrative had been heading the whole time, if I'm honest.'

'What did you do?'

'I told them to go fuck themselves.' He shook his head. 'My mother had worked too hard for what we had for it to just be given to scum like them. For weeks I expected to see the police converging on my house. But no one came and I began to wonder whether the threat had been an empty one. Then Mother was exhumed . . .'

'Why didn't you tell us?' Süleyman asked.

Uğur shrugged. 'Mother was a shock. I thought that was probably them, and so I confronted them. They denied it, citing all sorts of religious stuff about not disturbing dead bodies. They came across as highly offended. I didn't believe them.'

'Do you now?'

'I don't know. There has been no further contact with them since. I know nothing about Kasımpaşa except the old myth about them being tough down there. But the more I thought about what had happened, the more I began to think that perhaps I was right about them in the first place. Maybe they were just . . . nothing. And I spoke to people who know the area who told me that since the previous gang boss's death some years ago, the district had been in a power vacuum. Then this ineffectual man-boy . . .'

'You didn't consider coming to us?'

'What with? My brother owed them the money I gave them.'

'For harassment?'

He shook his head. 'I'm sorry now that I didn't tell you, of course. But after Mother's exhumation, I didn't want the situation to get worse. I thought if you went to see them, it would. Also . . .'

He looked up at Süleyman, who could see what he wanted to say in his eyes.

Also, he was a proud Kurd who should be able to look after his own.

Leah Delmonte ran along the balcony towards the Kazantzoğlus' apartment, struggling to keep upright on her high-heeled shoes. She was following Çetin İkmen, who had declined her idea about speaking to the landlady, Fatima Hanım, first.

Quite why all the windows and the front door were open now that the family had departed wasn't something the burqa-wearing landlady had been prepared to discuss with Leah earlier, when she'd gone and asked her about what was going on.

'They gave notice last week,' was all Fatima Hanım had said.

'To go where?'

'I don't know!' Then she'd shut her door in Leah's face.

Panicked, Leah had phoned İkmen, who had decided he wanted to see the Kazantzoğlus' apartment while he could.

'Çetin Bey!' she puffed as she ran after him. But by the time she caught up with him, he was already inside, heading towards the living room at the end of the little hallway where Ceyda Hanım used to have her landline on a table with a magazine rack underneath. It was strange to see the Kazantzoğlus' apartment almost empty, stripped of all their personal effects. In the past it had always looked so small and full, what with all the equipment they had for Devlet so they could take him out, toilet him and put him under the shower. Leah had always wondered at how cheerful her old friend had been in the face of this misfortune.

Çetin was standing by the window, looking down into the street below. When Leah walked into the room, he turned. 'Did they have any friends here?' he asked. 'Anyone they might have told where they were going?'

'No,' she said. 'With the exception of Ceyda Hanım, who always talked to everyone, they kept themselves to themselves. But even Ceyda was only actually friends with me.'

'Mmm.' He looked around the room. 'It must be strange for you being here,' he said.

'It is.'

He went over to a fitted cupboard, opened it and then, finding it empty, closed it again.

'It's the same size as my place,' Leah said, 'Two bedrooms, small bathroom and kitchen.'

He walked into the room adjacent to the one they were in, which was entirely empty except for a stained double bed. Some ragged net curtains hung at the window and the carpet on the floor was full of holes.

He was about to leave when he looked up at the ceiling. Heavily nicotine stained, with some bald patches where the ceiling paper had come away, there was a slight bulge right in the middle.

'I will be honest with you, Uğur Bey, we have become rather interested in Yaşar Akgün of late,' Süleyman said.

'In what context?'

'That I can't tell you. But it would be most useful to me if I had reason to legitimately bring this man in for questioning.'

Uğur Bulut frowned. 'You want me to report them? Now?'

'I do,' Süleyman said.

Uğur sighed. 'Would it put me in danger? I've got my sister staying with me.'

'It could. I can provide you with some protection, but of

course I cannot absolutely guarantee your safety. If I did, I would be lying.'

Uğur sighed again. Trying to run the business around this anxiety as well as his family issues meant he was hardly sleeping, and he was shattered. Also, the police had a patchy record on dealing with organised crime. He was grateful that this Süleyman seemed to be at least attempting to be honest with him, but it was still a big decision to make. He'd have to speak to Eudokia. But then he knew what she'd say, which was that he should let the police do their job.

'Mr Bulut?'

'If we don't try, we'll never know, will we?' he said. 'All right I will make a formal report. God help me.'

Fatima Hanım had provided a ladder. As she stood beside it, watching İkmen remove the hatch and climb arthritically, and not in silence, into the loft, she said to Leah, 'He looks ever so old to be a policeman.'

Leah didn't answer. She'd had to tell her landlady that İkmen was still a serving officer so that she wouldn't lose her temper and start making accusations about trespassing.

'He's quite fit,' she lied as they both heard İkmen swear because his knees were buckling.

'Are you all right up there, Çetin Bey?' she called out.

For a while, he just grunted. Then, breathless, he said, 'Pass me the torch, someone.'

Fatima Hanım gave Leah her torch, which she passed up through the hatch. Both women heard İkmen turn it on.

Fatima Hanım said, 'Only walk on the wooden struts; don't put your feet on the ceiling. It's only plasterboard, and the last thing I need is a policeman falling through into an apartment I need to rent as soon as possible.'

People who knew her said that Fatima Oz had always covered,

even as a young girl. It had caused her family some embarrassment at the time because her father had been a civil servant in
the old secular Kemalist administration. But she'd persisted, even
back in the 1970s, when covering had been frowned upon. She'd
never married but she had always been good with money, which
was why she'd been able to buy this block when her parents died.

'I will be careful,' İkmen said. Then he made some more
grunting noises and swore yet again.

'Less of the cursing!' Fatima Hanım called up through the
hatch.

İkmen didn't reply. But Leah said, 'It's horrible up there. Old
Avram Bey who used to live in number twelve once found a
wasps' nest.'

'What was he doing up there?' Fatima Hanım asked.

'I've no idea.'

'No one should go up there,' the landlady said. 'Unless it's
the police. I've never been up there. I wouldn't want to. Your
old friend Lilli Hanım used to say she heard ghosts.'

'What? From the attic? We live downstairs,' Leah said.

Fatima Hanım shrugged. 'I just say what I've been told,' she
said. 'Only God knows the truth.'

They both looked up again. Every time İkmen moved, or so
it seemed, the ceiling shook.

'Be careful!'

'I am!'

'Do you need help?' Leah asked.

'No I do not! If anyone else comes up here, the whole fucking
ceiling will cave in! You do know that a considerable number
of these wooden beams are rotten, don't you, Fatima Hanım?'

She shook her burqa-covered head and muttered, 'You're
wrong, but . . .'

A great groan from above told the women that İkmen was on
the move again.

Fatima Hanım said, 'Oh, how long . . .'

'Police,' Leah said, by way of explanation. 'As long as it takes, Hanım.'

Leah wiped sweat from her forehead. Another blistering day. How, she wondered, did women like Fatima Hanım manage to function muffled up in what looked like kilometres of black in weather like this? And she wore thick tan-coloured tights. Leah could see them, wrinkled around her swollen ankles.

A brief shower of dust, or plaster, came down through the hatch and Fatima Hanım yelled, 'Hey! Don't damage my building!'

İkmen didn't reply, but they heard him move again. Then, so Leah thought, came a loud intake of breath.

She said nothing for a moment, but when he still didn't say anything, she called up, 'Çetin Bey?'

There was another long pause, and then he said, 'Call the police, Leah Hanım. Now.'

As she climbed slowly and breathlessly up the hill towards İstiklal Caddesi, Deniz kept looking over her shoulder. She was paranoid because she was coming down. Whether someone was really following her, she didn't know, but she was afraid.

She didn't have any money. Nothing! She had no gear, no money and Can wouldn't wake up. It was his own fault for not taking the antibiotics she'd got from Dr Fixit. The doctor probably wouldn't be at the community centre, as he had a proper practice to run somewhere, but she needed help and didn't know where else to go. She also needed money, or he'd do nothing. She'd have to rob someone.

İstiklal would be packed with people at this time of day. Either walking on the street, window-shopping, or sitting outside cafés eating and drinking with their bags down on the ground or on chairs while they chatted to friends. She'd been one of those people once. Moneyed and secure, not even noticing the street

226

people swarming around her. But if she was being watched, it was a risky strategy; even if she wasn't being watched, it was dangerous. The fact remained, however, that she couldn't see Dr Fixit if she didn't have any cash. And she still hated him. She hated them all, because they'd taken Didem away from her. Although she knew deep down inside that wasn't true.

She watched the young people going in and out of the music shops on Galip Dede Caddesi, the tourists going into the Mevlevi Dervish lodge on the corner with İstiklal, and tried not to think about her old life, when she'd done normal things like that. Getting more antibiotics for Can probably wouldn't cut it; she'd have to ask Dr Fixit to get him into a hospital, which would cost more than she'd get from a straightforward handbag snatch. But it would be a start. She'd have to back it up with promises, like she'd done the last time. Maybe she'd say she was pregnant again. But he'd know; he was a doctor. Then again, there were other things she could sell . . .

Lokman and Eudokia had got there before him, but they weren't speaking. As he ran into Cihan Bey's waiting room, Uğur Bulut kissed his sister and then sat down. His brother, dressed like a teenager – which irritated Uğur – didn't so much as look at him.

'Do you know what this is about?' he asked Eudokia.

'No,' she said. 'Where did you go this morning?'

The lawyer came out of his office and smiled at the family. 'If you'd like to come in . . .' he said.

'I'll tell you later,' Uğur told Eudokia.

When they entered Cihan Teke's office, they found an elderly bearded peasant man already there. Uğur frowned. 'Who's—'

'I will explain everything,' Cihan Bey said as he sat down behind his desk.

The old man, who wore a collarless shirt underneath a woollen waistcoat and şalvar trousers, cracked his knuckles. It

227

was something Uğur remembered his elderly relatives doing years ago, back in their village. It always made him think of poverty and ignorance.

They all sat down in the chairs the lawyer had arranged for them around his desk. Cihan Bey smiled.

'As you may recall, I informed you that in relation to your late mother's will, there was another beneficiary you were not allowed to be informed about.'

'You didn't tell me,' Lokman said.

'With respect, Lokman Bey, you were not here,' Cihan said. 'At the time you were, as I understand it, pursuing alternative legal advice.'

Lokman shrugged. But Uğur noticed he was smirking, too. His sister, seeing his agitation, took his hand.

'But to continue,' the lawyer said. 'I took the initiative, on your behalf, to ask said beneficiary if he would be prepared to waive the anonymity Perihan Hanım had afforded him. He said that he would, and further, that he would be willing to meet with you.'

They all looked at the old man, whose face reddened.

'I will keep you waiting no longer,' Cihan Bey said. 'This gentleman is Ara Bulut.'

The three siblings looked from one to the other. Eventually Uğur addressed the old man. 'I thought you were dead.'

When Ara Bulut spoke, his voice was gruff, but much softer than Uğur remembered. 'I was in a way,' he said.

'You got your hands on Mother's money,' Lokman put in.

The old man shrugged. 'She left me some,' he said. 'I never asked. She was a good woman, your mother.' He addressed Eudokia, 'You the little girl she adopted?'

'Yes.'

'She leave you any money?'

'At her own request, Sister Eudokia excluded herself from

228

Perihan Hanım's will,' Cihan Bey said. 'As you can see, Ara Bey, she is a nun and lives in a convent.'

'I have no need for money.'

The old man shook his head. 'Perihan could smell an outsider needing care wherever she went,' he said. 'I imagine she gave you a good life, young lady.'

'She did.'

'She was way too good for me,' he said. 'I was a drunk, I was useless. When Perihan threw me out, it was the best day's work she ever did.'

'So why are you here now?' Lokman asked, 'After all these years. I don't even remember you.'

'I'm here,' he said, 'because Cihan Bey has told me that you need my help. And I owe you, all of you.'

'Where have you been?' Uğur asked. 'What have you done?'

Cihan raised a hand to interject. 'If I may, Uğur Bey, we are here for a set purpose. You may discuss other matters with your father once we have finished. But for now . . .' He looked at Ara Bulut.

The old man fixed the siblings with his eyes. 'Cihan Bey has told me what has been going on. I am truly sorry for what has happened to your mother. I am also truly sorry that it has thrown up the issue of your birth mother, Uğur. You were never meant to know this. Your mother, Perihan and I all agreed.'

'My mother?'

'Your aunt, Filiz,' he said.

'What, the one who was the old maid?' Lokman asked.

'She wasn't always like that. Perihan was very distant at the time, and Filiz, well . . .'

'Were you drunk?' Uğur asked.

'What? When . . . Probably,' he said. 'But I'd be lying if I told you it was just a drunken fumble. I cared for Filiz and she cared for me. We thought at the time that maybe Perihan couldn't have children.'

229

'Which is your excuse for adultery?'

'No!'

Uğur shook his head. 'You lied to us,' he said. 'You, Mother, Filiz . . .'

'Filiz is your mother,' Lokman said.

Anger that had been waiting to express itself burst out. 'Oh shut the fuck up, Lokman, you spoilt little shit!' Uğur said. 'You've nearly driven me mad with your demands, all the trouble you've got yourself into over money since Mother died!' He pointed at his brother. 'This idiot has got himself involved with gangsters. Borrowing money from the mob. Money I've had to pay out for him in order to save his useless life!'

'Which is why I have revealed myself to you now,' Ara Bulut said. 'Cihan Bey tells me you are to contest your mother's will, Lokman, and I feel this is a mistake.'

Lokman's face flooded with blood. 'You've got nothing to do with this, old man! Nothing!'

'Except that he's father to you and to Uğur,' Eudokia said. 'Listen to him, for God's sake.'

'Inasmuch as it means anything, I will support Uğur's right to continue running your mother's business,' Ara Bey said. 'Not because I want anything from any of you in return, not because I suddenly want to be back in your lives once again. I left you all years ago, but now that Perihan is dead, I want my sons to do what is right.'

'I don't know who it is,' İkmen said to Kerim Gürsel when he met him in front of the Kazantzoğlus' apartment. 'But it is definitely a human form. It's heavy and it's wrapped in black plastic bags.'

'Does it smell?' Kerim asked.

İkmen raised his eyebrows. 'Not now, but when the bags come off, I imagine it will reek. If it is the body of Ceyda Kazantzoğlu, then it could have been up there for a month.'

230

'Oh.'

He'd found the body lying on a board between the beams. It hadn't actually had anything to do with the bulge in the bedroom ceiling; that had been merely incidental.

'The landlady is downstairs with Leah Hanım having a glass of tea and a nervous collapse,' İkmen continued. 'Both women will answer any questions you have, but I thought it was important to get them out of the way before the doctor and the forensic team arrive.'

'Absolutely.' Kerim shook his head. 'Dr Sarkissian is less than fifteen minutes away, or so he reckons. The traffic is as abominable as ever.' He paused. 'Thank you, Çetin Bey, as always. However . . .'

'You've had heat from Özer over my appearance, I know.'

'Did Mehmet Bey tell you?'

'No, but I can see it from the expression on your face,' Çetin said. 'I don't want to make trouble for you, and so I will go.'

Kerim laid a hand on his shoulder. 'I've put out an alert for the Kazantzoğlu family,' he said. 'I have this under control.'

İkmen smiled. 'Tell the doctor to be careful up in the attic,' he said. 'Those supporting beams are rotten.'

'He's not here.'

Deniz could have cried.

'He doesn't live here, you know,' the man said. 'He does have his own practice.'

'Where?'

'I don't know.'

'So how do I find out?'

But he just walked away, leaving her slumped on the floor, the Dolce & Gabbana handbag by her side. Everything had gone to plan until she'd arrived at the community centre. She'd grabbed the bag from underneath a table in Tünel Pasaj and no one had

231

even noticed. It had been a good haul. The owner must have just been to the ATM, because she'd found two hundred lira in the purse and she could still sell on the bag and the credit cards. Normally she'd be delighted. But not now. Can was sicker than ever, and yet there was no sign of Dr Fixit.

Another man, a thin, weird-looking character, came out of the room they called their office and stared at her. She'd seen him before, but unlike the previous man, she'd never had any dealings with him. He walked over to her and Deniz pulled the handbag close to her body. The people in the community centre had done her many favours, but they had come at a high price. These were men who, like her, lived beyond the limits of the everyday.

When she couldn't stand his staring any longer, she said, 'What are you looking at?'

'You.'

'Why?'

'You're on the floor,' he said.

She shrugged. 'I've had enough,' she said.

'Enough of what?'

'Everything.'

He sat down beside her. 'What's wrong?'

Should she tell him? There didn't seem to be any harm in him, and besides, how could telling him her problems make them any worse?

'I'm looking for Dr Fixit,' she said.

'Oh, he's not here today,' he said. 'Tomorrow.'

'I need to see him today. Do you know where he has his surgery?'

He looked at her blankly for a moment, and then said, 'Kartal.'

Deniz felt her mood begin to pick up. She took hold of his thin shoulders. 'Where?'

'He's at number 85, Kordonboyu Mahalle, Ankara Caddesi, Kartal. And his name is Dr Özdemir. You can call him Alp if you are a friend. I do.'

232

Deniz stared at him. The man smiled.

'I know you,' he said. 'You had a baby.'

'Yes . . .' She began to feel her eyes sting with tears.

He nodded. 'A pretty one,' he said.

She turned away. She heard him stand up. 85 Kordonboyu Mahalle, Ankara Caddesi – could she remember that?

Then she heard him say, 'I can take you there, to Dr Alp, if you'd like.'

'Yaşar Akgün?'

Süleyman had known that the old man who had come to Akgün's front door wasn't the godfather himself.

'Is he in?' he continued.

'No.' The man peered at Süleyman's police ID. 'What do you lot want with him?'

'None of your concern,' Süleyman said.

'You're not coming in . . .'

'Really?' He pushed past the old man and entered a hallway rich in faux-baroque decor. Knowing that their superior didn't have a warrant to search, the squad of uniformed police officers behind him initially held back.

'Come on!' Süleyman said. 'Don't disturb anything, but look in every room.'

'You can't—'

'I can and I will,' Süleyman told the old man as his officers streamed into the wooden house. Once the abode of the gangster Paşa Beyaz, the place didn't look as if it had changed in fifty years. Süleyman noticed there were even gas lamps on the walls.

'Look for Akgün,' he called out to his men. 'You know what he looks like.'

'He's not here!' the old man reiterated.

Süleyman turned and looked at him. 'Who are you?' he said.

'Me? I'm . . . I do stuff.'

'For Mr Akgün?'

'Yes.'

'What's your name?'

'Why?'

'Just answer the question.'

'Abdülkadır Soyar.'

One by one, Süleyman's officers returned.

'No one here, sir.'

Süleyman looked at Soyar. 'Any idea where Mr Akgün might be?' he asked.

'Driving,' the old man said. 'He's a taxi driver.'

'So I hear.'

Soyar looked away.

Süleyman gave the old man his card. 'Well, if you see him before I do, ask him to give me a call,' he said.

'Is he under arrest?'

'No. Should he be?'

'No!'

'I need to speak to him,' Süleyman said. 'That's all. And the sooner he contacts me, the better. Tell him.'

Arto Sarkissian couldn't decide which was worse: being in a hot, cramped attic that by the look of it could collapse at any moment; or the smell of the degraded corpse he had just released from its black bin bag shroud.

As he cut through the plastic and felt liquid from the body on his surgical gloves, he was aware of his stomach turning. Two forensic officers assisted him, one holding a powerful torch trained down on the body, the other holding the doctor's voice recorder. As he opened the bags to reveal the body, he heard the one holding the torch gag.

Holding on to his own lunch wasn't easy, and the doctor was aware that if one of them threw up, they probably all would. The only way to get through this was to be as businesslike as possible. He looked at his watch and spoke the time into the recorder. Pulling the plastic to one side, he commenced his examination.

'Body is severely degraded and beginning to liquefy,' he began. 'The face has started to blacken but appears to be that of an elderly woman. Also clothing suggestive of a female – light-coloured cardigan, floral şalvar trousers . . . Can you please bring the torch a little closer.'

The officer holding the torch moved it slightly forward.

'More than that!' the doctor said, grabbing the man's hand and manoeuvring the torch into position.

Kerim Gürsel called from below, 'Doctor? Can I come up?'

'You can, although it's hell up here and these beams don't look too healthy.'

Gürsel was with him in seconds, and although the doctor knew the inspector was younger and fitter than he was, it still amazed him.

'The smell is . . .'

'Ah, yes,' Arto said. 'It is bad, but believe me, it was much worse when I first opened the plastic covering.'

'God!'

'It's all right, you'll get used to it.'

'Doctor's not wrong,' the officer with the voice recorder said. 'I hardly notice it now.'

Kerim, for whom displays of Turkish toughness were anathema, said, 'So. What do we have here?'

'Elderly woman by the look of it,' the doctor said. 'I think she's been dead for some weeks, although placing anything or anyone in plastic always accelerates the process.' He looked down at the body again. 'No wedding ring . . .'

'The woman who went missing from this apartment was called Ceyda Kazantzoğlu, aged seventy-five,' Kerim said.

'Possible.' The doctor nodded.

235

'Very well, I'll leave you to it. I've put out an alert for the Kazantzoğlu family, but I ought to go and speak to the landlady and the neighbour. Any idea about cause of death?'

'None so far. I'll have to get her to the lab to find that out, I suspect,' Arto said. 'She's lying on a plank of wood, which is basically holding her together. The body is very wet, so I'm wary of decanting it into a body bag without that support. It will be no easy task.'

Kerim was halfway through the hatch when he said, 'Do you want more help?'

'I think it might be wise.'

'I'll organise it.'

When Kerim Gürsel had gone, Arto Sarkissian wiped the sweat from his brow and asked once again for the torch to be brought closer to the body.

Chapter 18

The young man didn't look like Professor Aşık Tolon's son. Although why should he look a certain way, whoever's son he happened to be? Just because the father was a rabid neo-Ottomanist didn't mean that his progeny necessarily shared his views. But the boy with the T-shirt bearing the legend Fuck Power, man bun on his head, fingernails painted black, looked as if he was rebelling in quite a big way, which was often the case with kids from very strict backgrounds.

Although Sevval Kalkan had been found and Çetin's involvement with the Moral Maze was over, he still felt a responsibility towards the group, and this boy and his friend's bullying of Gold Bey was wrong. It needed to be stopped. He hadn't come deliberately to Tarlabaşı to do that. He'd actually driven over from Ayvansaray in the hope of dropping in on Sugar Hanım. But she'd been asleep. He'd seen her, just, through her filthy window, snoring with her mouth open in her chair.

Cuckuk Sokak was full of activity. He'd spotted at least two drug deals going down, men and women were coming and going to work, to shop and to gossip, and the street was, as ever, full of kids. A man like him, in a cheap suit, smoking a cigarette, blended right in. But how to approach this boy? Related to power, what the hell would he care about the opinions of an ex-policeman?

But then the young man wasn't alone. Another, similarly clad man came and sat down beside him, passing him a joint, which

Serkan Tolon took with a grunt of thanks. When he'd inhaled and slowly exhaled, he said, 'So what happened?'

The other man shrugged. 'You couldn't make it up,' he said.

'What?'

'We got to Cihan Bey's office, and there was my father.'

Serkan Tolon shook his head. 'I thought he was dead.'

'We all did! Cihan Bey's known about him for years, the crooked old twat! Apparently Mother left some money for the old bastard in her will.'

'Where's he been?'

'With some whore in Gebze.'

'So why has he turned up now?'

The other man sighed. 'To fuck me over,' he said. 'Cihan Bey went to see him and brought him back here to lend support to Uğur's claim over my inheritance.'

'What a fucking bastard!'

'Yeah.' He shook his head.

'But . . . Uğur's not your mother's child, is he?'

'No. But he is our father's child. The old man fucked Mother's older sister, Auntie Filiz. He was probably drunk at the time.'

'Was he drunk today?'

'No. But what I don't get is that we're talking about Perihan's money, not his.'

İkmen felt his ears prick up. Perihan was the name of the woman who had been removed from her grave in Karacaahmet cemetery. This was her son. He took another cigarette out of his pocket, lit up and pretended to look at his mobile phone. Nobody ever took any notice of people staring at those.

'Your dad doesn't trust you, then?'

'No. Even though he doesn't know me. What a shit!'

'And yet you started all this, didn't you?' Serkan said. 'You wanted that DNA test.'

'I took a gamble.'

'Don't you feel a bit responsible for your mother . . .'

'I didn't dig her up!' the other man said. 'What I did by requesting her exhumation was bring a crime to light.'

'Yeah, I guess so.'

'You're like my fucking brother. Everything's my fault! I suppose you think the business would be better under Uğur too.' He shook his head. 'Fuck you! God, you're not so innocent yourself.'

'I play the game with my family, Lokman.'

'At the expense of other people, yeah!'

'Oh, you don't mean Zeynep, do you?'

There was a pause, and then Lokman said, 'You know she's dead.'

İkmen saw Serkan raise his hands as if in surrender. 'Nothing to do with me,' he said.

'Oh no?'

'No,' Serkan reiterated. 'And anyway, it was you who found her, wasn't it?'

Lokman got up and walked away, while Serkan shook his head and then went into his house. İkmen leaned against the wall behind him and wondered who Zeynep was. He thought he might know . . .

Dr Özdemir's surgery waiting room was very familiar. It looked just like those high-end so-called addiction specialist places her father had taken her to when he was intent upon breaking up her marriage to Can and getting her clean. Full of plush carpets, magazines in English and French and patients wearing Gucci, Prada and Savile Row suits. There were also, in this case, a couple of covered women, but they were very modern. Designer modest coats and layers of thick, dramatic make-up.

The receptionist had told them that the doctor was currently with a patient but would see them next. Deniz wondered how the other patients would feel about this. She also wondered how they'd managed to jump to the head of the queue. It couldn't have been because of her. She was just a junkie with a posh handbag. It had to be because of him. She looked at the man who had driven her the thirty-four kilometres from Kasımpaşa to Kartal. All the way there he'd counted something; she didn't know what and had been nervous about asking. And who under the age of fifty still wore nylon trousers? They stank in the heat and looked terrible.

Deniz recognised Dr Fixit as soon as he came out of his office, leading his elderly patient towards the reception desk. Both God and the Devil, he fixed his green eyes on her face and beckoned her in. Her driver came with her.

Once inside his office, the doctor addressed her companion. 'You shouldn't come here, certainly not without calling first.'

'She needs antibiotics for her husband.'

The doctor looked at Deniz, finally. 'I gave you antibiotics. Is he still ill?'

'He threw them away,' she said.

'Threw them away! Why?'

'He wouldn't take them unless I scored, and I couldn't because I didn't have any money.'

The doctor glared at her. 'You people,' he said. But he sat down to write another prescription. 'I'll need twenty lira for this.'

'I think he might need to go to hospital,' she said.

'So take him to a public hospital.'

She wondered whether he was so fixated on money with his legitimate patients. But she knew the answer to that. Once he'd given her the prescription and she'd paid him, he stood up to indicate that the appointment was at an end.

'And make sure he takes it this time,' he said.

There were times when Deniz was prepared to be abused in order to get what she wanted, and times when she wasn't. She said, 'It's all about money with you, isn't it? You use people like me to get things rich people want.'

'You sell, others buy. I just do my job,' the doctor said.

The strange little man who had driven her there said, 'Come on. We should go.'

'Yes, you should,' the doctor said. 'I come to you, not the other way around, Yaşar Bey. No disrespect intended, but you know how this thing works as well as I do.'

And then Deniz realised who he was. 'You're Yaşar Akgün,' she said.

He smiled and said, 'Yes.'

As they left the doctor's surgery, Deniz Palandoken remembered that people said Yaşar Akgün controlled everything in Kasımpaşa. She hadn't really believed that until now.

The queue for the Zurich flight was full of people with heaps of luggage. A lot of people going back to their jobs in Switzerland carrying gifts from the folks back home. But not all.

It was easy to spot the Kazantzoğlu family. A covered woman with a man in cheap market clothing wasn't an uncommon sight. It was the child making cawing noises in an oversized buggy that singled them out.

When Eylul Yavaş had been taken to İstanbul's largest airport, Atatürk, as a child, it had usually been to visit her uncle and his family in Washington. She and her parents had never joined the long queue for economy. It had been first class every time. As she and three uniformed officers made their way towards the security staff at the entrance to the flight desk, she felt rather sad that soon Atatürk would be closing, once the new super-sized airport was completed on the other side of the city.

She showed her ID to the young woman administering security checks and said, 'We've come to take a family called Kazantzoğlu off this flight. They're wanted for questioning.'

The young woman didn't say anything and just let the four officers through. In spite of air conditioning and cool, smooth marble floors, the international terminal was sweltering, and many of the people in the queue were fanning their faces with their e-tickets.

Two of the uniforms ducked under the queue control tape and approached the couple and the child from behind. Eylul and the remaining officer pushed through until they stood in front of the family. She held her ID up for them to see.

'Mr and Mrs Kazantzoğlu?'

'Yes,' the man said.

'Police.'

'Oh.'

Everyone around them was staring, and it made Eylul feel sorry for the family. But it had been unavoidable. The police had only heard from the airport authorities half an hour before that the Kazantzoğlus were heading for Zurich. Eylul and her team had raced to get there, sirens blaring, lights flashing. Now she looked at this small, dark-skinned couple with their screaming damaged son and felt nothing but pity. Whatever they had done.

'We need you to come with us,' she continued.

The woman said, 'We're going to Switzerland. They have a clinic there where they can make children like Devlet better.'

The child was, as far as Eylul could see, brain damaged. Probably from birth. She doubted whether anyone could do very much for him. But then again, the Swiss were a clever, and rich, nation.

'I'm sure you can get another flight.'

'We have an appointment tonight,' the man said. 'We've booked into a hostel—'

The woman interrupted, 'Are you arresting us?'

'Not if you come now,' Eylul said. 'We need you to come to headquarters to answer some questions.'

242

'What about?'

She put a hand on the woman's arm. 'Let's just go quietly,' she said.

Those behind them in the queue moved their bags and trolleys out of the way as the officers escorted the family away from the check-in desk. Eylul saw the woman, Ece, look at her husband with tears in her eyes.

İkmen ordered coffee for both of them.

'Thank you for coming so quickly,' he said to Süleyman.

His friend smiled. 'Sounded like you had something important to tell me.'

'Maybe.'

İkmen had suggested they meet at the Vatan Kafe. Close enough to police headquarters to be convenient, far enough away to be relatively discreet. Because they wanted to smoke, the two men sat outside in the small, slightly sun-bleached garden.

While they waited for their coffee, İkmen told Süleyman what he had overheard pass between Serkan Tolon and his friend Lokman in Tarlabaşı. By the time the drinks arrived, Süleyman had an almost full account of their conversation.

'I knew that there were problems within the Bulut family, but I didn't know the father had turned up,' he said. 'Like everyone else, I assumed he was dead. So tell me why you were there, Çetin.'

'I'd gone to visit Cumhur Polat, Gold Bey, and heard the pair of them lean on him to produce a funky watch for Lokman. Cumhur Polat is in this group I was working for . . .'

'The Moral Maze.'

'Yes. And even though my involvement with them is now at an end, Kerim Bey having been placed in charge of finding who is responsible for Sevval Kalkan's death, I felt I owed Cumhur Polat a little backup with these boys.'

'Did you.' Süleyman offered İkmen a cigarette and they both

lit up. 'Putting yourself in danger is something you don't need to do any more, Çetin.'

'Yes, well, I didn't do that, because I've come to you instead.'

'Good.' Süleyman cleared his throat. 'Lokman Bulut is a young man who has in the past owed money to the mob. He gets an allowance from his older brother, but it's never enough. Now he is challenging Uğur for sole control of his late mother's business and estate. I'd like to know what his father thinks of his antics.'

'The father, from their conversation, is supporting Uğur.'

'Interesting. Perihan Hanım wasn't Uğur's mother, but Ara Bulut is his father. It's Perihan's legacy, but I imagine the old man must worry that Lokman will fritter it away. Oh, and by the way, the mob involved are a strange, relatively new crew from Tarlabaşı.'

'Paşa Beyaz's old turf,' İkmen said. 'God, I remember him! The world's worst mobster.'

'This present bunch coalesce around a character called Yaşar Akgün, a taxi driver. Looks like a relic of the seventies and lives in Paşa's old house. Apparently he's quite a player, but from what I've heard, he's not exactly out of the usual mobster mould. I tried to catch up with him earlier because Uğur Bulut has made a statement to the effect that Akgün is leaning on him to sell his business. But no luck so far. I'm not keen to actually arrest him yet, because I'd like to know first whether I'm actually dealing with him or a bigger organisation behind him. I'm also keen to protect the Bulut family inasmuch as I can. Uğur Bulut is no easy mark, but I don't fancy his chances against people who I am told can get really rough. Ömer is watching Akgün's house to try and intercept him when he returns. If he returns. So this conversation between these two young men: interesting, but . . .'

'Not relevant? I thought so, but then at the end of their meeting, they argued,' İkmen said. 'Serkan Tolon made the point to Lokman that if he hadn't requested the exhumation of his mother's corpse, then none of what has followed would have happened. Lokman lost his temper and said that Serkan wasn't exactly an innocent because of someone called Zeynep who was now dead. Serkan then countered with the phrase "it was you who found her". Now the name Zeynep was unknown to me at first. I thought for a while they were talking about some old girlfriend of Serkan's. But then I remembered that it was the name of the character Sevval Kalkan played in Family Is Everything. It may be a coincidence, but then again, it may not. I'm telling you this instead of Kerim Bey because he's dealing with another unexplained death in Ayvansaray.'

'Which you discovered,' Süleyman said.

'I fear it may be that friend of Leah Delmonte I told you about.' İkmen shook his head.

'You know, at the back of my mind, I wondered whether Ceyda Kazantzoğlu might be my heartless body,' Süleyman said. 'But now it seems not. It does show, however, that I am, albeit unconsciously, reaching out for something to mesh together with something else to give shape to all these disparate pieces of evidence I possess. Maybe I should pay a visit to Lokman Bulut.' He smiled. 'Maybe you should come with me.'

'Ha! I think not,' İkmen said. 'Not if you want to keep your job.'

Süleyman shook his head. 'But seriously,' he said. 'Lokman Bulut is connected to some dangerous people, and I don't just mean this Yaşar Akgün. Have you ever read anything by Professor Tolon, Serkan's father?'

'I've seen him on television, and that's enough,' İkmen said. 'He wants to remake the Ottoman Empire.'

'Not militarily, but politically, yes,' Süleyman said. 'Using—'

'Religion as the glue, of course,' İkmen said. 'How very unoriginal. Isn't it Tolon who also wants to reinstate the monarchy?'

'Yes. And he has powerful friends, some of whom, shall we say, break bread with people who should by rights be imprisoned for life. Tolon has been dismissed by some as an unhinged joke, but if his friends are anything to go by, he also has the potential to be a dangerous adversary.'

'Gone quiet on TV lately, though,' İkmen said.

Süleyman lit a cigarette. 'Maybe he's planning something new. But whatever is going on, I feel I am not yet done with Lokman Bulut, or his friend Serkan. I am seeing Lokman and his siblings in the morning. I will drop the name Zeynep. I'll also speak to Kerim Bey; he should know about this.'

Yaşar Akgün walked in the front door and took off his shoes. When he saw the Özince brothers, Ekrem and Ali Haydar, he smiled.

Ekrem stepped forward and said, 'You take that woman over to see Dr Özdemir?'

'Yes,' Yaşar said. 'She needed antibiotics for her husband. He'd thrown the ones she gave him before away. We help where we can, don't we?'

'Yes,' Ekrem agreed. 'But not people like that woman.'

'Not people we've helped?'

'No. Ordinary punters,' Ekrem said. 'They'll pay you properly.'

'That woman paid me.'

'Yes, but . . .' He let it go. There were several junkies they'd helped who had turned out to be pains in the arse. He'd always been wary of them, but his brother had a little habit himself. That had to stop.

'And there's the police,' added the old man, Abdülkadır Soyar.

'Police?'

'They came here to see you,' Ekrem said. 'They want to ask you some questions.'

'What about?'

'I don't know! Traffic violations?' He turned to Abdülkadır. 'What was he called, the policeman?'

246

'Inspector Süleyman,' the old man said. 'I told him nothing, Ekrem Bey.'

Ekrem handed the card the old man had given him to Yaşar and said, 'Well, you'd better call him, hadn't you?'

'What do I say?' Yaşar asked.

'You say,' Ekrem said as he moved in very close, 'that you're sorry you weren't here this morning when he came, but you were working. Then you ask him what he wants to see you about and we take it from there.'

'We?'

'Me and Ali Haydar will be listening in,' he said. 'Looking after your interests.'

Chapter 19

Once the child had been taken away, it was clear the couple didn't have a thing to say to each other. Of course the stress had much to do with it, as well as the presence of a constable standing in front of the door of Interview Room 5.

Sergeant Eylul Yavaş sighed as she watched them through the one-way mirror that allowed direct viewing of activity during interviews. Inspector Gürsel was due any minute and would of course take the lead on this interrogation, but Eylul still felt nervous. The husband, Ateş Kazantzoğlu, had refused legal representation. His wife, Ece, had cried. He'd clearly gone to hit her until he realised where he was and stopped himself. Had he got her into this, whatever it was?

Kerim Gürsel burst through the viewing-room door.

'Sir.'

'Sorry, Sergeant,' he said. 'Just wanted to get as much information from Dr Sarkissian as I could before I left the scene. Seems it's a woman's body, elderly.'

He looked through the one-way mirror.

'That them?'

'Yes, sir. There's also their child, but he's being looked after by social services. They have other children still at home, but they've not been mentioned.'

'Well, they're not in Ayvansaray.' He sat down. 'Just need a moment. Mehmet Bey called me and I missed it. Have to deal with it later.' He ran a comb through his hair. 'How are they?'

248

'Nervous,' Eylul said. 'Ateş Kazantzoğlu tried to hit his wife when she cried. He stopped himself, but the way she flinched made me think he's probably done it before.'

'Probably.'

'How did you get on?'

'Let's put it this way,' he said, 'when I do finally get home tonight, I may monopolise the shower for many hours.'

His phone rang. It was a welcome distraction from the gridlocked traffic. Situation normal on Vatan Caddesi during rush hour.

'Süleyman.'

'Sir, Yaşar Akgün has returned home,' Ömer Mungun said.

'Good. I'm on Vatan and it's hell, but I'll turn round as soon as I'm able.'

'And he wasn't alone when he got back,' Ömer continued. 'He had Deniz Palandoken with him.'

'Really?'

'No idea why. When she got out of the car, she ran off.'

'Well then maybe Mr Akgün will be able to tell us about that when I get there.'

He ended the call and tried to decide whether he wanted to put the not very efficient air conditioning on or open the car window. He'd just decided that he'd make do with the air con when his phone rang again.

'Süleyman.'

There was a pause, and the caller cleared his throat.

'Süleyman. Yes?'

Eventually a voice said, 'You wanted to speak to me.'

'Who are you?'

'I am Yaşar Akgün.'

Hesitant and quite small, it wasn't the sort of voice one usually associated with the popular image of a mobster.

'Ah, Mr Akgün,' Süleyman said. 'I was just coming to see if I could find you at home.'

'I am here.'

'Good.'

He heard whispering, other voices in the background, but he couldn't make out what they were saying. Then Akgün said, 'What . . . what's it about?'

'I will tell you when I get there.'

Not wanting to get drawn into further conversation, Süleyman rang off abruptly. Other people had been with Akgün when he made that call. Maybe just the old man, maybe others. But then the prevailing wisdom on Akgün seemed to be that he was controlled by others. Or perhaps they just thought they controlled him . . .

Süleyman switched off the air con, opened a window and lit a cigarette. All but deafened by car horns, he closed it again immediately.

Deniz shook Can until he opened his eyes.

'Wha . . .'

He stank. God knows how many times he'd pissed and shit himself in his sleep. She took a pill out of the box Dr Özdemir had given her and tried to slip it into his mouth. But he spat it out.

'What you doing?' he mumbled.

'You need to take antibiotics,' she said. 'I went and got more. It's that or go to hospital.'

He sat up slowly and opened his eyes.

'Did you score?'

'I had to steal a bag to get enough money to get your pills,' she said.

'Where is it?'

'Where's what?'

'The bag.'

250

'I gave it to that man from the community centre, the skinny one. He had to drive me to the doctor's. Take your pill.'

'You—'

'Look, I'll go out again and get money and I will score, I promise!' she said. 'But please, please, please . . .'

Slowly, taunting her, he took a pill out of the box, pushed it into his mouth and swallowed it. Deniz almost cried. Can smelt of shit and the floors beneath them reeked of rot and heaved under even the slightest weight. As the sun went down, the old house started to come alive with the rats that emerged to torment them every night. But her husband was complying with the doctor's instructions. At last.

All she had to do now was go out again and score. Which meant she had to either rob someone or beg. Or she could go back to the one-eyed man and offer him something . . .

But she knew the dealer in fine opium didn't want anything she had. She baulked at the idea of returning to Tarlabaşı, but maybe a promise of something in the future would get her enough money to fund a night of oblivion for herself and Can. She'd considered it before, but remembering the one-eyed man had brought it to mind again.

Abdülkadır Soyar brought them tea. 'Them' being two heavy-set men, Ekrem and Ali Haydar Özince, and Mehmet Süleyman. Apparently Yaşar Akgün was in the bathroom; hence the tea party, in what Süleyman had previously observed was the most floridly baroque room in the house.

The old man put the tray with the tea glasses and bowl of sugar down in front of the men and said, 'Yaşar Bey won't be long.'

Süleyman sighed. The idea had been to pick Akgün up and take him to headquarters. But this was traditional Turkish hospitality, even if it was in the presence of what had to be Akgün's heavies. Were these the men who had attempted to terrorise Uğur

Bulut? If this was the calibre of soldier Akgün employed, Süleyman had to hand it to the Kurd. He'd been a brave man to stand up to this pair. Not only big, but also obviously tooled up, Ali Haydar and Ekrem Özince looked at the policeman in the same way a lion looks at a gazelle.

Süleyman had never crossed paths with them, but he would look them up when he got back to his office, as he was pretty sure they both had a record. It was judgemental, but probably true.

When Yaşar Akgün eventually appeared, the Özince brothers stood up. Süleyman remained seated. 'Mr Akgün.'

'Oh, er, yes.'

Yaşar Akgün was just as he had been described. Thin, nondescript – a bit vacant, to be honest. And he smelt. For a man who had just spent almost half an hour in the bathroom, this seemed a little strange. But then Süleyman saw the dampness and heavy staining on the front of Akgün's polyester trousers.

Now Süleyman stood. 'I'm Inspector Süleyman. I'd like to speak to you,' he said.

'Oh, so yes, I'm here.' Akgün tried to smile, but for some reason his face just couldn't manage it.

Süleyman began to make for the door.

'Where are you going?'

He turned. 'My car is outside, I need to interview you down at headquarters.'

He noticed that the Özince brothers were standing in front of him.

'Can't we talk here?' Akgün said.

Fixing his eyes on the heavies, Süleyman said, 'No.'

'Why not?'

There was something child-like about Akgün. Süleyman couldn't put his finger on it.

'Because I need to talk to you formally, Mr Akgün,' he said. 'If you don't come voluntarily, I will have to arrest you.'

The two heavies stayed where they were. Süleyman walked towards them, and when they didn't move, he pushed his way out between them.

'Gentlemen,' he said.

'I believe,' Kerim Gürsel said, 'that you have two other children still resident with you.'

'They live in Cankurtaran,' Ece Kazantzoğlu said. 'With my sister.'

Her husband looked at her angrily, and she lowered her eyes and fell quiet.

'Not going to Switzerland, then?'

'No,' Ateş Kazantzoğlu said. 'Just my wife and I and Devlet. There's a doctor there who can cure him.'

'So why did you give up your apartment?'

'That's our business.'

'Is it?' Kerim said. He leaned back in his chair and looked quickly at his sergeant, just to make sure she was prepared for what came next. 'Because earlier today, Mr Kazantzoğlu, we found a dead body in the attic above your apartment, which makes it my business, don't you think?'

For a moment there was complete silence. Then Ateş said, 'Don't know anything about it.'

His wife, whose face had gone first white and then red, burst into tears. Either forgetting or not caring where he was, her husband slapped her. 'Shut up, woman!'

Kerim got up and moved their chairs apart. 'Mr Kazantzoğlu, if you do that again, I will charge you with assault. Do you hear me?'

He grunted.

Kerim sat down. 'So, the body, Mr Kazantzoğlu . . .'

'What body?'

'The one I told you about.'

253

Silence again, save the sobbing of Ece Kazantzoğlu.

'We have to catch our flight or Professor Klein will cancel our appointment.'

'Don't change the subject, Mr Kazantzoğlu.'

The two men glared at each other while Eylul Yavaş just looked at Ece Kazantzoğlu. Shouldn't they have been interviewed separately? Inspector Gürsel must have had a reason for seeing them together . . .

'Professor Klein is the world's leading doctor on this damage that Devlet has,' Ateş said. 'He is the greatest brain surgeon. We are very lucky he can fit us in.'

Still staring into the man's eyes, Kerim said, 'The body, in your apartment . . .'

'Every kurus we have we spend to make our son well. Every kurus!'

'The body is that of a woman, elderly. Our doctor has found significant wounds to her head.'

'So we have to give up our apartment . . . It's nothing!'

Ece Kazantzoğlu, still crying, was getting smaller and smaller in her chair. Eylul, caught between looking at her and being mesmerised by the way Inspector Gürsel just wouldn't let the woman's husband's gaze drop, began to feel shaky, as if something uncanny had just entered Interview Room 5. She'd heard, when she'd first got this job, that Gürsel had once worked for Inspector İkmen, whose mother had been a witch. Was this . . .

'We killed her!'

Ateş Kazantzoğlu threw himself at his wife.

The djinn looked slightly different. More transparent. It still hissed at him when he went into the kitchen, though, and İkmen hissed back. Çiçek wasn't due home for another couple of hours, and Samsun was . . . somewhere. İkmen settled down with a glass of tea and a cigarette in his chair on the balcony, opposite his wife.

'Do you remember someone called Professor Tolon?' he asked her, expecting, as ever, no answer. 'I suppose he started appearing on television about five years ago. Supposedly a historian. He had an awful droning voice, but he always said the right things, if you know what I mean. And I don't mean about religion. No, not directly. His thing was always how great the Ottoman Empire was, how we should bring it back and how the republic was an evil aberration. One of those people you used to shout at me for shouting at when they were on TV.'

She smiled. She always did. It was all she ever did.

'Well, his son, from what I can gather, is an entitled little shit. Lives an "alternative" life in Tarlabaşı, smokes weed, goes around with other rich kids. But there's a chance he may be mixed up in the disappearance and death of Sevval Kalkan. Don't know how he would have known her, Sevval being a dissident, if you will. But then again, Serkan Tolon might have liked mixing with those people. Maybe being around people like the Moral Maze, effectively his father's enemies, made him feel bold and excitingly transgressive. I've never been excitingly transgressive myself; I think it may be something only rich people do.'

He put his cigarette out and lit another. Fatma's smile dropped.

'Oh, I'm sorry,' he said. 'But I can't think unless I smoke. And yes, I know it will kill me. But . . . According to what I overheard, it was Lokman Bulut who found this Zeynep. It was he who knew she was dead, and not Serkan Tolon. So Tolon didn't kill her, but he was indifferent to her death. I didn't get the impression Lokman Bulut was particularly bothered either. But if these men didn't kill her, then what did they do?'

Mehmet Süleyman could see the two Özince brothers out on the street. They'd followed his car. He turned away from the window and looked at the man sitting opposite him. Yaşar Akgün had been completely silent in the car. Sitting in the back with Ömer Mungun, he hadn't said a word.

'So, Mr Akgün,' Süleyman began. 'I've brought you in here today to give you the chance to answer an accusation that has been made against you.'

'What?'

He looked bewildered, as if he'd just woken up. Süleyman looked at Ömer Mungun, who raised his eyebrows. This was, they both knew, a very different type of crime boss. If indeed that was what Yaşar Akgün was.

'An accusation has been made against you,' Süleyman repeated.

'You said. What is it?'

Although his behaviour was unusual, it was at least to the point.

'You've been accused of attempted extortion,' Süleyman said.

'Who by?'

'Before we get into that, do you deny that you are a man with some power in your community?'

'I help people,' Akgün said. 'People like me.'

He seemed, inasmuch as Süleyman could tell, to actually believe that. The inspector looked down at Uğur Bulut's statement. 'The complaint concerns the Gaziantep pastane on İstiklal Caddesi.' He looked up.

Akgün shrugged.

Süleyman frowned. 'What does that mean?' he said. 'Do you know this place or not?'

'Everyone knows the Gaziantep pastane. It's famous,' Akgün said. 'I've eaten there.'

'Owned by a family called Bulut. It has been brought to my attention that you and your agents have allegedly attempted to apply pressure to the owners in order to obtain the Gaziantep pastane at less than market value. Is this correct?'

256

Yaşar Akgün visibly turned it over in his mind. He put his hands in his lap.

'No comment.'

Then there was a knock on the door.

A glass of tea plus some liberally applied antiseptic cream made Ece Kazantzoğlu appear calmer, although who knew what was bubbling underneath? When her husband had attacked her, Kerim Gürsel and Eylul Yavaş had pulled him out of the room and thrown him into a cell. Now the two officers waited in silence for her to fully regain her composure. Eventually she said, 'Ateş isn't a bad man, you know.'

There was nothing either of them could say that would either affect that statement, and so they said nothing. Ece sipped her tea and continued. 'I'm not making excuses, but money has always been a problem for us. And when Devlet was born, it just got worse.'

'Devlet suffers from . . .'

'His brain was damaged at birth,' she said. 'We were told it was incurable. We were also told there was little we could expect by way of assistance. Ceyda Hanım, my mother-in-law, helped, and our children who work would send money when they could, but it was never enough. When a child can't move or communicate without help, when he's incontinent and can't even feed himself, there's so much that he needs.' She wiped her eyes. 'We coped, but that was all we ever did. Until Ceyda Hanım took me to the auctions in Balat, I never went out. Do you know the Balat auctions?'

'No,' Kerim said.

'They take place in an old coffee house. They only sell cheap stuff, but it's fun. And the people there accepted Devlet; they even seemed to like him. Ceyda Hanım knew some of them. Ladies she said she would meet sometimes in Kasımpaşa. I thought nothing of it. She was often out by that time, often with Leah Hanım from downstairs.'

'Leah Delmonte?'

'Yes. They were friends. Always in a huddle, talking. I thought Leah Hanım knew everything, but I was wrong.'

'Everything about what?'

'My mother-in-law and her gold,' she said. 'That was why she went to Kasımpaşa, to buy gold. She'd been doing it for years. Not there to begin with, but in the Kapılı Çarşı. She went to Kasımpaşa because it was all women. Although she loved going out with Leah Hanım, she was still a traditional woman at heart.' She sighed. 'Back in the spring, my husband read an article about a doctor in Switzerland who was claiming he could repair brain damage. He contacted the clinic, but the treatment was too expensive for us. To be honest, I felt it was too good to be true. I know my mother-in-law felt the same way. I mean, how do you repair a brain that doesn't work?'

'I don't know.'

'I forgot about it, but Ateş didn't. He talked his mother to death about it; he brooded on the injustice of us not being able to afford to take Devlet to Professor Klein's clinic in Zurich. Then he found out about his mother's gold. He'd always known she had some, but he hadn't realised she had so much.'

'How much?'

'We sold it for half a million lira.'

'You sold it?'

She averted her eyes from both of them. 'It was the last week in May,' she said. 'Ceyda Hanım and I had been to the auction in Balat.'

'With Leah Delmonte?'

'No, she had a hospital appointment.' Ece began to cry. 'We got home, and there was Ateş, in his chair, counting these gold coins. There were hundreds of them. Ceyda Hanım screamed when she saw him. She told him to put down what wasn't his. But Ateş was furious. He asked her why, if she had all this gold, she wasn't helping with Devlet. She said she wasn't prepared to give money to some fake foreign clinic. Ateş told her he was going to sell her gold and buy the treatment for Devlet anyway.' She put her head in her hands.

Kerim Gürsel leaned forward. 'What happened then?'

Her face still hidden, she said, 'Ceyda Hanım tried to take back what was hers. My husband hit her and she fell to the ground.' She lifted her head and looked Kerim straight in the eye. 'Ateş was not himself. He loved his mother!'

'But . . .'

'He picked up his ashtray, which is made of glass and very heavy, and hit her with it until her skull cracked. All the while Devlet was screaming and I just stood there. I just stood there and watched my mother-in-law die.'

The two officers let her cry, and then Eylul Yavaş said, 'Ece, did you at any time strike or assault Ceyda Hanım?'

'No.'

'But you let your husband kill her,' Kerim said. 'Did he threaten or hurt you at all?'

She sniffed as she attempted to stop herself crying. 'No,' she said. 'We both just stared at her, I don't know how long for. There was blood everywhere. On the carpet, up the walls . . . I remember putting Devlet to bed and then cleaning. She lay there while we moved things around her.'

'Where were your other children?' Eylul asked.

'Out,' she said. 'They don't know anything. Ateş told them their grandmother had gone to stay with their uncle. They're young, they have their own lives.'

'So how did you explain to them that you were moving out?'

'That came later,' she said. 'It was like the worst nightmare you can imagine. Ateş began to wrap the body in bags. He said

259

we'd have to get rid of it. So we put it in the attic. I was terrified it would smell. I've been terrified for weeks. But what could we do? If we told the truth, we would go to prison, and who would look after Devlet then? He'd be sent to one of those hospitals where they leave them all day naked and screaming and starving.'

Cases of children with learning difficulties treated like wild animals in institutions set up to care for them had come to light in recent years, and so her fears were not unfounded.

'I understand that—' Kerim began.

'No you don't!' she shouted. 'No one does!'

The two officers let her regain her composure before she continued.

She said, 'The only way forward was to use the money to go to Switzerland. Ateş said that if we could get to Professor Klein's clinic, then at least, even if Ceyda Hanım was found, we'd be out of the country. At least Devlet would have a chance. We told the children we were going to sell everything to do this, and that they would have to stay with their aunt in Cankurtaran, near the old railway station. Don't go after them. They know nothing.'

'We will have to question them,' Kerim said. 'I'm sorry, but that is just procedure.'

'Oh God!'

'Ece Hanım,' Kerim said, 'I have to ask you formally: are you confessing to being present when your husband, Ateş Kazantzoğlu, killed his mother, Ceyda Kazantzoğlu?'

Suddenly quiet, she looked down at her hands. Often when confronted by the bald fact of what they had done, those who had killed or assisted a killer went into shock. Eylul took her hand. What had happened could not be excused, and provided the evidence supported Ece's claim, even if her husband didn't admit to killing his mother, he would eventually be convicted of her murder.

'Yes.' Her voice was small and weak, and both Kerim and Eylul felt desperately sorry for her.

Chapter 20

There were lawyers and then there was Eyüp Çelik. Tall, handsome, and perfectly groomed, he was known to be aggressive and ruthless inside and outside court. It was rumoured that he had every celebrity and many government ministers on speed-dial. It was also said he knew a lot of people involved in organised crime, had appeared in a porn video and had mistresses in three cities. And he was only twenty-nine.

'This allegation is something you must investigate before you bother my client with what could very well be complete nonsense,' he said to Mehmet Süleyman.

Yaşar Akgün, who very obviously didn't know who he was, stood behind him looking bemused.

'And how,' Süleyman countered, 'do you suggest I do that without questioning the object of the complaint, namely your client?'

Çelik smiled. Or rather, his face moved. 'Inspector Bey,' he said, 'my client, as I'm sure you have deduced by now, is a vulnerable adult. He is also a local philanthropist who performs good works in his home neighbourhood of Kasımpaşa. He is loved.'

'And so who called you?' Süleyman asked.

'That is irrelevant,' Çelik said.

The lawyer had walked into police headquarters demanding to see his client, who had not, he pointed out, been formally arrested. Süleyman had been obliged to tell him about the complaint, which he hadn't wanted to do, and now Akgün, with Çelik's assistance, was leaving.

'You need to get your evidence in place, Inspector Bey,' the lawyer said.

'I am aware of what my job involves.'

Süleyman was visibly bristling, and Ömer Mungun took a calming breath as he anticipated the explosion that could result from this stand-off.

'Further,' Süleyman continued, 'I was merely wishing to speak to your client at this stage. Nothing formal.'

'Which is why I am removing Mr Akgün,' Çelik said. 'Until and unless you have evidence that allows you to arrest my client, I would do the smart thing, which is to leave him be.'

He turned, took Akgün by the arm and left. Ömer said nothing. Süleyman walked back into his office and slammed the door behind him.

Night shifts were a pain in the arse. There was generally nothing much to do except listen to Münir Sever drone on about his illnesses, who he hated and why; and think about the possibility of ghosts. Then, in the early hours of the morning, it would get really cold, even in summer, and he'd have to muffle himself up in multiple jumpers. No wonder the poor homeless people who got into the cemetery to sleep lit fires.

Raşım Dorsay sauntered past Türgüt Bey's office, where, to his relief, the gatekeeper was otherwise engaged poring over paperwork with Münir Sever. After his clandestine meeting with Inspector Süleyman, Raşım didn't want to see Türgüt Bey and have to answer any questions. He had no doubt the gatekeeper had seen him with Süleyman. He walked out into the cemetery and breathed in the comparatively fragrant air and the silence. Soon Münir would join him, schedule for the night in his hands as usual, and the whole night-work horror would begin again.

Raşım lit a cigarette. Would Inspector Süleyman be able to find that poor snivelling necrophiliac he had described? And even if he did, would it help him solve the mystery of who had been placed inside Perihan Bulut's grave? Maybe graveyards, by their very nature, were places where dark and unnatural things occurred. His mother had once told him that the Roma people believed that death was not a natural state, and so they avoided cemeteries in case they 'caught' it. He didn't know whether that was true or not, but what was true was that the Karacaahmet was not the easy-going place it had been when he'd first worked there. That had been before Türgüt Bey had taken it into his head to produce his schedules, his routes and his clock-watching. It made the job a grind. Not that Münir seemed to mind.

'Raşım Bey?'

And here he was now. Raşım put his cigarette out and said, 'There seem to be fewer policemen here today.' Usually there was a small gang of them clustered around the entrance whenever he came on shift.

'Called back to direct traffic and stop old ladies tripping over paving stones,' Münir said, and smiled. 'Up to us to protect our sainted dead, as it should be. Even if we have to guard bloody Alevis too.'

'I'm glad you've had such a good result,' Süleyman said as he put his coffee cup down and leaned back in his seat. 'Albeit a very sad one.'

Kerim Gürsel, now celebrating with a glass of rakı, toasted his colleague. 'Thank you. I wish—'

'Oh, I'll get him in the end, the shit!' Süleyman said through his teeth. 'Bastard!'

'He looked rather timid when I saw him,' Kerim said.

'Not Akgün!' he exploded. 'Çelik! Bloody man's the person-ification of arrogance! God, does he love himself!'

They'd come to İkmen's favourite haunt, the Mozaik bar in Sultanahmet, not because their former colleague was sometimes there, sitting outside with his cat, but because it was one of the places they could go in order to talk freely. Neither a traditional police haunt nor the sort of place that routinely descended into rowdiness, it was a good place to be on a warm evening. Later, when she got home from her shift at the café, Çiçek would have to walk past the Mozaik in order to go home. And Süleyman could do with seeing his girlfriend.

'He talked down to me,' he continued. 'Even though I'm taller than he is. Standing there with his slicked-back hair, smelling of Sauvage . . .'

'Is that an aftershave?'

'Yes.'

Kerim could remember when he had been talked down to by Süleyman. Most people had. But he didn't say anything. Everyone knew that Prince Mehmet Bey had a bit of a blind spot when it came to his own faults.

'Ignore him,' he said. 'He'll work for anyone with enough money to engage him. Doesn't mean he's any good.'

'But he is! He gets people off all the time!'

'Only because he knows which palms to grease,' Kerim said.

Süleyman lit a cigarette.

'Anyway, what's this about the Bulut kid?' Kerim asked.

'Lokman? He's hardly a kid, he's thirty-six. But . . .' Süleyman exhaled. 'Çetin Bey overheard a conversation between him and the son of that so-called historian, Professor Tolon.'

'That the one who writes books about reinstating the monarchy?'

'Yes. Anyway, this man, Serkan Tolon, was talking about someone called Zeynep who was now dead. Zeynep was the character played by Sevval Kalkan in that soap whose name escapes me.'

'Family Is Everything,' Kerim said.

'It may be her or it may not be,' Süleyman said. 'I've asked the Bulut family to come and see me in the morning for an update on our investigation at the Karacaahmet. Bad news on that front, as Özer has, as you know, asked me to reduce the number of officers on the site. But I'm going to talk about Sevval Kalkan in terms of a possible connection to their mother's death and see how Lokman reacts.'

'I have to be with Dr Sarkissian in the morning for Ceyda Kazantzoğlu's autopsy.'

'I'll let you know what, if anything, I find out,' Süleyman said.

There was a silence between them, then Kerim said, 'Tell me about Yaşar Akgün.'

'Oh, what's to say?' Süleyman shrugged. 'If I were asked to describe him, I'd say he was some kind of savant, if there wasn't a note of what I can only call cunning behind his odd manner. I can't work out whether the henchmen he has around him are using him, or whether he's using them. It must have been them who called Çelik, or maybe that was Akgün when he was supposedly in the bathroom. His personal hygiene leaves something to be desired.'

Kerim smiled. 'What are you going to do about him now that Çelik is involved?'

'Watch and wait,' Süleyman said. 'See if Uğur Bulut has any actual proof that Akgün and his people leaned on him. Apparently his staff saw Akgün and his heavies monopolise tables at the pastane and then leave without paying. Uğur told the staff to leave them alone, which they did. But of course his employees wouldn't know whether he was being leaned on or not. A lot of proprietors deal with difficult customers by simply letting them have a little of what they want for nothing.'

'It was ever thus.'

The house was dark. In fact, the whole quarter was dark and quiet and eerie. Unlike its rowdy neighbour Tarlabaşı, Kasımpaşa didn't have a seedy nightlife. At least not one that could be easily found. But it was here that the truly desperate came to trade, as Deniz Palandoken knew to her cost. Not a day went by without her thinking about the baby she had named Didem. She'd given birth to her in one of those rooms on the first floor of the community centre. Coming to Kasımpaşa was always a trial for her. But it was also a place where money could be made.

The first time she'd been to this quarter she'd met a man called Ali, who had set her up with Dr Fixit. He had promised her that the child would go to a good home, and indeed, when she'd handed Didem over, it had been in an office in Gümüşsuyu, which was a wealthy area. Not that she remembered much about that day. It had been a blur, mainly because she'd had to get very high to do it.

Peering through the darkness, she looked again and again for signs of life inside Yaşar Akgün's house, but saw nothing. If she woke him up, would he be angry? He'd been nothing but kind to her in the car and the doctor's surgery, but people said he could also be cruel. She hadn't met him that first time, when she'd had the child. People had spoken about him, but they'd never communicated.

She sank down onto the broken pavement. If she waited it out, Mr Akgün was bound to appear at some point. Then she could tell him what she was offering and go back and inform Can. That would make him happy because it meant that soon they'd be able to score again for a while with no problem.

Kerim Gürsel had been gone for almost an hour when Çiçek turned up at the Mozaik. Mehmet Süleyman, who had moved on from coffee to a glass of wine, greeted her with a kiss.

'What are you doing here?' she asked him as she sat down and lit a cigarette.

'I've been talking to Kerim Bey,' he said.

'Oh. Where is he?'

'He went home.'

'And so . . .'

'I knew you'd be here soon and so I decided to wait for you,' he said.

Light from the string of multicoloured bulbs that ran around the awning over the entrance to the bar reflected in his eyes, making them look glassy and a little strange.

'Have you seen Dad?' Çiçek asked.

'No.'

'I'm sure he would've joined you for a drink . . .'

'I know, but I wanted to see you on your own.' He leaned towards her. 'I've got the car; do you want to come back with me?'

She did – and didn't. Of course she wanted to be with him, but she was exhausted. Also, she had thought about what Samsun had said about not appearing too keen, and it did make sense. And if she was honest, being a little aloof was more where she generally was with men these days. She said, 'I'm shattered. Maybe tomorrow?'

He smiled, but not with his eyes. He was disappointed, and she was instantly alarmed.

'Oh . . .'

'No, that's fine,' he said. 'Of course you're tired, you've been working late.' He put his hand in his jacket pocket and threw a bundle of notes down on the table to pay for his drinks. 'At least let me see you safely home.'

She put her cigarette out and stood up. Laughing, she said, 'Even if it's only a few steps away.'

'Even if it's only a few steps away.'

He opened the tall metal gate that gave access to the apartment block and they both went into the scrubby little garden that surrounded the building. The İkmen family lived on the fourth floor.

She said, 'You don't have to come up.'

They walked towards the front entrance, which he sidestepped, pulling her into the shadows beneath the fire escape. Slightly unbalanced, she tripped into his arms.

'Oh!'

While his kisses were never perfunctory, this was a particularly passionate example, which she leaned into with pleasure. Did she want to touch him as much as he was touching her? He pulled her buttocks towards him and she felt his cock against her stomach. Her heart began to race. This was not what she'd planned. That had been more along the lines of soaking her sore feet. But he was clearly psyched, and she was aroused.

He pulled her more deeply into the shadows and lifted up her skirt, then entered her with a grunt. His cock was hard and hot, and she pressed herself still closer so that she could feel every bit of him. Usually a gentle, skilled lover who liked to give pleasure as well as receive, tonight he was tense and focused, and when he came inside her, it was quick and strange. It felt as if by having sex this way, he had relieved himself of an almost unbearable tension.

And yet even though this violent, wordless sex had surprised her, what came next did not. Aware that her own pleasure was incomplete, he put a hand between her legs and his lips around her nipples until she too reached her climax.

When it was over, she said, 'That was unexpected.'

'But not unwelcome, I hope?'

'No, just . . .'

He kissed her and said, 'I had to.'

But he didn't say why, and she didn't ask.

Whether it was better when Münir droned on about his military exploits was a good question. Usually it was not, but on this occasion, Raşım could have done with a bit of conversation, however poor, to help take his mind off the way the moon shone down on the gravestones, making them look eerily luminous.

Although he'd not been particularly aware of their presence, Raşım missed the background noise from the police officers assigned to search the graveyard. They still didn't know who the woman in Perihan Bulut's grave had been, and now that they were leaving, they probably never would. Unless of course they were pursuing other lines of inquiry elsewhere. Raşım didn't know, although it would have been wrong to say that he didn't care.

The route Türgüt Bey had given them was well away from the perimeter wall. Towards the middle of the site, things became quieter and more creepy.

'I'm going to relieve myself,' Münir said. 'I'll catch you up.'

'OK.'

Raşım began to move, slowly.

'And don't lurk about. A man needs to be alone sometimes.'

He headed back to the path. Most men weren't so touchy when it came to pissing against a tree, but then Münir was old and grumpy, and his dick was probably small and shrivelled.

The stones in this part of the cemetery were mainly written in the Ottoman script. It was said that some of them were quite poetic, even racy, but it was impossible for most people to read them. When Atatürk had changed the Turkish alphabet from the Arabic script to the Roman, back in the 1920s, the nation had lost touch with much of its written past.

Raşım trained his torch on one very large stone that was topped by a crest made up of numerous flags and a crescent moon. Obviously the grave of someone important, it must have cost a lot of money back in the nineteenth century or whenever. Now, half sunk into the earth, it was covered with dirt, moss and bird shit.

'Fuck off!'

He looked up. That was unmistakably Münir's voice. Had he found someone attempting to get in? Raşım switched his torch off and began to slowly approach the tree he had seen Münir disappear behind. If whoever it was thought Münir was alone, they might be alarmed enough to just scarper when they saw him. But then there was another voice, and it was foreign. For a moment, Raşım couldn't identify it; then he caught one word, which he recognised as being English. The word was 'hungry'.

He attempted to get closer, but was afraid to move too much in case whoever Münir was with heard him. He thought he picked up the sound of crying, but he couldn't be sure. Then Münir said, 'Fuck off!' again, and followed it with something that sounded like a name. There was the sound of moving feet, and Raşım just managed to make out a stocky figure walking towards him. A second figure was heading in the direction of the perimeter wall.

'What are you doing?'

He looked up into the face of Münir Sever.

'Why didn't you go up to the path? Were you watching me piss? What are you, some kind of homosexual?'

In spite of what he'd seen, Raşım felt himself blush. 'No . . .'

'So what are you doing?' Münir said. 'Fucking fairy!' With one hand on his night stick, looming over Raşım, he looked intimidating. And even though Raşım knew he had every right to question his colleague about what had just happened, and who the other man had been, he didn't feel able to do so. Also, he was shaking too much.

Çiçek had hoped to get back into the apartment unseen. With her head all over the place, she didn't want to have to talk to anyone. Had she consented to the sex she'd shared with Süleyman, or had she just allowed him to do what he wanted to her? And if it was the latter, then why had he done it and why had she allowed it?

She was just about to creep down the hall to her bedroom when she heard her father's voice coming from the living room.

270

'Çiçek?'

'Yes,' she said. 'I'm really tired.'

'Can you come in here a moment, please?'

She felt her heart sink. Her father missed absolutely nothing, and he would know, if only by the smell of her. But she walked into the living room anyway. Resistance to Çetin İkmen was generally futile.

'Dad.'

He was sitting on the sofa reading a commentary on Mary Shelley's Frankenstein. He held it up. 'Thought it was apt, given that grave robbing appears to have returned to the city.'

She sat down opposite him.

'I'm really tired . . .'

'I know,' he said. 'But I have to ask you something.'

She felt her heart sink. He wouldn't judge her for her recent indulgence in al fresco sex, but she still didn't want to talk to him about it.

'Yes?'

'Has anyone been here lately?' he said. 'Anyone new? Maybe Samsun brought someone home?'

'Have you asked her?'

'No,' he said, 'I'm asking you.'

He knew, of course he did. She said, 'She had a man in here, an Arab. He was an exorcist. But before you blow your top, he didn't do anything. I came home before he could, and Samsun threw him out.'

Her father didn't say anything.

'I told her you'd lose your shit,' Çiçek said. 'But she was desperate. I don't know why, but it creeps up on her. Her nerves are frayed. I mean, we both, Samsun and I, we know why you—'

'Yes, yes.' He silenced her with one raised hand, then shook his head.

'Has it gone?' she asked. 'The djinn?'

'No, but its brightness is fading,' he said. 'Whatever this Arab did has worked, in part.'

'I'm so sorry.'

He smiled. 'It isn't your fault. Or Samsun's, really. It's mine.'

She frowned.

'What fun can it be for you and Samsun to live with a djinn and a dead woman?'

'Mum . . .'

'Your mother is dead, Çiçek,' he said. 'She will never cook food for us again, never hug us or moan at us for leaving our shoes in a mess by the front door. She'll never keep my poor old body warm at night again, and it's hard. It's so hard I am even prepared to make do with this echo of her I see out on the balcony. But it isn't real.'

Çiçek went and sat next to him, putting her arms around his shoulders and kissing his cheek.

'And so what has happened is for the best,' İkmen said. 'For me as well as for both of you. If we ignore the djinn and . . . my ghost, they will fade, and I think I want them to do so. Samsun has to live here too, and I should respect her need not to be startled. It's not good for me either, and although you will one day leave . . .'

'You think?'

He laughed. 'One day,' he said. 'Whether into the arms of Mehmet Bey or . . .' He shrugged. 'Maybe when the world turns again, as it will, you'll find yourself a new direction, with another or alone.'

'Dad!'

'Oh don't get me wrong, I would happily let you live here for ever, but it's not right for you, Çiçek. You're too bright to be home alone with your ancient dad and his cousin.'

She put her head on his shoulder. 'You're not ancient,' she said. 'And I love being back at home.'

'Even if you do go to stay with Mehmet Bey,' he said, 'you know that isn't a problem for me. I just want you to be happy.' He kissed her hair. 'Now I'll let you get to your bed,' he said. 'I'm sorry I detained you; you must be exhausted.'

She didn't respond, although she felt her face colour. Did he know? Probably, but he wasn't going to say.

She stood up, and he went back to his book. Just before she left the room, she asked, 'What does that book say about Frankenstein?'

'It's interesting,' he said. 'It looks at the book through the prism of loss of innocence.'

Çiçek showered and then went to bed, but she couldn't sleep. Mehmet Süleyman had admitted to her long ago that he had gone through a phase when he used prostitutes. She couldn't get away from the idea that, had she not met him at the Mozaik, he would have gone elsewhere for the sex he had clearly needed so urgently.

Chapter 21

'Arto!'

It was 6.30 in the morning and İkmen sounded elated. Given that Arto Sarkissian had really wanted to wake his friend up in revenge for İkmen having woken him the previous morning, the Armenian was disappointed by the brightness of his tone.

'You weren't asleep?'

'No,' İkmen said. 'Not been to bed. But in a good way. I was just about to call Kerim Bey.'

'Oh.' The doctor didn't ask for an explanation. Instead, he said, 'I told you I'd get back to you regarding the gentleman who goes to my church. The one who works at the Forensic Institute.'

'Oh yes!' İkmen said. 'Silivri prison!'

'Are you on drugs?'

'No, but I've had some thoughts,' İkmen said. 'And I've got my second wind. Tell me about Silivri.'

'Well, as I'm sure you're aware, prisons have their own medical provision. So, although blood and other test samples will be sent to the Forensic Institute for analysis, the actual taking of medical samples is done in house. Doctors and nurses are only brought in from outside if an inmate has a specific medical need.'

'Like diabetes?' İkmen asked.

'No, I think it has to be more serious than that,' Arto said. 'My friend Tigran Bey tells me that a cardiologist does go in from time to time and sometimes orders blood or urine tests, plus administering ECG tests. In addition, there have been some requests for HLA tests.'

'What, the bone marrow thing?'

'Yes, to test for suitability.'

'Why would a cardiologist do that?'

'She wouldn't. Not as far as I can see. Though if this test was part of a wider patient profile request, then it's possible. Cardiologists can order tests for almost anything they deem relevant to their patient's health. However, in the last year this test has been requested more often than would be expected.'

'All from this one doctor? A woman?'

'No, not just from her. There's also, according to Tigran, an oncologist who visits from time to time. Dr Yavuz, works out of the American University Hospital.'

'Means nothing to me,' İkmen said. 'What about the cardiologist?'

'A Dr Çoban from the Koşuyolu Medipol Hospital in Üsküdar,' he said.

'No bells are ringing,' İkmen said. 'So how would you read this? Or rather, how would your friend read it?'

'Unusual but not unknown,' Arto said. 'The oncologist may have a patient who requires a transplant. Of course, strictly speaking it would have to have been done with the inmate's permission, but who knows. Quite what a cardiologist would do it for, I don't know. But then I'm not involved in either cardiology or oncology. Things move at such a rate in medicine these days; it's amazing how many drugs intended for one condition have been discovered to actually be more effective when used to treat other pathologies. I know of at least one ancient antidepressant now used to calm the symptoms of irritable bowel syndrome.'

'Well, that's all very fascinating,' İkmen said. 'But do we know whether Sevval Kalkan had an HLA test?'

'No. Unless Inspector Gürsel orders an investigation, it's going to be hard to match a result to an inmate,' Arto said. 'Such data is coded to protect the identity of those being tested. Some of the inmates at Silivri are famous, and certain media outlets would be extremely excited about getting hold of medical data that they would undoubtedly speculate upon in totally inappropriate ways. Kerim Bey will need a warrant. But he's due at Ceyda Kazantzoğlu's post-mortem at nine, so I'll tell him then.'

'You're sure the body in the attic is her?'

'Not a hundred per cent; we won't be able to say that until DNA has been analysed. The state of the corpse doesn't really lend itself to positive identification.'

There were lots of stories about mothers-in-law having no boundaries when it came to their daughters. Sinem Gürsel's mother, though born and raised in İstanbul, was a typical village mother-in-law. This meant that she was forever either feeding people or preparing to feed them. In addition, nothing was off limits to her, and that included the bedroom her daughter shared with her husband. That Sinem and Kerim's marriage was entirely one of convenience was completely unknown to her, which made the way she habitually burst in on them all the more unforgivable.

'Pınar Hanım!'

Pınar, who was 108 kilos of pure baklava laced with a dash of spite, looked at him as he shot up, bare chested, in the bed beside her daughter. 'Why don't you wear pyjamas like a decent person?'

Her husband, poor old Binali Bey, wore pyjamas and a vest when he went to bed. Many old men did. Kerim usually slept naked, especially when his lover Pembe was at home. With Sinem he wore boxer shorts; after all, they might only be married in name, but they were still close friends, and she particularly liked a cuddle. She'd had a wretched night with the pain. Her fingers twisted into arthritic spirals, she'd drunk as much oral morphine as she was allowed while Kerim cradled her in his arms. What she didn't need now was her mother yelling. She tucked herself into her husband's side.

'What are you doing here?' Kerim asked. He looked at his phone and was horrified to see it was only 6.40. 'I don't need to be up for another hour!' he said.

Pınar left. Kerim got out of bed.

'Kerim!'

He looked round to see that Sinem was looking at his loins. He had an impressive erection.

'Sorry. Sorry.' He put his dressing gown on. 'These things happen.'

She laughed, and sat up slowly and painfully.

'People must think I'm so lucky,' she said.

'What do you mean?'

'To have you,' she said. 'Handsome husband with a good job, hung like a horse.'

When they were teenagers, Kerim and Sinem had both tried to be straight. They'd even had sex, once. But it hadn't been very good and they'd both decided they'd never do it again. But in spite of preferring women, Sinem did appreciate male beauty, and sometimes, these days, Kerim did wonder whether she occasionally wanted him.

His phone rang. 'What is this today?' he said. He looked at the screen and saw that the caller was İkmen.

'Kerim Bey,' İkmen said. 'I was reading a commentary on Frankenstein last night and it got me thinking about loss of innocence.'

'Loss . . .'

'Yes,' he said. 'By creating the monster, by engendering, if you like, a miracle, Dr Frankenstein basically robs all those

277

around him, and himself, of his innocence.' He didn't wait for Kerim to respond, but went on, 'So I was thinking of those two young men in Tarlabaşı, Lokman Bulut and Serkan Tolon. Both wealthy, spoilt, no real stress in their lives, and yet they seem to me to be operating in a kind of darkness . . .'

'A kind of what?'

'They live amongst the poorest in the city, they drink, take drugs, get in debt . . . I know they smoke cannabis, because a neighbour told me, and then I remembered the graffito . . .'

If Kerim hadn't known better, he might have thought İkmen was on amphetamines.

'Gonca Şekeroğlu, when I showed her the photograph of Sevval Kalkan's graffito, was convinced it was inside and not in the street. So if we could get into these young men's apartments . . .'

'Just a minute,' Kerim said. 'Get into their apartments? How?'

'Cannabis,' İkmen said. 'Everyone knows they smoke it . . .'

Kerim sighed. 'Çetin Bey, I'd need a warrant,' he said. 'And quite honestly, for a gram or two of weed, is it worth it? You know as well as I do that we leave Tarlabaşı alone most of the time just so that we know where to find the dealers should something like a bad batch of coke suddenly appears. Is this the graffito of the—'

'Don't even say it over the phone,' İkmen said. 'Yes, it is. Do you see where—'

'Yes, but unless you have reasonable suspicion that this man has such a thing on his wall, then getting a warrant from a prosecutor will be hard. Look, I'll float the idea if you like, but I can't do anything this morning.'

'Yes, but—'

'I know you're looking for connections between the death of Sevval Kalkan and Mehmet Bey's organ-trafficking investigation, but we must proceed with caution. You know this! If we make a wrong move, we could lose an albeit tenuous hold on something

278

far bigger and more impressive than just a weed bust or a one-off case of organ trafficking.'

He heard İkmen sigh. He didn't sound as if he was in a good way.

'Çetin Bey, are you all right?'

There was a pause and then İkmen said, 'I'm not sleeping.'

'So go to bed now,' Kerim said. 'I'll bear what you've said in mind. But I hope you can see—'

'Yes. Yes.'

İkmen ended the call, leaving Kerim slightly stunned.

'What was that?' Sinem asked as she lit her first cigarette of the day.

Kerim sat down on the bed again and stroked her cheek. 'I don't know,' he said. 'Not really. Don't worry about it.'

'Will you kiss me?' she said.

'Of course.'

He went to kiss her on her forehead, but she grabbed his chin and made him kiss her on the mouth.

'I'm sorry, all right?'

'I know,' İkmen said.

Samsun threw herself down in the chair directly in front of the television and picked up the remote.

'The exorcist was only in the kitchen on his own for a few minutes,' she said. 'He can't have done much.'

'He did something,' İkmen said. 'You saw the damn thing! Its head has all but disappeared.'

Samsun switched the television on.

'Oh for the love of God . . .'

'What?'

'TV on already?' İkmen said. 'Seriously?'

'Well, what else is there to do?' she snapped. 'You won't let us change anything in this mausoleum!'

That hit home, because it was true. Nothing had changed since the day Fatma had died. And while the place was occasionally cleaned and tidied in a minimal way, for the most part the İkmen apartment was given over to ghosts and djinn.

He said, 'I was going to get rid of the djinn myself, eventually.'

'And Fatma Hanım?'

He shrugged. 'Her too.'

'Because she's not here. You know that, don't you, Çetin?' Samsun said. 'What you see is an echo of your wife, something that comforts you.'

'It's not fair on Çiçek, to live with a dead woman . . .'

'It's not fair on me either, or you!' She began clicking through TV channels. There were such a lot. Back in the seventies, when Samsun had bought her first television, there had only been one. 'How can you move on with your wife still in the house?'

'What do you mean, "move on"?'

Her eyes still firmly on the TV, Samsun said, 'You know . . .'

'What? Find another wife?'

'Yeah, well . . .'

'The only thing further from my mind than finding another wife is fathering another child,' İkmen said. Then, seeing which channel Samsun had settled on, he added, 'Oh surely not?'

Samsun turned the volume up as a very large audience on the screen burst into ecstatic applause.

'I love my chat shows,' she said. 'And İsmet Bey just makes me howl with laughter.'

İkmen looked at the screen, which showed a close-up of a middle-aged man wearing a collarless shirt and expensively tailored trousers.

'He's a fraud! Like all of them.'

Tele-evangelist İsmet Satar was a one-time heroin addict from the eastern city of Harran who had experienced a religious epiphany when he had visited Aya Sofya back in the 1990s.

Quite what had occurred, nobody really knew, but ever since that visit Satar had been born again in Islam, giving up drugs, drink and women – what he described as 'earthly delights'. In spite of this, rumours about cocaine-fuelled sex parties abounded, though they were not believed by anyone who mattered.

'I know,' Samsun said. 'I just like the way the women in the audience almost come when he walks past them.'

'That's cruel.'

'They believe his bullshit and so they deserve it. Anyway, he's got some "experts" on today, so I'm expecting conspiracy theory overload. Last time they had this nutter from Mersin who reckoned the Pope was actually a Jew and a member of Mossad.'

İkmen shook his head. 'I'll leave you to it,' he said.

He'd begun to walk back into the kitchen when something on the screen caught his eye.

Having already established that Ceyda Kazantzoğlu's skull had been fractured in two places, Dr Arto Sarkissian was examining what remained of her brain. Gently pulling aside the folds of the cortex, he searched for evidence of the blood clot he suspected had killed her.

'I think that's probably the culprit,' he told Kerim Gürsel as he pointed with a probe to a small discoloured lump.

Kerim, who was slightly colourless behind his face mask, just grunted. Attending autopsies wasn't something he looked forward to, and in this case, the corpse in question was extremely odiferous.

The doctor picked up the brain and placed it on a set of scales, then typed its weight into his computer.

'How are things progressing with the Kazantzoğlus?' he asked.

'Ece has given us a statement to the effect that her husband, Ateş, killed his mother in a fit of rage,' Kerim said. 'This is not, however, corroborated by the husband.'

281

'What's his story?'

'He doesn't have one. At first, when we interviewed the couple together, he insisted his wife was lying, but now he's gone silent.'

'But you managed to obtain a DNA sample.'

'In the end, yes.'

'Mmm.' The doctor picked up a fresh scalpel and a set of rib spreaders. 'Let's see what else ailed this woman, shall we?'

One of the two men and the nun looked expectant; the other, Lokman Bulut, simply looked bored. Mehmet Süleyman, innately suspicious of anyone stupid enough to go to a loan shark, regarded the young man as little more than a spoilt rich kid. A silly poseur who felt the world owed him a living.

He dived into his subject without preamble. 'I'm afraid I have to tell you that our investigation at the Karacaahmet cemetery is being scaled down,' he said. 'This doesn't mean it is at an end – far from it – but it is felt that tying up so much manpower cannot be justified. Although your mother's body has been removed without authorisation—'

'By whom? We still don't know!' Uğur Bulut looked wrung out. His face was grey and unshaven and he seemed to be on the verge of tears.

'I appreciate there are still questions—'

'Damn right!'

Sister Eudokia put a hand on her brother's arm. 'Let him speak,' she said.

'I know this is disappointing, but please do be assured that we are not dropping the case. The woman who occupied your mother's grave was killed unlawfully and we are pursuing all and any lines of inquiry.'

'And we can't even respectfully re-inter Mother's body!'

'My mother's body,' Lokman corrected.

They all looked at him and he averted his eyes.

'The investigation at the gravesite is at an end,' Süleyman said. 'And so within a few days it will be possible for you to re-bury—'

'A leg bone and some vertebrae? What's the use of that?' Uğur said. 'That isn't our mother!'

Süleyman wanted to say that even if they'd discovered Perihan Hanım's skeleton in its entirety, it still wouldn't constitute her, but he didn't.

'As I have said, sir, this investigation is ongoing. You may call me any time . . .'

'Oh, to hell with this!'

Uğur Bulut stood up and stormed out of the office. Sister Eudokia rose and began to follow him. But not before saying to Süleyman, 'Thank you. I understand and so will my brother when he's calmed down.'

'Sister.' Süleyman bowed.

This left the policeman alone with Lokman Bulut, which was, in a way, quite fortunate.

Raşım Dorsay had done everything he could. He'd told Türgüt Bey about Münir Sever's late-night meeting with someone to whom he'd spoken English, and the gatekeeper had said he would deal with it. So why couldn't Raşım just go to sleep and prepare for his next night shift like a normal person?

He knew why. Seeing Münir and Türgüt Bey together before last night's shift had come as a surprise. By the look of it, they'd been planning the night-time rotas. Did they always do that? Münir was usually at work before Raşım, but that alone didn't mean much. And even if they did plan rotas together regularly, it didn't prove anything. Not on its own. However, it did mean that the two of them could, in theory, be directing the guards away from any illegal activities that might be taking place on the site. But to what purpose? Türgüt Bey had been a lawyer

and had plenty of money, and while Münir claimed to be perpet-
ually broke, he was also surely too floridly patriotic to do anything
that might damage his reputation.

Then Raşim remembered how angry Münir had been. Everyone
knew he had a temper, but Raşim had never actually felt frightened of him before. And what was the speaking in English about?
He poured himself another glass of tea and lit another cigarette.
It was then that the name of the person Münir had been speaking
to, or what he thought might be the name, popped into his mind.

'Do you still intend to contest your mother's will?'

Lokman Bulut, while not wanting to accompany his brother
and sister out of Süleyman's office, only wanted to stick around
long enough to make sure he didn't catch up with them.

'Yes,' he said. Slumped in his chair, he looked like a sulky
teenager.

'Do you not think that might be divisive?' Süleyman asked.
'Your brother gives you a very generous allowance . . .'

'He's not my mother's son. She built the business and I'm
her only child.'

'In recent years your brother has expanded the business.'

Ömer Mungun came into the office. Lokman ignored him.

'So? That was his choice. He got lucky. I'll have my own ideas.'

'You know that legal battles like this can be costly?'

'Yeah.'

Süleyman shrugged. 'Sergeant Mungun will drive you home,'
he said.

'I'll make my own way, thanks.'

'No, I insist.'

They stared at each other for a moment. Lokman knew he
shouldn't do this. But it was hot and he was tired.

Chapter 22

Her mouth was dry and tasted of dust. In spite of the fact that the sun was shining, she was as cold as the dead. Was she dead?

A face from the past went in and out of focus, mouthing something. Deniz Palandoken raised herself on her elbows. She was outside. Where was Can? Her head seemed to be in several places at once and she felt a bit sick. Where was she?

'Are you all right?'

Why was this character asking her whether she was all right? She wasn't.

'Do you want to come to my house and rest?'

Instinctively she pulled away from him.

'I want to help you,' he said. 'That's what I do, I help people.'

And then Deniz realised who he was, and she kissed his hand. 'Oh yes,' she said. 'Help me! Help me, please!'

Sergeant Eylul Yavaş could only hear Inspector Kerim Gürsel's side of the conversation. He'd barely been back in his office when his phone had rung, and so they'd had no time to discuss the autopsy he had attended that morning. All she knew was that the caller was Çetin İkmen, because when Gürsel had picked up, he'd smiled and said, 'Ah, Çetin Bey.'

Now, however, her superior looked grave. She heard him say,

'I take your point, but a warrant could still be knocked back due to lack of direct evidence.'

There was a pause, and then he continued, 'Yes, but he'd have to be prepared to make a complaint, and if we find nothing, that is where he lives. It's risky.'

Now that she had been separated from her husband, Ece Kazantzoğlu was talking freely. Eylul had spent much of the morning with her, learning about her terrible life. She could have been allocated an attorney, but she had refused, saying she preferred to speak to Eylul. Everything she said was recorded.

'Well, if you want to do that then you'll have to bring him in,' Gürsel said. 'And only when I've taken a statement will I be able to apply for a warrant. I doubt we could do this today.'

Ece's husband's family had been Greek originally. But with the collapse of the Ottoman Empire and the coming of the republic in 1923, the Kazantzoğlus had opted to convert to Islam and stay in Anatolia. According to Ece's dead mother-in-law, they had become 'more Turkish than the Turks'. One of the things Ateş had screamed at his mother when he killed her was 'rayah', which was an old Ottoman term of abuse used against non-Muslim citizens of the empire. Back in those days, some non-Muslims were resented because of their ability to lend and trade money. Muslims were forbidden the 'sin' of usury, but the Greeks in particular had a reputation in this trade. As far as Ateş Kazantzoğlu was concerned, his mother, by hoarding gold, had committed a great sin. But other influences were at play too.

'Ateş watches a lot of those evangelist shows on TV,' Ece had said. 'I think some of them may have turned his mind. Especially the ones that talk about bringing back the Ottoman Empire. He says he'd like that. But then I think the strain of being with Devlet has played its part too. You feel so alone and helpless . . .'

On the phone, Kerim Gürsel said, 'Well, if you can find him, but don't put any pressure on him. This has to come from him . . . No, I'm not happy about it, but I do take your point. If there's the slightest chance . . . Yes, of course. Bye.'

Eylul watched him put his mobile down on his desk and then exhale.

'Have you heard,' he asked her, 'of Professor Aşık Tolon?'

'Yes,' she said. 'Believes we should bring back the empire, doesn't he?'

'Yes. He's been off our screens for a while, but now, according to Çetin Bey, he's back.'

'Oh.'

'His absence was, he claims, due to ill health. When pressed by his interviewer this morning, he admitted it was cancer. But now he is cured.'

'Oh.'

'Yes,' Kerim said, 'by God.' There was a pause before he continued. 'I realise that you and I may have different views regarding alleged miracles, but in this particular case we should pay attention.'

'What do you mean?'

'I mean that the professor's son, Serkan Tolon, may have a connection to Sevval Kalkan.'

'That's very tenuous, sir.'

'Perhaps, but Çetin Bey—'

'Didn't that connection come from Çetin Bey when he overheard a conversation between Serkan Tolon and a member of that family Inspector Süleyman has been investigating?'

'Yes,' he said. 'And now, for better or worse, he thinks that perhaps Professor Tolon's recovery has rather more to do with an intervention from his son than with the hand of God.'

* * *

287

The building stank of damp. But then a lot of the old Tarlabaşı houses did. Still puzzled as to why his police driver wouldn't let him walk up his own stairs alone, Lokman Bulut said, 'You don't have to come to my door.'

Ömer Mungun looked sheepish. 'Well, actually I was hoping to use your lavatory.'

'Oh.'

They stood outside the door into the apartment. Ömer knew what Lokman was probably thinking, and so he said, 'Look, you're a victim of crime. I don't care if your place smells of weed. Where doesn't around here?'

Lokman Bulut paused for a moment, then said, 'All right.'

He opened the door and the unmistakable smell of stale cannabis assaulted them. The bathroom was at the end of the corridor beside the small galley kitchen. As he walked towards it, Ömer saw that the living-room walls were covered in graffiti.

He went into the bathroom and shut the door. He heard Lokman go into the kitchen.

When he had washed his hands, he returned to the corridor. There was one room, on the left, that he hadn't seen. Lokman Bulut appeared behind him and said, 'You done?'

'Yes. Thanks.' He began to walk forward, thinking about where this unseen room, probably a bedroom, was positioned in the building. He said, 'Do you get a view of the Golden Horn from that room?'

'A bit. Not much.'

'Can I see?'

'It's my bedroom, I'd rather—'

But Ömer had opened the door. And yes, there was a very small sliver of a view from the window. There was also an even stronger smell of cannabis. He left and closed the door. 'Thanks.'

When he got back to his car, he called Süleyman.

'There's some graffiti in the living room, but it's all very small and amateur. Nothing like that mural Çetin Bey showed us.'

He heard Süleyman sigh.

'What are you doing?'

Yaşar Akgün turned. 'Getting drinks.'

He'd just come out of his kitchen and was headed for the small patio at the back of his house, where he'd left Deniz Palandoken.

Abdülkadır Soyar shook his head. Some days he wished passionately that he was back in Rize.

'You shouldn't bring that woman here,' he said. 'You shouldn't bring any of them here.'

Yaşar frowned. 'I helped her,' he said. 'She's grateful. And I think she needs help again.'

Abdülkadır toddled after Yaşar on sore, swollen feet.

'Yaşar Bey,' he said. 'If the boys come back and find her here, they won't be pleased . . .'

'Her husband is sick again,' Yaşar said. 'And so she has come to be part of the helping that we do.' He smiled.

Outside, he handed a glass of orange juice to Deniz Palandoken, who drank the whole lot in one go.

Yaşar smiled. 'You must have been thirsty,' he said.

'I was.' She put her head down for a moment as the sudden rehydration made her feel dizzy. Then she said, 'I told you my husband is sick. I need some money.'

Yaşar shook his head. 'I'm sorry to hear that,' he said. 'We've helped you before and we shall help you again.'

'Oh . . .' She took one of his hands in her filthy paw and kissed it.

This was too much. Abdülkadır grabbed her by her reeking hair and pulled her away.

'That's enough of that,' he said.

'Abdülkadır Bey, you're hurting her!'

'I know.'

He dragged her towards the house and then pushed her into the hallway.

'Get out!'

'But I want to—'

'We don't want you!' the old man said. 'Get out!'

She opened the front door and ran. Yaşar turned to Abdülkadır. 'Why did you do that? She wishes to donate. She wanted to help.'

Abdülkadır shook his head. 'You've been told, Yaşar Bey,' he said. 'We're helping no one at the moment. We will do again, but we have the police making up stories about us and so we must do nothing for now.'

'Why do the police make up stories about us?' Yaşar asked.

Abdülkadır couldn't remember what that celebrity lawyer had said to him last time, so he just said, 'Because they're bad people. They're fascists. They don't care about the people like we do.'

'Oh.'

İkmen walked up the stone steps into the battered, slightly sagging old building that was Rifat's bar and was assaulted by the reek of rakı and a dense cloud of cigarette smoke.

He'd tried to find Vedat Bey, the alcoholic, at his building on Cuckuk Sokak, but a woman hanging out her washing in the street had told him that the old man had gone out. Since the government had started to tax alcohol heavily, paying for booze had become burdensome, especially for alcoholics. Luckily help was at hand in the shape of people like Rifat Sasmaz, who knew people who could get alcohol more cheaply. It was that or home-brew, which could be lethal.

İkmen went straight up to the bar and called Rifat over.

'What can I help you with, Çetin Bey?'

İkmen cleared his throat. 'I'm looking for a man called Vedat, who lives on Cuckuk Sokak. Could be fifty, could be seventy, he's lived a life, likes a drink . . .'

'Vedat Oktay,' Rifat said with absolute certainty. 'He's been coming here for years.'

'Is he here most days?'

'He used to be.'

İkmen passed a cigarette to Rifat and they both lit up. 'So why doesn't he come so much now? Your prices are keen, to say the least, Rifat Bey.'

The bar owner smiled. 'Indeed they are,' he said, 'but even I can't compete with moonshine.'

'Ah.'

Rifat shook his head. 'Since the tax increases, the most unlikely people have been setting up stills. I know of at least one priest who does it. Mind you, his stuff is safe and good, and he just keeps it for himself and his friends. Wherever Vedat goes will be much more downmarket.'

'Not a wealthy man?'

'If you've seen him, you'll know.'

İkmen nodded.

'I've no idea where he might be,' Rifat said. 'I mean, take your pick round here. He's probably gone to ground. He does that when he runs out of money. He may even be at home, unless he's not paid his rent.'

'Does he have friends here?'

'No, not really. Alcoholics don't tend to have friends.'

'So when he comes to the bar, he just sits down and gets blind drunk.'

'That's about the size of it. Try going to his place. If he's in, he's in. If not, you've lost nothing but a little time.'

Süleyman steepled his fingers underneath his chin and said, 'What do you know about Türgüt Bey?'

'Nothing much,' Raşım Dorsay replied. 'When he first came, before I worked here, people were surprised that such an educated man wanted a job like that.'

'He was a lawyer.'

'Yes. Weird. Before Türgüt Bey, the guards didn't have rotas and so people thought he was going to be more efficient. Apparently a lot of the older guards left then because they didn't like it.'

'But not your colleague Münir Sever?'

'No. But then if he's doing the rotas with Türgüt Bey, I can understand that,' Raşım said. 'Inspector Bey, I don't want to get anyone into trouble . . .'

'And yet the appearance of this Hafız or Hafez last night unsettled you?'

'If it was the same person I saw hanging about in the grave-yard the other night, then . . .' He shrugged. 'I don't know. But Münir was really angry when he saw me and he was quiet for the rest of the shift.'

'Türgüt Bey hasn't tried to contact me yet,' Süleyman said. 'Although I assume he's home by now.'

'He worked the night shift too, so yes. I don't want any trouble,' Raşım said. 'And yet . . .'

'And yet what?'

He sighed. 'Things have been different at work this last year. This business about not officially recording break-ins or sight-ings of unauthorised persons on the site. Everyone feels under pressure to cover things up. I mean, take that boy, Hafız, I caught lurking about. He tried to resist when I took him to the office, and then Türgüt Bey tells me to just tip him out on the street. He could've been doing anything! It's as if Türgüt Bey is frightened of being human.'

'What do you mean?'

'Well, of course people get into lonely places like graveyards at night. They always have, and yet he seems to be frightened of even admitting it's possible. He has to keep a perfect record. He says it's because he's worried we might lose our jobs if there are incidents.'

Süleyman knew the type, sadly. In almost every walk of life there were people prepared to break the rules and falsify data in order to maintain a clean sheet. On the other hand, few jobs were secure and there were always people willing to take advantage of a less than perfect record.

'Would you recognise the boy you saw last night?' he asked.

'I don't know. It was very dark and I was not close. But I would recognise the boy, Hafız. He was an Arab, probably a Syrian, about my height and really young. A teenager. He didn't speak Turkish, only Arabic. The person Münir met spoke English.'

'Do you speak English?'

'Not well, and I didn't try it with the boy,' Raşım said. He paused for a moment and frowned. 'Inspector Bey, I've been wondering whether Türgüt Bey and Münir have . . . whether they know more about what happened to Perihan Bulut's body than they are saying.'

'You think they may . . .'

'I don't really know what I think, but I've felt for a while that something is wrong.'

'Mmm.' Süleyman nodded his head. 'Tell me, Raşım, does Türgüt Bey ever meet any members of his family at his place of work?'

'No. Not that I know of. Why?'

'No reason.'

And yet there was. Süleyman still wasn't convinced that Türgüt Akgün wasn't related to alleged gangster Yaşar Akgün from Kasımpaşa. Although Turgut had been born in Hasköy, both men's families had originated in Rize. . The inspector looked at his computer and brought up his notes pertaining to the gatekeeper.

* * *

She saw the water bottle first. A full two litres, untouched. Ever since he'd become ill, Deniz had never left Can without water and, if she could, some food. Usually, especially if she'd been gone a long time, he'd drunk all the water, even if he'd left the food. But not this time.

In spite of the shade afforded by the boarded-up windows, the ruined house the couple squatted in was hot. As soon as she clambered through the hole in the wall, Deniz wanted a drink. Can had to be asleep. Asleep and dehydrating. She picked the water bottle up and removed the lid, then squatted down beside him.

'Can. Can?'

He usually started to stir when she spoke to him, but not this time. She looked at him hard, but he didn't move. Was he breathing? She put her hand to his mouth, but felt nothing. She shook him. Nothing. She shook him again, and it was then that the vomit remaining in his mouth spilled out all over her and she screamed.

The door banged open to reveal the youngster with the man bun. And while his eyes were very clearly stoned, his face was red with fury.

'What do you want?' he shouted at a very humble-looking İkmen. 'Who are you? I told you to fuck off! Why didn't you?'

'I am most awfully sorry,' İkmen said with more than a nod to his family's five hundred years of subservience to their Ottoman masters. 'But I'm looking for Vedat Bey. He's not at home . . .'

There was nothing to see in the apartment's hallway.

'What do you want with him?' Serkan Tolon said.

'Well . . .'

'Well? I'm busy. Spit it out!'

'He owes me money,' İkmen said.

'Oh does he? Well don't expect me to reimburse you.'

'No, of course not.'

'He owes me rent, the drunken tosser!'

İkmen had knocked on Vedat's front door before he'd gone to Serkan's apartment. Of course the alcoholic could be in there, but he could also be dead – or just out. Not that it was Vedat or his apartment that he wanted to see. After witnessing Professor Aşık Tolon's evangelical performance on that chat show, he was now in search of any evidence he could find to connect the Tolon family to Sevval Kalkan. Only someone with real power could have silenced a woman facing her own demise as thoroughly as Sevval had been silenced. Someone like Professor Tolon.

'I've tried knocking on his door . . .'

'Oh for God's sake . . . I'll get the key,' Tolon said. 'Wait there.'

He walked down the corridor and entered a room nearly at the end, on the left. İkmen had to be quick, and he had to assume that Tolon was alone. He heard him throwing things around and swearing as he hunted for Vedat's key.

İkmen stepped over the threshold and opened the door directly to his right. A small kitchen that stank of stale food. He shut the door.

'Oh for fuck's sake!' he heard Tolon growl.

His breathing coming short now, his heart hammering, İkmen placed a sweaty hand on the handle of the door to his left, right next to the one Tolon had disappeared into.

Dark, because of closed curtains, the room wallowed in the afternoon heat. İkmen switched the light on and saw a bed. Then he saw what was above the bed. Having seen it, he had to stop himself looking at it.

By the time Serkan Tolon had found Vedat Oktay's key, the man who had been at his front door had gone.

* * *

Nobody who lived in the brightly coloured wooden houses of Kuzguncuk needed money. The place was stiff with lawyers, doctors and captains of industry. Only such people could afford to eat at the restaurants with stunning Bosphorus views or buy chocolates from the gourmet chocolatier or browse in the bookshops cum coffee joints.

Türgüt Akgün, still in his pyjamas, returned from his kitchen with three glasses of tea and put two of them down on the small carved table in front of Süleyman and Ömer Mungun.

'I honestly do not want any trouble,' he said. 'My previous career was nothing but trouble and I don't need any more of it.'

'What kind of trouble?' Süleyman asked.

'Oh, where to start?' he said. 'Any kind of law practitioner gets his or her share of threats. But when you work in property law, you get more than most. Especially in land disputes. Whether your client wins or loses doesn't matter; someone will threaten to break your arms.'

'Did you go to the police?' Ömer asked.

'What, three times a day?' He shook his head. 'What would be the point? Anyway, that's ancient history. When I gave it up and got this job at the cemetery, I thought I'd have a nice restful time until I retired. But the directors want a quiet life too, and so you soon find yourself in charge of a team and a site that has to present zero problems.'

'Which is why you didn't report last night's intruder?' Süleyman asked.

'Yes,' he said. 'Probably a friend of Münir's. I'll speak to him about it. He's been at the Karacaahmet for years and I trust him completely, even if he's a bit of an old thug. He's helped me to compile the guards' rotas ever since I took over at the cemetery. He cares about the place a great deal, but he's not well, which is why I don't want to confront him over meeting a friend.'

'Guard Dorsay said they argued, in English.'

Türgüt shrugged. 'I don't know. A lot of people speak English . . .'

'Yes, but they argued,' Ömer said.

The gatekeeper threw his arms in the air. 'Münir has a short temper!' he said. 'He's not exactly a tolerant man. Can't stand people if they're different from him. There's a lot of it about.'

'So why do you consult him regarding the rotas?'

'I told you, because . . .' He looked down and then sighed. 'Look,' he said, 'in my attempt not to make any waves, I think I may have told you an untruth.'

'As in a lie.'

He shrugged. 'You wanted to know whether I have any family in Kasimpaşa and I said no.'.'

'So you do?'

'Yes. But I never see them. They're my cousins, but I wish to God they weren't.'

'Why's that?'

'Because, well . . . Look, only one of them lives in Kasimpaşa. But . . . Yaşar Akgün, the one in Kasimpaşa, is . . . I don't know what, there's all sorts of rumours about him being involved in crime. I don't think that can be right. İzzet, his brother, he lives in Rize but he visits. He's someone I could believe anything about . . .'

This was a breakthrough he hadn't expected, but Süleyman nevertheless couldn't get it out of his head that this man had suddenly come clean when he had wanted to talk to him about Münir Sever. Why?

Can couldn't be dead. It was ridiculous. Deniz had been sitting beside him for over an hour, occasionally shaking his arm. Every time she did it, his torso just flopped forward and she began to cry. If she'd had any gear, it wouldn't have been so hard, but there was nothing to take the pain away and so she just hurt and wept and then hurt again.

What did you do with the dead anyway? Her father had always dealt with that. And why had Can died? Why? She'd got him antibiotics! She looked in the box she'd given him and he had taken them. Why had this happened? Perhaps the medication had been tainted in some way. Maybe it was the wrong sort. After all, what did Dr Fixit care? How could she trust these people anyway? Hadn't they promised her they'd give her five thousand lira for her baby? She'd only ever got two. Something about the child being less than perfect . . . What did that even mean? She'd taken the money because Can was howling for a fix. They'd both been exhausted and broke and she'd not been able to stop crying.

She had hated herself ever since. She hated herself now. She took Can's penknife from his coat pocket and cut her arm as deeply as she could bear.

'Abdülkadır Soyar is Yaşar and İzzet's uncle on their mother's side,' Türgüt said. 'He left Rize years ago to come and work for a man called Paşa Beyaz in Tarlabaşı.'

Süleyman looked at Ömer Mungun, who raised his eyebrows. Now that Türgüt Akgün had opened up about his relatives there was no stopping him. And it had been Türgüt himself who had named Yaşar Akgün with no help from Süleyman . . .

'I don't know why Yaşar came to join him,' Türgüt said. 'İzzet remained in Rize and took over his father's gold business when Uncle Ramazan died. My father was Ramazan's brother, but even he kept clear of them.'

'Why?'

'Because they're idiots. Uncle Ramazan was ever so pious, but he swore like a marine, and if no one would fight him, he'd start a fight with himself. They're thugs and they're stupid.

What more can I say? Some years ago, İzzet had a land dispute involving his shop. He asked me for help, but just the thought of assisting him made me sweat. If I lost his case, he'd probably beat me up, he certainly wouldn't pay his bill, and if I won he'd recommend my services to every scumbag in Rize. I spoke to a colleague in Ankara who agreed to take him on. He won, thank God. My father brought us to İstanbul to get away from his family.'

'Do you think Abdülkadır Soyar obtained a job for Yaşar with his employer?'

'I've no idea,' Türgüt said. 'And while we're talking about Yaşar, I assume that if you've met him, you'll know he's not right.'

'He's different.'

'You could call it that. My opinion is that he's autistic. Infuriating, but not a bad bone in his body.'

'Not like other members of his family?'

'Oh no,' he said. 'One of the reasons we all disliked Uncle Ramazan and İzzet was because they made fun of poor old Yaşar, especially after his mother died. Treated him like an animal. Maybe Abdülkadır Soyar did him a favour bringing him to the city.'

Or maybe he brought him here to use him, Süleyman thought. But this wasn't helping with his immediate problem.

'I understand Münir Sever is on duty tonight,' he said. 'I should like to observe his activities.'

'If you must.'

'Sergeant Mungun and I will watch Sever and Dorsay from a distance.'

'How do you know this boy will show up again?' Türgüt said.

'We don't. But according to Dorsay, he had some sort of issue with Sever that was left unresolved, so there is a chance he may return. Needless to say, I don't want you to say anything to anyone about this,' Süleyman added. 'Not even to Guard Dorsay.'

It was clear when they left that Türgüt Akgün wasn't happy about the arrangement, but he agreed to keep his mouth shut. Once out on the street, Süleyman said, 'I wish he'd told us what he knew about Yaşar Akgün before. I wonder what Abdülkadır Soyar did for old Paşa Beyaz.'

'And what Yaşar did,' Ömer said. 'I wonder how he actually inherited Paşa's patch.'

There had been rumours for years that Paşa Beyaz was partial to a younger man.

'Who knows?'

As they began to make their way back to the car, Süleyman spotted someone he recognised. He made as if to greet Dr Sibel Çoban, but when she saw him, she turned away.

Chapter 23

'It doesn't prove he had anything to do with her death.'

'Yes, but he knew her,' İkmen said. 'He had to know her to have her paint that mural for him. It's exactly the same as the Polaroid I was given. He talked to his friend about Zeynep.'

Kerim Gürsel leaned back in his chair. 'Çetin Bey,' he said, 'taking on these people . . .'

'Professor Tolon, Serkan's father, had cancer. He now claims that he's cured. Bone marrow transplants are used to treat some forms of cancer.' İkmen looked behind him to make sure that no one was listening. 'People like Tolon have an agenda.'

Kerim Gürsel hadn't been pleased to see İkmen waiting for him outside his office. Commissioner Özer would know about it – he had eyes everywhere – and there would be consequences.

'Look,' İkmen said as he took an empty cigarette packet out of his jacket pocket and placed it on Kerim's desk. 'There are two names here, doctors who have performed medical examinations in Silivri prison. Both these doctors, Yavuz and Çoban, have ordered HLA tests on prisoners from time to time. That's the test for—'

'Yes, I know. Was Sevval Kalkan tested?'

'The way the data is stored means that the prisoners are simply numbers,' İkmen said. 'But you can request full disclosure as part of your investigation.'

'I'd have to have good reason.'

'You do have good reason,' İkmen said. 'Kerim, a woman

has died needlessly, and a man, Tolon, is basically defrauding the public.'

'You don't think God can cure people?'

'I don't know,' İkmen said. 'But I'm pretty sure that if He does take a hand in our affairs down here from time to time, it is not to the benefit of people like Tolon who divide society with their rhetoric about an empire that is dead and gone. You know this!'

And although he didn't say it, Kerim also knew that İkmen, like him, was inwardly quaking at the thought of challenging the assertions of such a powerful figure. It was one of those moments when his public persona as a police officer and a member of a minority of gay officers brought about a level of dissonance he found hard to bear. To put his head, figuratively, above the parapet could potentially invite unwelcome scrutiny. That said, İkmen was right.

'I'll have to take advice,' he said.

'From whom?'

'I don't know. I should, strictly speaking, go to Özer.'

He watched İkmen put his head in his hands.

Kasımpaşa looked normal, except for her. Women, their heads and sometimes their faces covered, doing their shopping, men talking in small, subdued groups on street corners, somebody constructing a shonky-looking shack on top of a tall nineteenth-century building that appeared close to collapse. And then there was Deniz Palandoken. With her one good hand, she'd knocked and knocked on Yaşar Akgün's door until her knuckles burned. Now she was on her way to the community centre. Soon it would be öğle namazı, the midday call to prayer, and all the men in the coffee house would be at the local mosque. Would Akgün and his people be with them?

As she walked up the stairs and past the door into the coffee

302

house, Deniz saw the men stir. Holding tight to the rag she'd tied around her arm, she continued up to the first floor. The man who'd given her money for her newborn flesh and blood stood in front of her. He said, 'Get out!'

Deniz shook her head. 'Can is dead,' she said. 'I want to see that doctor.'

The man, Ali Haydar Özince, wasn't looking at her, but at the floor. 'You're bleeding!'

Deniz looked down. He was right. The cut she'd made on her arm was still bleeding in spite of her attempts to bind it up.

'Then get me that doctor,' she said. 'I want to see him.'

Ali Haydar walked towards her. 'Go to the fucking hospital,' he said.

'Where is Yaşar Bey?' Deniz asked.

'Doing better things than talking to a junkie.'

'Get him!'

He took hold of her arm and began to push her back towards the stairs. 'Get out! Filthy old slag!'

Deniz was unsure about what happened next. She couldn't remember letting go of the rag around her arm, but she must have done, otherwise she wouldn't have been able to stab Ali Haydar in the guts with Can's knife.

'Do you think Türgüt Akgün was telling the truth about his family?' Ömer Mungun asked his superior.

Traffic was stationary on the 15th July Martyrs Bridge. It had been renamed to commemorate the victims of the attempted coup of 2016, and like all the bridges across the Bosphorus was a victim of almost permanent traffic jams.

'I can't see why not,' Süleyman said. 'He'd successfully hidden his connection to them in the past. That said, did he do it to take attention away from Münir Sever?'

'You know, sir, I never cease to wonder at how seemingly

diverse people almost always turn out to be so interconnected in this city. Mardin is much smaller and of course we all know each other, but here . . .'

Süleyman smiled. 'İstanbul, the biggest village in the world,' he said. 'And like a village, it gossips.'

It was almost midday and the sun beat down on the unmoving car with a fierce intensity. Süleyman turned the air conditioning up.

Ömer said, 'Do you think this Münir Sever could be involved in Perihan Bulut's disappearance from her grave? I mean, what do you hope to find tonight?'

'I don't know,' Süleyman said. 'I imagine the cemetery guards do meet people they know in the Karacaahmet from time to time, but when Guard Dorsay described what had happened, the elements of violent language combined with fear struck me as concerning. Dorsay is convinced that something has been wrong for the best part of a year, although I got the impression he felt the main reason for this was Türgüt Akgün, who may yet be involved in illegal activities.'

Ömer, whose brain was too hot in spite of the air con, said, 'And yet in spite of being the biggest village in the world, we still can't find out who the woman we found in Perihan Bulut's grave is.'

'We do know that she's on the margin between the gossips of the biggest village and the omertà of the criminal fraternity.'

'Omertà?'

'The code of silence that originated with the Sicilian Mafia,' Süleyman said. 'Every gang of thugs everywhere uses its own version to silence and terrify its members.'

'Yaşar Akgün doesn't look very terrifying to me,' Ömer said.

'I agree,' Süleyman said. 'But when a person, however timid, can command the services of someone like Eyüp Çelik, then one must take that person seriously.'

'You think?'

'I think Akgün has a lot of power behind him,' Süleyman said. 'He may even have a violent side.'

'I can't see that,' Ömer said.

Although he had first been engaged on the hunt for Sevval Kalkan by Machine Bey, it was Gold Bey, the jeweller Cumhur Polat, to whom İkmen now turned. After leaving police headquarters, he'd driven to Tarlabaşı, ostensibly to check up on Polat, though he knew there was more to it than that.

It was as hot as hell in the basement apartment, and so Polat took İkmen outside to the tiny stained mattress and discarded oil tin that he called his garden.

'I never really bought into the idea of Sevval as graffiti artist,' he said as he placed a glass of tea on the wall İkmen was sitting on. 'Certainly not one who commands ten thousand lira for her work. We are exploited, people like us. I can't enforce my prices for the pieces I make any more than Machine Bey can for his sculptures. You saw how those two young men treated me over that watch. Now I've made the damn thing, the buyer is nowhere to be seen, and yet he wanted it yesterday! Maybe I've made it for no reason.'

'I know who those young men are, 'İkmen said. 'The friend of your customer is Serkan Tolon, the son of Professor Aşık Tolon.'

'Ha! The so-called academic,' Polat said. 'Why am I not surprised?'

'It was in Tolon Junior's apartment that I saw Sevval's graffito.'

'I thought that was out of doors . . .'

'So did I,' İkmen said, 'until a friend pointed out that there was wooden flooring below the image.'

'But why would Tolon have a picture of . . . I mean, he's in favour of the status quo.'

'I think Tolon Junior wants to appear edgy and alternative,' İkmen said. 'But look, I've come to pick your brains. I know I've done it before, but . . .'

'Pick away.'

'Do you have any idea at all about how, why or where Sevval may have met Serkan Tolon?'

Polat frowned. 'She was very full of herself when she sold that graffito,' he said. 'I was happy for her, but when I asked who'd bought it, she clammed up.'

'Completely?'

'She said she'd sold it to an art collector,' he said. 'She didn't say where she met this person or how, and I didn't ask.'

'What about the others?'

'I don't know,' he said. 'Maybe she told Olimpio. I know that Sevval liked to tease her with stories about her romantic conquests to make up for all the criticism she got from her. Olimpio is a funny old thing, but she's as upset about Sevval's death as the rest of us. Talk to her.'

'I will. Gold Bey, to take you back to your time at Silivri, do you remember your medical examination upon entry?'

Polat sighed. 'Not well. I know my blood pressure was high and I was too wound up to give a urine sample. I think I told you before, I don't know what I was tested for.'

'The doctor who performed the test . . .'

'A woman,' he said. 'Couldn't tell you her name if my life depended on it. All I do know is she kept taking my blood pressure and frowning.'

'Did she give you any blood pressure medication?'

'No,' he said. 'I think it must've come down. I defy anyone to have a normal reading under prison conditions.'

'She took blood?'

'Oh yes,' he said. 'A lot of that.'

'What do you mean?'

'I don't know what she was testing for, she didn't say, but she must have taken five or six of those vial things they use.'

'Did you ever get any results?'

'No.' He thought for a moment. 'But last time you were here, with Machine and the Designer, Olimpio did say something about her results after you'd gone.'

'Do you remember what it was?'

'No, but I can message her if you like.'

The screaming was so loud, it hurt her head. Deniz Palandoken put her hands over her ears and closed her eyes. Maybe if she cut everything out, it would go away. But it didn't. She could hear it through her bloodied hands, and when she opened her eyes, he was still running around the room like a raving madman.

For the most part he said absolutely nothing, he just screamed, but whenever he stopped to look at the body on the floor, he shouted, 'What am I going to do? What am I going to do?'

Deniz had reached a sort of strange, detached calm. She wondered whether it was something to do with cutting herself. Had she lost so much blood she was about to die? Like Ali Haydar Özince. His blood had gone everywhere; it had just poured out, as if someone had left a tap on.

All the men downstairs had gone to pray, and Yaşar Bey had come up here on his own. Deniz wondered whether people in the street could hear him screaming.

'What am I going to do?' he yelled. Over and over and over again.

She tried to form the words to say that she didn't know, but she couldn't. What was more, she didn't care. Can was dead and so her reason for carrying on had gone. What did she care whether this crazy man knocked himself out running around and screaming? And yet she couldn't stop watching him.

When the whispers on the opiate grapevine of İstanbul had

reached her about the men in Kasımpaşa who would buy anything that came from the human body, she had imagined a coterie of butchers. But in amongst the thugs there had been a doctor, and a godfather nobody ever saw who, she was always told, just wanted to help people. But now he'd gone mad, and it was her fault.

Still nobody came. Then Yaşar Bey slipped in Ali Haydar's blood and fell over. Deniz wondered at her own lack of empathy for the man she'd killed. She just kept on thinking how toxic he had been while alive, and how dangerous he was now he was dead.

People could sometimes surprise. Not generally people like Commissioner Özer. But when Kerim Gürsel had entered his office his superior had looked different, thoughtful.

Before Kerim had even sat down, he'd said, 'When I was a young man, the world was in many ways more brutal than it is now. If, for instance, one fell foul of those in power, one could very easily end up dead. Not that we always knew about such things. Communication systems were limited back in the seventies and eighties. Now we know so much more. Now we can disseminate our own opinions, if we so wish . . .'

Kerim suspected he meant via social media, a vexatious issue for the state, to say the least. A vexatious issue for all states, he felt.

'And yet,' Özer continued, 'is that a good thing?'

'I—'

'The question was rhetorical.' He stared at the ceiling. 'However true some things may be, do we really have to share them with others? Is that always a good thing?'

Kerim didn't move or speak. What was going on here? Was Özer having some sort of epiphany, and if so, what about?

But then it was as if a switch flipped in the commissioner's head, and he trained his eyes on Kerim and said, 'What do you want?'

'Ah.' Caught off guard, Kerim found himself having to marshal his thoughts again. 'Sir, it's about the Sevval Kalkan case. It's come to my attention that when she was in Silivri prison, she was given a medical.'

'What of it?'

'I'd like permission to gain access to the results of those tests.'

'Why?'

'We know that Kalkan donated bone marrow to an unknown person. As yet, there is no record of her having attended any hospital in the city in the last six weeks.'

'What about outside the city?'

'Sergeant Yavaş is working on that.'

'Continue.'

'It's possible she may have been operated on in a private home,' Kerim said. 'Reports from places where organ trafficking is common confirm this phenomenon.'

'You're hitting a brick wall.'

'You could say that, yes.'

There was a long silence as Özer rubbed his chin really quite hard. Kerim began to wonder whether he might make it bleed. Then he said, 'And the prison . . .'

'In order to determine whether someone is a suitable donor, a blood test called an HLA test must be performed,' Kerim said. 'We have no idea when or where or even if such a test may have been performed on Kalkan, but the prison is a possibility.'

'Is it a standard test?'

'No.'

'So you're looking at some kind of conspiracy.'

'I wouldn't go so far . . .'

'But it's possible. If a doctor or nurse employed by the prison to perform medical tests was looking for a bone marrow donor for themselves or someone else . . .'

'Precisely.'

Another silence rolled across that small, stuffy office. Kerim began to feel himself sweat.

Then Özer nodded. 'Do it.'

Kerim breathed. 'Thank you, sir.'

Özer shrugged. Kerim got to his feet. 'I'll go and . . .'

'Yes,' his superior said. 'And . . .'

He went off into what looked like a trance again.

'Sir?'

'Tell İkmen we are grateful for his intelligence,' Özer said. 'Cases like this, Gürsel, represent how far we have fallen. Do what you must to find the truth.'

'She says,' Gold Bey read off the screen of his phone, '"I was told I might develop something called ankylosing spondylitis. It's a spinal disease. Far as I know I haven't got any problems with my back." So . . .'

İkmen rubbed his face. He was tired, and this message from Olimpio hadn't clarified anything as far as he could tell.

'Don't know what that is,' he said. 'But thank you. Sevval and Olimpio were arrested round about the same time, weren't they?'

'About. They came for me a couple of months later,' Gold said. 'Machine Bey served more time than any of us. He was arrested a year before I was.'

İkmen went home. He'd written the words 'ankylosing spondylitis' on the back of his cigarette packet with the intention of finding out what the hell it was later. However, when he returned to Sultanahmet, he found someone waiting for him outside the front door of his apartment building.

'I did not know what to do,' the young boy said. 'You are police but not police. I come to you for help.'

310

He was still wearing the same filthy and inappropriate T-shirt. İkmen recognised Hafız the Syrian boy immediately.

They both heard the men return from the mosque. Quietly at first, then, as they began to settle back into their familiar routines of gossip, tavla and television, a buzz of sound began to build. Deniz looked at Yaşar, who was still lying on the floor, quiet now, covered in Ali Haydar's blood. If someone came in, would they think he had killed that thug? She looked down at the knife in her hand. No.

What was Yaşar thinking? His eyes were closed and blank, but then they'd been like that when he'd taken her to see the doctor. Not that it mattered. Can was dead; it was almost irrelevant what happened next.

She thought she might react when she heard footsteps on the stairs, but she didn't. Both she and Yaşar turned calmly to look at the man who appeared. Deniz recognised him, even if she didn't know his name. He was the man who ran the coffee house. Poor thing, he looked very pale.

Chapter 24

Süleyman had just managed to drive off the Martyrs Bridge when his phone rang. He took the call.

'Is that Inspector Süleyman?' The voice was female, unfamiliar and cautious.

'Yes. Who is this?'

'Constable Aksoyer.'

From Kasımpaşa; the only cop over there who'd told him the truth about Yaşar Akgün.

'What can I do for you, Constable?' he said.

'I have a situation, sir.' She was clearly, from her tone, in a place where she couldn't speak freely.

'What kind of situation? Can you say?'

'No, not really, sir. But I can tell you I'm at the community centre in Kasımpaşa, and although I know I should call my colleagues for backup, I'd rather have you. I think you need to be here.'

Ömer, who had been listening in on the conversation, mouthed, 'All guns blazing?'

Süleyman nodded, and then said, 'We're on our way, Constable.'

Although God knew how they'd plough through all this traffic to get over to Kasımpaşa in less than an hour, even with the car's sirens shrieking and blue lit to the hilt.

* * *

'This man, he owes me money,' Hafız said. 'He will not pay.'

'This isn't Machine Bey, is it?' İkmen asked as he placed a glass of tea and a plate of börek in front of the boy. Hafız stuffed half the pastry into his mouth in one bite.

'No.'

İkmen put a hand on his arm. 'Go easy,' he said. 'I'm not going to take the food away from you.'

The kid was clearly hungry, but if he carried on like this, he'd give himself stomach ache.

'When you've finished, we can talk,' İkmen said.

He lit a cigarette and slowly drank his tea. Hafız had, by the look of him, been sleeping rough and İkmen resolved to let him take a shower before he left. Kemal, his youngest son, still kept a few T-shirts and pairs of jeans in his old bedroom; İkmen was sure he wouldn't mind if he donated them to the boy.

When he'd finished eating, Hafız said, 'Cigarette?'

İkmen threw one across the table at him. 'I shouldn't, but . . .' He lit it for the boy, then said, 'So tell me why you're here. What's this about a man owing you money?'

'One thousand lira,' Hafız said.

'That's a lot.'

'It is. But he won't pay.'

'What does he owe you money for?' İkmen asked.

The boy said nothing.

'Hafız?'

He appeared, although İkmen couldn't be certain, to be making something up. His face had just the kind of look one might see when a person was concocting a story.

Eventually he said, 'Really he owes my grandmother money.'

'Your grandmother? What for?'

He shook his head. 'Berat Bey, he told me you are good man, safe man.'

313

Berat Aznavoryan owned the carpet shop below which Machine Bey lived, the place where this boy had first taken İkmen.

'Yes?'

Hafız began to cry.

Even if he could find the right words, Kerim Gürsel's written application for the release of Sevval Kalkan's medical records from Silivri prison would take time. Over the past twenty years, the notoriously glacial Turkish public service administration mechanisms had improved considerably. But there could still be hold-ups, and of course, a successful outcome probably meant that one's application was uncontentious. Which this one certainly wasn't.

He sat in front of his blank computer screen and felt his mind drift back to what had happened that morning with his wife. Had she felt duty-bound to kiss him like that because her mother was in the apartment? Or was she broody? They'd both hit forty earlier that year, and while Kerim occasionally inspected his face for wrinkles, Sinem hadn't shown any signs of being concerned about the passing years. Birthdays had never featured heavily in her life. She'd been diagnosed with rheumatoid arthritis as a child, and pain consumed her every waking hour. Children had never even come into the equation as far as Kerim knew. But maybe they did now.

Eylul, still on hold to yet another hospital administrative department, drank from a huge Starbucks mug and closed her eyes. If Sevval Kalkan had donated her bone marrow to Professor Tolon, then getting anyone to provide evidence of that, much less speak about it, was going to be tough. People like Tolon had followers, which meant there was a whiff of the cult about his operation. And his message was approved by some in high places. Kerim knew that if there was any truth in the Sevval Kalkan theory, his evidence for it would have to be unequivocal.

And unequivocal evidence was as rare as true love.

* * *

Hafız's grandmother was, apparently, dead, and Hafız reasoned that the man who had owed her money now owed it to him. But whenever İkmen tried to find out more about it, the boy just cried. So he tried a different tack.

'Tell me about your grandmother, Hafız,' he said. 'What was she called?'

'Kelebek.'

'That's a nice name.'

'She was nice. She come from here,' he said.

'Turkey?'

'Yes. We come here because that.'

'But you don't speak Turkish.'

'No. I live with mother and father until they die. Grandmother bring me here. We run from the war, you know?'

Like everyone else, İkmen knew about the endless war in Syria. His country had taken in more than two million refugees from the conflict. Now that they were speaking Grandmother Kelebek's name, İkmen took the conversation back to the money someone owed her.

'You had no money when you came here?' he asked.

'Little.'

'Where do you live?'

Hafiz shrugged.

'On the street?'

'Sometimes in the park. Graveyard . . .'

'Not frightened of ghosts?' İkmen asked with a smile, and yet he felt a prickling on his skin that was more than a little spooky. 'Hafız?'

'This man . . .' the boy began, and then he swallowed hard.

'The man who owes you money?'

'Yes. He work in the graveyard.'

* * *

In spite of what Constable Aksoyer had told him about not contacting her colleagues, he was surprised that no other police officers were in evidence around the Kasımpaşa community centre. To all intents the place was working normally. As Süleyman and Ömer Mungun stepped into the entrance hall, the only indication that something might be wrong was the appearance of a white-faced man who turned out to be the owner of the coffee house.

'Upstairs,' he whispered when the two men showed their ID. 'The officer is alone with them.'

They climbed the stairs. The smell of blood reached them before they saw anything.

Süleyman called up, 'Constable Aksoyer, it's Inspector Süleyman and Sergeant Mungun.'

'Thank you, sir.'

The relief she clearly felt was obvious from her tone. After all, it had taken them well over an hour to get to her.

When they reached the top of the stairs, Aksoyer was standing there, her firearm raised, looking at a figure lying face down in a pool of blood. Beside the figure was a bloodied woman they both recognised to be Deniz Palandoken, holding a knife to her own neck and panting. A man was curled up in a corner, whimpering. He too was heavily bloodied. He was also Yaşar Akgün.

Süleyman approached Aksoyer and said softly, 'What's happened here?'

'Victim on the ground is one of Akgün's men. The woman says she killed him. She's threatening to kill herself. She's a user and she's come right down. Found her husband dead this morning . . .'

'What are you talking about?' the woman said.

'This is Inspector Süleyman and Sergeant Mungun, Deniz. They've come to help you,' Aksoyer said.

'Help me!'

For the moment Süleyman ignored her. 'And Akgün?' he asked.

'I've no idea,' Aksoyer said. 'But that is why I called you. He's involved here somehow, I think. This may be your chance . . .'

Süleyman began to approach the woman on the floor until she would tolerate him moving no further. She raised her knife and he stood still.

'Hello, Deniz,' he said. 'I'm Inspector Süleyman, and this is my colleague Sergeant Mungun.'

'And?' she said. 'That stupid man downstairs went and got her . . .' She pointed to Aksoyer. 'I've told her I killed this piece of shit and I'm not sorry. Now if you'll all just fuck off, I can die in peace.'

'Why do you want to die, Deniz?'

'I've killed someone,' she said. 'Which means prison. Oh, and I've lost my child, and my husband's dead.'

'And you've come down . . .'

'Oh yes, and that,' she said.

He squatted down so that he could look her in the eyes. 'I can help with your physical state,' he said.

'What? You going to go and score for me?'

'No, but I can get access to methadone.'

She shook her head. 'I'll pass.'

'Why?'

She put the knife to her throat.

He backed away. 'OK.'

'What's the point?' she said. 'What is the fucking point?'

Which told Süleyman all he needed to know.

'We have no money,' Hafız said.

'When was this?'

'I don't know. Three, four months. Grandmother is very upset. Soon we will die, she thinks. We are sleeping in the graveyard then, with the dead. It was cold then.' He shook his head. 'I do

317

not know this man because he is Turkish and he speaks only to grandmother. She tells me he is the big boss of the graveyard and he says we can stay.'

'For how long?'

'I don't know. He bring us some food for maybe a week, and then one day he talk to grandmother a lot. She tell me she must go for operation to the hospital. I say I didn't know she was sick and I am very upset. But she tells me this man will take care of everything. That she will be paid to go to the hospital. I tell her I know what this is.'

'What is—'

'When we come here, people do this all times. Sell parts of the body. I say her no, but she say she don't need it.'

'What?'

'One kidney,' he said.

İkmen felt his face pale.

'Then she tell me, if anything happen to her, I must get the money they promise. And so that is what I do.'

'We will take this one step at a time,' Süleyman said.

Ömer Mungun had called for discreet backup, plus a small bottle of methadone, which would be released from the headquarters medical facility.

'Firstly, I have methadone on its way,' he continued. 'Let's get you more comfortable before we do anything else.'

Deniz said nothing. Yaşar Akgün began to hum tunelessly. Süleyman didn't take his eyes off the woman, relying on his colleagues to look after Akgün.

'Why don't you tell me what happened, Deniz?' he said. 'You say you've killed this man, but who is he?'

She said, 'He's called Ali Haydar Özince. He's a terrible person.'

Süleyman realised that of course he'd met the victim. He was one of Yaşar Akgün's henchmen.

'You killed him because he's a terrible person?'

'He sold my daughter,' she said. Her eyes filled with tears. 'I sold her . . .' She looked up at him. 'I sold her, to him.'

Although he wanted to reach out to her, Süleyman didn't move. Then he said, 'I know.'

'You know?'

'Deniz,' he said, 'we want to stop these people. We've been watching them.'

'You know?' She shook her head. 'Can and me, we use. Junkies can't have children.'

'They can,' Süleyman said, 'but they need help.'

'And we were desperate,' she said. 'I gave her to them and I took their money and we both got high. How could I have done that?'

He saw her push the knife into the flesh of her neck so that it started to bleed.

'But you can help her now . . .'

'I don't even remember her name! I can't remember it! I can't remember her name!'

'You will. You will now—'

'No!' she screamed. 'No! This is not happening! No!'

A tension had been invoked that would not subside. Briefly Süleyman looked up at Constable Aksoyer, and then he launched himself towards Deniz, who screamed and slashed her knife wildly in front of her.

Cigarettes were being smoked thick and fast now. İkmen put a hand on the boy's shoulder. 'What happened?' he asked.

Hafız began to cry again.

İkmen poured the boy another glass of tea and placed it and more pastries in front of him. When he was able to speak again, Hafız said, 'She died.'

'How?'

'I do not know.'

'Where did this happen? In a hospital? Did you see her?'

Hafız shrugged. 'I know nothing,' he said. 'They just tell me she die. They say she was old and weak. I know this.' He shook his head again. 'This man . . .'

'The man in the graveyard?'

'Yes. He tell me they will bury her as a Muslim. I am alone, what can I do?'

İkmen wanted to hug the kid and try to take some of his pain away. The fact that a young boy should have to even know about such things was heartbreaking. But he kept his distance. Hafız needed to tell his story, and when he was done, İkmen needed to make sure it reached the right ears.

'So you had a funeral for your grandmother.'

'No.'

'No?'

'No, they tell me they bury her. I don't know anything.'

'Where?'

'I don't know,' he said again. 'If I know it I would be there.'

It was all too easy to imagine that Hafız's grandmother had been put into Perihan Bulut's grave. But İkmen didn't know that. He said, 'Go on.'

'So then the man say they have to use money grandmother was given to bury her. I have nothing.'

'They'd given her money already?'

'Before operation, they say.'

'But she didn't give it to you?'

'No,' he said. 'I never see it. The man say she is not doing what they want.'

'What do you mean?'

'She died,' he said.

İkmen frowned. 'You mean before they managed to remove one of her kidneys?'

320

'They say so. The man say the burying is a gift. I ask him again and again and he say this.' He waved his hands in the air to emphasise his point. 'I know things, I say him! I know grandmother does not need to be alive to do this! I think someone have her kidney now, for nothing!'

The boy clearly knew that organ trafficking was illegal, and so he had to also know that İkmen, even as a former police officer, couldn't help him to get his money back. But then this wasn't really about the money; this was a cry for help from a child who had been left alone and destitute.

Ömer Mungun ripped off his jacket and held it to Süleyman's face. In the distance, the wail of sirens announced that backup was on its way. Once he was sure that Süleyman could hold the jacket on his own, albeit with shaking fingers, he took his phone out and called for an ambulance. Constable Aksoyer held her gun slightly unsteadily against Deniz Palandoken's head.

'I'm all right! I'm all right!' Süleyman said as he pushed Ömer away and pressed hard on the jacket against his cheek. Blood was everywhere, from the dead man on the floor, from Deniz Palandoken, from the inspector's face . . .

Deniz had dropped her knife as soon as she'd slashed at him. The cut had been deep, and his blood had poured over her fingers as she screamed in sudden horror at what she had done. In the far corner of the room, Yaşar Akgün had stared at the scene in what to Constable Aksoyer looked like silent fascination.

As he rose slowly to his feet, supported by Ömer Mungun, Süleyman said to Deniz, 'You must tell your story now. You know that, don't you?'

She nodded.

Chapter 25

Kerim Gürsel pressed send, then leaned back in his chair and closed his eyes. Either his request for Sevval Kalkan's medical records would be successful or it wouldn't. In the meantime, Eylul had gone to get them both some restorative coffee, and he should now turn his attention to Ece and Ateş Kazantzoğlu.

While Ece had pointed the finger of blame for Ceyda Kazantzoğlu's death firmly at her husband, Ateş was still not budging. Kerim doubted whether he would ever admit his guilt, even though denying it was ridiculous. If one's mother disappeared, one would notice at the very least, one would ask around. He'd have one last crack at him and then let the mounting forensic evidence hang him, figuratively speaking. Capital punishment didn't happen in Turkey any more, even though some people seemed to want it to return. Kerim found the whole idea of state-sanctioned murder absolutely horrifying.

His office door opened and then closed on Eylul Yavaş carrying two Starbucks coffees. Kerim would have preferred the cheaper and, in his opinion, better options that were sold by locally run coffee shops. But he knew Eylul was addicted.

She put the cups down on her desk and said, 'I've just seen Sergeant Mungun downstairs. Apparently Inspector Süleyman has been taken to hospital.'

* * *

'Just stitch it up, will you.'

'Don't be a hero,' the doctor said. 'We get them in here all the time and it's boring.'

It wasn't the reaction Mehmet Süleyman had been expecting when he presented himself for treatment at the Okmeydanı hospital.

The doctor gently pushed the sides of the wound together. 'Do you want a local anaesthetic?' he asked.

'I want you to stitch it up without comment,' Süleyman said.

'You are the boss, Inspector Bey.'

'Yes, I am.'

It was childish and Süleyman knew it, and when the doctor began to stitch the wound, it hurt. Of course it bloody hurt! But he didn't show it, even though it made him sweat, even though he knew he was being ridiculous. He had to get back to work because he had to be the one to interview Deniz Palandoken, not to mention Yaşar Akgün.

'There will be a scar,' the doctor said as he inserted the needle into Süleyman's flesh. 'Don't know whether that's a problem for you or not.'

He clearly had an issue with macho men, but Süleyman wasn't in a position to comment.

'Ideally you should rest,' he continued. 'But I imagine I'm probably speaking to myself on that issue. However, I am going to give you a course of antibiotics, which I would urge you to take in case of infection, and I'd also like to take a blood sample.'

That made sense, and Süleyman grunted his assent. Now his eyes were watering and he knew he probably looked as if he was crying. It was unavoidable, although he wished it wasn't so. This doctor, a small, disapproving man in his fifties, wasn't the most friendly individual. But then that wasn't his job. In a way, being a doctor was a lot like being a police officer – one was dedicated to the public good while not being in the business of necessarily being anyone's friend.

Ömer Mungun had supervised the transfer of Deniz Palandoken and Yaşar Akgün to police headquarters, where they would be offered the opportunity to engage legal representation. This probably meant, in Akgün's case, another visit from the odious Eyüp Çelik. Although this time Süleyman would have rather more power in the room than before.

Was the idea of another confrontation with Çelik behind this ridiculous refusal to have a local anaesthetic, or had he done that simply to save time? He knew it was probably the former and was annoyed at himself for it. The celebrity lawyer had got under his skin like no one else had for many years. He'd made him feel small, powerless and old. Indirectly, he'd made him use Çiçek as a form of stress release, a way of reasserting his manhood in his own eyes. Unlike his previous lover, Gonca, Çiçek wasn't the sort of woman who enjoyed rough sex and he knew it.

'Well,' the doctor said as he tied his handiwork off, 'that's it.' He taped a large gauze pad over the wound. 'I'll give you some spare dressings. Try not to get it wet for at least forty-eight hours.'

Süleyman stood up. He swayed very slightly but hid it well.

The doctor took his plastic gloves off and threw them into a bin. Then he turned to his computer. 'You can go,' he said.

'Thank you.'

Without turning away from his computer, he added, 'And if you're wondering why I'm not fawning all over one of our "heroes", then know this: my little brother was a police officer, years ago. He was shot and refused analgesia. He died of a heart attack before the surgeon could even get him on the table. He was twenty-four.'

Süleyman's phone was switched off and so İkmen had a choice: he could wait for it to be switched on again, or he could take Hafız to police headquarters himself. He chose the latter, and arrived just as Kerim Gürsel was speaking with officers on the front desk.

'Çetin Bey!'

The two men embraced.

'I'm sorry to be here again, given your superior's disapproval,' İkmen began.

'Ah, I shouldn't worry about that too much,' Kerim said. He looked at the boy. 'Hello.'

'Oh, he doesn't speak Turkish,' İkmen said. He explained why he was at headquarters, and why he had Hafız with him.

Kerim took his phone out of his pocket and began to compose a text message. 'I'll let Ömer Bey know you're here,' he said. 'I'm sure this young man would be more comfortable speaking to someone in Arabic.' Then he took İkmen's arm and pulled him to one side. 'Something has happened, I believe in Kasımpaşa. Don't know what, exactly, but Ömer Bey is apparently processing a couple of prisoners. Inspector Süleyman was injured and is being treated in hospital.'

İkmen felt himself go cold. 'Treated for what?'

'Word is he was cut across the face,' Kerim said. 'I've no details. All I know is that he's due back to interview these two detainees sometime soon, so it can't be serious.'

Serious no, but if the wound was to his face, İkmen wondered how it would affect his friend – and his daughter. He knew that Çiçek would love Süleyman whatever, but how would Süleyman himself take it? His good looks had always been a big part of his life. His appeal to both women and men was legendary. If he lost that, would he lose part of himself? And why, İkmen thought, was he thinking like this before he even knew the extent of the injury?

'You have a right to legal representation . . .'

Deniz Palandoken didn't much care.

'You need to go to Can,' she said. Her husband was still lying dead in that shithole in Cankurturan.

'We will,' the officer, Sergeant Mungun, said. 'But about a lawyer . . .'

She wouldn't even have been able to understand what he was saying until a few minutes ago. All she'd been able to see was the police officer's face when she slashed it with Can's knife. But then the methadone had arrived and she'd begun to understand things.

She said, calmly, 'I'm going to go away for ever; what's the point?' A murder, an attempt on the life of a police officer – they'd throw away the key.

'The point is,' Sergeant Mungun said, 'that you know things about Akgün and his people that could help us bring them down.'

'I'll still go to prison.'

He sighed. 'Think about it. I'm sure your family will be able to provide you with the best legal representation available.'

But Deniz shook her head. 'I'm a junkie, Sergeant Mungun,' she said.

'You are also your parents' child,' he replied.

Kerim Gürsel's office was smaller than Süleyman's. It was also messier and seemed to contain a huge number of used Starbucks cups.

'You can wait here,' Kerim said as he offered İkmen and the boy chairs. 'Sergeant Yavaş is with the Kazantzoğlus and their legal representative.'

'Oh?'

'Ateş Kazantzoğlu has to be made aware that, quite apart from his wife's evidence, he really has nothing tangible to support his plea of innocence in his mother's death. All he can sensibly do is plead mitigation.'

İkmen shuddered, the memory of that plastic-wrapped body in the Kazantzoğlus' attic still fresh in his mind. Plus he needed a cigarette and knew he couldn't have one. He said, 'Are you sure I can be here without Özer . . .'

Kerim sat down. 'I honestly don't know what's the matter with him,' he said. 'He actually asked me to thank you for your help on the Sevval Kalkan investigation, and he gave me the go-ahead to apply for her record from Silivri. Maybe I'm reading too much into this, but I'm wondering if he's having something of a change of heart.'

'About what? Me?'

'Not just you,' he said. But before he could continue, there was a knock on the door.

'Come in.'

It was Ömer Mungun. When he saw İkmen, he smiled, then said, 'I got your text, Kerim Bey.' He looked at Hafız. 'Is this the boy?'

'Yes. He's called Hafız.'

Ömer raised his eyebrows and said, 'Is he? Interesting.'

He said something, presumably in Arabic, and the boy replied. Ömer smiled, then turned to his colleagues again. 'I can't do anything now,' he said. 'The inspector has just returned from hospital and wants to get these interviews under way.'

'Interviewing who?' İkmen asked.

'Deniz Palandöken and Yaşar Akgün. Long story.' Ömer said something else to Hafız, then left.

When he'd gone, İkmen realised he'd not asked him how Süleyman was. But then he had to be reasonably all right to go into interview. İkmen didn't know Yaşar Akgün, the supposed godfather of Kasımpaşa, but he had been acquainted with Deniz Palandöken for many years. He wondered what she'd done but also how she would cope with interrogation.

Hafız interrupted his thoughts. 'We stay here?' he asked.

'For the moment,' İkmen said.

'Yes. The man who speak Arabic say I must.'

Without the methadone, Deniz knew she would have fallen apart. When Inspector Süleyman came into the interview room with half his face hidden under a thick gauze pad, she could feel the regret, the shame and the fear rising inside her. Fortunately the meds held it, for the moment. And then there was the lawyer her father had sent, a woman called İris İmamoğlu. She was very smart and very young and Deniz felt like a bundle of rags sitting beside her.

Formalities of name, age and residence completed, Mehmet Süleyman said, 'Wishing to clarify the events of today, why were you present at the community centre in Kasımpaşa this morning?'

'I went to see Dr Fixit.'

'Dr Fixit?'

'I don't know his real name,' she said. 'He has his office in Kartal.'

'We'll go back to that,' Süleyman said. 'Why did you want to see this doctor today?'

'I wanted to ask him why my husband was dead.'

'Can Palandoken?'

'Yes,' she said. 'I got him antibiotics from Dr Fixit days ago, at the community centre. Can's had this infection for ever and . . . But when I took them back, he got angry because I didn't have any gear as well, and he threw them all over the floor where there's rats and shit.'

'Can you clarify what you mean by "gear"?' the sergeant, Mungun, asked.

'Heroin. Or, when we can get it, opium.'

İris İmamoğlu looked at her.

Deniz said, 'What?'

Süleyman interjected. 'To go back a bit, what happened after Can Palandoken destroyed his antibiotics?'

'I got him more,' she said. 'I found that Yaşar Akgün and he took me over to Kartal. Don't think Dr Fixit was best pleased, but he sold me another lot. This was yesterday. Can took some and then I left him to go out, and when I got back, he was dead.' This time she didn't cry, because she was high, and up

328

there you felt nothing. That was why she did it, and why Can had done it too.

'Why did you go to the Kasımpaşa community centre if you wanted to see this doctor in Kartal?' Süleyman asked.

'Because he told me not to come to him in Kartal,' she said. 'He comes out to the community centre.'

'When?'

'Sometimes.'

'Do you know when exactly?'

'No. But he comes on gold sale day.'

'What's that?'

'When a man comes from Rize to sell gold,' she said. 'People say it's Yaşar Akgün's brother. I don't know, I've never bought any gold.'

'Why does this doctor come on gold sale day?'

'To do business.'

'What kind of business?' he asked.

'Flesh business,' she said.

'You're early.'

Cemetery Guard Raşım Dorsay turned and saw the grim-faced gatekeeper behind him.

'So are you,' he said as he took a work circular out of his pigeonhole and put it in his pocket. Ever since he'd been to see Inspector Süleyman, he hadn't been able to get to sleep, and so he'd come into work. Türgüt Bey looked almost as tired as he did. Raşım was anxious, too. What was the inspector going to do about Münir Sever? If anything?

Türgüt Bey looked down at his ledger as he spoke. 'I didn't manage to contact the police today,' he said. 'I thought about that situation too, and I . . . I don't think there's any reason to think the person we discussed was doing anything wrong last night.'

329

'Oh.'

'No,' he said. 'So I think it's best if we just forget about the whole thing.'

Deniz Palandoken looked at the smart lawyer sitting beside her and said, 'You won't understand this, Hanım.' Then she looked at Süleyman. 'I sold my daughter; Didem, she was called. She was just days old and I sold her to Dr Fixit to give to a couple who couldn't have children, so he said. I sold my child to buy gear.'

Süleyman, for one, hadn't ever heard anything so sad in his life. He said, 'That must have been hard.'

It was a pointless thing to say and he chastised himself for saying it as soon as the words were out of his mouth. Deniz Palandoken said nothing.

Süleyman took a deep breath. 'Who brokered this deal?'

'Can,' she said. 'He was getting some gear from a man in Kasımpaşa. Through him he met the Özince brothers.'

'Ali Haydar and Ekrem.'

'They said their boss, this Yaşar Akgün, was always looking to help people. If you wanted to get a baby, he was your man; if you wanted to lose one, again he could do it. He'd make whatever ailed you better. I never met him, not until yesterday, when he took me to Kartal, but he didn't seem to know much. I don't think he knows anything about what's really happening.'

'Who do you think does?'

'The Özinces.' She looked up. 'The old man who lives in Akgün's house.'

'Abdülkadır Soyar?'

'I don't know his name.'

Süleyman said, 'Take me through what happened to you when you found out that you were pregnant.'

'It was at the end of 2016,' she said. 'It was never meant to happen. Neither of us knew what to do. I was all for having an abortion, but then Can met this dealer in Kasımpaşa. They said—'

'Who said?'

'Ekrem Özince said they'd get me a doctor and once the baby was all right we'd get five thousand lira. Even today, that's a lot of gear.'

'It is. By "once the baby was all right", you mean . . .'

'She had to be withdrawn,' she said. 'I had her upstairs in the community centre, then they took me to that house where the Özinces live. But it's his house, Akgün. I didn't know that at the time. The doctor came every day to check on her, and then one day he didn't come but the brothers came instead. They gave me a big hit of heroin and we went over to Gümüşsuyu. I handed her to this woman . . .' She looked down, but she didn't cry. 'Then the Özinces gave me the money. Not all of it, though. They said Didem wasn't perfect. She was, but . . . Can and me, we were high for two weeks.'

Solid with the misery of her story, the room almost seemed to stop in time. Even the clean, smart lawyer looked on the verge of tears.

'When I went to the community centre this morning, I wanted to kill Dr Fixit,' Deniz said. 'He helped to take my daughter away from me and now he's killed my husband.'

'Did Can not die because he wouldn't take the doctor's pills?' Ömer Mungun asked.

She shook her head. 'I don't know. I think maybe he puts shit in the stuff he gives to junkies.'

She looked agitated again. Süleyman whispered to Ömer Mungun, 'I think the meds are wearing off.' Then he looked up. 'Let's have a short break now.'

* * *

Why had that woman killed Ali Haydar? Yaşar had helped her find somewhere for her baby to go. They all helped everyone, all the time. Ali Haydar, Ekrem, his uncle, him . . .

And now he was in prison. Would İzzet come and get him out? And what about Dr Özdemir? Would he be sent to prison too? Yaşar didn't understand. He'd come to İstanbul when he hadn't wanted to, to work for Paşa Bey. He'd done everything he was told to do, even when he didn't want to. And then, when the old man had died, he'd become someone people respected because of all the work he did for them. Paşa Bey had never made people better like he had. What had gone wrong?

The police had told him he could have his lawyer, but he didn't know how to contact him. The brothers and his uncle always did those things, and so he'd said he didn't want a lawyer, because if he told the police the truth, they would think he was silly.

Maybe if Ekrem or his uncle found out where he was, they could come and sort it out. But neither of them had appeared, and really Ekrem needed to be there because Ali Haydar was dead and Ekrem was his brother and so the police would have to tell him.

The key to the whole operation was to do things calmly. Abdülkadır Soyar had been in İstanbul for thirty years, and so he knew that colluding with its default setting of blind panic in times of trouble was not the thing to do. He packed the same small suitcase he'd brought from Rize when he first came to work for that old pervert Paşa Beyaz, taking only his money, a few clothes and his medication.

The police would soon discover the truth about Yaşar, if they didn't already know. He'd only ever wanted to help people, even old Paşa, whose ghastly cock the poor simple thing had serviced almost until the day the old man had died. Yaşar had deserved what Paşa had bequeathed him. Now he'd service everyone else's guilt.

Abdülkadır would hail a taxi to the bus station and remove

himself to somewhere like Olu Deniz or Bodrum, where he could have a shave, purchase some new clothes and blend in with tourists from across the world. He'd decide what to do next once he'd settled in to a nice hotel. He'd cleaned out the safe, and so Ekrem Özince would just have to live off any savings he might have, until the police came for him. Abdülkadır didn't know where he was and cared even less. His brother was dead, and so it was possible he was crying or distressed or something. Possible but not probable.

As for the rest of them, Dr Özdemir and his associates . . . Those people got away with murder, literally. Why should he care?

He had, of course, made a short call to his nephew, İzzet. Now there was an intelligent man! He'd always seen that boy's potential even if his father had been a useless waste of skin. Always with an eye turned towards trouble, İzzet had told his uncle he was already on his way out of his door. And if Abdülkadır knew his nephew as he thought he did, he'd have most of the stock from his gold shop with him.

Methadone wasn't as good as proper heroin, but it did the job for a while. When the two police officers returned to the interview room, Deniz smiled.

'Feel better?'

She nodded.

'Can you take us to these places you've told us about?' Süleyman asked. 'This house in Kasımpaşa, this doctor's surgery . . .'

'Yes,' she said. 'But I don't know where the apartment in Gümüşsuyu was. I was too high.'

'It's all right.'

'Later I wondered if they'd given my baby to paedophiles,' Deniz continued. 'You hear about it sometimes. But then it would go out of my head again. When you have to score every day, it takes every bit of your concentration, you know?'

'How . . .'

'I steal, I beg, I sell everything,' she said. 'Even my own flesh and blood. What kind of person am I, eh?'

The two officers said nothing.

'Can can't do it. He used to score, but now he can't.' Then she remembered and said, 'Of course now that is impossible. But he's been tired for a long time. He sleeps . . .'

'Deniz,' Süleyman asked. 'Do you know where Ekrem Özince might be?'

Kasımpaşa was already stiff with police officers, but so far, neither Abdülkadır Soyar nor Ekrem Özince could be found. What was more, officers on the ground had reported that people were not exactly forthcoming.

'Only if he's at that house or the community centre,' Deniz said. 'And they're the only people I know, apart from Dr Fixit.'

'From Kartal?'

'Yes,' she said.

Süleyman said, 'He's called Dr Alp Özdemir and a warrant has already been served for his arrest.'

'Good.' But then her face fell. 'Although you know he'll get away with it, don't you? I come from that world. Doctors, lawyers . . . They look after their own, they know people . . .'

Süleyman decided it was the right moment to tell her what he'd done during their short break.

'Deniz, as your next of kin, your father has the right to see you,' he said. 'I've spoken to him again. He would like to come and speak to you.'

She was angry, but she didn't show it. Instead she just said, 'He's worried it will get into the papers and spoil things for him. You know he wants to go into politics, don't you?'

Süleyman didn't. 'No.'

'It's about that,' she said. 'So tell him no. Have you found my Can yet?'

Chapter 26

The room, if it could be called a room, was completely enveloped in the stench. Even if Dr Arto Sarkissian hadn't known that a dead body was inside that wrecked house in Cankurturan, he'd not have been able to miss it. This was what happened when the temperature topped thirty-five degrees: the dead began to speak in the only way they knew how.

Two scenes-of-crime officers were already in attendance, and Arto took a few uncomfortable moments to struggle into a white forensic suit, which made him sweat all the more.

'Good afternoon, gentlemen,' he said to the attending officers.

'Doctor.'

'This is I believe a Can Palandoken.'

'Yes, sir.' One of the officers walked over to him. 'Inspector Süleyman has been told that he probably died last night.'

'By?'

'His wife. She too was a user.'

'I see.' He put on a pair of plastic gloves. In his experience, if an habitual heroin user told you something, you should usually treat that information with caution.

'He's got some powerfully infected wounds,' the officer continued, 'which could explain the intensity of the smell. The wife apparently tried to get him to take antibiotics, but he wouldn't.'

It was an odd phenomenon the way a lot of drug addicts would refuse to take regular medication. But it was common.

Some even claimed that meds like antibiotics were unnatural and would damage them.

The doctor picked his way over piles of rotten plaster, broken wooden beams and the bodies of dead rats until he came to the body, which was propped up against a wall. He knew of the Palandoken family; in fact he didn't live far from their vast modern villa on the Bosphorus in the trendy village of Bebek. As a very young man, Can Palandoken had been one of the country's most eligible bachelors. Rarely out of the gossip columns twenty years ago. What Arto saw now, however, was a far cry from that. A man so thin his ribs could be seen through his shirt, his hair grey and filthy, his face that of a man twice his age, reeking of infection and stale piss. And while he was disgusted, the doctor was also deeply sorry for this man who had been born with every advantage money could buy, only to die broken, in a reeking house infested with rats.

İkmen didn't even allow Süleyman to speak. As soon as he saw him, he jumped to his feet and examined what he could see of the wound on the side of his face.

'It's nothing,' his friend said.

But İkmen hugged him. 'Don't be such a fucking hero,' he said, echoing the words of the doctor who had stitched up the wound.

But Süleyman's eyes were already on Hafız. 'Who's he?'

'Ah, this is Hafız,' İkmen said. 'He has a tale to tell about organ trafficking at the Karacaahmet.'

'Hafız, eh.' The name was familiar.

Ömer Mungun translated for the boy, who was much happier speaking in his native Arabic than in English.

When he'd finished, Süleyman said to his deputy, 'Well, it would seem that our visit to the cemetery this evening will be plus one. Ask him if he will be able to identify this man.'

Ömer asked, and was told that Hafız was sure he could do that. Then, while the boy, whose appetite appeared to be insatiable, ate the food that İkmen had bought for him on the way to headquarters, the men talked. İkmen was sorry to hear how far the Palandokens had fallen, and what they had done in order to survive.

'Ah, she was such a pretty young woman,' he said of Deniz. 'And Can, dead.' He shook his head. 'A high price but hopefully now you can expose this organisation.'

'Run by a man who seems, well, on one level simple,' Ömer Mungun said.

'I think Yaşar Akgün has a form of autism,' Süleyman said. 'We'll have him assessed. On the one hand, he is clearly a very bright man, but on the other, he is rather like a child. By that I mean he is trusting and wants to do good.'

'Do you think he's been used?'

'Almost certainly. Those who work for him control him. The Özince brothers, his uncle, Abdülkadır Soyar, maybe his brother in Rize. We have the doctor from Kartal in custody.'

'Has he made his call to his no doubt high-powered lawyer yet?' İkmen asked.

'Oh yes.'

But Süleyman knew that Dr Alp Özdemir was also very afraid. He wasn't a surgeon himself, but according to Deniz Palandoken, he knew the surgeons the Akgüns used. He also provided the patients' after-care. He'd either drop his colleagues from a great height or he wouldn't speak at all. It would depend upon who the said surgeons knew in high places.

Kerim Gürsel's office fell quiet at İkmen's next words. 'What about Deniz's child?'

Süleyman sighed. 'We're still looking for Ekrem Özince and Abdülkadır Soyar,' he said. 'If we find them, perhaps they'll be persuaded that it's in their best interests to give up that information. Yaşar Akgün, if he knows, will probably tell us when we interview him.'

'Which will be when?'

The inspector lifted the glass of tea Kerim had got for him. 'When I've finished this.'

İkmen remembered relentless days like this. When suddenly and often unexpectedly a whole series of disparate events came together to make a whole so terrifying and important one had no time to breathe.

Kerim's phone rang. Just before he picked it up, he said, 'Prosecutor's office.'

Access to Sevval Kalkan's prison medical records was at stake here, they all knew it. They also all knew, from Kerim's face, that it had been denied.

When the call was over, he sat down.

'Did they give you any reason?' İkmen asked.

'No, they don't have to.' Kerim rubbed his face with his fingers.

İkmen said, 'Get Serkan Tolon in. We know he knew Sevval; the evidence is on his bedroom wall. He's a spoilt little rich boy, never had to face real life.'

'But if you're right about what Sevval may have done for him, then he won't be able to talk,' Kerim said. 'Given that it's his father we think was the recipient.'

'At least it will be a step towards the truth,' İkmen said.

'It might be.'

Knowing that some people in society were basically untouchable engendered a sense of despair. When taking on such people, many gave up before they'd even started.

Ekrem Özince had always been a thug. Back in the days of Paşa Beyaz, he'd been the one who had dished out any beatings the old man needed to inflict. Not that there had been many. But that was pretty much all the Özinces ever did for their boss, who they basically robbed blind. Abdülkadır Soyar knew that he hadn't been much better than the brothers, but at least he'd given poor old Paşa his nephew to play with.

Esenler bus station was a vortex of movement, noise and stench. Everybody going everywhere, all wanting to get there before anyone else. Abdülkadır had finally opted to go to Antalya on the Mediterranean coast. He'd never been there before, and according to TripAdvisor on his phone, it had a lot of very luxurious hotels. With a big comfortable bed to lie on plus room service to take the bother out of eating, he'd plan his next move there.

In the meantime, however, he had to try and maintain his place in the unruly knot of people lining up for the bus: a gang of screaming children, a pregnant woman who looked as if she was just about to drop and a gaggle of men carrying carpets. There were a lot of police in evidence and it was likely they were looking for him. He kept his head down even when a child at his elbow splashed a carton of ayran on his coat. He couldn't stand kids. When the Özince brothers had got into that business, he'd almost got out.

Travelling on his own kimlik was risky, but there had been no choice. Old Paşa had known a few forgers back in the day, but there hadn't been time to contact any of those. He watched a group of police officers get onto the bus going to Trabzon. They'd probably look at transport to the Black Sea coast first of all. After all, that was his home. But he wasn't an idiot. By the time they'd gone through that vehicle, he was slightly closer to the door, and watched as they moved on to the bus journeying to the far eastern city of Kars. He'd been there once, years ago. It was a dump. But then he'd gone in the winter when the whole place was covered in thick snow and looked like Russia. In fact it had once been part of Russia, just after the Great War.

It took longer for the police to check everyone's ID cards on the Kars bus. But then he could see that it was far more packed than the one going to Trabzon. And then suddenly there was a shout. He couldn't make out what was said; his ears were giving up the ghost these days. But his eyes were not, and so when two officers brought a man in handcuffs off the Kars bus, he could easily see who it was. Ekrem Özince.

Abdülkadır smiled. Now they had him, maybe they'd call the search off. He put a foot on the bottom stair of the entrance to the bus and thanked his lucky stars the fool had decided to go north.

Raşım Dorsay felt sick. Inspector Süleyman still hadn't got back to him, and he felt anxious about what was going to happen at work that night. The last he'd heard, the police were going to watch Münir Sever. But what if he didn't meet that boy again, or what if his contact with the kid had been entirely innocent?

He picked up his truncheon and slipped it into his belt. He was aware that Türgüt Bey was watching him, and wondered what he was thinking. Did he know what was going on, or had the police decided that he was in on whatever this was too?

When he walked outside, he saw Münir waiting for him.

'No fucking about hiding behind gravestones tonight,' the older man told him.

Raşım said nothing.

Süleyman had expected the odious Eyüp Çelik to have arrived by the time he and Ömer Mungun interviewed Yaşar Akgün. But apparently Akgün had refused legal advice.

'That woman, Deniz, I don't know why she killed him,' Yaşar said, alluding to the death of Ali Haydar Özince. 'He helped her.'

'By this you are referring to the trade in human infants that you ran?' Süleyman said.

'We find parents for babies who are not wanted,' he said.

'And organs, like kidneys, for those who need them.'

'People have to wait years for such things and sometimes they die. We help them.'

'But they have to pay.'

'Yes,' he said. 'But they only pay the doctors. We don't make any money.'

'Then how do you live?' Ömer asked.

'I drive my taxi,' he said. 'And of course Paşa Bey very kindly left me his house. They're good people, the Özinces, they provide help for nothing, and so does my uncle.'

'Abdülkadır Soyar.'

'Yes.'

'Was it your uncle's idea to provide this help to the people of Kasımpaşa?' Süleyman asked.

This time Yaşar didn't answer.

Süleyman leaned forward. 'What's the matter?'

Still he said nothing.

'Yaşar?'

He turned away. But as he did so, Süleyman noticed that something about his demeanour had changed. His eyes had darkened, and hardened. 'I can't say any more.'

'Why is that? Has someone told you not to talk to us?'

He fell silent again.

A knock on the door relieved what was becoming a tense situation, and Ömer got up to answer it. When he opened the door, an officer leaned in to whisper in his ear.

When Ömer returned, he said, 'Ekrem Özince has been found. He was at Esenler bus station on board a vehicle going to Kars.'

'Ah,' Süleyman said. 'So, Yaşar Bey, if you won't tell us whose idea this . . . charitable organisation of yours was, then it is very possible we will find out from Mr Özince.'

'Oh, I don't think so,' Yaşar said.

'And why is that?'
'Because İzzet will have told him not to.'
'Your brother, İzzet Akgün?'
Once again Yaşar lapsed into silence.

What would happen to Hafız after Süleyman's investigation was at an end? Smoking in his kitchen, this was something Çetin İkmen couldn't get out of his head. Since his grandmother's death, it seemed the boy was alone in the world and not coping.

Of course while he was involved in giving evidence to the police, he would be protected. But what about afterwards? And what if they never managed to find his grandmother's body?

The djinn reared up in front of him and bared its teeth. The confounded thing seemed to be back with a vengeance, as was his wife. Was that because the exorcist Samsun had engaged hadn't completed his rituals?

İkmen went out onto the balcony to talk to Fatma.

'I know we can't have the boy here,' he said, carrying on the conversation he'd had with her earlier. 'But I would if I could, in spite of the language barrier.'

He sat back in his chair and looked up into the still clear blue sky. 'I wish I could help Kerim,' he said. 'I know in the depths of my shrivelled soul that the awful Professor Tolon was Sevval Kalkan's bone marrow recipient. And yet if Kerim isn't allowed to look at her prison medical records, then how does he prove that? I know it's not enough that Tolon's son knew her. Our only hope is that the doctor or doctors who performed the procedure will come forward. But that's not likely. We can get to a gang of organ traffickers in Kasımpaşa because they're basically chancers, even if they do live in a famously pious district. They're working class and they're nothing. The Tolons of this world shape people's thoughts.'

Fatma just smiled, as she always did. In terms of communication, she was even more mute than the djinn.

'Of course you're not even aware of what I'm saying,' he went on, 'but just looking at you is nice. In reality you're not much more than a photograph.'

He lit another cigarette, wondering what exactly he was doing. But then he knew that. 'I'm holding on to you for now,' he said. 'I won't for ever. It wouldn't be fair.'

But even saying that hurt him, and so he changed the subject.

'Try as I might,' he said, 'I can't stop worrying about Çiçek. I know it's ridiculous when the woman is over forty, but there it is. You know how much I love her and how much I love Mehmet Süleyman, but I wrestle with this feeling he might not be good for her all the time. Because I'm sure that he isn't. Not to say he's a bad person, not at all. It's just that she's been through so much. I don't want her hurt and I'm not sure I can trust her to protect herself. You know?'

Fanatically riffling through all the evidence he had accrued about Sevval Kalkan wasn't going to get him any closer to finding out why she had died. Poor Eylul had spoken to almost every hospital in the country and had now gone home with what he hoped wasn't a migraine.

Kerim Gürsel wondered whether he was doing this because he was genuinely obsessed by this case or because he didn't want to go home to his wife and her mother. If her mother was indeed the reason behind Sinem's new amorous feelings towards him, he wanted the old girl to leave as soon as possible. He knew she wouldn't. He also knew that he loved his wife, just not physically. Would Sinem, if she genuinely did feel amorous towards him, get between him and his transsexual lover Pembe? Pembe was also Sinem's carer, so how that would work out he couldn't imagine.

He turned back to the information on his screen. It didn't help that Sevval Kalkan had been effectively a non-person. It made him wonder how many of those very vulnerable people there were now. If they had indeed all been involved in the attempted coup of 2016, then surely it would have succeeded?

Denouncing people was all too easy in this still febrile post-coup atmosphere. And anyone who was in the least bit different, like Kerim himself, was at risk. He should go and see these associates of Sevval Kalkan, the people who had employed Çetin İkmen. Outcasts all of them. But he didn't have anything new to tell them and his mere presence would alarm them. So what was the point?

Unless they had information about Sevval they hadn't yet shared . . .

The figure took them both by surprise, Münir as well as Raşım. Although it was a shock to Raşım that he was so young. He hadn't remembered him quite like that. Maybe it was because he looked clean now.

'You owe me money!' the boy said to Münir in English.

Münir looked at Raşım. 'Fuck off while I deal with this!'

'Deal with what?'

Münir pushed him so hard that Raşım fell over onto the grass. 'Mind your own fucking business and fuck off!' he said. Even in the twilight, Raşım could see that the older man's face was red and seething with fury.

As he picked himself up, he heard the boy say, 'You owe me money for grandmother!'

Münir took hold of the boy by his T-shirt. 'She's dead,' he said. 'Let it go.'

'Because you kill her!'

Raşım looked around to see whether any of the police were in the vicinity. What was this about Münir killing his grandmother?

'No I didn't!' Münir said. He turned to Raşım. 'I've told you to fuck off, so fuck off or I'll fucking kill you!'

344

Münir often made threats involving death when he was angry. Raşim had been alarmed by him before. This time, though, he felt genuinely scared, and so against his better judgement, he turned and sprinted off. As he ran, he glanced back over his shoulder. It was then that he saw two figures move out of the trees and take the boy out of Münir's grasp.

Chapter 27

The whole exercise had been futile. None of the other members of the Moral Maze had been able to tell Kerim anything about Sevval Kalkan that he didn't already know. Although there had been one thing Olimpio the Designer had told him that had piqued his interest, and when he got home, he looked it up on his laptop while his mother-in-law tidied compulsively around him.

Ankylosing spondylitis was a spinal condition that resulted in chronic pain. The description given was of a nasty if non-life-threatening condition. What interested him, however, was how it was diagnosed, which was complicated.

Pınar Hanım ran the vacuum cleaner around and underneath his desk for maximum inconvenience. 'You should,' she whispered in his ear when she got close enough, 'make my girl pregnant. A woman of forty without a baby! It's a disgrace!'

Kerim ignored her. He had to in order to give his attention to what he was reading on the screen. Apparently key to the diagnosis of ankylosing spondylitis was the identification of a gene called HLA-B27. And for that the patient had to have an HLA blood test . . .

'I can't afford to pay, and if I go on a waiting list, I'll probably be dead by the time I reach the top of it.'

Münir Sever, cemetery guard and coup hero, was a sorry sight, sitting in front of Süleyman and Ömer in Interview Room 6.

When Hafız had identified him as the man who had encouraged his grandmother to sell her kidney and then refused to pay the boy when she died, he'd held up his hands.

'My kidneys have been dodgy for years,' he continued. 'My family come from the Black Sea coast originally and so I know Kasımpaşa well. I knew old Paşa Bey. But when he died and I found out that the Akgüns of Rize were providing medical services, I went and paid my respects.'

'To Yaşar Akgün?'

'No, to İzzet.' He shook his head. 'Yaşar is just the human face of the operation. İzzet arranges everything from Rize with the help of the Akgüns' uncle, Abdülkadır Soyar, and the Özince brothers. You know them?'

'Yes.'

'I told them what I needed but that I had no money. Abdülkadır Bey said that if I would help them, they'd make sure I got my operation as soon as a suitable donor appeared.'

'Kidney donor?'

'Yes.'

'So how did you help them?' Süleyman asked.

He shrugged. 'I helped identify suitable donors.'

'Like Hafız Barakat's grandmother?'

Münir put his head down. 'Yes,' he said. 'How was I to know she'd die?'

'She was almost eighty,' Ömer Mungun said. 'If you didn't think about her, you should have thought about the recipient.'

Münir shrugged. 'Ali Haydar Özince said she died before they could take her kidney.'

'And so what did they do with her?' Süleyman asked.

'They asked me if I could bury her in the cemetery.'

'Which you did.'

'Yeah.'

Süleyman looked at Ömer, who said, 'In Perihan Bulut's grave?'

Münir was silent for a moment, and then he said, 'Yes.'

'Did you see the body? Did you notice they'd taken her heart?''

He looked away.

Süleyman leaned forward. 'If you tell us, it will go easier for you.'

'Yes, yes, I knew, but . . .' Münir clutched his side and groaned in pain. 'This is what happens! This . . .'

'You knew they'd taken her heart and yet you carried on working for them?'

'I'm sick, I—'

'Oh, you're sick all right,' Süleyman said. 'And what about the original occupant of that grave, Perihan Bulut? Why did you remove her bones? Burn them?'

Still gripping his side and sweating now, Sever said, 'An Alevi, why should I care? There wasn't much left of her anyway.'

Both officers wanted to punch him; neither of them did.

'But I didn't burn the bones,' the guard continued. 'That was probably homeless scumbags.'

'Oh, well that's all right then!' Süleyman said. 'Did it ever occur to you that the woman you buried for Yaşar Akgün and the Özinçes could have been murdered?'

'They told me she died on the table.'

Süleyman's temper flared. 'Whilst allegedly having an illegal kidney donation operation!' he said. 'They killed her! Whoever is walking around with her ancient heart inside them is probably dead by now too!'

'I don't know! I don't know! Ask them!'

The officers waited for his pain to abate. Then Ömer said, 'So the body you buried in Perihan Bulut's grave was Hafız Barakat's grandmother, Kelebek Hanım?'

'Yes.'

'And was that the first time you'd done something like this?'

'No,' Münir said.

'How many . . .'

He closed his eyes, his hand clutching his side. 'I don't know,' he said. 'I don't know anything about any of them. All I was concerned about was when it was going to be my turn. This fucking diseased kidney is killing me.'

'In spite of the fact that they preyed on the elderly and the sick?' Süleyman said. 'Didn't you worry that they might try to give you some ninety-year-old's kidney?'

He shrugged. 'When the pain is as bad as it sometimes gets . . .'

'Do you know which doctors they use?' Ömer asked.

'No,' he said. 'But there's a proper surgeon.'

'Who is it?'

'Don't know. But they told me he works in a hospital. Not when he does this work, but . . .'

'He?'

'He or she, I don't know.'

'But he or she has a proper practice in a hospital?'

'Yes. I don't know where.' Now the pain had eased somewhat, he sat up straight. 'I do know they perform surgery in that community centre, but I've never seen where or been there when it's happening.'

Süleyman nodded. 'And you were willing to entrust your life to a criminal gang who use a non-sterile environment as an operating theatre?'

Münir shook his head. 'I'm desperate,' he said.

And that was the crux of the whole issue.

Çetin İkmen knew how these things worked and he knew that Kerim Gürsel did too. But he also stood by his conviction that getting Serkan Tolon in was a punt worth taking. The man was already at headquarters and under caution when Kerim called him.

'With his lawyer,' Kerim added.

349

İkmen, who had been attempting to make himself a late-night sandwich, sat down at his kitchen table and glared at the djinn. Çiçek had gone to bed, and so he was alone with it, which wasn't ideal. Also Çiçek had been upset about something.

'Who is he? The lawyer?' İkmen asked.

'Eyüp Çelik.'

He let out a long stream of air from his lungs. 'Celebrity attorney to the stars . . .'

'And the corrupt.'

'Good luck with him,' he said.

'Oh, he's already blinding me with so-called evidence and running rings round me, as he did with Mehmet Bey,' Kerim said. 'I needed a break even if they didn't.'

'But if you can shake the bastards . . .'

He heard Kerim sigh. Then he said, 'Even if Tolon's father was Sevval Kalkan's recipient, we'll never get him. I know that cardiologist Dr Çoban ordered an HLA test for Olimpio, because the Designer has told us herself. But I'd have to get access to Sevval's medical records to see whether she also had that test via Çoban. And I can't do that.'

'What about Serkan Tolon's mural?' İkmen asked.

'He paid Sevval ten thousand lira for that. He even has a receipt from her. I've seen it. Everything and everyone who matters is taken care of.'

İkmen didn't reply, not even to encourage Kerim to carry on regardless. Because he knew that what he'd said was correct. They'd get those low down on this hellish food chain of organ trafficking, but those at the top were another matter.

It was two o'clock in the morning when Mehmet Süleyman and Ömer Mungun finally got a break from interviewing the sick, the venal and the unwilling. In an attempt to lift their spirits, Süleyman drove them both to the twenty-four-hour café on Vatan

Caddesi, where in the shade of a plastic palm tree they discussed what had taken place so far.

Süleyman, who had a cup of coffee, a glass of water and a bottle of Pepsi, lit a cigarette and said, 'They're both terrified.'

He was right. Ekrem Özince had answered all their questions with 'no comment', ditto Dr Özdemir, while Yaşar Akgün was somewhere else entirely, tucked away in a place where their words meant nothing. Süleyman had called for a psychiatric assessment.

'I don't understand why Dr Özdemir won't name the surgeon they used,' Ömer said through the froth of his cappuccino. 'That would show willing to the public prosecutor.'

'Professional solidarity,' Süleyman said. 'Doctors don't inform on each other. Also I think we know this operation goes higher than just picking off a few junkies and old people. If there is a connection between the Akgüns' organisation, the death of Sevval Kalkan and Professor Aşık Tolon, this goes to the top.'

'Yes, but we don't know that.'

'No. Kerim Bey has been questioning Tolon's son, but I doubt he's had much luck with that. Not with Çelik on Tolon's side. If neither Dr Özdemir or Ekrem Özince will talk to us, and the neighbourhood has closed ranks . . .' He shrugged. 'Putting Akgün's uncle Abdülkadır Soyar to one side, we know that the only other person missing from this line-up is İzzet Akgün, and my question for him would be: did he start the gold-selling business in Kasımpaşa as a cover for his organ-trafficking work, or was it the other way around? His brother just wanted to help people as far as I can tell. What do you think?'

'I don't know,' Ömer said. 'I can't work Yaşar Akgün out. Mad or bad, do you think?'

'Hence the psych assessment,' Süleyman said.

They both drank in silence. Luckily the heat had dropped to a manageable level, even if the streets were still full of roaring, hooting, polluting traffic.

'Where do you think İzzet Akgün might be, sir?'

'Probably out of the country by now,' Süleyman said. 'Rize is handy for all sorts of places. Georgia, Armenia, across the Black Sea to Ukraine – or is it Russia these days? Yaşar is clearly frightened of his brother, so I feel İzzet was probably the brains, or at least the driving force, behind the operation. Messy.'

'Messy?'

'Things like this, where codes of silence are at play, always leave loose ends. With the confession of the guard, Sever, we should have enough to put Özince, Dr Özdemir and Akgün away. Not for long enough, but . . . The surgeon will walk.'

'You think so?'

'Who is the surgeon?' Süleyman said. 'I know who I think it is, but I can't prove it. I can't even bring in Dr Sibel Çoban, the cardiologist who ordered Olimpio's HLA test. You know she came to the Karacaahmet once to tell me about a fire she'd seen at night? Then I saw her again when we visited Türgüt Akgün at his house in Kuzguncuk.' He laughed. 'How she must pity us lesser mortals!'

'If she was the surgeon . . .' Ömer said.

'Kerim Bey has been trying to get hold of Sevval Kalkan's medical records from Silivri, but without success. I can't see that changing. So Çoban ordered an HLA test on Olimpio; so what? Doesn't mean she even saw Sevval.'

'But she may have.'

'Precisely. She may. We can tie the small fish to the boat, but not the big ones. I so wanted to do that, but . . .' Süleyman shrugged. 'We'd best get back. Maybe someone has decided to talk to us properly while we've been away. I hear miracles can happen.'

It was easy to see why Mehmet Süleyman hated lawyer Eyüp Çelik so much. Not only was he arrogant and superior, he was also handsome and he knew it, as well as clearly very rich, with his Savile Row suit and Rolex watch. His client, Serkan, son of the famous Professor Aşık Tolon, was of a similar type, if fashionably scruffy. Kerim felt the full force of the ruling elite staring at him across his desk.

'Mr Tolon,' he began, 'can you please tell me about your relationship to the actress Sevval Kalkan?'

Serkan looked at Çelik before he spoke, then he said, 'I didn't have any relationship with her.'

'And yet you have one of her works of graffiti art on your bedroom wall.'

He frowned. 'I didn't know what she was going to draw.'

'So why didn't you ask her to change it?'

'One doesn't dictate to an artist. That belies the whole reason behind artistic endeavour.'

'You paid her?'

'You know I did. My lawyer has given you her receipt, made out in her own handwriting.'

'How did you meet Sevval Kalkan?' Kerim asked.

'Through my friend Lokman Bulut. He recommended her.'

'And you took his recommendation on trust and paid her ten thousand lira without even knowing what she was going to do until it was finished?'

Tolon looked a little confused for a moment, and then he said, 'I'm a bit of an airhead, to be honest, Inspector. Ask my father . . .'

His face dropped at the same time as Eyüp Çelik's hardened. To invoke the father, Kerim felt, had not been in their plan.

'About your father . . .' he began.

Before Tolon could even draw breath, Çelik had his client on his feet.

'My client's father is not pertinent to any of this,' he said. 'You wanted to discuss my client's artwork, as I understood it, Inspector Gürsel. That is fine. Referring to his father, a man only recently recovered from a life-threatening disorder, is not.'

Then he bundled his client out of the office door before turning and grabbing Kerim's tie, pulling his head in very close to his own minty-fresh mouth.

'You drop this, you vile little poof,' he hissed. 'Drop it or I will end you!'

One month later

Thank God the evenings were not as hot as they had been. Çetin İkmen, sitting in his favourite seat outside the Mozaik bar, gave his cat Marlboro a plate of flaked bonito and then looked at his new toy.

He hadn't owned a cigarette case for decades, and so it was nice to have one again. And this one was special. Made for him by Cumhur Polat, Gold Bey, it was a token of the thanks the Moral Maze members felt they owed him for his work on tracking down Sevval Kalkan. Not that he felt he'd done a particularly good job. But that was hardly his fault.

Two sets of closed communities – doctors and the ruling elite – had actively mitigated against ever apprehending the person who had operated on and killed Sevval. If, as he suspected, Sevval had donated her bone marrow to Professor Aşık Tolon, the truth would only come out when those protecting him lost their power or died.

He turned the case over in his hands. It was made from the rose-gold back of an iPhone and the top of a Dolce & Gabbana spectacle case. Decorated with electrical wire filigree, it also featured a diamond stud welded into the clasp. Gold Bey was of the opinion the diamond was real.

'The rich decorate their phones with all sorts of valuable things these days,' he'd said when İkmen had expressed his amazement. 'Keep it, you deserve it.' No argument about how the diamond could keep him in food for months would shift him.

İkmen lit a cigarette and stroked the cat, which purred as it was eating. It was actually nice to be away from the apartment for a while, especially when he was meeting friends. He ordered another glass of rakı and was about to close his eyes when Mehmet Süleyman arrived.

'Good news for once,' Süleyman said as he embraced İkmen and then sat down opposite the man and his cat.

'I'll always drink to that,' İkmen said, and indicated to the waiter that another rakı was required.

'İzzet Akgün has been detained in Georgia,' Süleyman said. 'It will take us a few months to extradite him, but hopefully when we do, we will learn a lot more about the Akgüns' organ-harvesting operation.'

'That's excellent.'

'Isn't it.'

He lit a cigarette as his drink arrived. Pouring water on top of the rakı and watching it turn milky was something that always delighted him. It was a funny little quirk he shared with Çiçek. Not that the two of them were together at the moment. She had called for a break two weeks before. She needed time to think, and he understood that. He also knew that this thinking was largely about the way he had behaved that night after he'd been humiliated by Eyüp Çelik.

Çetin İkmen knew about the break and so there would be no talk about it. But Süleyman knew it had to be worrying him. He'd seen Çiçek in her café several times since the split, and she'd looked thin and miserable. But she was probably doing the right thing for her. He knew that because he'd already been to see his ex-lover, Gonca, for a friendly conversation, and ended up having sex with her. He wasn't a nice man. He certainly wasn't nice enough for Çiçek.

He heard İkmen say, 'Kerim!'

356

He looked up and saw Kerim Gürsel walking towards their table.

'I tried again to make a case for the records to be released from Silivri,' Kerim said as he sat down and poured himself some water.

'Using the information you'd got about Olimpio's condition?' İkmen asked.

'Yes. It's very unusual to be tested for ankylosing spondylitis,' Kerim said. 'It's a side product, if you like, of an HLA test. My question, of course, being: why was Olimpio given an HLA blood test, and was Sevval given one too? But that got me nowhere.'

İkmen shook his head. 'Do you think this doctor, the one Mehmet Bey thinks might be the female heart surgeon, was looking for a donor for someone?' He lowered his voice. 'For Tolon?'

'Seems so,' Kerim said. 'But we can't prove it.'

'Well, we can, but . . .'

'Exactly.' He ordered himself a gin and tonic and smiled as he watched İkmen's cat eat its fish. The lawyer Eyüp Çelik had telephoned a few times since Serkan Tolon's interview. Kerim had tried to speak to Lokman Bulut, Serkan's friend, but Çelik had become his attorney too, so it seemed.

As if reading his mind, Süleyman said, 'I've heard Lokman Bulut is no longer contesting his mother's will.'

'Thank God!'

'It would seem that his father's objection to his proposed action was enough to bring out the dutiful son in him,' Süleyman said. He smiled. 'These kids think they're so alternative and rebellious, but the great and powerful Turkish family code of honouring one's parents persists. Even if said parent is a waste of space.'

'Maybe,' İkmen said, 'he'll be a bit more careful with money from now on.'

'I doubt it,' Süleyman said. 'But I'm glad that family can rebuild itself now. Perihan's bones were put back in her grave last weekend, and I believe the nun, Sister Eudokia, has returned to Greece.'

'I'm just relieved we were able to find the remains of young Hafız's grandmother,' İkmen said.

'It was good of you to pay for her reinterment,' Kerim said.

İkmen shrugged. 'It's only money.'

That was so typical of Çetin Bey. Kerim smiled. But he said nothing, because, entirely unbidden, his mind was still full of the images of his wife lying beneath him as he'd tried to impregnate her. He'd come inside her twice, but was that going to be enough? And enough for whom? For Sinem? For her mother? Or for himself, to show that bastard Eyüp Çelik who was and who was not a poof?

İkmen cut across his thoughts. 'Now, gentlemen,' he said, 'I've ordered a meze, my treat, and I want you to eat as much as you like.'

A small, clean boy waiter came over and placed a tray full of bread, hummus, anchovy, beans and other delicious-looking small dishes down on their table.

'Thank you, Hafız,' İkmen said.

'Çetin Bey, Mehmet Bey, Kerim Bey,' Hafız Barakat said. He smiled and bowed, and left them to their food.